OTHER PEOPLE'S CLOTHES

Calla Henkel

SCEPTRE

First published in Great Britain in 2021 by Sceptre
An imprint of Hodder & Stoughton
An Hachette UK company

This paperback edition published in 2022

1

A CIP catalogue record for this title is available from the British Library

Paperback ISBN 9781529357677

Typeset in Sabon by Palimpsest Book Production Limited,
Falkirk, Stirlingshire

Printed and bound by Clays Ltd, Elcograf S.p.A.

Hodder & Stoughton policy is to use papers that are natural, renewable
and recyclable products and made from wood grown in sustainable forests.
The logging and manufacturing processes are expected to conform to
the environmental regulations of the country of origin.

Hodder & Stoughton Ltd
Carmelite House
50 Victoria Embankment
London EC4Y 0DZ

www.sceptrebooks.co.uk

For Mom and Dad
+
Max and Mia

1

'Start from the beginning,' she insisted and if I were allowed to smoke, I would have lit a cigarette. I was never good at telling stories and this one always felt like it belonged to someone else; *I had been young and stupid. I had been idealistic. I was twenty.* Maybe I could start from the first slide of art history class – a black diorite pillar. Hammurabi's code: two hundred and eighty-two laws and sliding punishments for 18th-century-BC justice, some seemingly logical, an eye for an eye, a surgeon's hand for a botched surgery, a builder's life for a collapsed building, some more bizarre – the guilt of the adulterer judged by whether or not they sank when thrown in water – all etched out onto a seven-foot column. But there was nothing for me on the cold black stone. No law had been engraved to deliver due process for what happened to me last year. I had no idea whose hand to chop off.

'OK. Well, what about her first words? What did she say when you got here?'

I sat silent, arms tightly folded, unable to understand Frau Klein's persistent interest in the beginning.

The Spa was only for women, all of whom were present for different disorders, and some diseases, most unknown to me. But everyone knew why I was there. I was famous, and the angular whispers of the nurses and patients followed me through the concrete building. However, I found comfort in their efforts to mask these remarks, knowing all too well that outside of The Spa there was no reason to whisper. By the time Berlin's summer was blazing, we – Hailey Mader and myself, Zoe Beech – were all anyone could talk about.

Sprawling and old, The Spa was situated in a converted primary school somewhere in northern Brandenburg. Its hallways still smelled chalky like the inside of a brick, and most of the bedrooms, once classrooms, were shared by two to three girls. But I was alone, living in what I assumed had once been a very generous broom closet, with my own square window, blue painted chair with matching desk, and a porcelain sink adorned with a halo of dark-brownish mould. I liked to imagine that the ring of mould was a well-run city of tiny spores, filled with good, non-violent mould citizens, maybe even with mould artists and mould curators doing coke at tiny mould clubs.

I spent most of my time in this sort of useless daydream, elbows pressed into the soft wood of the desk, staring out at the unbearably still farmland and then, lightning, an interruption to my doldrums: a body writhing in a lake of blood, flashes strobing, sound blaring, like a Rihanna music video, or a trailer for a horror film. And just as fast as it crested, I'd snap back to the barren field or mildewy sink or the constellation of moles on Frau Klein's neck.

Frau Klein loved the word *par-a-noi-a*, letting each syllable slip like a ping-pong ball out of her wet mouth. She was in her early forties but dressed for her sixties, with roadkill-brown hair and potato-sack skirts. We had at this point spent many hours together and I was certain she was living vicariously through me, filling the void of her own existence with my answers and traumas, extracting information she would eventually sell to the tabloids, or her own tell-all.

'Zoe, how did sex make you feel?'

'Did you ever fantasise about Hailey?'

Her voice sounded scripted as if she were recording an audio cassette from a language class.

'What drugs did you do?'

'What pushed you to do them?'

I watched in disinterested horror, as the saliva began to surface at the edges of her thin lips, thirsty for my reply.

'I did what was around.'

She nodded. More questions. Whenever I mentioned the name Beatrice her eyes flickered and she would take her stubby blue pen and quietly draw a shape in her notebook. Frau Klein entertained my theories but she always returned to the same head tilt: 'And what makes you so sure Beatrice was watching you?'

'She read my emails.'

'And how can you know that?'

'I told you already—'

'But is it possible you imagined it?'

'No.'

Frau Klein made another shape in her notebook then checked the clock. The stainless-steel lamp on her desk cast an orange circle on her over-moisturised cheek, her skin hanging loose like the Mask of Agamemnon or a glob of half-baked cookie dough.

'And whose story do you believe you are in right now?'

'Yours,' I said, motioning towards her notepad.

Frau Klein made a suggestive nod. 'And, let's go back to the beginning again. What were her first words to you when you arrived?'

2

'*G*uten *Tag*, Dumpster!' Hailey called, waving a frantic freckled arm across Hauptbahnhof with an ochre hiking-pack strapped to her athletic frame. She looked ready to move camp every night, which terrified me. While buying our train tickets she perkily explained that Hostel Star was in the East side of the city, a bed cost twenty-two euros a night and each room held eight people with four bunks. I didn't really understand the intricacies of East or West, but I knew it meant something specific here. The grog of the Dramamine I'd taken somewhere over the Atlantic was wearing off and I felt helpless for relying on all of her arrangements, following, a mute dog, as she babbled, pointing things out on the train: the art museum on our left, Alexanderplatz, the TV Tower.

I rolled my hand-me-down suitcase on the cobblestone sidewalk while Hailey bounded ahead until she abruptly stopped under a neon star winking from a crumbling concrete facade. I followed her in and the smell of mildew and lemon floor cleaner wafted over us.

'I liked the name Hostel Star,' she said with a hint of embarrassment while looking around the fading lobby. Finally clutching our new keys, we entered our room on the third floor where we found three guys our age, spread across the furniture, duffle bags and rolling papers littering the dark-blue linoleum. They greeted us with rotund Australian accents.

'We are only here until we find something more permanent,' Hailey whispered after the initial pleasantries, unbuckling her

Gore-tex straps and taking a sip from her Smart Water bottle. The three Australians went on to tell us their names, which all sounded like Aaron, Oron or Erin. We reluctantly introduced ourselves. I was relieved when she yawned. Human, after all. We lay down on our bunks and I fell into a syrupy sleep. When I woke from my jet-lagged nap the sky had already turned black, and the reflection of the neon star bounced into our room like a hiccuping sunset. The Aarons asked us if we wanted to go to the club with them. Hailey and I exchanged *fuck no* glances. They shrugged and began snorting speed off the lip of the top bunk. In one last attempt to persuade us to join them, the tall one bellowed, 'Every night you miss in Berlin is a night you miss in Berlin.' We burst into laughter after the door thudded shut.

This became our mantra for when things were either absolutely miserable or absolutely amazing. Every night you miss in Berlin is a night you miss in Berlin. I watched from the top bunk as Hailey scrawled the lines in her orange diary. She was always scribbling, pausing from our conversations to pull out the soft-covered book, her red ponytail a bobbing paint brush as she wrote.

'All of the great artists kept a diary,' she'd said to me on our second afternoon, croissant flakes fluttering from her cupid's-bow lips, 'I'm taking it really seriously while I'm here.' I nodded, not sure what I was going to take seriously in Berlin. I wasn't even sure why I was there. I peered at Hailey over my chai latte, she was so muscular in her certitude, confident of what she wanted from the next months and probably years. I began mentally drafting an email to Jesse, my boyfriend, telling him I would come home early – that Berlin had been a huge mistake, and I had no idea what I was doing.

I had met Hailey in art history class at school in New York, she was from Rhode Island and somehow also Kentucky and Nebraska and Colorado, her dad owned a chain of successful supermarkets inexplicably called *Biggles*. She was a magazine-cover redhead, always running her fingers through her hair as if there were cameras filming. In class, her freckled limbs were constantly springing into the air to answer questions. *Why was Cimabue significant?* BECAUSE HE WAS THE SINGLE MOST IMPORTANT TRANSITIONAL FIGURE BETWEEN MEDIEVAL AND RENAISSANCE PAINTING. She was usually right and had a schizophrenic way of switching accents, mutating herself to fit situations; a Southern drawl for asking to borrow a pen, or an 'r'-less East coast to dish answers.

Hailey had invariably showed up to 9 a.m. class in bright lipstick, either wearing Victoria's Secret PINK sweatpants or tight lowrider jeans – nothing in-between. Even occasionally donning a Von Dutch hat, arguably retro for 2008, and an absolute anomaly in art school where the average collegiate uniform consisted of paint-stained Carhartts, oversized concert tees and Doc Martens. Like me, she hadn't grown up on the teat of the avant-garde. She believed pop culture was paramount. She idolised Andy Warhol, and didn't hesitate walking into the cinephile mecca Kim's Video on St Marks and requesting *Notting Hill* from the clerk, who openly eye-rolled.

The only time I had been to Kim's, I'd buckled to the pressure of the employee favourites and rented a Czech New Wave film, which I'd paid double for after trying, but failing, to watch it four nights in a row.

On Fridays, after art history study group, a pack of us often went to Asian Pub in the East Village, a dive bar with cheap cocktails and a relaxed ID policy. One night a few drinks in, Hailey caught me staring at her nose. It was too perfect, like a children's ski slope. She leaned in, wafting strawberry daiquiri, and told me that in high school she'd been hit in the face with a lacrosse stick and persuaded her dad to let her get a nose job. She took a slurp of her pink drink, holding my eyes, clearly wanting the subject to linger.

'I tried out for, like – three Neutrogena ads, kept getting rejected and – I knew.'

'Oh,' I said, unsure of what to add.

'So I took care of it,' she said, making a batting motion towards her head, her words ringing with high-pitched adolescent pride.

'You're saying you did it on purpose?' a guy next to us butted in.

'Yup,' Hailey clucked.

I excused myself to the bathroom, but the image had lodged itself into my brain; Hailey bracing herself as the aluminium shaft throttled towards her sweet teenage face. A few weeks into the semester when I swung by her dorm to pick up a hand-out on Byzantine mosaics, I noticed her modelling pictures taped to the wall above her bed: young Hailey in a plaid mini-skirt in a Delia's catalogue, drinking a Capri Sun on a soccer field, surrounded by other redheads and a miniature bull terrier for a Target campaign.

'See, the nose worked,' she said while digging through her desk; I nodded, both repulsed and intrigued at her pubescent drive.

By the end of sophomore year I desperately wanted to get out of New York. I felt crushed. The slump. The blues. Whatever it was, Carol Gaynor, the guidance counsellor, a slender woman with flawless skin who was married to a famous dermatologist, was going to help plot my escape. Carol would let you curl up in her office as she'd chatter on about irrelevant amenities of far-off universities available for exchange years.

'There is an orangerie with a cafe near the school that makes really spectacular scones,' or another, 'with the nicest sauna just about a mile up the road, and it splooshes right out onto the sea.'

I wanted to go to Helsinki, the one with the sauna.

'You know everything can be fixed by a good schwitz,' Carol hissed over her coffee mug. I had a Montessori-esque fantasy of hard wooden floors and fractured Finnish light streaming onto a circle of well-mannered art students fiddling with string. I believed Europeans were people of dignity and history and reason. The opposite of my school, which orbited around the sculpture boys, who built mammoth objects with 2x4's in the woodshop and got drunk in class on whiskey decanted into Pepsi bottles.

Our school was extremely competitive. Critiques of artwork were a sanctioned system for attacking one another. All grievances could be played out in the second-floor classroom, or as most students called it, *the pit*. Friends were inspired to undercut each other with personal tidbits: Republican parents, unread seminal texts, porn predilections, leveraging weakness and sharing anecdotes that were wholly irrelevant to the work in question, all in the pursuit of power. What power exactly, I still wasn't sure. Some of it lay in the hands of the professors, who could support a young artist's move into the misty abyss of the gallery world. But the sculpture boys were untouchable, they screamed profanities at freshmen, misquoted Joseph Beuys, ripped each other's work off and everyone still wanted to fuck them.

David Chris was the leader of the sculpture-bros, he was the tallest with a big broad face, and looked like he'd just climbed out of a prehistoric cave in France, his hands still wet with paint from his latest renderings of buffaloes. My Aunt Caroline always said in her two-pack-a-day Southern accent, 'Never trust anyone with two first names.' And David Chris was no exception. He was the lead architect on a multi-generational mural of freshmen girls in jizzy Sharpie that wrapped the ceiling adjacent the senior studios. Each figure had a nickname scrawled below, sometimes charting who they'd slept with or important facts; *Muppy has herpes* or *Ken-doll has a tight pussy.*

My nickname did not have a sexual origin. On Halloween, dressed as a zebra in an American Apparel jumpsuit, I had teetered down eight flights of tight Chinatown stairs, only to trip on the last, landing on a pile of very forgiving trash. David Chris, who was dressed as Paul Bunyan, but did every day anyway, was standing at the bottom with a big grin. And now, in half-dried red Sharpie, my nickname *Dumpster* is scrawled under a not completely unflattering sketch of me emerging from a trash can looking somewhere between a demented Botticelli Venus and a horny Oscar the Grouch. It wasn't the worst. Hailey was called *Holey* because she'd let a guy named Moses finger her on the roof.

I had finally built up the courage to bring in one of my assemblage sculptures to *the pit*. A hulking, piss-stained, most likely bedbug-infested piece of plywood that I'd found on the Bowery. I drilled hundreds of holes in the warped board, and with silver wire I'd carefully threaded all the pocket-sized debris that I had found on the streets over the month: keys, candy wrappers, little earrings, coins, hair ties, a baby shoe, tarot advertisements, receipts, plastic straws, Lego. It was December. I thought of it as a New York City advent calendar. David Chris was drunk.

A soft lull fell over the room while my fellow students circled my sculpture. Inspecting it, David flicked the splintering edge. I waited, fear strumming my veins. My piece was the last in a long night of heavy spelunking. We'd just spent two hours debating the *inherent sentimentality* of a still-damp plaster-covered doughnut.

David finally broke the silence, saying the words into his paper cup mid sip, his voice lightly distorted by the echo, 'Zoe – you realise – this is decorative.'

'How?' I asked, softer than I'd meant to.

'It's like, domestic . . . it's *cute* . . .'

'How is this domestic?' I asked again, firmer.

'You can't escape it.'

'The hair ties,' said Jeff gruffly, whose ratty flannel matched David's.

'And the way you fastened the wire, it's so dainty. Like clinging on to past stuff. It's like a dream catcher – or a jewel box, or—'

'I think there should be more stuff too,' David said. He took another sip, ending his presence in the discussion, then turned to a girl who had a brand-new tattoo, still puffy, of a sparrow on her neck and refilled her cup. A few others chimed in their agreement.

'It seems underdeveloped.'

'More of a proposal or proposition.'

'Watered-down Rauschenberg.'

In *the pit,* the easiest way to dismiss a female's work was by calling it domestic. Or decorative.

The double D's. Or as David Chris pronounced domesticity, *dumb–ass–titties.*

When I'd found the battered piece of plywood on an overcast Wednesday, it was swollen with the liquids of the city and lodged behind a bike rack, anything but the double D's. I hauled it back to the studio, my fingers still ringing with its weight while I began to scrutinise the board. For all its gritty ugliness it was smooth like driftwood, its jagged edges rounded by its movement through the concrete tides. Every paint fleck and indentation seemed important, telling some traumatic story only I could hear. It felt obvious to me that this board would be home to all the other bits, the treasures I had been finding in the daily currents of the sidewalks and stairwells over the past month. But I didn't know how to say any of this to the class. I just let their comments wash over me, afraid that if I said any of those things, and they still dismissed it, I would have nothing.

I was jealous of all the students who had grown up in big cities. They seemed to have the tools for living in New York. Everyone's parents were interesting: cartographers, novelists, costume makers, environmental lawyers and projectionists at MoMA. My mom worked at a cheesy real-estate agency in Florida. I still tried to perform the New York City stereotypes – I wore a black leather jacket, I rarely washed my brown hair, I drank coffee even if I didn't like the taste, I had a fake ID, and I was perfectly comfortable saying *fuck you*. But the alien-hot-air rushing from the subway grates could petrify me. The psychic weight of all the people waiting at the stop light at 14th Street could render me unable to move my legs. Grocery shopping at Trader Joe's was horrifying, and going to the post office overwhelming. I reminded myself that in some ways I was more equipped for all of this than a lot of my classmates, most of them had never done a load of laundry in their life. I'd explained to at least three pyjama-clad students how to add soap to the big white machines in the basement. I had a nearly full scholarship, I could make an omelette and I knew I wanted to be an artist. I believed that should be enough.

When I was younger, my ability to draw was the only thing that made me, even vaguely, popular. I rendered crayon princesses and dolphins jumping through flames, whatever my peers required of me. It was like printing money. In fifth grade my cross-hatched drawing of the playground won a school-wide competition for the cover of the 2001 calendar. I turned my skills to collage in middle school, covering binders, lockers and pre-pubescent walls with cut-outs of Destiny's Child, Leo, Christina and Britney. And in eighth grade, my best friend, Ivy Noble, a ballerina, decided she wanted to go to New York City and dance at Juilliard. Ever competitive, and ever willing to follow her, I decided that I too would go to the big-scary-pick-pocket-city, for art. So I threw myself into

11

studying – she had rehearsals and training, but I had the library. I discovered Man Ray, Basquiat, and the otherworldly collages of Hannah Höch, who pushed me to pervert Leo and Britney into dramatic teenage abstraction.

At least I didn't cry in class. I had gulped for air in the bathroom after a critique but I'd never cried. And I'd often meet up with Ivy, who had, despite the nearly impossible acceptance rate, made it to Juilliard unstressed. I even had a few friends, and my then boyfriend, Nate Kai. He was one year older than me, a cynical computer dork with an intense MacBook stare – whenever he'd launch into talking, his turtle-green eyes would get a dark zoom while he rummaged for words, like a hand silently dipping into a Scrabble bag, feeling for the next vowel. Nate, the debate champion of his boarding school in Massachusetts, maintained his tradition of choosing an argument-a-day to spar over: *Was it morally corrupt to sell your work in a gallery? Was computer-generated painting still painting? Was everything a ready-made in our current age of art-supply manufacturing?*

Our relationship scared me. But I thought that was how artists' relationships should be; unpredictable, tortured, intense. And Nate's East Coast-ness was the complete oppos-ite of the sunburnt beach brains I had grown up with. I'd even briefly met his parents at the Four Seasons before a UNICEF charity function. They were icy at best, but totally regal. Nate's father, Ken Kai, born in Japan, was a Wharton-educated banker and his mother, the lemon-meringue-haired Barbra Kai, was an heiress to a small chemical fortune.

Nate had a habit of leaning over my sketch book, his mouth squishing Orbit gum, critiquing me, 'Zoe – I just think there is – *chew* – too much going on, don't be – *chew* – afraid to waste paper.'

I was afraid to waste anything, I was on scholarship. Nate loved waste. He had his parents' credit card, and when he got into a fight with his dad, as he often did, we'd take a taxi up to the Carlyle Hotel and order two of the Dover soles deboned table-side on a silver platter. Nate had desperately wanted me to have a fetish. I didn't. He did. And he wouldn't tell me what his was unless he truly believed I had one. I googled *fetish*.

Arousal by insects.

Arousal by stone and gravel.

Arousal by amputees.

I had no idea what to pick. I was with Nate because he made me feel a part of another world, not because I wanted to step on his face in high heels. But I was afraid to lose him, his tickets to the opera and boarding-school anecdotes. One night after colour theory class, we were walking past a grocery store. I told him he could pick out a zucchini and fuck me with it. Vegetables would be my fetish, sure. His eyes lit up, his hands excitedly moving through his iridescent black hair as he inspected each zucchini, measuring it with his index and thumb, squeezing it, finally settling on one with a slight curve. Back at his apartment, mid-act, he suddenly looked down at the squash in horror, certain I was trying to shame the size of his truly normal-sized cock with the girthy vege-table, he began crying and told me to leave. I walked back to the dorms mortified. I googled *fetish,* again determined; *role-play, tentacles, feet, toilet paper, rubber, medical supplies, teddy bears.*

A few days later things had calmed down, the squash remained unmentioned, and we were peacefully watching a Kenneth Anger movie he'd already seen, but insisted I see. He ran to get more beer, leaving his phone on the stone counter, it began to shriek, a buzzy hyena. I tried to ignore it, focusing on the Nazi bikers sinking into the blue highway, but it began its electric-howl again. And again. I finally picked the phone off the desk, about to silence it when the text messages popped up. They were from a girl, *Sam Cassady,* scheduling a time to meet and what he should be wearing. *Leather pants and white button-up.* When Nate came back up the stairs and saw me holding the phone, his face dropped. His eyes enlarged, the green zoom, he was momentarily speechless, then he dumped me.

Per Carol's email instructions, I prepared the documentation of my work for the abroad application, pressing each slide into its little plastic sleeve saying an inaudible prayer, which quickly mutated into inaudible fuck-yous.

FUCKYOUDAVIDCHRISANDNATEANDALLOFTHE SCULPTUREMOTHERFUCKERS.

Repeat. I would leave Manhattan, the isle of rotten man.

A few months later, with joyous exuberance, Carol Gaynor called me to her office, which was slender like her, and informed me that I had been accepted to Helsinki for a study abroad year. I would walk to the sauna on the sea and continue my studies with students of dignity. Carol did an embarrassing little dance with her index fingers shooting up above her head. High on my impending exit I treated myself to a box of sushi and a bubble tea and called my mom while sucking down tapioca balls.

I ran into Nate sitting on the steps of the school. And because I was happy I said hello. And he took my smile, my little opening after three months of cold-shouldering, to begin talking about himself and his life, a roaring faucet of banality. Enjoying the tapioca balls expanding in my stomach while staring at his dull face, I was pleased at my ability to ignore him. And then, as if dropping a brick on my sandalled foot, he mentioned how he had just heard he had been accepted to Helsinki. I said nothing, spun around, and walked back to Carol's office, my brain thudding. Nate had known I was applying to Helsinki. I had even showed him the campus on Google Maps, zooming in on the sauna that splooshed out at the sea. The manipulative prick. Carol informed me there was one spot left at the art school in Berlin.

I had really only known her from a distance, I never imagined spending a year in a foreign country with Hailey Mader. I knew she wore Chanel Mademoiselle – a ubiquitous Windexy vanilla scent that was popular with dental hygienists, gallery assistants and other women proximate to benign power. I knew she possessed the frightening fortitude to break her own nose, chewed Dentyne Ice gum, and decorated her dorm with 1930s posters of Italian liquors – but I had no idea what Hailey's artwork was like. I'd never seen her in *the pit*. She'd told me once with an air of deep seriousness that her work was *conceptual*, as if that explained everything. At school, to me, she was a character in a poorly acted TV show with only the edges of an identity.

Apparently Hailey could speak German, a fact that Carol had been excited to relay while she handed me a wad of brochures. I was relieved I wouldn't be alone. Relieved someone else might have a plan. I still had Hailey's number from a study group so I called, and she'd sounded genuinely excited, rattling things off – her tickets were booked, she'd found a hostel, she'd get a new sim card when she got there. But there had been a slight falter in her voice towards the end of the conversation, a barely noticeable shift in tone, as if it were just dawning on her that she would no longer be alone. I imagined Hailey might have wanted to re-invent herself in Berlin. Maybe she'd watched *Cabaret* with Liza Minnelli too many times. Or planned on cutting short bangs and producing techno, or maybe she too hated the sculpture-dicks. Whatever it was, by the end of the call she knew we were stuck together.

Our first meal in a proper Berlin restaurant was at a fondue place near the hostel, a dark hobbit hole with knobby wooden chairs, thick menus and flickering candles. The waiter was cute in a teenage-heart-throb way, and kept theatrically checking in to make sure we were *OK*, then retreating with a wink. I asked Hailey why he was being so nice.

'We are hot and barely twenty. And foreign.' She stared the waiter down with a *fuck me* grin while sopping a square of bread through the thick bubbling cheese, he reciprocated with a head nod as if he were going to jerk off in the back room.

'So, what happened with Ivy?'

I stuttered. I hadn't realised she knew about Ivy. I'd missed my final crits for the funeral, so I guess everyone in my studio classes knew, but I had somehow hoped to keep her for myself here. Just before I'd left for Berlin I was still regularly forgetting, thinking of things to tell Ivy, pulling out my phone – and only after I'd begun typing would it hit me that she was gone.

'She was murdered,' I said matter-of-factly, startling myself.

'I know,' Hailey said, subtly gesturing her knife towards her neck. 'Do you know who did it? Like do you have any ideas?'

'They think it was random.' I was mushing the remnants of food on my plate. I wasn't ready to trust Hailey with Ivy.

She was holding my stare, she wanted more, she jabbed a chunk of bread, 'Nothing's random.'

I shifted my focus to the drone of the refrigerator holding chocolate cakes iced in what appeared to be whipped concrete.

'Did you dye your hair to look like her?'

'How do you know she was blonde?' I asked, startled.

'I looked her up on Facebook,' she paused, 'everyone loves a dead girl.'

I nearly choked, Hailey continued. 'And anyway, we can be best friends now. I've never really had one – my family moved around a lot.'

I was relieved when the waiter interrupted my silence and Hailey began speaking in overly enthusiastic German. The language frightened me, every sentence felt like a car being compressed into a cube. It seemed impossible to flirt but the waiter was laughing and Hailey was coquettishly tracing her collarbone. The situation embarrassed me. I stared out the argyle stained-glass window until he left. We counted our shiny new currency, like terrified goblins. Hailey whispered that we didn't have to tip too much, that it was different in Germany, but it felt too weird, so we tipped like Americans, regretting it as we trudged back to Hostel Star.

Two days later we heard back from a potential apartment on Craigslist, advertised as a fall-to-spring sublet. The Australians had been getting more aggressive, one of them lunging into my bed reeking of cigarettes and urine. Hailey had written explaining that we were students and clean and respectable and so forth. The subletter, who had posted no photos of the apartment, was apparently 'a fellow ex-pat' and asked if we could meet later that evening. We took the mustard-coloured subway across town to Schöneberg. The building sat on the end of Bülowstrasse with a ribbon of raised train tracks running directly in front of it, and nestled across the street was a plump brick church surrounded by a pleasant little park with a wooded area. It looked like the Europe I had imagined.

'See those women?' Hailey asked, snapping me from my fantasy, pointing to a cluster of bodies clad in neon stockings with corsets pulled tight over puffed jackets. 'They're prostitutes. It's legal here. They even pay taxes.'

I nodded, not sure if that meant it was a good or bad neighbourhood. Hailey was full of facts, which I was grateful for. I knew nothing. Earlier that morning she calmly informed me that the reason most German toilets have a shelf instead of a water-filled bowl at the bottom is because they liked to inspect their shit.

'I think it's a perfect backdrop for our time abroad,' she said, gesturing towards the street and the stone facade in front of us. I nodded again. We stomped our boots at the door, then trudged up to the second floor. When the door creaked open we were hit by the smell of flowers, like at a funeral, sharp and final. A jet-black-haired woman stuck out a hand equipped with five crimson fingernails, and introduced herself as Beatrice Becks, her B's popping when she said her name, 'Beee-atrice Beee-cks.'

I smiled cautiously, tossing the name in my mind like a coin.

Tall and elegant, in a billowing white Oxford, Beatrice ushered us into the entrance hall, her flowery scent intensifying as she extended her arm, pointing towards the coat rack. Her fragrance was something I couldn't place from my countless hours behind the perfume counter at the mall – maybe Diorissimo by Dior, but that was too creamy, this was pointed; peppery even. She watched closely as we peeled off our coats.

When we knelt to take off our boots, Hailey leaned her head towards mine, 'She looks like Uma Thurman from *Pulp Fiction*, right?'

I held in a laugh. I'd never seen it, but knew the poster from Kim's Video – it was the exact same haircut and red lipstick. I stole another look, Beatrice was waiting for us with her arms crossed, she checked herself in the hallway mirror, lifting her hand to adjust her bangs, then relaxed her jaw and cocked her head. Clearly aware of her best angles.

Hailey stood and I followed her socked feet, then glanced to my right and caught a view of a green-floored kitchen. Beatrice turned left, we trailed, entering the living room, warm with light flickering from a chandelier of candle-like bulbs. Hailey gasped at the beautiful room. The ceilings were at least three times my height with trim that looked like cold butter carved with a spoon. I had seen enough photos from the other options on Craigslist to know this was not normal.

We both jumped. There was another woman sitting in the room, dressed in the same style of Oxford with the same bobbed hair and bangs, but hers a dull grey. Hailey, bowed nervously. The grey haired woman dipped her head in return. I let my eyes fall to the couch she was seated on, which was bright red and lip shaped, in a plump surrealist pout. Beatrice, who had seemed so tall at the door, diminished as she took her place on the couch. The other woman was introduced as Beatrice's mother, Janet. I stood transfixed by the odd expression of the couch, one corner seemed to be turned up towards the ceiling as if caught in a fake laugh.

The mother and daughter stared at us with the focused eyes of a Renaissance painting. I shivered, noticing the windows were open, but the cold was seemingly unregistered by the two perfect wax figures.

Beatrice broke her silence, 'I am a writer.' She said it as if it were a fact we already knew well. 'And I am leaving my flat to take refuge from the Berlin winter in the warmer climate of Vienna.'

I stared blankly. Hailey chuckled, it was a joke. I followed in a forced burst. Beatrice regained the floor, 'And we are from *California*.'

There was an old-world elegance to the way she tongued the word *Calii-four-nia,* it vibrated with the sound of expensive cars turning on rock driveways and grapes blowing on vines. I assumed she was in her early forties.

'I will be in the throes of works at the Austrian Federal Chancellery Writers' Schloss, a mouthful, I know, but a fabulous place to focus.' Beatrice looked to her mother, searching for something. Janet dipped her pointy chin approvingly, Beatrice seemed to relax, moving her index finger over the red line of her lips. I noticed that Janet, despite her grey hair, didn't seem that much older than Beatrice and they shared the same features – a strong nose, and nearly black eyes, but everything on Janet was sharper, almost ridged.

We discussed New York, we discussed art. *Yes*, we were both studying here. Hailey listed her origins from Rhode Island to Kentucky. *Yes*, we were new to Berlin. *Yes*, we were new to everything. When Beatrice and her mother weren't looking Hailey shot me big moon eyes, she wanted the apartment. Hailey switched into her Southern story mode, regaling them with the horrors of the Hostel Star and the Australian Aarons: *Every night you miss in Berlin is a night you miss in Berlin.* The pair released matching laughs, their necks now oscillating, moving from one another and back to us. They were warming up. You could see Beatrice beginning to see herself in us, the young ex-pats full of wonder. Her questions became rapid as if the clock was running out in a game of charades.

'Why Berlin?

'What sort of art do you like?'

Hailey talked about Warhol.

'Have you ever been abroad before?'

Hailey nudged me, I told them about my Mexico City trip in high school, twenty-two girls and one boy.

'What do your parents do?'

Hailey began a lengthy explanation about how her family's supermarket chain, Biggles, was re-shaping American consuming.

'Are you involved?' Beatrice said, ignoring Hailey's monologue on perishables. It took us a beat to realise what she meant. Hailey happily told her about her boyfriend Zander, 'the genius', trailing on about their open relationship and how he had been recently nominated for a prize for his work in robotics. Beatrice began to inspect her fingernails. Janet yawned and shot a look at her daughter. In a panic, Hailey clicked her tongue, 'Zoe is dating her murdered best friend's ex-boyfriend.'

I flushed. How had Hailey found out? I had only told her I was dating someone named Jesse. She must have put the pieces together from Facebook. Beatrice's eyes flashed, she looked towards me with a tight smile and Janet seemed to finally truly come alive.

'Oh. I'm terribly sorry. How did it happen?' Janet asked.

'Stabbed,' Hailey said, as if explaining how she wanted her steak cooked. Beatrice and Janet both raised their eyebrows, clearly wanting more.

'Where?'

'In the neck and chest, fourteen times,' Hailey responded.

'I mean geographically?'

'Florida. She was a ballerina.' Hailey glanced at me to continue. I looked down at the ground, a wide silence settled in the room, I hadn't told Hailey any of that. Why was she doing this? I wanted to scream. Beatrice cocked her head with faint pleasure. Everyone was looking at me. A train rumbled by, casting a yellowish glow into the room. It was just close enough that you could make out the silhouettes of passengers gazing dimly out into the night. I wondered if they could see us, if they also knew the room was waiting for me to speak.

'Why do you live in Berlin?' Hailey asked Beatrice, finally claiming the emptiness after the train's whooshing exit.

Beatrice sat up, turning her cheek to the side in thought, but before she could answer, Janet cut in, 'It's a wonderful place to write, one can still entertain darkness here – but we keep our main residence in *Calii-four-nia*, and my favourite – a Friesian cottage on the coast of Sylt.'

Hailey smiled as if that explanation made perfect sense.

'What's a Friesian cottage?' I mumbled, trying to make up for my earlier silence. Hailey glared at me like I was an idiot.

'It is a style of thatched farmhouse, ubiquitous on Sylt – an island up north,' Janet explained.

21

'I love those cottages,' Hailey added.

'They are darling, but need constant maintenance.'

'All right then,' Beatrice clipped, clearly annoyed at her mother's blabbering. She lifted her bony figure off the couch and beckoned us to follow, her crimson nails flying around as she pointed things out – the brand-new washing machine, a windowless bathroom, a nice nook for reading. The kitchen was clad in fading '70s floral wallpaper and floor-to-ceiling books. I lingered, peering out the window near the sink at an empty courtyard.

'And here is the bookshelf with all my own works,' she said, gesturing to the twelve-tier rainbow that stood behind her in the foyer. I shuffled out of the kitchen just as she paused in front of the shelf as if for a photograph, her black hair reflecting the overhead light.

Beatrice ran to answer her phone, leaving us momentarily alone in the foyer.

'I fucking knew it. She's famous, her books are in airports,' Hailey whispered with zeal. Her love of pop extended to the literary, with a penchant for carrying around fat brick-like books with embossed covers and bloody fonts. She was giddy.

Beatrice returned. 'So as you can see there *is* a primary bedroom, but the living room has a lovely day bed.'

'Fantastic,' Hailey said with a shit-eating grin.

I flushed with anger at her empty exuberance. She had thrown Ivy on the table like a poker chip. She had no filter. No breaks.

'Take a look around,' Beatrice said, bangs fluttering as she nodded towards the entrance to the bedroom.

Separated into two enormous rooms, the once ballroom was partitioned by carved double doors painted white with gold handles, pre-war, or as Beatrice had said, *Altbau*. The floors were patterned in parquet diamonds with thin strips of dark cherry running along the edges and covered in a smattering of carpets. The biggest room, the bedroom, had a bay window overlooking the park, a wrought-iron bed, and a glossy upright Blüthner piano. And the slightly smaller room, the living room, where Janet sat rigidly on the lip-shaped couch, boasted a large oak dining table and a collection of bookshelves. Both rooms had a massive ceramic-tiled rectangle in the corner.

'Ah yes, the proverbial elephant in the room. It's the only drawback, girls – coal heating. But it's terribly efficient once you get the knack,' Beatrice said gingerly as she caught Hailey side-eyeing the tiled mass.

After the tour we headed towards the entrance hall and retrieved our jackets, Beatrice gave us each a stiff embrace, covering us in her mutant floral scent. 'It would be so nice to have you girls stay here, *my fellow travellers,*' she cooed. Janet joined her daughter in the door frame, both women now backlit, their matching bobs silhouetted.

'So we – can – have it?' Hailey asked nervously.

'Yes, I don't see why not,' Janet said, leaning her neck out.

Beatrice shot her mother a look. 'I'll be in touch with the details.'

'And I do hope you girls will enjoy our library,' Janet added just before the door shut.

Hailey hummed excitedly, releasing a, 'Fuck yes,' as we hit the street. I couldn't celebrate. As the apartment faded into darkness I felt choked in anger at Hailey for mentioning the 'murdered friend's ex-boyfriend'. I snapped at her, 'Hailey, that wasn't—'

She didn't even let me finish. 'Oh, come on. It's Beatrice Becks, we needed to tell her a good story so she'd give us the apartment. Look at what we got – it's insane, it's the best apartment in Berlin. What, do you have a better plan?'

I didn't. This was the invisible weight between us. It was Hailey who spoke German, it was Hailey who understood the map of the city, who wasn't afraid to ask strangers directions and send emails about apartments. I sighed, letting her comment melt away on the train.

Later that night, after receiving the confirmation and details from Beatrice, we were on a cloud, even joining the Australian Aarons in smoking weed out the window, while they regaled us about a club called *Berghain*.

'You gotta try, man. No one gets in, we've been rejected two nights in a row.'

'It's just a roll of the dice – the hardest club to get into in the world.'

'It's a motherfucking church of sound.'

'Oy, we will – and we'll get in,' Hailey said, making fun of their accents while passing the joint to me.

Ten minutes later the Australians were putting on jackets and straightening beanies, readying their luck.

Hailey called to them just as they were opening the door, 'I have ecstasy. It's the good stuff, if you want it.'

The boys yipped. Hailey dug into her toiletries, removing three blue pills.

'Thanks, babe, you're the best,' the tallest said, palming the pills and knocking a peck on her cheek.

The door shut behind them, Hailey wiped her face.

'You have ecstasy?'

'Sleeping pills. I scratched off the logo.'

I snorted, then was hit with concern for the Australians and their impending lethal tox reports.

'Revenge, served with a yawn,' Hailey laughed.

We finally drifted off, the door knobs of Beatrice's apartment dancing like sugar plums in our stoned heads.

We had a week until we could move into Beatrice's apartment. We drank beers in the lemon-scented lobby bar of the hostel, which consisted of a mini fridge, sloppily muralled map of Berlin pubs and a TV Tower-shaped honour box chained to the window. Hailey turned to me, 'You know what we need?' I shook my head. 'We need to go out, it's our last weekend before school – we'll probably be too busy once it starts.'

'Where?' I asked, contorting my neck, sarcastically motioning to the map of cartoon bier-steins above us.

'Berghain.'

My image of European clubs was mainly derived from *Alias* episodes where Jennifer Garner donned short black wigs and spoke in Russian to meaty bouncers and snaky women, the Australians being rejected made perfect sense; they didn't belong.

'Come on, we can prove to them that they're losers.'

'Yeah, let's,' I said.

Hailey settled on a pair of purple low-riders and an iridescent butter-cream blouse, me in silver American Apparel tights under ripped jeans and a leather jacket with hoop earrings. The club wasn't far from Hostel Star. We bought a small-ish bottle of vodka and drank it as we walked, its rim slick with Hailey's ruby Dior lipstick.

The industrial building stood alone in a field dotted with chain-link fence and locked bikes, it was well past midnight and the line was at least a hundred people long.

'Everyone's ugly,' Hailey said too loudly towards the queue, 'we'll definitely get in.' We had drained the bottle of vodka. My legs felt loose but waiting for our fate at the door made my nerves stretch like piano wire.

'I know we'll get in,' Hailey kept saying to no one in particular. She popped another wad of her imported Dentyne Ice into her mouth and began smacking. We got closer, we could see clumps getting rejected and some let in.

'Let me do the talking in German, I'm sure they hate tourists.' I nodded, picking at my cuticles. 'And here, put on my lipstick.'

25

I obeyed, squishing the plastic wand into the bright-red hole, then rimming my lips. 'God, everyone's in black,' she gestured towards the fifty or so people who stood, winding back and forth in the cattle-corral between us and the door. 'We shouldn't have worn so much colour.' A hooded guy swooped in and offered to sell us cocaine. Hailey shrugged and exchanged two twenties for a white plastic baggie.

'We have to do it before we get in, I heard they really search you . . .' she said, fondling the baggie, panic ricocheting through her voice. A group of four were rejected. A lanky guy in a bomber was let in. Hailey and I hid behind the lumbering bodies in front of us and snorted rough wet mounds off of her plastic wallet. I knew immediately it wasn't coke. Maybe speed. Something intense. We became way too high. 'I'll put the rest in my underwear,' I suggested. Hailey nodded, her face anaesthetised. Finally, the three tall bodies in front of us were let in. The bouncer, with a thick neck and mean stare, looked us up and down quickly, '*Heute leider nicht.*'

I didn't need to speak German to know. I began walking away quickly, my eyes glued to the dirt, my heart sunk deep into my stomach. Nostrils burning. Where was she? I looked back. Hailey was arguing with the bouncer. It sank further. 'Hailey come on,' I called, desperate for the situation to fade behind us. Desperate to be anywhere but standing in front of that line, all those other eyes, calculating the signifiers of our rejection. She finally turned and left.

'Asshole told me it's 'cause he hated my shoes.'

I looked down at her strappy Marc Jacobs gladiator boots. They were hideous.

'But I think it's because we weren't wearing black. And maybe it's because we were too sexy. Apparently you have to look like a garbage bag to get in there. Fuck him,' her face was hard, her pupils huge, 'let's go somewhere else. I hate techno anyway—'

I nodded. Hailey bought another bottle of vodka and we walked to the train. She was on a war path. I was too high to talk. Hailey's nose began dripping blood, pooling onto the breast plate of her blue coat, the synthetic surface turning amethyst. She cleaned it up with napkins from a kiosk at the train station, assuring me it happened all the time, a side-effect from the nose job.

'There is an artist club I heard about, on Skalitzer, let's go there,' she said, holding the now red heap of tissues to her face. Sipping from the bottle, I followed obediently for what felt like hours, until we found ourselves in a parking lot, music thumping from a brick building just beyond. There were only a dozen or so people in line, again, all dressed in black. I flushed with the possibility of a second rejection. 'We could also just go drink at the hostel, I'm high—' I deflected.

'No,' she spat. The drugs made her mean. Ten gruelling minutes later the bouncer, a guy in a denim jacket with floppy hair, let us in with a smile. Once through the door we erupted.

'Oh my god, yes. See!' Hailey squealed, pushing her way to the bar.

The menu was written out in Sharpie on glitter board, the bartenders, four men, were nearly hairless and all shirtless. Hailey's drug eyes had softened. The dance floor was packed with bodies, glistening limbs swinging, while all the surrounding crevices under chairs and above windowsills were plugged with sweaters and jackets. We shoved our coats under a bench. Hailey ordered vodka sodas, she paid. We bobbed on to the dance floor. The music was more disco than techno, and we soon found ourselves enmeshed in a group of four ex-pats who had the studied ease of having hundreds of nights out together – their hands multiplying like Hindu gods, sliding in and around each other, exchanging drinks, smirks, comments and key bumps.

'Hi, where are you from?' the tall one of the group, with curly brown hair and proud designer glasses, asked Hailey.

'New York,' she said, tucking her hair behind her ear.

'I'm Christopher, I'm from Connecticut,' I heard him say before spinning her ironically as if in a '40s swing movie. *Christopher from Connecticut*, it had the ring of a fancy hand-towel brand. I watched Hailey's red hair release from behind her ear, swooping back and forth, neck elastic, in sync with his. Hailey was pretty. I knew that. I understood what that meant, but seeing her on the dance floor made it real. Like a currency that could get exchanged at the airport. People were drawn to her. She winked at me and I felt a shimmer of pride, we were in this together. I danced off to the side of our new group, nervous, sweaty. Still too high. A Donna Summer song played, it was one of Ivy's favourites, which she kept on repeat in her copper Bravada, blasting it with the windows down – *I feeeel love.*

I reached for the ribbons of Ivy lacing through me. She felt close. The music climbed. I closed my eyes and I could see her, tanned and focused, moving her shoulders in scientific rhythm. I felt her heat braid into mine, and when I returned to the room, my lids fluttering, Ivy was there, just another bouncing body. I stopped moving and she shot eyes into me, they'd always had the effect of Nerf guns, softly capturing whoever they were pointed towards – I held my hand out, dumbfounded. She was solid, flesh, bone, blood pumping. Euphoric, I wove my hands around her wrist, pulling her towards me. We moved in unison, I had ten thousand questions I wanted to ask. *What happened? Who killed you? Where are you? Are you mad at me?* I leaned in, my lips suddenly Saharan. Ivy held her finger up, shushing my fumbling mouth, then slowly backed away. She began to slip, dissolving into the room. Panicking, I grabbed for her wrist, but this time it was Hailey's, she smiled before turning back towards Christopher from Connecticut.

Donna Summer faded out but Hailey and Ivy's merge felt permanent, diluting the confused venom that had been pumping through me since the funeral. I continued to dance, staring at Hailey as she flipped her hair back and forth, her tits jumping from her push-up bra with each step, my heart expanding every time her eyes met mine. Only then did I realise how desperate I was for her friendship.

Thirty minutes later Hailey pulled her face close to mine, 'They want to get out of here. I like this guy, he's a filmmaker – I think maybe famous. They're all really cool and like – we should go, they have a taxi outside—'

I would have followed her anywhere. We found our coats, which were now wet with spilled drinks, and followed as the group of four jumped into a pale-yellow van. As the door slid shut, Hailey and Christopher's tongues began making watery whale sounds. The girl seated next to me, dressed in stretchy layers of black that gave her the outline of a bat, extended her hand in an expression of deep boredom without even offering her name.

'Where are we going?' I asked her.

'Berghain,' she said nonchalantly, her angular haircut shifting towards me as she turned to look out the window.

My heart sank. Hailey looked up at me in horror, her tongue still in Christopher's mouth. The car rode on.

After a few minutes, Christopher released himself from Hailey's face, smeared in her lipstick, 'Let's do some lines.'

On cue the bat-shaped girl whipped out a silver cigarette case and expertly cut dashes, her wrist gyroscopic as the car's wheels spun on the pavement below us. In terror, I obliged, pulling my hair back. After some silence, Christopher and Hailey returned to the spit swapping.

'So what do you do?' I asked the bat-shaped girl.

She rolled her eyes. 'I'm a trend forecaster.'

I nodded like I knew what that was.

'Has no one told you yet that's a rude question to ask people in Berlin?' The taxi slowed. We were right back where we'd started.

Jostling from the jaws of the sliding door, Hailey whispered, 'Let's just switch clothes, they won't remember. We can't tell them we got rejected, it's too – humiliating.'

'Did you not ask them where they were going?' I nearly screamed.

Hailey shook her head quickly in an effort to quiet my outrage.

The mass of people waiting in line had tripled. We took our place on the sidewalk, nearly a block from the club. When the others in our group seemed occupied, Hailey and I traded coats. I put my hair down. Hailey put her hair up. After forty minutes she insisted we switch shoes.

'No, you said he hated them,' I moaned.

'He hated them on me.'

The whole night felt like an uncontrollable waterfall. My body suspended in motion, propelled towards an out-of-sight drop, I sighed and slipped my feet in. The boots were two sizes too big.

'It's best if we go in two smaller groups,' Christopher said, splitting Hailey and me apart. When we were near enough that I could see it was a different bouncer, I exhaled in relief.

The bat-shaped girl removed the drugs from the cigarette case and stuck them in her sock. The Spaniards in front of us were rejected. Hailey and Christopher were first. Just then the bouncer with the thick neck, from earlier, returned. He started laughing. Hailey turned to me, a thin river of blood began dripping from her nose.

'I told you two – *not tonight*. You can switch clothes, but those boots.' He pointed to me, 'Go home—' he turned to the stunned group, 'and same goes for the rest of you.'

The bat-shaped girl looked mortified. Christopher's mouth hung open. 'Look, we come here all the time—'

'I understand but I already rejected these girls once tonight.'

Tears were welling in Hailey's eyes as a red geyser shot from her rhinoplastied nose. Christopher turned calmly, clearly not wanting to make a scene at the door. But ten paces away he began screaming in Hailey's direction, 'Why wouldn't you tell us that you had already been rejected? Are you insane? You'll be lucky if any of us ever get in again.' He was looking at the bat-shaped girl, shaking his head.

'You're the one who insisted we bring them, Chris, this one's on you,' she snapped, already headed back to the taxi line, she turned her asymmetrical haircut towards us, 'that's what you get for picking up randos.'

Hailey looked as if an axe had split her into two, she tore off running, blood flicking like rain behind her. I followed. She was fast. Five warehouse-ish buildings later she finally stopped, I hobbled behind, my toes smashing against the leather insides of her boots. She was crouched near a bush peeing, crying. I paused, catching my breath, unbuttoned my pants and joined her squatting, our lazy streams of piss floating down the cold sidewalk, peaceful and unaware of the night's drama.

'Let's just never talk about it – ever,' she said, wiping a mixture of snot and blood from her nose.

I nodded and whispered, 'Every night you miss in Berlin is a night you miss in Berlin,' then buttoned my pants back up.

School was barely existent. There was no Carol Gaynor, no friendly coddlers to help us along. Just a series of massive metal doors painted in thick lacquer that remained locked or banged shut right before we could catch them. When I finally managed to pick up my school ID from a woman with a tight black braid who presided over a red filing cabinet, she simply pulled out a quarter sheet of paper and asked me to sign at the bottom by tapping her pen. Her parting words were a choppy *Gud luck*.

I held my breath as I entered the Hogwarts-esque facade, hoping for glowing torches and over-stuffed chairs, but instead found a labyrinth of unheated, debris-littered hallways that reeked of turpentine. My class was in the outermost 'Hof', which apparently meant 'back building'. The room was the size of a small airplane hangar and paved in offcuts of rough lumber with brown vines crawling up the windows. All of the artworks spread out on ancient desks had a shared earthy tone; piled moss sculptures, unfired clay smooshed around barbed wire, stuffed birds with their heads attached backwards, indigo barrels, rotting water in labelled glass jars. It all had the air of an experimental natural history museum. Standing in the middle of the room, I tried to remember how I had ended up here – after I had switched from Helsinki to Berlin, a voluptuous goth girl had overheard me talking about the Berlin school in the elevator, she'd turned her painted neck towards me and informed me that Klaus Simons was the best teacher there. I scribbled his name on my hand, grateful for the scrap of information, and submitted my request for his class that day. I hadn't even googled him.

A swanlike boy approached me with skittish English and informed me that Klaus was only coming in for classes every third week and, *Yes*, it was all in German. Roughly calculated, I would have nine classes while in Berlin. I had four classes a day in New York. The swan offered to show me the cafeteria, we both ate potatoes, his mashed, mine fried. We smiled a lot and nodded.

Four days before school officially started, Hailey and I moved into Beatrice's apartment. 'Which room do you want?' she asked, taking her backpack off. I shrugged, knowing it was going to be one of those passive-aggressive games. Obviously I cared and so did she. Hailey was untangling her backpack from her hair, she went into the slightly larger room with the bay window and real bed, letting out a sigh, 'If it's OK I'll take this one.'

She didn't even play the game. I rolled my eyes and suitcase into the room with the lip couch and day bed, which was still by far the nicest place I'd ever lived.

We both knew we were not the respectable clean girls we had dutifully promised, we were artists with India-ink, rubber cement and travel paint sets – the white shag trapezoid carpet wouldn't have lasted a week so we rolled it up and shoved it under Hailey's bed along with the Persian one from my room. For those first hours we were royalty, striding around the open spaces of the apartment, arms outstretched, savouring our good fortune, but the opulence began to fade as soon as we tried to build a fire. Each white-tiled stove was topped with a series of glazed reliefs depicting budding flowers and curling branches and fitted at the bottom with a little metal door that creaked to reveal a space where the alleged 'fires' were to be made. Beatrice had left behind one ton of coal in the basement, an orange mesh bag filled with ten-inch sticks, two bricks of a marshmallowy fire starter that reeked of kerosene and a pile of the *New York Times*. Dropping to our knees, we began balling up paper; several smoky attempts later, we had our fires burning.

We added greasy black bricks of coal and sure enough, after a few hours they glowed like bars of gold – meaning it was time to add the next round of bricks, and so on and so forth, until we died or summer came.

On the fridge we found a note outlining housekeeping details, how trash was to be sorted, the coal ash disposed of, the water heater turned on, and ending with a forwarding address for the mail to Janet in Sylt who apparently took care of the minutiae of her daughter's life while Beatrice focused on writing. We had gathered up the tumble of white envelopes upon our arrival. Hailey wanted to open them before forwarding.

'We can seal them back up.'

'I'm pretty sure that's a felony.'

'We can just say it was a mistake,' she said as she slipped her index finger in, popping the bonded flap.

'Boring, electricity bill.' She picked out another, tearing it open.

Her eyes lit up. 'It's from her editor in New York, *Mabel Henderson*, it looks like Ms Becks has postponed her next book—' she paused, scanning the rest of the letter, 'Twice!'

I walked into the other room, making a mental note not to leave my mail around Hailey.

On our third day in the apartment Hailey came home with a Schlecker drugstore bag full of small cardboard boxes. 'We're going to dye everything black,' she announced, filling up the tub with steaming water. She dumped the powdered contents in, then began bringing armfuls of clothes: T-shirts, white tights, a light-blue dress, a grey sweater, the bruise-purple pants. 'Come on, there is *literally* no point in having any colour here,' she said, prodding at the lumpy mass stewing in the now jet-black tub. I threw in a striped tank top, a yellow pair of tights and a baby-pink T-shirt my mom had given me.

'You should dye those dance shirts you have,' Hailey said without looking up.

'They're Ivy's—' I replied uneasily.

'I figured. You don't think it's weird that you wear them?'

I flushed and turned, leaving her to push the mound of fabric with a broom handle. I didn't want to explain that I only felt like myself in Ivy's clothes.

No matter how attentive we were to our precious coal fires the air still felt thick with the impending winter. And Hailey, like me, rarely had class – so we were both always home. We took to hanging out in the kitchen with the door to the gas stove open to keep warm, where we'd empty jugs of gluhwein into a thin metal pot, careful not to boil the alcohol off. The mulled wine tasted of Christmas and we'd slurp it down while the oven purred its soft blue heat. Hauling coal was its own hell. Coal was stored in the basement that reeked of WWII, with creepy messages burned in frothy candlestick on the low ceiling, and notices about rats in old German Gothic font. We only had the nerves to go down there when we were completely wasted, giggling while hauling the fifty-brick stacks stair by stair.

It was tenuous and still new, but we had forged a friendship on our coal-heated island. I had forgotten to buy eggs, she had eaten the last of my muesli, I had relied on her too much for her German, she'd left a bloody tampon in the toilet, I'd locked myself out and she'd come home to let me in – but it somehow always balanced out. I decided that even if this was all Berlin was, just us, drinking and talking, it seemed good, better than being in New York where everything reminded me of Ivy, who was no longer a subway ride away. But one late night after building our fires, Hailey was splayed out in a starfish shape on the floor of my room while I lay curled in bed. We'd drunk two bottles of wine and had exhausted most topics of conversation and were both zoning out as Kanye West whined from Beatrice's crappy speakers.

'I'm bored,' Hailey pronounced at the end of the song. 'Tell me something about Ivy.'

I shook my head, returning to my computer screen. I still wasn't ready, and didn't want Ivy to be the bubble wrap to Hailey's boredom.

Amy Winehouse began howling, her voice ricocheting around the room. We downed another glass each without talking.

'You happy?' she asked. 'I mean here.'

I waited for a break in the guitar riff, 'It's better than New York, I guess. You?'

'My brother learned French, so Paris was his thing. And I learned German so I always knew Berlin was going to be my thing. I just had a feeling, that like . . .' She tilted her head and her heart-shaped face was softly illuminated by the train rushing by. 'I just always had the feeling that my *story* would take place here. It's just not turning out yet – how I had imagined.'

I was annoyed at how she said the word *story*. As if I, and the rest of the city, were mere set pieces in her high-school fantasy. Hailey had a way of making everything seem like it was for some larger purpose. Not God, but self-narrativising.

After all our drinking my jaw felt loose, it slipped out. 'Did you watch a lot of *Cabaret*?' I asked with more sarcasm than I'd intended to reveal. I had only seen snippets of it – Liza Minnelli twirling her translucent flesh around a chair in a smoky club, or drooling German in a feathered robe – a distinctly annoying spectre of Berlin.

'Of course I did, Zoe.'

My sarcasm had flipped a hidden switch.

'You think it's funny,' she took a sip then shifted her body towards me, 'you think you're *alternative,* and outside of the system. You rented the interesting movies. And went to the noise concerts in Bushwick. And you, like everyone at that school, thought you had to be dirty and weird to be a good artist. But that's not true.'

'I don't think I'm *alternative*,' I said incredulously.

She was seething. 'I know you were the creative-weird-moody-girl in high school. But you weren't the weird one in New York. Nope. Not by a long shot, you were just another in a circuitous line. And that probably made you feel worse than Nate Kai, or whatever you thought you didn't like about

New York.' The bottle of wine was showing itself in the roundness of her words. I remained silent, not sure if I should protest. She continued, 'Being an artist is about selling stories, and selling stories is commerce. There is nothing alternative about it.'

Hailey had pulled herself off the floor and was already looming in the door frame.

'I don't think I'm—'

'You do,' she said, before turning to leave for her room.

I sat silently ringing in hurt, that whatever this was, and whoever she thought I was, wasn't enough.

3

Last May swept into New York City on an ecstatic warm current, bra-straps and bare legs emerging en-masse. I didn't think I'd end up going on exchange to Berlin – and not because I'd wanted to go to Helsinki but because Ivy was murdered and I fell in love. I was on the train and my hand sanitiser had exploded in my bag, when my phone rang it was soaked in green apple-scented alcohol. I wiped it off on my skirt but when I held it to my face I still felt nauseous from the fumes. It was James, one of my best friends from high school. He'd been the star of the musical theatre programme, and he had just fulfilled his dream of moving to Orlando and performing in a gay club. He'd put up with hell in high school, way more than me, but he'd made it. James was uncharacteristically quiet.

'What's up?' I asked again. He never had trouble finding words. I knew something was wrong.

'It's Ivy.'

She had been stabbed fourteen times on her way home from *The Fish*, a nautical-themed bar with two-for-one Natty Lights, on the south side of Sebastian. They didn't know who did it or why. I thought I could feel a hand coming up from the inside of my body, jamming its fingers out of my mouth – I began coughing. A large lady in a pristine white polyester suit pulled a wad of tissues from her purse. The train creeped over the East River. Ivy was my best friend, the ballerina who'd twirled her way through our adolescence. She was supposed to be stretching in a lilac leotard Uptown, drinking water from a turquoise Nalgene, preparing for her next leap, spin, jump, triple axel whatever.

I had seen her the week before. She'd been stressed about finals and wasn't sure if she should take the weekend off to go back for her Grandma Jane's eightieth birthday. *You'll regret it forever if you don't go* – that string of words I'd said to her I've since turned over and over, an anxious rosary. She had sighed agreeing, then, as she always did when uncertain, began furiously bouncing her leg.

We both loved Grandma Jane, she was a self-described *feisty old girl*, who wore only pastels and swore in Southern-isms. *Shit*, was *Sweet Honey Ice Tea*. In middle school she'd taken us for frozen yogurt every Friday, teaching us among other things that the rudest thing you can say to someone is usually polite – her favourite was, *I'll pray for you*. I pulled out a pink wax-paper envelope, and pushed it towards Ivy. Earlier that day in the Lower East Side, trolling flea markets for art supplies, I'd found a gold chain bracelet, with an italic cursive nameplate spelling – *Jane*.

'Zoe, she's going to love it. It's very Carrie Bradshaw.'

'So is Grandma Jane.'

Ivy slipped the bracelet on her wrist, admiring it in the reflection of the window. 'Or maybe I'll keep it.'

'Wear it till her birthday.'

'Zoe, I really might not go – finals are crazy.'

'Then how's she going to get her present?' I chided.

She inhaled. 'I know, you're right.'

When Ivy transferred to my school in fourth grade I was stung with jealousy by her hair. It took two elastic bands to secure her Coke-bottle-thick ponytail, which shimmered like underwater treasure. She was instantly popular. Good at making the girls who sat under the gazebo at lunch laugh, good at geography, theatre, cheerleading and she even spoke fluent Spanish. My grade-school envy was so palpable, some days it made my teeth itch. How could she simply arrive and be friends with everyone? After school I'd stare at myself in the mirror. Practising scrunching my nose when I laughed as she did. When she came to school wearing a light-pink plastic Roxy surf watch, I swooned with jealousy, and begged my mom to buy me one. When she finally caved, and Ivy noticed the identical timepiece proudly strapped on my young wrist, I lied – and told her I'd had it for months, long before her. And when Ivy began wearing headbands, I forced my mom to take me to Eckerd's drug store to pick out a rainbow pack. It went on and on, until we became eerily similar, twins. Me mirroring every decision Ivy made.

And finally in the fifth grade, due to a fortuitous seating-chart, the object of my youthful obsession turned into my best friend. Later that year we won second place in the school's science fair testing salt levels in the Indian River Lagoon. To celebrate, Ivy's mom Ana took us to the Disney Hotel pool for virgin Piña Coladas. The drinks were served in bong-shaped glasses sprouting Mickey Mouse ears, and when all the white syrup was slurped I slipped the exotic swizzle straw into my beach bag for a future life on my windowsill – a token of our union. Ivy and I spent every weekend together from then on.

In New York we were both busy but we texted every day. She thought my art school friends were snobs and I disliked most of her dance friends, who all seemed to survive solely on miso broth. But it didn't matter, we continued Grandma Jane's tradition, proudly eating froyo at Union Square each Friday, swapping stories, disappointments and mundane trivia about our new lives. We were planning to move in together, I was pushing for Williamsburg, she Yorkville. We would start looking in summer.

The airplane to Orlando was cold and quiet. I wanted

peanuts, something salty. I shakily asked the flight attendant, who responded, 'The peanut days are over.' The phrase felt like an epitaph. It had only been two years since our final summer before college. We had been invincible windmills dancing at sweaty punk shows, borrowing our moms' cars to drive to whatever friend's beach house was empty for the weekend.

I retraced the steps of that summer. Heavy-drinking 40's on the side of Wabasso bridge, letting the bottle whisp and crack into the rocks below. I met up with Molly, Ashleigh and Alexa, we waded into the stretch of beach where we'd hung out after school, passing a sandy bottle of Bacardi raspberry, lamenting – if only one of us had been there to loan her ten more bucks for another round or walk with her home or call her a taxi. Ashleigh was convinced it was her fault because she had bailed on Ivy that night to study for her nursing final. Ashleigh could barely speak unless completely liquored up, then she couldn't stop the low sobby bursts – ITSsnortMY-FAULTITSMYslopFUALTITSMYsobFAULT. Alexa wanted vengeance, at least vengeance was a direction. I felt still and useless. Alexa and Ashleigh and the others were interviewed, the police asking insensitive questions. *Did she have a history of picking up men in bars? Would you describe her as a party girl? Did she always wear such short skirts? Did she have any enemies?*

I went to visit Ivy's mom, Ana, every day I was home. I'd remembered her as bronzed and strong, wearing three thin silver necklaces and making jokes in Spanish at our expense while fixing sandwiches in a bikini top. Ana was completely ashen, fingers chalk sticks, eyes two dark stones. My mom insisted on making food. I delivered the tupperware, feeling stupid and angry, as if a plastic cube of egg salad could ease any of this. But Ana let me sit in Ivy's room as long as I didn't disturb anything and it comforted me that it would

41

be an air-conditioned tomb I could visit forever. I'd flop into the ballet-slipper beanbag she'd gotten for her thirteenth birthday, the pink ribbon handles dirty from slumber parties, and flip through our yearbooks and read the things Katie Newman and Beau Alter had written: *Never Change*. I looked through her clothes, shoving a few of her T-shirts and two pairs of jeans in my bag. I was numb. How were people supposed to feel when they lost their best friend? I had fought so hard for her, for us. Our friendship. I sprayed myself with her perfume. Clinique Happy Heart. What a horrible name.

In high school I worked weekends behind the perfume counter at the Indian River Mall. Ivy would often visit, leaning against the glass vitrine slurping down a Jamba Juice – and we'd take bets on what customers would choose. CK One was easy. And Tommy Girl, in head-to-toe Abercrombie, you could pick out in a crowd. The older ladies went for Shalimar or Chanel, and we assumed drank from their bottles of Elizabeth Arden's Red Door based on the speed they went through it. But we were often wrong – surprised by the sophisticated taste of the teenager wearing a bedazzled bandanna as tank top. Ivy liked the cheesiest scents. Clinique Happy Heart, cucumber and orange, Miss Dior Chérie, a strawberry cream-pie that brought to mind a banquet of teenage girls in white cotton panties. I tried them all, Mugler's Alien, Stella, Escada, Flowerbomb and Versace Bright Crystal – but in the end I wore nothing. Everything always reminded me of someone else. Some other girl with glossed lips and Dillard's bags hanging from her wrist.

The whole town was trying to find meaning in the murder, which had no suspects, no motive, no theft, no missing wallet, no rape. I had watched enough *CSI* to know the Sebastian Police Department had no idea what the fuck they were doing.

Ana would answer their calls, give the *mmmhmmm*s, and then put the phone down. How could there be nothing? How could they not know the kind of knife? Couldn't they pour some sort of resin or plaster into her wounds and remove the shape of the blade, fingerprints in tow?

No one I had loved had ever died. I didn't know how to act. My mom and I weren't religious. We were Unitarian Universalists when people asked. Ivy's murder made me feel in-between, unable to connect. I couldn't cry and didn't like getting hugged. At the funeral James sang with a rag-tag mix of theatre kids and band nerds – dressed in his full Stevie Nicks, slinky dress and lots of scarves. It's what Ivy would have wanted. James's blonde wig hanging to his shoulders, one of the spaghetti straps falling as he gripped the microphone. The opening notes of 'Landslide' by Fleetwood Mac teetered off the piano. James's voice was thick and booming, warming the refrigerator of a church. You could feel the conservative Christians squirm, whispering that not only was this inappropriate for a house of God, but *a black man can't be Stevie Nicks*. It was the song James and Ivy had choreographed a dance to during that last summer. They'd spent every afternoon in her mom's garage. 'Zee studio,' Ivy liked to say in a cartoon French accent. While they rehearsed I'd photographed, framing their tight bodies as they drifted through the summer air, thumbs locked together, fingers fluttering.

Cause I've built my life around you.

The funeral was a premature high-school reunion, the freshmen fifteen barely hanging on our bodies, thickets of parents standing like reeds on the edge. Ivy's mom stood stoically in a dark-green dress pierced by a silver button with a picture of a young Ivy in a cheerleading uniform. Ivy's father Eric, who ran a carpet-cleaning business, was unable to make eye contact with the mourners, instead releasing a high-pitched humming sound as he accepted hugs.

Grandma Jane got up from her chair when she saw me, her white cotton-ball hair fluffed to perfection, tears in her eyes.

'I'm so sorry,' I said, embracing her small form.

'Mother of pearl, I'm sorry for the whole world.'

'Did she give you the bracelet?'

'What bracelet?' she asked, head shaking, looking confused and suddenly elderly.

'Ivy was supposed to – never mind, I'm so sorry.'

I hugged her again and let her return to her seat. I'd forgotten. Ivy was killed the day before the birthday party. She'd never had the chance to give the bracelet to Grandma Jane. Walking away my mother grabbed my arm and whispered to me, 'I don't know what I'd do if anything happened to you.' I squeezed her back, unsure of what to say, unsure of how to behave even with my own mother.

I had told Ana I couldn't give a speech, words seemed unimportant, she said she understood but I felt lame, as if I were letting Ivy down. What could I say? *The peanut days are over.* Ivy would have given a great speech at my funeral. I bet she'd already had it planned out – at least an outline or some bullet points. I had nothing, and yet I knew I wouldn't even exist without her. I'd never have gone to New York or had the courage to go to portfolio reviews or apply for scholarships. The slideshow of Ivy cycled endlessly. The cap and gown. 'Zee studio', with its wobbly Ikea mirrors leaning on crates. Ivy with a hairsprayed bun at the premier of *Swan Lake*. Ivy clutching a bouquet in a parking lot, squinting. Her first recital. Ivy embracing Grandma Jane on the beach.

Falling in love at a funeral was wrong, but it happened. Jesse was sitting to my right. I could feel him fall in love with me. And I was ahead of him by a full few seconds, like a rocket looking back just to make sure the second had launched. His eyes kept darting over, holding mine, his lids heavy with tears.

I had seen Jesse Waylon just before the holidays in the parking lot of Publix when I was home for Thanksgiving. He was picking up a Key Lime pie, his wrap-around sunglasses glaring. When he called my name over four lines of parked cars, I smiled, recognising his voice before seeing him. He bounded over, hugging me and my mom. After initial parentally-acceptable pleasantries, I told him *no*, Ivy hadn't come back, she had rehearsals, but *sure* I'd be happy to get a drink with him and catch up.

The next night Jesse and I met at a beach bar with a sand floor, he wore a dress shirt and was sweating profusely. He animatedly told me about his latest BMX competitions and the dystopic protein-powder-pyramid-scheme his brother had been roped into. Jesse's teeth were disturbingly white, and popped against his sunburnt skin. Like everyone in the town, he was a redneck – a lover of deep-sea fishing and duck hunting – but BMX made him something else, it gave him edge, and a pack of like-minded vanilla vandals to roam the streets.

I told him about school, about New York, and Ivy, who I admitted I wished I saw more – she was busy, I was busy. Each time I mentioned Ivy his eyes grew focused, leaning in. A pang of jealousy shot through me. I didn't tell him about Ivy's new dancer boyfriend, instead changing the subject, dazzled by his smile. He radiated coolness, his tattoo of E.T. biking over the moon peeking out on his chest from his now mostly unbuttoned shirt. I insisted we leave after the third round, I had to fly back in the morning. He drove me home and asked when I'd be back next, I said I didn't know. When we got to my mom's he leaned over, my heart skipped – he opened the door, and told me he hoped there would be a reason soon.

After the prayers and songs and the endless hugs, teachers, parents, ministers and scantily dressed teenagers filed out, we ended up at Hurricane Harbor, a pastel crab shack on the Indian River, just a few miles down the road from The Fish where Ivy had been stabbed. Barry, the owner of The Fish, had offered to host the event but no one felt it was right and I didn't want to be surrounded by the silent objects that witnessed her last moments – the scalloped napkins, the red plastic pitchers of ice water, the corner of the bar where she balanced her last drink.

Hurricane Harbor was a fading tourist dive with peeling murals of tropical birds and Jimmy Buffett calypso covers on loop. It was packed but no one quite knew what to say. Faint gossiping about how the police had no idea who did it, statistics of murders, meth heads, dealers, and the favoured perpetrators *the tourist or outsider* – because after all no one wanted to believe someone in Sebastian would do this.

Jesse was on the other side of the bar, looking anxious in his ill-fitting suit. He pointed to the bartender and ordered me a beer, cracking a big sad smile. 'Margaritaville' began plink-plonking on a steel drum. The room was sweltering, even with the ceiling fans thudding above us. Everything was melting. Looking at Jesse made me feel closer to Ivy. He held my gaze, scooping my eyeballs like liquid sorbet. I could feel him consume me. Jesse had dated Ivy for all of high school, he had been her big love, all the milestones – prom, her virginity in his parents' condo, break-ups, make-ups. The summer after freshman year, when Ivy had just gotten her licence, she would pick me up, then Jesse, and then we'd drive down A1A to pick up my boyfriend, Brian Delters. We'd spin our way to the ice-cold mall to aimlessly wander or we'd slather ourselves in coconut oil at the beach while Ivy and I passed watermelon Lip Smackers back and forth.

My feelings for Jesse had drifted in the tangled depths of high-school friendships, only surfacing once, while Ivy and he had briefly broken up junior year. Jesse was driving me home from an uneventful house party. Pausing at a stop light, he kissed me, or I kissed him, I couldn't remember. The betrayal had rooted itself as a dark sinking bomb in my stomach. I called him crying the next morning and made him promise to never tell, he agreed. And now, standing at the bar in Hurricane Harbor, it seemed that night had happened in another lifetime, to other people, with stupid problems, kids.

Jesse walked towards me with my beer, his eyes swollen from crying, taking my hand and flipping it around in his, slowly pulling me through the clumps of friends, who having moved on from signing the guest book, were now pressing the soft-tipped markers into their flesh, writing Ivy's name. Their arms and legs covered in looping I-V-Y's looked like baseballs after a Little League season. The smell of the marker reminded me of the green apple alcohol from the hand sani-tiser, the beginning of this trip that we would all walk away from back to whatever it was we did, but Ivy wouldn't. Nursing my beer, I felt sick. I wanted to leave. The room was spinning. I couldn't find my shoes but couldn't remember taking them off. I left barefoot.

Jesse wanted to drive.

'Let's just call a cab?' I pleaded.

'I drive best buzzed, Zoe. Honest.' Jesse held his hands over his head and performatively walked a straight line.

His insistence on driving drunk was a leftover bad-boy streak from high school. But he had buried Ivy's cat, and helped her mom put up storm shutters, and always remem-bered birthdays. Ivy said it frequently – *one of the good ones*.

I shrugged and got in. Jesse lived on the other side of town with a bunch of skateboarders, who were sprawled out in the formica kitchen drinking canned beer. The guys all nodded. I guess they approved of scoring a fuck at a funeral.

Everything in his sand-coloured room was in moving-boxes and the walls were dotted in tape marks from ripped-down posters. We made out in sloppy bursts, his fat lips pressing on mine. He smelled warm, a mixture of cedar and suntan lotion. He had the biggest dick I'd ever seen, Ivy had not exaggerated. He cupped my chin and pressed himself into me. He felt like a drug, we didn't sleep, lying in bed tracing each other's palms while I periodically used my fingers as windshield wipers on his cheeks. I loved watching his eyes well. His wet lashes, thick and black as Betty Boop's. When the birds began chirping their rapid morning melodramas, he motioned to the boxes with a heavy sigh as if admitting a huge secret, as if I only now could see them towering in the corner of his little room.

He was moving to Wyoming to work at his stepdad's pavement company, learning how to grade driveways and hot-pour asphalt. This was his last night in town. He had already delayed leaving for a week because of Ivy's funeral, and had to be there by the first of June. He told me he loved me. He said things that sounded like they were from movies. *I've always known it's been you.*

His room was cold from the buzzing air conditioner, I slipped into his Thrasher hoodie. He became sombre, dipping back into the mood of the funeral, his eyes flooded. More movie lines: *We already lost too much, let's not lose this – for Ivy. No one loved her like we did.* He licked his lips and asked me to come with him to Wyoming. I hid my face, not sure what to say. I was relieved, relieved to be with someone who truly understood and was capable of processing the hurt. Rolling me into his arms he pulled the hoodie off, I was naked again, he climbed on top.

When we were too hungry to stay in bed we ate waffles in his filthy kitchen, and then I helped him carry his boxes to his Malibu. Sitting on a broken half-pipe in his driveway I watched while he loaded his trunk, realising if I didn't go to Berlin I'd have the year off. I hadn't *really* wanted to go there anyway. I told him *yes*, he picked me up, lifting me onto the hood of his car. Happy to at least have a direction.

When I got back to my mom's house she was standing on the patio, her arms sharply folded. 'You could have at least called.'

I scoffed, a teenager again, 'I texted.'

'I wanted to hear your voice.'

I knew everyone was anxious. Still reeling from Ivy. I should have apologised. Instead I let the screen door slap behind me, forcing my mother to follow as I hoisted myself onto the kitchen counter, my usual after-school position. I was fidgeting with a box of Goldfish.

'What is it?'

It had always been just the two of us, we'd established early on that we didn't need to tell each other everything, but she'd always listened when it mattered, and she could tell this was one of those times.

Still in my black dress from the funeral, I told her I wasn't going to Berlin. I told her it felt too far, I didn't feel strong enough, all the things a mother couldn't disagree with. Then I told her about Jesse. I saw her body tighten, she took a breath and moved away, just slightly.

'Ivy's boyfriend?'

It stung. But Ivy had dumped Jesse months before we'd moved to New York, that was almost two years ago. It felt like a lifetime ago. She recrossed her arms and I could see her running through the situation like a slot machine, the combinations, the probable outcomes. She had never loved the idea of me going to school in Berlin, but she definitely didn't love the idea of me moving to Wyoming to be Jesse's housewife. She released a long thin breath, looking defeated. I heaved myself off the counter.

'But you'll go back to New York after—'

I nodded.

49

'It doesn't look good,' she paused, 'the two of you.'

'I don't . . .'

I let whatever response I had trail away as I disappeared down the carpeted hallway.

In the bathroom I stared at myself in the mirror. I had always been the brunette to Ivy's deep honey blonde. The Veronica to her Betty. We both had bikini bodies but my tits were bigger and her ass was nicer. I burned, she tanned. And I shaved and she waxed. We'd grown into our skin together. I followed her lead, systematically trying out waterproof mascaras, only using Herbal Essences shampoo, mine in the pink bottle, hers in yellow. Staring at myself, I realised I had always existed in comparison to her, and now my reflection was left holding both of us. She was inside of me, I assumed Jesse knew it too. Being with him felt like being with her, like she was a secret only we truly knew.

I wanted a bubble bath. Naked, I rifled through the remnants of my cosmetic youth; half-used pack of Clearasil pads, cherry-scented hand cream, a bag of cotton balls, nail polish remover, electric-green aloe – and a box of blonde hair dye. Without thinking, I took the box and opened it, spreading its contents on the ledge of the tub. Putting a toe in the burning-hot water I slowly lowered myself in, as my skin turned scarlet I wondered what Ivy would actually think of me and Jesse. I hadn't told her about our drink a few months prior, it hadn't seemed important. Now it did. If I told her now she'd probably just have wanted to hear all the details, then drive to Barnes & Noble and buy a stack of wedding magazines, then google beachfront venues on her blue plastic MacBook. I dunked my head back and squirted the blonde dye into the little bowl, it stank of ammonia.

After a dreamless nap I slipped into the humid air of the back patio. It was already night. I glanced over at the beach chair next to me, the woven pink stripes sagging towards the concrete. The scream of the katydids hole-punched my thoughts. I couldn't understand her murder. I didn't know what to say to anyone. How was I supposed to be able to talk about the grotesque moment that had transpired; a knife stabbing fourteen times into her body? How had the ingredients aligned? How had Allen Sternbuckle, a retired accountant, and his boxer *Trixie* found her that morning? And why had Allen described it in such mechanical detail to the newspaper? I couldn't get myself to read any of it; the dunes, the blood, the pattern on her chest, the time it took the police to arrive. All I could do was understand the small deaths – the empty chair, or the fact that she would never shower after the beach. Forget her towel. Steal my mom's wine coolers or call me to tell me she was waiting in the car outside. I wished I could cry.

The next morning I was greeted with the news that Chelsea Benedict, an insect with tits, had found out from one of the skateboarders that I had gone home with Jesse the night of Ivy's funeral. Chelsea hated me. Among other grievances, she blamed me for Ivy quitting cheerleading the year they lost the State Championships. She had made it her mission to destroy me, even personally derailing my first art show the summer before my junior year. Craig, my then boss at the ice-cream shop, had offered to let me install whatever I wanted on the walls for the month of August, so I'd spent June and July and most of my paycheques on framing. I photographed Ivy in her dance studio, her slender arms and legs stretched in different poses. I made eight collages. Chopping up Ivy's limbs, mixing them with scenes from environmental disasters I'd cut from *National Geographic*s. A pair of tan legs en pointe shooting out from a crude-oil-encrusted egret, the *Exxon Valdez* emerging from Ivy's torso. I'd even written a press release about 'the human impact on the natural world' and sent it to the local newspaper.

Chelsea found out about the show and started a rumour

that my practice of cutting up photographs of bodies was satanic, and the cherry on top – that I was gay and in love with Ivy. Sebastian is a small and very Christian town, it spread like a hot knife through butter. There was a message board, a petition, and a protest with a few cheerleads and megaphones. Craig freaked out. He claimed the ice-cream store had a *no controversy policy*. He made me take the framed collages down the night before I was supposed to have the opening. He couldn't even decide what was worse, the possibility of me being gay or worshipping the devil. That night Ivy found me at the beach, drunk off the cheap cabernet I'd persuaded my mom to buy, because all *real* openings had wine. Ivy sat down into the sand next to me and took a swig from the bottle.

'Why did you let her bullshit get to you?'

'Craig cancelled. She won.'

'Craig's an idiot, it's an ice-cream shop, I promise you would have deleted this off your CV after one year in New York.' She paused and looked at me seriously, 'But you could be gay, that would be OK.'

'Why does everyone think I'm gay?'

'Well, I for one know you usually date guys out of spite. Everyone else thinks it because you wear cargo shorts and that ugly messenger bag.'

'Jesus, Ivy—'

'Let's go home,' she said, slapping my knee and tossing the wine bottle into the boardwalk trash can.

I was angry about the show until I got my revenge. I fucked Chelsea's baseball-playing boyfriend, Brock Hansen, after a Spanish field trip in the back seat of his immaculate Chevy Impala, leaving my thong as a gift to be discovered in the passenger-side cup-holder.

And here I was, nearly halfway through college and still getting bullied by the same *rah-rah* girls, but they'd exchanged their pompoms for hymnals and were cheering for Jesus Christ with the same lunatic self-righteousness they had for the Sebastian Sharks. I almost felt bad for them at the funeral, sitting in their too-tanned-over-plucked-eyebrow clump, they were stuck in this hot boring town with nothing to do but preach shit. All my sympathy evaporated after reading Chelsea's not-so-subtle Facebook posts about the art of grieving.

1 Thessalonians 4:14
   For we believe that Jesus died and rose again, and so we believe that God will bring with Jesus those who have fallen asleep in him.
   ****A little reminder to those who need an etiquette lesson on mourning – The bible wasn't talking about falling asleep WITH him, him being the ex-boyfriend of your dead best friend – THE NIGHT OF HER FUNERAL.
   ****Stay classy Sebastian X Chels

I ignored it. I was leaving and the sharks would find some new chum or just get knocked up. It wasn't my fault I didn't cry and didn't want to hug every bloated ex-classmate of mine. None of them knew her like I knew her. None of them loved her like I loved her.

The drive to Wyoming was long, thirty-one hours via I-75 north, and Jesse only had one CD – *Californication* by the Red Hot Chili Peppers. By the time we reached the Georgia State line, the endless drum riffs were driving me insane. I offered to buy another CD at the next rest stop in Valdosta, but Jesse refused. He said he preferred having one soundtrack for each major experience in his life, because it meant he could return to this moment whenever he wanted, he'd listened to *Is This It* by The Strokes for three months straight before his first big BMX competition and now whenever he listened to it he could still 'feel the rush'.

When I rolled the window down, I could hear the hitched bikes on the back of the car bucking in the wind, I dipped my head out, watching my blonde hair fly. Jesse reached over to reassure me, grabbing a tress as he flipped on the AC, and I rolled my window up. I asked if I looked like her. He nodded, not taking his eyes off the road. I knew he saw her in me. I could feel her coiled like a spool of pink ribbon around my bones. I was wearing her ripped-up Hollister jeans and one of her shirts, lilac with puffy white letters arched above ballet slippers: *NEVER GIVE UP.* Just outside of Kansas, traffic slammed to a stop, a chain of horns blaring. I craned my neck over the front of the dash and could just make out a toppled grey semi-truck hugging the pavement. After an hour of creeping in one lane, we saw what the bent rectangle had released: thousands of pale pimpled chicken carcasses. I screamed at the fleshy lumps sweating in the afternoon heat.

Jesse began smiling, 'See now, every time I hear this song, I'll think of all those freeway chickens and your cute face.' He turned up 'Otherside' and began singing.

Slit my throat it's all I ever

Wyoming was a martian landscape – an ocean of churning rock grass and tree that made me feel small and safe. We unpacked into a rented tiny two-room house. I spent most of my time engrossed in books from the Casper Public Library waiting for Jesse to finish paving a strip mall off the highway. I was reading about sacrifice and death, tracing ancient Greek masks with charcoal, poring over books on the Chinese practice of burning fake paper money and other desirable objects for the afterlife: Corvettes, cell phones and carefully glued-together mega mansions complete with closets bursting with Balenciaga shoes.

The little house with eggplant carpet sat behind a larger

house that was a home for mentally unstable adults. I felt mentally unstable but not adult. I tried to make pasta without a press. Jesse humoured all my attempts at home-making. At a yard sale I'd found a heavy cookbook with long recipes that I was never patient enough to complete, but I got good at making peach pies – Ivy's favourite. Everything was for her. We didn't have much money so we mostly drank beer in the house and we had a lot of sex. We'd fuck before he left for work, and after in the shower, where I'd help scrub black tar splatter off his ankles. I was faking all of my orgasms but I was sure I loved him.

On a sticky July day we went to the central Wyoming fair. The fat bellies and peeling shoulders of the town were lazily sifting from one brightly coloured stand to the next. I won a pink plastic necklace by catapulting floppy frogs onto moving lily pads. Jesse won a fish in a glass orb from a man wearing an oversized T-shirt that advised us to *Go Big or Go Home*. I was working on freeing my molars from a caramel apple when I saw two girls who were fourteen, or maybe an over-developed thirteen. They looked just like us. Ivy and me. Shorts too short, awkward tube tops, platform jelly sandals, my heart stopped. They were laughing and snipping at each other, carrying little backpacks bursting with the change of clothes they'd pull over their tiny outfits when their moms came to pick them up. Jesse looked at them, then me, she was everywhere. He began to bawl. Heavy jerking sobs. He steadied himself on a tent pole. I held him, thankful for his eyes, which felt like an extension of my own, capable of what mine weren't. As the weeks pushed on Jesse seemed more and more engulfed in sadness. Often I'd wake up next to him in foetus position crying. I'd pull him towards me, whispering that I understood, that we both loved her, promising that our love kept her alive.

We named our goldfish 'Slugger', and kept him on the fake

fireplace. Sometimes after work Jesse would pick me up in his mud-licked car and we'd drive out to some giant glowing mountain. Or we'd wade into a stream that was so spectacular and clear it felt as if we were starring in an Anheuser-Busch ad as we'd crack our silver cans against the neon-blue sky. And every day, no matter the weather, Jesse would stop on his way home and pick a bouquet of wild flowers – calling to me from the car as he turned into our drive.

'Where's my buttercup?'

'Where's my poppy?'

'Where's my prairie clover?'

And I'd come running with a washed-out tomato can, or beer bottle to add to the line of bouquets on the windowsill. Most days we'd bike to the skate park where kids ripped around the concrete swells. They loved Jesse and his sticker-covered bike, he had always teetered on the edge of being a professional, a slipped disk, a broken leg, a dog's death always stood in the way. But on those hallowed cement curves, sputtering whooshes and tyre screeches, he was a god. I would dangle my legs as if I were Narcissus, drawn to the pool to fall in love with my love all over again.

In early September the days turned long. I felt aimless. I made collages for Ivy, sacrifices of things I thought she would want for her afterlife: Kate Bush and Janis Joplin lounging poolside, a dance studio filled with flowers I'd cut from a garden magazine. At first I took to burning these offerings in the backyard of the little house, the smoke curling up to the great blue Wyoming sky – until, mid-burn, a man from the big house in a tweety-bird hat charged at me, grabbing both my shoulders and informing me with ten thousand megawatts of fear: 'THEREARETOOMANYWILDFIRESFORYOU TOBESOSTUPID.'

I moved to burning my sacrifices in the bathroom, letting the black soot trail into the toilet.

After one long silent day scooting around the eggplant carpet I tried to imagine what Ivy would say if she walked through the door, her perfect posture slouching down to greet me.

'Ugh, Zoe. Look at yourself.' She'd kick me with her tightly laced trainers and tanned leg, 'All your major decisions in the past months are about boys – or me.' She would savour saying the 'me' part, she had always basked in my devotion. 'School doesn't start in Berlin until October, you still have time – you're an artist, go be one.' Then she'd walk to the fridge and grab a beer, done being gentle, and say something crass, 'You're only with him to be near me. I know it's hard to give up dick that nice, but this place sucks.' I knew she was right. For the rest of the day it felt like she was there, like we were hanging out, suspended in one of our lazy summer days, painting toenails and talking trash.

Three days later, I still couldn't shake her. I baked a pie, and told Jesse that I was going to go to Berlin after all. He cried, his Betty Boop lashes flaring. I promised we could make it work, and really believed we would. Skype every day. Emails. He asked me to marry him. My stomach dropped. When I told him I wasn't sure, his eyes shuddered dark – he picked up the still-hot pie tin and threw it at the fake fireplace. I sat frozen, as the glistening peach slugs inched towards the carpet.

4

Berlin was like living inside of a freezer, there was rarely light and it was always cold. For those first weeks on Bülowstrasse Hailey and I had to go to the jazz cafe on the corner to use the wifi, it was a grotesque background for my fragile conversations with Jesse. He took each botched Skype personally – fuming as if I had paid the four-piece band to lurch into a creaky version of 'Fly Me to the Moon' while he was talking about his stepdad's benign tumour. I found out Hailey could really speak German when she screamed at the internet provider with the bravado of a New Yorker in rush-hour traffic. And then again, later that week, as she managed to sort our registration – *Anmeldung*, at the citizens office. It was electrifying and made her seem somehow finally like herself. I'd grown to love watching her red lips push out the harsh sounds. There had always been something puritanical in Hailey, something crazy and fresh off the *Mayflower*, but adding in the angry German tied the bow.

Lacking any meaningful school schedule, I wondered if I should go back to Wyoming. I imagined Jesse would just arrive. Would buzz the terrifying buzzer that sounded like an electrocution. And there he would be, standing on the steps of Bülowstrasse in his torn Vans, asking me to come back to the little house with eggplant carpet. And maybe that's where I belonged. With him, closer to Ivy.

The cold was exhausting, we wondered how others in the

building managed, but we'd never seen any of our neighbours. At night we swore we could make out voices, the walls creaked and moaned. One evening, well past midnight, certain we heard footsteps, Hailey sprinted into the pitch-black hall and found – nothing. The next morning Hailey wrote Beatrice about the neighbours. A week later we received a reply, from Beatrice's mother Janet, who sternly informed us her daughter was not to be bothered while working, and explained that we had no neighbours, something to do with the impending sale of the building. At first, this was news we celebrated – we could play music loudly, dance, scream – but it soon dawned on us that heating the apartment was as impossible as melting a single ice cube in a frozen tray.

We tried to get out of the apartment when we could. We went to a few gallery openings that Hailey found out about online, but we were invisible, dejected flotsam circulating at the edges of the painted white boxes. The cheap red wine only seemed to appear for those who had the confidence to go into the back rooms, which we never did. Whatever insecurities I'd had in New York were magnified. And Hailey, who seemed so cocksure when it was just the two of us, shrank to a wordless thimble.

One night after returning home from filtering through several fluorescent galleries, Hailey was enraged, wiping her feet on the door mat, 'I hate openings here. At least in New York you don't feel like you're outside of some secret society.'

'It does seem like the same thirty people at each opening,' I added.

'Yeah, fuck them. They all have old face anyway,' Hailey said as she turned into the kitchen, ripping the oven door open and flicking the pilot light to warm her hands.

I went to my bedroom. My fire had dissolved into a dusty orange mound.

*

The rectangular water heater suspended above the tub sounded like a bowling ball bumping down a winding staircase as it warmed. It took well over an hour to heat one bath's worth of water so we were resigned to leaving it on. Waiting felt primitive. Each night we took turns soaking, then jumping into our slippers and sitting in front of the stove to gulp more gluhwein. We were easily drinking several bottles a day. The alcohol made the cold more tolerable. I learned how to cook a bit from Hailey, she knew what a leek was, and how to roast vegetables and how to make macaroni and cheese from scratch. Her mom had gone to some famous cooking school with a French name, and would even do tutorials in the aisles of the original Biggles.

Ever since moving into the apartment I had been experiencing a rumbling nausea. A dog-whistle, just a few octaves out of range of simmering discomfort. One Tuesday night, after too much wine, and too much of Hailey's lasagne, I threw up. My gag reflex was a pause button on my self-loathing, a tiny bit of control. One of my friends, Molly Webster, had been a blend of bulimic and anorexic in high school, it had always annoyed me – a disease of the middle class that meant we never got to eat anything spicy. Yet, here I was – not an excellent bulimic, not religious about it and often too lazy to throw up, but I was good at hiding it. It turned the apartment into a part of my body; the bathroom had other meanings, my fingers new uses. I got to eat my food twice. A whole new hole. Anorexia takes too much work on the front end, I enjoyed the idea that you could correct your wrongs, like going to confession. And yes there they are, the gummy bears and the falafel; now I have atoned.

I didn't want to tell Hailey – it was my secret, one of the few things I didn't have to share with her. One night, drunk after jamming my hand down my throat, I thought about writing Molly Webster who was off at veterinarian school in

Gainesville. How would you say it? What could one possibly write in an email to an old friend letting them know that – you, too, were regurgitating regularly? I imagined Molly's perfect fingernails holding a scalpel and slicing a cat spleen then slipping off to the bathroom, violently hand-sanitising before gagging herself. She loved to talk about it. She used to puke in the shower because she hated having to look at the toilet, but she'd become paranoid that she'd clog the drain and her dad would find out, so she switched to puking in Ziplock bags and tossing them into the dumpster behind school. I started to type.

Hi Mol.

Hope Animal school is riveting. Bulimia – it really is just as fun as you made it out to be. Do you have any fresh tips for a virgin throat banger? lol.

I closed the email without finishing. It wasn't funny. It would never be funny.

The Academy System in Germany was structured on the old apprentice philosophy in which a student studies with the same professor for the entirety of their schooling. *They came from the class of* _____ was the common identifier when describing artists, as if *the class of* _____ were a small and prestigious town. In the few conversations I'd had at school, it seemed all of German art history could be traced through lineages of classes, the teachers producing students like little drummer boys of ideology. Nevertheless all professors are forced into retirement at sixty-five. One would assume forty years of teaching was enough, but not for Klaus Simons.

Klaus argued incessantly. 'Look around you, all I see are questions! My work is clearly not done here.' His sense of urgency and bureaucratic martyrdom seemed to fill most of his time, leaving little to no room for his students, and certainly not a new one. For the first class of the semester he sauntered in wearing a thick wool sweater, acknowledging me by pointing a dog-eared copy of Goethe's *Faust* in my direction, switching briefly to English, he said, 'You, new student, can be here, of course you can partake in this class, but you must understand this is a year of war.' I nodded, a soldier, as he pointed to a desk. I remained for an hour or so, wondering who had sat there before me, maybe a Japanese student with a penchant for woodworking or maybe an unhappy Brazilian. Klaus met with students in his office, his voice briefly booming over them until they'd scuttle back, returning to their little desk universes to divinate.

I wanted the first day of school to mean something. Class had felt pointless, so I decided to go to Hannah Höch's house, which had been converted into a museum and was apparently open for visitors. It was on the outskirts of Berlin, and already dark when the bus dumped me on the sidewalk. I pulled out the non-sensical map I'd drawn on the back of a receipt and kept spinning it as if it would morph into a compass and nudge me the right way. I took a left, instantly lost, surrounded by trees. I steadied myself and went right. Freshman year I had chosen to do my research paper on Hannah Höch. I knew all the facts. Her mother was an amateur painter. Her dad worked at an insurance company. She'd lived through both wars, was gay, born November 1st 1889 and one of the only female Dadaists, but the facts didn't matter.

It was the collages that mattered, they were intense, alienating, vibrating with violence – eyes floating, faces chopped, dragonfly wings emerging from mechanical gears. She took photography and all its repugnant 'reality', and shredded it into celestial oblivion. *I would like to show the world today as the ant sees it, and tomorrow as the moon sees it*, she had said, to whom I didn't know but I'd written the quote in bold at the top of my paper. I finally found a plaque pointing its way to her house. The beautiful garden I'd seen on the website looked spiky and charred. I walked up to the wooden gate and pulled, it was locked. I checked the hours next to the bell. It had closed ten minutes earlier. How had I not realised? I hated myself. Through the window of the vine-encased cottage I could see a dull orange light. I wanted to scream at it. To beg the orange glow to let me in, to give me some sign that today meant something, that I belonged in Berlin and I wasn't completely lost. Instead, I retraced my steps back to the bus – I was the ant, and there was no moon.

When I got back to the apartment I tripped over another package in the entry. Zander, Hailey's boyfriend, refused to Skype. Hailey didn't talk about him much, but I think she found safety in his extreme devotion. He sent her packages almost daily, each one more elaborate than the last. They were piling up. I only knew Zander from the school's metal-shop. He was quiet and wore all denim while he tinkered with his complicated kinetic sculptures. He had been accepted to every college he'd applied to: seven art academies, four Ivy Leagues, and a handful of engineering schools. He'd chosen our school in New York because he deemed it the most flex-ible, somewhere he could make sculptures and take physics. Hailey called him *The Genius* with audible awe – as if he were a retired general or an inventor of some universally celebrated household appliance.

In the kitchen, I cut a hunk of dark-brown bread and a few pieces of sweaty cheese, then settled in to check Ivy's Facebook. It had been five months since her murder and the pain was still searing. It confused me that people were posting on her wall. What was the point if Ivy couldn't respond in her signature charm bracelet of asterisks, smileys and hearts? Chelsea Benedict had been tagging her in photos from their cheerleading days, Ivy's cousin Darren shared a picture of her holding a bluefish still on a hook that glittered like a disco ball. Her Grandma Jane kept posting the same link to an e-card of a humpback whale that read, *I miss you a ton*. My trance was broken by the sound of Hailey's key crashing in the lock.

'Jörg Hefe is a middle-aged bumbling idiot. First, the class is all women, and it's clear he prefers it that way. And he wore linen pants and he literally made us do a "ritual stretch". Which was just downward dog while he checked out our asses. AND then he brought in three of his still-wet squiggle-paintings of landscapes for the class to critique for two hours.'

Her intensity seemed to shift all the molecules in the room. This was the version of Hailey I loved, enraged and unapologetic.

'You have no idea, like you can't even imagine. This man thinks he's some new-age god,' she ripped her grey scarf off, 'but really he is just another insecure-small-dick-pathetic-german-male-holocaust-guilt-painter. And I am the one paying for school. Why should I critique his work? Why on the first day would I invest my young intelligent brain in unpacking his decrepit shoe-box of a practice?'

Hailey pulled out a bottle of wine from her bag. It was much nicer than the one I'd bought. She stalked into the kitchen still screaming. 'And how was, whatever his name, Jan, Karl?' I waited for her to return, then watched as she began twisting the corkscrew in large thrusting motions that, with her down jacket still on, seemed somehow medieval.

'Klaus, also basically nothing, like studying under the direction of a slight wind. Every few weeks, the wind blows in, maybe gusts a few pieces of paper or words in our direction, then it's off.'

'Jörg is more of a dry fart,' she scoffed just as the cork plopped out. 'After the two morbid hours we spent on his work, we, his obedient harem, were allowed to show one slide each, but get this – we weren't even allowed to introduce it, all we could say was our name and he would make comments. There were five imitation-squiggle-landscapes, a photo of a construction site and then – I don't remember, whatever. When it was my turn I said I wasn't willing to simply show a slide, because conceptual work always takes an explanation. And he refused.'

I let out an overly dramatic gasp.

'He said if my work can't speak for itself, it doesn't speak.' Another gasp.

'I wasn't going to be one of his girls just slobbing on him, so I just flipped him off – and asked him to comment on that. You should have seen his face. You know what he said? "*Ich bin kein Fan von billiger Theatralik im Klassenzimmer.*"'

I waited for a translation.

'*I'm not a fan of cheap theatrics in the classroom.* And I know what he meant by *cheap theatrics*, he meant *Feminismus.*'

With her low-riding jeans and perfectly plucked eyebrows I hadn't pegged Hailey as a feminist, but I also knew she couldn't stand a muzzle.

'I'm not going to be from *the class of Jörg Hefe*, you know I thought he was famous but he hasn't had a gallery show in twelve years. I'm switching out but not before I destroy him – if there is one thing I understand, it's the power of *cheap theatrics*. Fucking landscape painter.'

I nodded, then retreated behind my computer. I found Hailey's love of revenge campy, like the exaggerated slap of a soap opera starlet – first the Australians rolling on sleeping pills, and now poor Jörg waiting for his punishment. But at least she'd had a response, all I did in Klaus's class was silently watch, an idiot bobble-head.

After my third glass, the excitement of Hailey's classroom antics had worn off and I was refreshing my feed every few minutes, deeply bored and a little drunk. The girl with the sparrow neck tattoo in New York had posted pictures from the most recent critique in *the pit*. I almost missed the sculpture boys. It seemed like another life, maybe even a good one. Hailey cut the silence with a hacking sound, calling my attention to the couch.

'Lindsay Lohan got another DUI!' She tilted the screen of her white MacBook so that the deflated tangerine face of the actress greeted me. Hailey was obsessed with the celebrity gossip blog *Perez Hilton*. 'She is of course going to rehab again, the new cold shower.'

'It seems sad,' I said, not sure how else to relate to Lindsay Lohan's vacant stare in an overlit California precinct.

'She's a total turnip. People say I look like her, but that's just because people think all redheads look the same. But she's bulimic—' she scoffed, 'like have some self-control, there's really nothing more pathetic. Bulimics should all be rounded up and shot, eat your fucking food or don't.'

I sank into my chair, cheeks burning, imagining an earthen pit filled with all of history's bulimics and myself, making a mental note to be even more diligent about covering my tracks.

Hailey took a sip of wine, assuming my indifference was about Lindsay Lohan. 'What's amazing is getting all of this gossip in real time. Can you imagine living abroad ten years ago, waiting in line to buy a month-old *People* magazine?'

I could imagine. It would have been nice to escape the inane bullshit of American culture. I wanted Europe. I wanted dignity and reason, but that had felt less attainable with each day we'd been there. But Hailey lived for the trash, to her it was art. She religiously checked the smutty Lower East Side blogs and followed the nightlife photographers on Flickr, filtering through endless images of close-range flash on young skin, cracked mirror and wet lipstick. I once asked her if she'd gone to those parties, the basement clubs were only a few blocks from our dorms, but she'd turned to me with distinct resolve, as if she'd been waiting for the question, 'At this point in my life, I would never let my image be used in the service of someone else's narrative.'

Hailey went quiet for a while scrolling through British tabloids, then chirped, 'It's insane she did cartwheels while waiting to be interrogated. Who does that? She has to be guilty.'

Amanda Knox was one of the main food-groups of Hailey's gossip bingeing.

Amanda had been one year ahead of us – picked out a study abroad programme, bought a travel-sized toothpaste, hugged her parents goodbye, and flown to Perugia – but she was now in prison and her roommate Meredith was dead. Hailey wanted to talk about it constantly. It was too close. Too real. The photos of Meredith happy and unaware, too similar to Ivy's slideshow at the funeral. I didn't want to look at Amanda's old Myspace, where she talked about loving wine and roller coasters. And I didn't want to think about Meredith's decomposing body, which – according to Hailey – got held up for days at the Italian airport due to botched medical tests.

I tried to talk with Jesse as much as I could but he was an avalanche of bad news. He had left Wyoming after a fight with his stepdad – *not his fault*, of course. Back in Sebastian he was plagued by Chelsea Benedict and the other adult cheerleaders who were filled with good Christian rage at him for dating me right after Ivy's funeral, something that hadn't bothered him when I was there to hold his hand and suck his dick. And to top it all off he was pulled over drunk, coming home from The Fish, and had his licence suspended. I felt bad for Jesse, stuck in his dad's tiled living room staring at his laptop and unanswered texts: *where's my buttercup? what you doing? miss you baby! wish I could bring you a bouquet of wild flowers!*

Hailey thought I should break up with him.

'I mean he could send you a bouquet of flowers, there are literally thousands of services to fulfil that very thought. Just end it,' she had said. 'He has no relationship to your real life.'

'What is my real life?'

Hailey was doing yoga poses on the floor, 'New York, Berlin whatever, not living in bumfuck Wyoming. You fell in love at a funeral. You were being an emotional vampire.' I frowned at the phrase *emotional vampire*.

'You said it yourself, you liked to watch him cry, it's nuts he asked you to marry him.'

I'd forgotten I had told her about the crying, now that I was regularly regurgitating I often blacked out towards the end of our evenings. The train passed by, my mind drifted to the tiny dining room table in Casper. The swollen slice of peach pie I had been staring at when Jesse asked me to marry him, his words had awoken a dormant rodent in my stomach, and a gnawing need to get away as fast as possible.

'What did you even say when he asked you?'

'I don't know, that we could talk about it when I got back from Berlin.' The truth was I couldn't imagine letting go of him or marrying him, both seemed like a betrayal to Ivy. I had been stuck, and Berlin had been my trap door.

Hailey looked directly at me, her green eyes electric as she pushed into cobra, back curved, shoulders open, 'Do you think Ivy really would have been OK with you marrying him?'

I took a breath. 'Ivy wasn't petty. She was dating a dancer at school. She said sleeping with dancers was better because they're so – limber or aware or something . . .' I trailed off, Hailey's droll tone of questioning made it feel as if it were just another episode of her favourite show *Law & Order*.

'No way to know now, I guess,' Hailey said on her knees, back arched.

Obama won the election. We bought cheap champagne at the Spätkauf and cried as the speeches rolled in at midnight.

'The Bush years are behind us – time to shave our pussies,' Hailey toasted.

'Maybe it's not such a bad time to be an American abroad,' I added rosily.

Hailey snorted, 'And maybe those fucking Canadians stop safety-pinning their flag on every bag they own, god forbid they be confused as one of us. I mean, they should be so lucky.'

I went to bed hopeful, but woke to the terrifying things my childhood friends in the military were posting, sunburnt Southern boys dusted in sand, weighted down by their M16A2 rifles and grenade launchers.

Neither Hailey nor I wanted to go on the three-and-a-half-hour bus tour for exchange students – but we didn't really have anything else to do. Hailey was wearing a push-up bra and a freshly dyed black sweater and I was in my black parka and Ivy's jeans.

'Maybe, we'll meet some people—' I said to Hailey with a flit of hope. She was staring at herself in the reflection of the train's window, gently pulling the V of her sweater lower. She pushed out her lips, eyes still fixated on cleavage, 'Yeah – well it's not just art students, it's also whatever else people study. Hitler nerds and mathematicians so it will obviously be annoying.'

A few metres from the train we found a growing tangle of people our age. It was drizzling and no one seemed to be in a good mood.

'I don't want to be stuck on this bus with—' Hailey said loudly, flicking her hand towards the group.

I looked down at my feet, embarrassed at Hailey. A skinny guy with a moustache moved away from us. Two Swedish girls in matching felted jackets, clearly in the fashion department, began talking quickly and laughing. A girl in a Ramones sweater and loose braid came bounding towards us, her purple-quilted purse sagging below her knees. 'Is this the exchange bus tour?' she asked. Hailey nodded, I nervously dug the curve of my index finger into my thumb's cuticle waiting for whatever nasty thing Hailey might say next. At home I slurped Hailey's cruelty like spaghetti, twisted and wet, but in public it seemed garish.

All the other students waiting for the bus seemed equally unsure of why, or what, we were doing. The tour had been the only olive branch of camaraderie the university had extended to our programme. There had been no introductory drinks, no phone tree or common lunch hour on the vast campus. We were a loose mass of perfect strangers hovering on cobblestone. I overheard a short fuzzy-headed guy describe his violin-practising habits to a girl with a square yellow backpack, 'Six hours a day, sometimes, sometimes, seven.'

'This is going to be the worst,' the Ramones sweater said, looking up at the rain-heavy sky.

Hailey laughed, 'Yeah, it probably will.'

The Ramones sweater extended her hand, 'I'm Constance. I'm from Montreal.'

'I'm Hailey,' she nodded towards me, 'this is Zoe, we're from New York. What are you studying?'

'Photography,' she said as the bus arrived. We shuffled on.

Hailey leaned her head in and whispered, pointing to Constance, 'No Canadian flag.'

I laughed. I was only a short step behind Constance, caught in a cloud of her perfume. It was plasticky and chemical rich. I inhaled again, it reminded me of a sculpture-class field trip to the MoMA restoration department where we had learned about *weeping Barbie syndrome* – when rubber disintegrates and bleeds plasticisers in new-car-smell pools, maybe it was some poorly constructed Paris Hilton scent, *Heiress* or *Dazzle* – or a boozy body spray like Miso Pretty. The bus lurched off.

'Hey stop – uh, *Halt*!' Constance screeched at the driver, the bus thudded forward then back, a girl with high cheekbones and brown hair was waving her arms. As the door opened, the bus dipped towards the curb and the girl, dressed like Annie Hall on a Nile cruise in well-tailored khakis, a flowy button-up and a cinched Burberry trench, proudly entered.

'*Danke*,' the girl said to the driver. She slipped into the empty seat next to Constance.

'I'm your hero. You should be thanking me,' Constance bowed her head with an air of ironic importance.

'Oh, well, thank you – I'm Viola, are you – American?'

'I'm Constance, Canadian.'

Viola gave her a nod as if she were supposed to continue. 'My parents hail originally from Iran if you *must* know.'

Viola looked embarrassed. The rumble of the bus took over. I watched as Hailey eyeballed Viola, whose pores seeped wealth, everything neatly styled – her leather bag monogrammed *VGG*, and her ears punctuated by two tight diamonds, but whatever perfume she might have been wearing was choked out in her proximity to Constance.

Hailey leaned over me to get closer to Viola, 'I'm Hailey and this is Zoe, we're from New York.'

'Oh, I'm from New York too, Upper East Side. You?'

'I mean – not actually from New York – it's just where we go to school,' Hailey said, flushed.

'Oh, I see,' Viola said. I could detect the edges of an amorphous British accent. 'What's your medium?'

'Photography,' Constance said, butting in, 'mainly self-portraiture and nudes.'

Viola smiled, 'I am also in photo, here to study in the country of the greats: the Bechers, Gursky, Ruff—'

'I'm a conceptual artist,' Hailey said, cutting her off.

The city zoomed by as skeletal trees bent in the wet wind. I pressed my forehead against the window, at a traffic light I watched steaming noodles heaped into red paper boxes at a kiosk, my stomach growled. I'd forgotten to eat lunch. Ten minutes later the bus rolled to a stop.

'All right, everyone. You have fifteen minutes at the Memorial to Murdered Jews of Europe,' the guide, a miserable grad-student in the process of fulfilling work-study debt, called over the bus's microphone.

We filtered into the sunken landscape, slipping through the alleyways carved by the memorial's large stone blocks. Constance, Viola, Hailey and myself – a nascent alliance – observed the bleak vista together.

'It's like a graveyard,' Constance said, the pads of her fingertips moving across one of the towering stones in front of us.

'It's supposed to disorient you,' Viola said, 'and the greyness of the slabs represents the loss of identity.'

We pushed forward. Glancing to our right, we caught the Swedish girls taking photos of themselves posing against the columns.

'No loss of identity there,' Hailey said, as the flash of their camera electrified stray pellets of rain. Constance and Viola snickered.

'I'm hungry,' I said, instantly aware of the pettiness of my desire in the stark landscape.

The din of the grad-student rang out over the slabs, 'Next stop, Hitler's bunker. Everyone back on.'

We exchanged looks.

'It's not that I don't respect the tragedy that is the Holocaust, it's just – raining. Shall we ditch?' Constance asked.

'Yes,' Hailey said, relieved, with a glance towards the bus. 'Where should we go?'

'I live on Wrangelstrasse, I just moved in—'

We all nodded at Constance, thankful for the invitation. Before we could change our mind, Viola had hopped out into the street and hailed a taxi and was holding the door open for us with delicate expertise. When we eventually stopped, Viola removed a crisp white envelope from her bag. Hailey shot me a look. Hailey loved reciting quotes from Andy Warhol, and had just read me the one about how *rich people don't carry their money in wallets or Gucci this-es or Valentino thats. They carry their money in a business envelope.* Sure enough, Viola parted the white flaps and lifted out a cut-from-granite twenty and handed it to the driver. Hailey ogled Viola, impressed by an art student more prissy and richer than she.

Fifteen minutes later in Kreuzberg, Hailey was seated on a fraying rug, Viola was politely patting down the duvet to cover a period stain peeking from the striped sheet, and I was settling in next to a suitcase of soft exploded shapes: tangled hoodies, socks and moth-eaten T-shirts.

'This guy I was sleeping with was going on tour, so he let me sublet. It's the best, right?' she called from the kitchen while holding a battered frying pan.

We all nodded. Despite the bachelor decor the apartment was light and airy with large windows and stalky green plants. We lazed around, trading stories. Viola name-dropping artists. Constance talking in absolutes: her father, 'the most boring man in Alberta'; her take on Berlin, 'the best place to be as long as you know what you want'; and what she wanted was 'to meet absolutely everyone, and make one thousand prints in the school's darkroom.' Hailey and I were impressed, she didn't seem to be having the same struggles that we were having, she appeared to be good at meeting people, good at weaving her way to the back rooms of galleries and retrieving the off-limit glasses of red wine. She cooked chicken and counselled us on the value of being a young woman living alone, 'It's just so important to explore yourself.'

Hailey rolled her eyes.

Building a daily coal fire was a good continuation of the sacrificial burnings I'd practised in Wyoming. I bought a few photo albums at the flea market, big crusty things that were falling apart, the photos brittle and fluttery like fall leaves. Old grandmothers, and young boys dragging logs through burnished farmland. They must have all been Nazis. Or at least all they probably talked about were Nazis, I tried to imagine a dinner table in 1951, what else could you say? I cut up the family pictures and rearranged them, pairing them with slicings from the *New York Times* that continued to arrive, Beatrice's name printed on a white label in the left-hand corner. Each night I'd take a photograph of the day's collage then burn it.

Hailey loved watching *Law & Order SVU*. At first it made me feel sick. I'd shut the dividing door but the sound still carried. It seemed like the cops were always talking about Ivy. And the saxophone was annoying. But after a while I got used to it and the generic responses to limp bodies in dumpsters would gently carry me off to sleep. On an early Sunday evening, bored, I caved. A Botox-lipped blonde was raped by a famous scientist but, in a gripping twist, turned out to be working at a sperm bank, electro-shocking semen out of genetically desirable dates after she roofied them. It was all so absurd. Within the safe shimmer of artifice I relaxed, and found the gore unexpectedly cathartic. It was theatre. Detective Olivia Benson was an empathetic vessel of persistence and justice, the killers were always found and the child-molesting-uncles girlfriend-stabbers guilty-priests were walked to the clink with a knowing bob of Ice-T's head.

We'd prop my computer up on the piano bench and lie, two worms in my bed.

'How do they come up with this shit?' I asked, rolling over. Hailey shrugged while rubbing crumbs off my sheets. 'How many rapes do you think we've watched this week?'

'Thirty, at least.'

Each crumpled female form discovered by a jogger helped turn Ivy's death into an episode of normality. This was something that happened to girls, their lives were swept away to the wheedling of saxophone, it was normal.

'It is truly a wonderful pop-culture-crossover that Ice-T parlayed his music career into playing a cop on this show,' Hailey said, hands on the keyboard as she expertly coaxed the next installment from a streaming site. 'But the only good episodes are with the dead girls – everything else seems like a stretch.' We belted out the opening credits as if Karaoke: *In the criminal justice system, sexually based offences are considered especially heinous* . . . arguing over the final notes. Hailey saying, 'BUM BUM.' Me, correctly saying, 'DUN DUN.'

The holidays started to edge in. Klaus Simons organised a big dinner, transforming the classroom into a banquet hall. Large pots of boiling potatoes on hotplates and a table that stretched the entirety of the room with candles and pine branches sticking out of wine bottles. The room had a sense of rustic German cheer and collectivity that I recognised from the photo albums I'd been chopping up. A big piece of butcher paper ran down the middle and everyone was making botanical drawings; ferns, curling wreaths and poinsettias – far from the sperm-laden frescos of the sculpture boys in New York. I felt a sliver of hope, but the next day all the students were off for the month to Bremen, Hamburg, and North Rhine-Westphalia to see their parents and horses and siblings and exes.

Hailey and I rarely left the apartment. I suppose we were, as Constance would have said, *exploring ourselves*. Since there was no school we turned inward – we became obsessed with Beatrice, poring through her private documents, tax filings, photo albums and letters. Whatever hesitation I'd had about opening her mail had long since evaporated. We dug through every box and binder on the one *real* oak bookcase, with glass door, that stood out in Beatrice's erudite Jenga of shelves. Our findings included a multicoloured folder with some old tax returns and visa information, a copy of her passport, a stack of unopened letters from her health insurance provider in the US and a recent letter from someone named Michael, who *longed for their late-night conversation*.

'Poor Beatrice, Michael sounds like a bore,' Hailey laughed.

We also found a close-up photo of Beatrice and Janet, poolside in what we imagined must have been Beverly Hills in the '70s.

'They look so similar,' Hailey said, inspecting the photo closely. I peered over. Janet looked our age, maybe younger.

'Was she a teen mom?' I asked, pointing to Janet's youthful glower.

Hailey shrugged, I took the photo from her and continued to stare at the mother–daughter duo in matching white shorts and light-blue T-shirts, their legs half submerged in pool water. Their bob haircuts were identical even then, and Janet's, which we'd only seen as grey, was a shock of black. Everything in the picture was bright and happy, five-year-old Beatrice beaming, but something hung heavy around Janet, as if it were the last place on earth she wanted to be.

'Did you hear that?' Hailey asked, looking up terrified.

'No, what?'

'Like a weird scream?'

'Just now?'

She nodded.

76

'No, but last night I swore I heard a couple fighting – I even went into the hall, but nothing.'

'I guess it's just the fucking wind blowing around this empty building.'

I huffed in agreeance. We kept digging, and found several clippings from a vintage lady's magazine, written by a *J. Becks*.

'Oh my god, Janet did advice columns,' I squealed.

When your husband is off at war, it's important not to bother him with trivial worries in your correspondence. What he needs to know is that you love him, and you are keeping a smart and warm home for his return. Do not bother him with queries like – what sort of linens he prefers. Instead, describe a fond memory, your wedding day, or a special picnic, something that can spark positivity. And if you want to have a little fun, invent a secret language, create images to represent your hearts' desires, or send crossword puzzles. Keep your husband stimulated, and keep him marching forward.

'Was Beatrice's dad in Vietnam?' I asked as a train rushed by.

'Yeah, he died in like the second year of the war – *Operation Silver City*. Good name, right?' She held up a photo of a teenage Beatrice posing with a cello, 'Born into tragedy, never met her dad.'

Hailey returned to her pile of letters.

'How do you know all that? About her dad.'

'I found an article online where Beatrice talks about it, Redbook I think.'

Hailey was now devouring a series of correspondence between Beatrice and her editor in New York, which made clear she was in danger of defaulting on her advance if she didn't have a book done by the end of the winter.

'Look at this. No wonder she is holed up in Vienna,' Hailey said, doing her best impression of Detective Benson. 'I knew it was impossible to write three fucking books a year.'

Only one drawer was locked. We tried to open it with a safety pin, not that either of us knew how.

'What do you think's in there?' Hailey asked.

'Maybe a birth certificate?'

'Why lock it up?'

'Why lock anything up?'

'I wonder what Miss Becks is hiding.' Hailey had found a tube of her lotion and was massaging it into her clavicle. I was struck with how trustworthy Hailey's face looked, it was the type of face anyone would believe. 'Come on, you know she is hiding something good . . .' She threw the tube at me, I opened it. It smelled old and lemongrassy.

From her Wikipedia entry we could verify that Beatrice had no kids and wasn't married, but this seemed wholly obvious from the information in the apartment. The lone desk lamp. The lack of closet space. The two sad plates, the two sets of silverware and the one *good* kitchen knife. But she did have five octagonal wine glasses, well, four. Hailey broke one doing dishes. I heard the crack, then the 'F-U-C-K.' Followed by Hailey running into my bedroom holding the broken stem like a dead rat, screaming, 'BEATRICE IS GOING TO KILL US.' I jumped, terrified, then burst into laughter. The broken glass seemed less violent than the hours of sifting through her cabinets, opening mail, and rubbing her lotion on our skin.

Hailey had become fused to the lip-shaped couch like a canker sore, methodically reading all of Beatrice's books. 'You know she wrote the first book when she was twenty?' she yelled across her room into mine, the large dividing doors ajar.

'How old is she now?' I asked.

Hailey made a nasal blow letting me know it was a dumb question, 'Forty-three.'

Hailey was reading *When Love Knows*, Beatrice's twelfth book, which, according to Hailey, was about a buxom co-ed who has an explosive tryst with her physics teacher, and when the teacher breaks off the relationship the blonde plots to kill his entire family with rat poison, framing him, but in an incestual twist ends up discovering she's actually his long-lost daughter. Hailey looked up from the bubble-gum-pink book, 'I just watched an interview with her, she's promoting one of her old novels for some book club, and they ask her about her next book – and if she has writer's block, and she gets this insane look.'

'Show me,' I said, shuffling over. Hailey heaved her computer onto her lap, pausing a singing Mariah Carey writhing in bed to find the tab with Beatrice sitting nervously on the set of a London morning show. Hailey skipped to the middle, Beatrice's black helmet hair bobbing up and down at chipmunk speed. Hailey stopped. A toothy brunette with bright fuchsia lips began her questions.

'And so, Beatrice, everyone wants to know about your next book. Do you see it as a continuation of the *Beach Death* series?'

'Not directly, but writing is always a continuation. A flow. No matter what we do, it proceeds from what came before. So it shares some elements, but it stands on its own – a real love story gone wrong.' She looked shaky, nothing like the wax figure we'd met. 'It will finally be out next fall, we are very excited.'

The news anchor was pressing her with the glee of an old boarding-school nemesis, 'It was supposed to be out last autumn! That must be so difficult.'

Beatrice's eyes flushed with terror. 'It was postponed – yes.'

'And would you call that writer's block?' The reporter was smiling a too-big smile.

'No, we don't agree with the term *writer's block*, you need to give yourself time to let things develop. As I said.'

Hailey rewound so we could watch that part again where Beatrice's eyes flashed with terror. 'Why does she keep saying *we*?'

Hailey shrugged, she had read seven of her novels so far. There was something about reading them that made me uneasy. We were already living in her apartment, eating off her lonely plates – it was too much. But Hailey loved the whole gory library. The day before, while I was scraping the last of our precious peanut butter from its jar, she'd paused from one of Beatrice's many murder-reference books stored in the kitchen's floor-to-ceiling shelving, to inform me that one can 'hotwire a urinal grate to electrocute a man via his *stream*'.

'Why does she need to rent us her apartment if she's on TV shows?' I asked.

'Only one of her books was actually big, *On Blue Peak*. The recent ones really aren't so good.'

'I thought you said her books were in airports?'

'Niche airports,' Hailey said, smirking.

'What was *On Blue Peak* about?'

'Well, it's an outlier for her, somehow,' she took a breath, her nose turned towards the window, 'less twisty and more emotional than the others. It's about a young Southern woman . . . who falls in love with an heir to a steel fortune. The beginning of the book is about their courtship in the mountains. Then they move to New York and live this big glam life – causing all this controversy throwing giant parties. And one day she comes home and finds her husband sleeping with his best friend, *a man*. And then she tries to kill the lover and accidentally kills her husband and she gets locked up in a loony bin. The book continues as she ages in the bin, it's quite sad and really beautiful and campy.' Hailey looked oddly pleased at her synopsis, as if she'd just let me in on some great secret.

'Wow,' I was trying to seem enthused. 'Sounds great.'

Hailey began to catalogue every book in the apartment with the drive of a deranged librarian, sorting, stacking and arranging piles of the rainbow spines, then clacking away at her computer with a deep scowl. Beatrice's library was mostly crime-related – Victorian forensics encyclopaedias, Tom Clancy, NRA gun catalogues from the '90s, Agatha Christie, James Cain, sociopath case-studies, but also classics: Greek tragedies, biographies of Presidents, and three shelves of theatre plays. Hailey's growing spreadsheet was titled in bold font, *The Library of Beatrice Becks by Hailey Mader.*

'It's a conceptual piece, not unlike a portrait,' she'd told me with an excitement I was jealous of, 'a trump card, in which all of her books become my book.' Hailey described all the ways she imagined it could be displayed: spiral bound on a pedestal, or under A4 pieces of glass held up with little metal nails.

There were two new packages from Zander, which were unopened on the table. The recent ones looked like Noguchi sculptures covered in postage stamps and black and white customs tape. The more intricate the package the more prone it was to being delayed at the German customs office, forcing Hailey to take the train to the *Zollamt* at the edge of town and explain to a miserable bureaucrat what was inside the ornate boxes. The reality being that she never knew what was inside, and she would be subsequently reprimanded for not knowing. She'd argue, 'The purpose of gifts is to surprise and delight,' something the packages were doing less with each trip.

5

Viola was coming over for dinner and bringing two friends. We were nervous, our first guests. We bought paper plates. I removed my duvet and pillows from the day-bed, and arranged candles on the dining table. Hailey, who had done most of the cooking while drinking a bottle of wine, teetered out to buy several bouquets of flowers, which she placed throughout the apartment.

Viola arrived punctually.

'Dears, this is Jens – from Stuttgart, a fabulous graphic designer. And Otto from Austria, a renowned pianist.'

'And I'm Hailey, the world's greatest artist – American,' she said, sticking her hand out with a smirk.

I mumbled my introduction and started getting the drinks together in the kitchen. Jens, who had just cleaned the fog from his glasses, explained that he studied in the visual art school same as us, and Otto was at the music academy. Otto nodded anxiously, slicking his fingers through his black hair. Hailey caught him eyeing the Blüthner in her room, which she was using as a convex clothes hamper.

'Can you play Rihanna?' she asked teasingly.

'He's amazing, he played my sister's wedding,' Jens said proudly. 'He can play anything.'

Otto blushed as Jens knocked him on his side.

'I can do "Umbrella".'

Hailey clapped.

Once at the table Jens and Otto voiced their curiosity about

Beatrice and the apartment. We told them everything we'd pieced together, fanning out a selection of novels, her black-banged face staring from the dust jackets.

'She has a sort of classic Weimar look, right?' Hailey asked, pointing to Beatrice's icy stare.

'Sally Bowles,' Otto said sheepishly.

Hailey lit up, 'Yes. Oh my god – can you play 'Cabaret'?'

Otto flushed, then nodded. Hailey smiled at him, and shot me an annoyed look – I assumed remembering my earlier comment on the subject. Hailey convinced him to play something. And I watched intently as the short, nervous twenty-year-old transformed into a confident swaying pianist. The apartment felt even bigger flooding with sound. Jens looked on with a grin, he was so German it almost hurt – blond hair, blue eyes, and a brick of a jaw.

Viola was bored, she wanted to discuss Amanda Knox. I sulked to my chair. 'All Italians think she did it.'

Jens was fast to volley, 'But we . . .' He paused, registering the disparate home countries in the room, 'The Germans don't believe in the Italian judicial process. So really anyone and everyone is innocent in Italy because there is no possible way to prove otherwise.'

'I do think it's very weird that she came home, saw blood on the floor, then took a shower WHILE there was a pile of shit in her toilet. I mean have you ever done that? Even your own shit?' Hailey said, opening the next bottle. I grimaced. She was now pointing at me with the corkscrew, 'I would have screamed at my roommate, and had her come flush it.'

Jens had turned bright red and was looking out the window, it was clear a drunk American girl talking about shit at the dinner table was more than he could handle. Otto was just returning to his seat. 'So wait, I haven't been following. Who is Amanda Knox?'

'Jesus Christ,' Hailey laughed, passing the roasted squash,

avoiding my eye contact. A train rushed by, filling the windows with yellow light.

Viola took over, 'Well, you see, Meredith Kercher was a British student on exchange in Perugia. She was studying . . .' She clearly couldn't remember what exactly she was studying but wouldn't let that stop her. 'Well, Meredith was living off-campus in a four-bedroom apartment with two other Italian women and one American; A-MAN-DA KNOX,' Viola said her name in a terrifying four-part drumbeat.

'Basically, A-MAN-DA-KNOX came home from her boyfriend's house. His name was Sauce-olitto.'

'Raffaele Sollecito,' Hailey interrupted.

Viola ignored Hailey, 'They'd only been dating for a week. A-MAN-DA-KNOX saw blood on the entryway floor of her apartment, noticed there appeared to be faeces in the toilet, and then took a shower anyway.' Hailey made a snort sound at the word *faeces*. 'Then she noticed more blood on the bathmat. Then she noticed the door was locked to Meredith's room, she knocked, no answer, so she called her boyfriend. The boyfriend, Sauce-olitto, called his sister, who was a police officer in Rome; she told them to call the general cops, which they finally did, and then after some unclear back and forth the cops broke down the door and found Meredith with her throat slit under the duvet,' Viola finally exhaled.

Jens was shaking his head in disgust at the Italian police. Viola kept going, 'And the prosecutors are pinning it on A-MAN-DA-KNOX because she is young and beautiful and American,' the words came out as a nursery rhyme.

Young and Beautiful and American
Young and Beautiful and American

Viola kept talking, 'They are saying the murder was enacted as a part of an erotic sex cult because she was seen buying condoms the week before.'

'Buying condoms. How horrible,' Hailey cackled.

'She obviously didn't do it, but there's something about her—' Viola added.

Jens slicked his hair back, 'Sounds like *The Crucible*.'

Hailey slapped the table. 'Yes! It's *The Crucible* as perfect pop-media-gore. By far my favourite piece of performance this year. Well, other than all the celebrity car crashes.' We all looked at her blankly. 'Come on, Lindsay Lohan got another DUI. No one has a publicist any more.'

Hailey went to the kitchen. I scraped the last of the potatoes out of a shallow metal pan, trying to shift gears by asking Jens if he knew much about the print studios, but before he could answer, Hailey came rushing back with a silver bowl of whip cream.

'The thing is, Amanda looks like a sexed-up Joan of Arc. You know that painting by Jules Bastien-Lepage.'

'Le-p-ah-ge,' Viola said in a French accent.

Otto shook his head, then patted his forehead with his napkin.

Hailey huffed, 'It's the one where she's staring out into the distance holding on to a tree, it's at the Met. She has the same watery eyes as Amanda, it's this ancient type of possessed sexuality that's been getting men off for years and they just want to watch these women burn.'

'You're really comparing Joan of Arc to Amanda Knox?' I asked, annoyed at our return to the subject.

'Yes. Think about it – Amanda, guilty or not, has joined the pantheon of women burned for our entertainment.'

'Meredith is the one who *actually* died,' I muttered.

Viola folded her napkin and set it into her tweed lap as if to address a courtroom, 'I mean Rudy Guede was found guilty, his bloody palm print was on her pillow. It should be over with but—'

'But the Italian court system is also racist—' Jens added solemnly.

'She had no idea how to mourn,' Hailey said, cutting him off, 'it's not hard to seem sad, you shouldn't be making out with your boyfriend at the crime scene, that *does* make her seem like a psychopath.' Hailey took a long look at me, 'But I guess Zoe knows about that. She basically did the same thing.'

I looked up at her, trying to gauge whether she would continue, what she would choose to reveal to these new acquaintances – I could see the words forming on her lips.

'Don't,' I snapped. A low silence fell, Hailey began concentrating on fluffing the cream in the silver bowl. Beyoncé crawled into the gestating pause.

Hailey looked to me for permission. I shook my head, teeth clenched.

'Oh come on, it's a good story,' she goaded.

I excused myself and went to the bathroom. I wanted to throw up my insides. To puke myself into oblivion. Hailey was a monster. I pulled out my Nokia brick, running through the empty contact list. There was no one to call, no one to text. I scrolled again. I realised I was looking for Ivy's name. I took a breath, washed my face, and returned to the table as if nothing happened.

'This is delicious,' Jens said as he pushed fluffy goo on his plate, trying to sidestep whatever bomb had been previously dropped.

Hailey and Viola slid into talk about their Christmas plans, Hailey would meet her family in Paris and Viola would fly Christmas Eve to London to meet her mother and sister who had rented a flat in Kensington where, apparently, Julie Andrews once lived. I had nothing to add to their conversation, I could barely afford to stay in Berlin. I concerned myself with draining the remainder of the wine on the table, sinking into the quicksand of Ivy, Hailey's barbed comment still stinging.

There had been no media circus for Ivy, no public speculation over her stabbing, it had all just slipped into silence. I wonder if she would have preferred it. Legions of people, young and old, speculating on her sexuality, her predilection for Spandex, her history with boys, the photos we'd taken with Jesse, posing with the garden clippers at the beach house. What would the Italian justice system have done with us?

'Earth to Zoe. You OK?' Hailey tapped my shoulder, gauging my anger. I ignored her.

Viola made a loud coughing sound that I think was supposed to be a yawn, then primly thanked us for the dinner and had her coat on within forty-five seconds, Jens and Otto trailing her.

'Do you think they are dating?' Hailey asked from the kitchen, dumping leftovers into a yellow bowl and covering it with plastic wrap.

Refusing to respond, I went into my room.

She followed me to the door blathering, 'Maybe it's a ménage à trois? Or was she into Otto? She's hard to read. Otto could be gay – showtunes. But I was impressed at Jens' ability to wear both a button-up and a turtleneck at the same time, such a violent thing to do to a neck.'

Hailey finally paused, putting her hand on my forearm. I turned to her, she looked like a Norman Rockwell painting, a dish rag over her shoulder, her red hair swept up in a loose bun – she seemed like she was about to say something meaningful, I readied myself for her apology.

'Viola is annoying. I think I hate her,' she took a beat, 'she just brings so little to the table.'

'What is wrong with you?' I snapped, turning away.

She seemed startled, then looked at the ceiling and cracked her neck, 'Oh – is this about the Ivy thing?'

I nodded.

'I was just trying to entertain our guests.'

'This isn't a fucking one-act—'

Without knowing how to finish my sentence, I grabbed the golden handle of the door and slammed it.

6

We started to get lazy about cooking. We bought overly salted tortilla chips in the American section of Kaiser's and stole Irish cheddar to make nachos. Stealing from the grocery store was easy, if you paid for one thing you could easily sneak something more expensive out in the bottom of a tote bag. Hailey enjoyed the thrill, I enjoyed the discount. After our ritual of nachos and a bottle of red wine, I'd turn the bathwater on, retch into the toilet, enjoying the corn chip splinters clawing their way back up my throat. Each night I methodically scrubbed the scent of bile off my hands with lavender soap while soaking in the tub.

Neither of us had directly acknowledged the fight at the end of the Viola dinner but Hailey had grown kinder, offering to do the dishes, suggesting we see a movie together – trying to smooth over the conflict without dealing. It was predictable. She was a pendulum, swinging into darkness only to return brighter and sweeter. She would never apologise.

On Wednesday Hailey, who dealt with all the sublet-related correspondence, received an email from Beatrice. She read it aloud as if giving a proclamation to a kingdom.

Dear H + Z,

I hope you are getting on well in the flat.

If I should happen to receive any mail from the Austrian Federal Chancellery Writers' Schloss, please forward it to me directly. No need to send it to my mother in Sylt as it's a time-sensitive matter.

Thank you in advance, B. Becks

'Maybe I should apply to the Austrian Federal Chancellery Writers' Schloss?' Hailey said, getting up from the couch, 'I bet it's super fancy. You know *Schloss* means castle, right?'

I pretended that, yes, I knew that, and googled – *Austrian Federal Chancellery Writers' Schloss.*

I was pleased to corroborate it was indeed *fancy,* and a castle, complete with pudgy-legged cherub frescos and geometric marble floors. The website boasted a long list of writers, a few I'd even heard of, but I couldn't find any info on the current session.

It was two days before her trip and Hailey was already almost packed; while reorganising her travel toiletries, she informed me that her parents would be coming to Berlin for a two-day visit after their stay in Paris.

'They'll take us out for a *nice* dinner.'

I flashed a nervous smile. I wondered what her parents imagined our life was like. Hailey had mentioned that her dad was one of those people who always found a way to work into conversations that he 'came from nothing', and success was 'just a matter of working hard'. I imagined if he found out about our utter lack of school he'd probably force her back to New York and enroll her in Econ.

Hailey had meticulously planned each outfit for Paris, and was careful to leave a fair amount of room for her future purchases, a process that I had observed from the couch, nodding as she held up combinations of skirts and sweaters. I was silently angry she was leaving me. I tried to hide it, fixed behind my laptop as she practised her high-school French. The idea of her leaving our bubble made me uneasy,

I was afraid she would come back to our world, our frigid island, less interested and less mine.

I was unsure if we would exchange gifts and I had no idea what to get her anyway. My feelings towards her were cloudy, still laced with frustration. But the day before she left, I chanced on a flea market on my way home. I became determined to find something. Maybe an old German poster or book, something poppy and graphic. After a few fruitless stalls, I found it – a vintage diary. The book was bound in red leather with black stitching, the spine gilded with a golden braid. I cracked it open, the paper was old and smooth, smelling of vanilla must. It seemed magic.

At home I put the book, wrapped in purple tissue paper, on the table. She erupted with childish glee and leapt towards the gift, I caught myself holding my breath, nervous as she peeled back the tissue. As the paper fell to the floor, she cried out, 'Like a spell book. I love it.'

I smiled, savouring her approval and her instinctual understanding that it was, in fact, *magic*. Hailey was complicated. Our friendship was complicated, but I understood her and this was proof. She hugged me, then loaded her hiker backpack onto her shoulders. On her way out she stuck a cream-coloured envelope to the fridge with *I know I can be dramatic xoxo* scrawled across it in her angular cursive. After she left I opened it; two tickets in bold German Gothic to see a play at a theatre called *Volksbühne*. I practised the name – *Volks-bü-hne* – my voice ricocheting in the now empty apartment.

I began to enjoy the silence. I could throw up with the door open and play 'Heartbeats' by The Knife on repeat. But after a few hours the vacant building, now without Hailey, seemed menacing. I didn't get out of bed at all the first day except to put things in and out of my mouth. I watched news reports about the financial collapse. Men exiting skyscrapers with cardboard boxes, staplers rattling – *subprime mortgages, securitisation, credit default swaps, bank bailouts.* Another foreign language. I felt safe in Berlin where time was still measured by coal briquettes. I kept my computer open, hoping someone would message. An old high-school friend. Anyone. Drinking alone felt sad.

I found a water-stained green rectangle that had once wrapped one of Hailey's bouquets and taped it to the wall, then browsed the newspaper but the pictures were all boring, nothing worth collaging. In the kitchen, underneath a pile of mail, was a plastic-encased leaflet of grocery store advertise-ments. I began clipping away at frozen berries and glass jars of pickles. I glued them in Dada combinations, radiating from the centre – sausages peeking out of cookie packages, coffee beans pouring from dish soap bottles. But I couldn't get into my usual trance. I stepped back. I hated it, at least the collages I made for Ivy had a purpose – a desired audience.

I went back to my computer and tried Skyping Jesse, the blue *S* bouncing as the underwater ring echoed, he finally answered – the whirring sound of a connection – his voice – far off – *Buttercup? Zoe, Zoe, Zoe?* – then the whooshing exit of the call disconnecting. I tried again. 'Buttercup!'

'Hi—'

'What are you up to?' he asked, the afternoon sun sparkling behind him. 'Just – working,' I lied, then choked. Unable to contain my sadness.

'Oh baby – I miss you. I wish I could hold you. Maybe you should just come home?' I nodded. I could hear his dad shouting in the background.

'Hey baby, I have to run. But I love you and just come home, OK? I really think you shouldn't be there any more.'

'I know,' I said, eyes burning as he waved at the camera.

When the call whooshed out, the apartment felt unbearably quiet. I waited for the tub to fill and swelled with hatred for my life, then I heard a pop from my computer. Constance, who was also staying in Berlin over the holidays, had sent a link to a party at a bar in Prenzlauer Berg. She wasn't going because she had a date, but she thought it might be fun. I turned the water off and got ready, music blaring.

I put on Hailey's Adidas top, shimmery silver with three thick black stripes, tilting my head to the right, I inspected myself in the mirror. Wearing her clothes made me feel in control. I dug through the pile at the foot of her bed, slipping on the bruise-purple pants, now a few shades darker, and sprayed an explosion of her Chanel Mademoiselle, watching as the tiny pellets of scent settled on my neck. Inhaling, I was hit with a rush – remembering all the self-assured women, their Tommy Hilfiger-clad boyfriends trailing, who had requested that square pink bottle of Chanel at the perfume counter. I joined their conga line of soft girl power. Tonight I was one of them.

I wrangled my hair in Hailey's signature high ponytail and my transformation was complete. I slipped on her puffy jacket and took the train to Bernauerstrasse, the bar was bursting. The dance floor was filled with languages and English accented in French, Italian and others I couldn't place, everyone expertly stepping to electronic music in quick sharp movements, all dressed in layers of black.

I found a locker in the hallway and jammed Hailey's coat in. Before re-entering I took a deep breath. Hailey's perfume was my gasoline. Courage from my second beer finally rippling, I felt unstoppable. I talked with a group of guys setting up their own magazine. A Venezuelan girl starting a gallery. A Croatian dancer making work-out tapes with artists. A spiky-haired guy in a black hoodie talking about Marx. I pressed my back against the wall. It reminded me of the bar in *Star Wars*, all these outer-space creatures from planets I had heard of grinding on each other and smoking cigarettes. How had they all gotten here? Where had they been? I was on my fifth or sixth beer when I started to feel woozy. I had nothing in my stomach but acid and beer. I wanted to stay but could barely stand. I grabbed Hailey's coat.

The Marxist was sitting on a bench at the train platform. In the light his tiny circular glasses gave him the look of a Russian villain in a Bond movie. On the train he was chatty and whipped out his laptop to show me a 3D rendering of a giant alien giving a peace sign that he was fabricating for his next art show. He, like most people in the bar, was both an artist and a DJ. I asked about the materials of the sculpture, and he launched into a lengthy explanation lubricated by amphetamines that carried him till I got up to get off.

'Hey what was your name again?' he said urgently as the yellow doors whirred shut.

'Hailey.'

I ate a döner in the street, bits of meat falling like hail. At home the fires were dead and we were out of coal. How could Hailey leave me without enough? I went to the basement terrified, unlocked the wooden door to the storage and jumped – staring back at me was a menagerie of cardboard objects, Hailey had been saving Zander's boxes. I ignored them, and dragged one of the brick stacks up the stairs, humming so as not to hear the sounds of the building. Once inside, I lit some newspapers and shoved the thin dry kindling on top, periodically blowing. I watched as the headline curled and disappeared: *Fed Shrugged as Subprime Crisis Spread*. Building a fire drunk has its merits. It lets you think, trance out into campfire mode. Staring at those pathetic flames, Berlin seemed bigger; a thick, black galaxy that had all these glittering stars, these bars filled with people and all I had to do was find them. The fire caught. I placed four bricks of coal with the sincere care of a drunk, and flopped to bed.

The next morning I woke up with a hangover and went to Kaiser's to steal fresh orange juice and pay for cereal. I stopped to check the mail. In the hall I leafed through the letters, a few bills and one with gold lettering from the Austrian Federal Chancellery Writers' Schloss. I put the mail in my coat pocket and dragged my dehydrated body back up the apartment steps, the bitter funeral-flower smell hit before I'd pushed open the door. I walked in slowly. She was home. I could see Beatrice sitting on the red couch, the afternoon light consumed in the black of her hair. She was perfectly still, shoulders rigid.

'Hello . . .' I stammered, 'I am so sorry, I did not realise you were . . .'

She remained seated, staring out the window, then began talking slowly, 'I could have written. I buzzed and knocked but assumed you were gone for the holidays, so I just let myself in.'

I wanted her to turn around, to look at me. 'I was just out getting orange juice, can I offer you a glass?' I awkwardly held the container in her direction, suddenly very aware that it was stolen.

'No, thank you. I'm just looking for something,' she said while rearranging out-of-sight papers, slipping whatever it was into her bag.

'Oh,' I responded. A chalky heat ran up my legs. 'If we had known you were coming we would have cleaned up,' I faltered, choked with embarrassment for the piles of clothes and books that were strewn across the floor.

'That is beside the point,' she said, raising herself from the couch as if her spine was connected to a metal cable. I straightened myself, trying to shuck my hangover. She slipped past me, and I was again staring at the back of her acorn-shaped head.

'Oh, this came for you from the Writers' Schloss,' I said, pulling out the letter and handing it to her. She reached back without looking and added it to her bag. On her way out, she motioned to the mountain of laundry on the piano, and said, 'I am happy you are at home here. I am back to Vienna this evening.' She paused almost out the front door, then said over her shoulder, 'An eating disorder is a serious thing. Do take care of yourself, and merry Christmas.' Her words were light and cool as a holiday greeting to a doorman. The lock thudded behind her.

What the fuck? I stood in the hallway in disbelief. I had to call Hailey. Did her phone work in Paris? How did Beatrice know about my throwing up? Hailey didn't even know. I barely knew. I ran to the bathroom to see if there was any evidence. Maybe I was being sloppy because I was living alone. I checked. There was nothing. I was a monk about cleaning the bowl. There were too many wine bottles in the recycling, but it was the holidays. That's normal. There was a wrapper from the döner I'd regurgitated. But there was nothing that would have given away my current experiment in finger-fucking my throat. My head throbbed. Maybe she could just tell. Were there cameras?

I inspected every object in the bathroom, turning over the soap canister, tracing the edges of the shelves looking for wires. Was I insane? Had I written it somewhere? It hit me. I ran into my room and looked at my computer. It was facing the wrong side of the bed. I grabbed it, thrusting the screen open, my drafts folder came into focus. It was open to the last one, highlighted in white, to high-school bulimic, Molly Webster. I deleted it.

The apartment reeked of Beatrice's perfume. White, Clorox clean, but still expensive, like flowers grown in a laboratory. It itched my nostrils, I wished I knew what it was. Then I could place her, bottle her, and shelve my uneasiness. I sat down on the red couch and drank the entire carton of orange juice. What was she doing here? Why had she looked through my emails? My cheeks flushed with heat thinking about Hailey and me poring through her drawers. Had she watched us? Was this her revenge? Despite her rigidity and reserve she had seemed slightly unhinged. She hadn't even made eye contact. I tried Hailey's phone again. It wouldn't ring through.

Christmas was spent at home, alone, in front of the oven, cooking a plate of roasted orange things. Carrots, squash, sweet potato, and six episodes of *Law & Order*. The apartment felt scary. I went to the bathroom to empty my stomach. Standing over the toilet, I thought about Beatrice and the last words she released, a venomous butterfly – *an eating disorder is a serious thing*. I couldn't make myself do it. I spat, watching my saliva sink into the slick bowl.

I missed Ivy, I wanted to crawl back to Sebastian and curl up on the ballet-slipper beanbag. I Skyped my mom. We talked about her psychotic boss and what she called the 'eroding' real-estate market in Florida. She went on to tell me about a couple, Brad and Marsha from Syracuse, who she'd been forced to entertain while waiting for the keys to a 'spectacular Spanish-style hacienda'. Apparently, she'd mentioned having a daughter studying in Berlin only to find out that Brad and Marsha had close friends living in Berlin with young girls in need of a babysitter – the Breitbachs.

'They seem *really, really* great,' my mom said, I could sense her desperation for it to work out. I knew money was tight. I emailed, and agreed to meet them two days later.

The next night Constance met me for dinner at a restaurant on Torstrasse. I got there before her and peeked in – too nervous to enter the tiny space, full of people who all seemed extremely *cool*.

'It's freezing, why are you waiting?' Constance yelled from the other side of the street.

I laughed. She darted through traffic and hugged me. We entered arm in arm and made our way to two seats behind a table full of people who all appeared to know Constance. After we put down our coats she bobbed and weaved through the adjacent crowd, accepting kisses and trading bits of gossip. When she finally returned I was stunned.

'How do you know everyone?' I asked in a hushed voice.

She leaned her head in, 'So the guy who I was fucking, Adnan—' I never knew who she was fucking.

She registered my blank stare, 'The one that makes music, who's on tour, whose house I sublet.'

I nodded.

'Well, before he left, he'd always host these big dinners, and like everyone would come. And Alexander, who runs this place, would cook.'

'And Pia his girlfriend, the woman at the end in the black sweater, she gave me an internship at her gallery. It's just one day a week, but lots of fun people.'

We ordered. I blurted out what happened with Beatrice, but left out her parting words on bulimia.

'She's American, right? There is a set of rules that go along with subletting, and I don't think dropping in and sitting on the couch is one of them.'

'I know.'

'Truly creepy.'

We talked about everyone I'd met at the party the other night – Constance informed me the Marxist was making internet art and going to have a big show in Braunschweig, and the Croatian dancer was supposedly pregnant.

'Honestly, what is internet art?' I asked.

'Pasty boys on laptops and – digital flames?' Constance laughed.

Dessert was *on the house,* baked pear and ice cream. We talked about high school. She'd also worked lots of jobs. I told her about the perfume counter at the mall. And she told me about the Jack Pot Casino, a windowless, dusty building in downtown Red Deer, Alberta. According to her, she looked a healthy-chested twenty-one at fifteen years old, a friend's brother made her a fake ID, and she got the job. 'I could have worked in a grocery store bagging groceries. Or I could make better tips, save money and get the fuck out of town. And here I am,' she smacked her lips, motioning around the restaurant, clearly still pleased with the ingenuity of her teenage self.

I found the Breitbachs' apartment in the central and bustling neighbourhood of Mitte, not far from the restaurant where Constance and I had had dinner. The white stone facade of the four-storey building had the look of a vanilla cake dusted in powdered sugar. The neighbourhood was chic. Nicer than ours, with little cafes and slick-fabric-covered prams. I stood at the buzzer trying to figure out which apartment was theirs but there was only one button in the brass trapezoid. I waited, unsure of what to do, then it hit me – they owned the whole building. A woman in a grey sweater and matching slacks opened the heavy gold door and looked at me as if I were delivering a pipe bomb. I tried to smooth my hair to match the unexpected elegance. The interior, a cross between a hunting lodge and Carrara marble quarry, was strewn with wrapping paper and toys. The woman in grey ushered me into a glass elevator and we whirred to the third floor. The doors opened to reveal *Claire*, the name scrawled above the address on my post-it, who came clicking towards me, her blonde waves bouncing in step.

Claire was wearing high heels the colour of Pepto-Bismol and an electric-orange dress dotted with fuchsia birds, topped off with a lime-green necklace. The tropical-housewife palette did nothing to soften her steel-grey eyes, she had the stare of a tennis champion in the final set of their life. She gripped my hand like she was weighing my worth. I wondered briefly if no words would be exchanged, this alone would be the interview – then she released.

'Hello, Zoe,' she tilted her head towards the woman in grey, who was saying something quickly in Spanish.

'This is Beata, she maintains our household.'

I extended my hand to Beata then followed Claire into the

white marble, peony-flanked kitchen. 'I am very excited about having another American in the house, a Floridian no less. I was born in Paris. Diplomat family. But I'm really from Miami, half Cuban. Do you speak Spanish?'

I nodded, then grew terrified she would test me. Claire sensed my hesitation.

'Beata and I speak Spanish with the girls, don't worry. I want them to be global. I have to do what I can to keep them from becoming too German – if you know what I mean.' She released a glassy laugh, 'Sorry, my husband is German, technically Swiss and German – so that's what he speaks with the girls. But German enough to still have a stick up his ass about everything.'

She laughed again. No wrinkles. I wondered how old she was and what plastic surgery she'd had done. Two brunette girls bounded into the kitchen with devilish smiles.

'Savannah, this is Zoe.'

'Hello, Zoe,' Savannah said with sarcastic politeness.

'Serena, this is Zoe.'

'Hello, Zoe,' Serena said, imitating her sister. They snickered.

'Savannah and Serena are the older set. Eight. Laurel and Leia are six. Also twins, but, much, much easier to manage.'

I nodded, shocked. I hadn't realised there were four kids. And I'd never spent time with twins before, let alone two different pairs.

'I know what you're thinking, it's a one in ten thousand chance. Having two – sets.' She looked towards Savannah and Serena as they began ripping paper-towel sections and throwing them at each other. 'In a few years I'm going to have to padlock my closet,' Claire said with a jocular smirk. It was a thought she clearly enjoyed. I watched as the clones shredded the soft squares, delinquent beavers, disturbing in their sameness, exchanging looks that might as well have been telegraphs in their own language. It made me miss Ivy, and Hailey.

'Hi, Mel, yes, absolutely we are on for fifteen hundred, Serena has been practising and is having some difficulty with Chopin's Prelude in E minor.' Claire looked away and up towards the ceiling, then gently touched her pierced ear, looking back at me, 'Sorry, Bluetooth.' She turned and began speeding through the house, pointing to different rooms, 'Play room. TV room. Dining room. The girls' rooms. We rarely use the first and second floors, generally we try to keep them a *girls-free zone*. They're still partially under renovation – a lifelong process, my husband bought the building after the Wall fell, I didn't want to live in Mitte but Tobi had a pioneer fantasy, covered wagons and schnitzel. I like to say *the neighbourhood grew up as we did*. Now I can get a cappuccino anywhere.'

Claire moved to the stairs, I followed. 'So, the second floor. That's where Tobi's offices are. He is into *electronic music*,' she let the words *electronic music* hover between us with obvious disdain. 'He's from an old Swiss family, he sold his holdings two years ago – and now he just – anyway, I used to be a lawyer, criminal, and civil defence.' She paused, focusing her battle-axe eyes on me, 'We strive for excellence with the girls. So never hesitate to ask me anything.'

'Great,' I said, realising I hadn't said a word.

'So you're an artist?' she asked as we zig-zagged our way back down to the first floor.

'I am.'

'What type?'

'Collage, I guess—' I faltered, in Claire's glistening world collage seemed too small, so I lied. 'And film.'

'Film is excellent, we go to Telluride every year. Do you think you can handle two days a week?'

'Absolutely,' I said, surprised at the speed of everything.

Claire held her gel-tipped finger to silence me. I crumpled, wondering what I had done wrong. She gave me a reassuring smile, then pointed to her Bluetooth, 'Yes. Yes. Brian, just tell Calvin to send Udo the calendar. There are no surprises, swim lessons are still at five. I need the girls' hair dry, we're having dinner at Borchardt.'

Unsure of where to rest my attention while Claire was talking, I began to look around the large entrance hall, my eyes rolling over framed photos, paintings and glass boxes holding artfully pinned-down butterflies. I was admiring the chandelier, a burst of violet bulbs, when I jumped, noticing a man staring me down from the curving second-floor staircase. His face was hidden in shadow except for his Terry Richardson glasses, which reflected the chandelier in two droopy moons. I smiled meekly, assuming the husband. Claire paused from talking, then looked up, 'Tobi, this is Zoe. She's going to be with the girls on Tuesdays and Thursdays.' He stepped forward, revealing a small mound of sandy hair on a mostly bald head, a puffed-pastry face, bovine gut, and a vague hipster moustache. A rush of disappointment. After meeting Claire, the tennis champion with her designer eyebrows and jack-hammered cheekbones, I had expected someone to match.

'Won-der-ful,' he said, leaning over the railing, the drawstrings from his red cashmere hoodie dangling towards me. I nodded. Tobi's gaze lingered longer than it should have before disappearing to the other side of the hall.

'OK, Zoe. See you Tuesday. Sorry this is so short, I trust Marsha and Brad, but I just wanted to make sure you weren't a lunatic.' Claire tilted her head, then screamed in Spanish for my coat. She gave me another tight handshake and within thirty seconds the gold door had swung shut, hermetically sealing their world behind me. I stood on the stairs dumbfounded.

7

Hailey returned two days later, the silver heart of her Tiffany's Christmas present vibrating below her throat as she talked. I sat in her room in rapture, deeply relieved to have her home as she described storybook scenes: *Walking along the Seine. Red wine in little cafes. Chanel window shopping.* Her sugary tone soured when she went on to describe how her parents had left early, cancelling their trip to Berlin, and abandoning her with her older brother. I was initially relieved that we would avoid having to defend our lives to Hailey's parents, but disappointed we wouldn't be going out for a *nice* dinner.

'I mean, of course, work comes first, I understand why they left, but being stuck with Brett in Paris. Jesus Christ. He didn't even want to go to the Louvre, he just wanted to chase after French pussy.'

It sounded as though they'd spent the holiday arguing and eating.

'Oh. And my brother and I were given completely horrible hotel rooms. So small. So I convinced the manager that I was handicapped and they gave me an upgrade.'

I searched her eyes, she was serious. I chose to ignore whatever she must have said to pull that off. All I wanted to talk about was Beatrice.

'So she was just sitting here?'

'Staring out at nothing, like in a trance. Then she started going through a stack of papers, which she put in her bag, and she wouldn't even look at me when we were talking.'

'That's weird,' Hailey croaked. 'I wish I'd gotten to see her. I'd have asked her why she killed Luke off in *The Devil's Dimples*.'

'I think she was angry, because it was messy and we moved the lip couch . . .' I was blabbering. I had left out Beatrice's comment on eating disorders. Too embarrassed, still reeling from Hailey saying all bulimics *should be rounded up and shot*.

'I just have this feeling she is watching us,' I paused, 'or something.'

'Eh . . . don't be paranoid, just because we are going through *her* stuff doesn't mean she is going through ours,' Hailey said, near laughing, as I poured her more wine into one of Beatrice's octagonal glasses.

'The weirdest thing is she wasn't even wearing a coat,' I added.

'What are you even talking about? Oh my god you're totally afraid of her . . .' Hailey was now really laughing.

Trying to change the subject, I told her about the bar where everyone was an artist or a DJ or both.

'I can't believe the one weekend I am away you go out and meet everyone *and* see Beatrice. Not fair.'

I liked her jealous. Hailey sat up and pulled my hand towards her, 'Guess what? I have a surprise for you, and you can't say no.'

I lifted my eyebrows.

'My parents weren't able to cancel their full hotel stay, so we have one night at the Hyatt Grand, with pool! And room service. Check-in opens in forty minutes.'

I jumped up and gave her a hug, smashing her back into bed. She had missed me.

Hailey offered to pay for a taxi to the hotel, feeling generous, or flexing her wealth – I wasn't sure and didn't care. I packed my bag quickly, digging out a black swimsuit

I had brought to Berlin in dumb hope. Hailey was tearing around the apartment looking for something, her backpack already strapped on.

'Have you seen my diary?' she asked.

'The one I got you?'

'No, the orange one. The one I *write* in.'

I hadn't. But I helped her search, then suggested maybe she'd left it in her handicapped hotel room in Paris.

'I didn't bring it to Paris and I haven't seen it since I fucking left.'

She had an accusatory tone and was staring at me stonily.

'Do you think I took it? Or what, read it?'

'No—'

'Maybe it's at school?' I asked, even though I knew she rarely went. A tremor passed through me, maybe Beatrice had taken it? I didn't want to seem paranoid – so I pushed the thought away.

'Whatever,' she finally said, deflating onto the edge of the couch, 'I guess, let's go.'

I was elated to be getting out of the apartment.

'It doesn't look so *grand*,' Hailey said as the taxi pulled up.

I didn't care, the lobby was immense with a sea-foam marble floor and the concierge smiled sweetly as he photocopied Hailey's passport and phoned to make sure the room was ready.

Hailey was bubbly, in the elevator she dug out a faux-retro Polaroid camera her parents had given her for Christmas, and we posed in the mirror. There was a new magnetic energy between the two of us. Everything felt heightened. The room on the sixteenth floor had a view of the whole city, a kitchenette and a baby-grand piano in the sitting area.

'I love that Berlin is paved in pianos,' Hailey said as she removed two fluffy robes from the closet. 'Straight to the pool.'

I went to the bathroom and changed into my swimsuit.

'Oh my god – the floors are heated,' I called.

Hailey laughed, 'Maybe we can convince Beatrice to make some upgrades?'

The rooftop pool was glassed in and topaz blue. There was only one other couple drifting around the shallow end, I dove in, the tension in my body releasing from all those weeks of cold. After lapping back and forth, we went to the sauna and then steam room.

On the lounge chairs Hailey turned to me, 'Let's raid the mini-bar, and order room service.'

I smiled, deeply grateful, and followed her back to the room, where we broke open a bottle of red and looked at the menu, lounging in the king-sized bed.

'Burgers and fries?'

I agreed. Hailey called the front desk, then walked to the piano, and began noodling off the opening lines of 'Seasons of Love', over and over at the top of her lungs. I took a Polaroid, the flash reflecting off her gold bikini. After her image emerged in the emulsion, I slipped the rectangle into the pocket of my coat, knowing I would add it to the collage with all the cut-out Dada groceries – the empress of Biggles, my goddess of commodity.

The food arrived on a metal cart and we ate in bed, our teeth matte purple from the wine. Hailey turned on the surfboard-sized flat-screen and chirped in glee when Amanda Knox's blonde ponytail popped up in a sea of blue-uniformed officers.

'She *finally* goes to court next month – a year after, can you believe it?'

'Change the channel,' I begged.

'Oh come on?'

'I'm serious.'

'Fine,' the TV went black, 'but let's talk about it.'

'What?'

'Ivy – I think it would be good for you to talk about her.'

I exhaled. She refilled my glass and opened another bottle, the world started to feel tiny, just her and me and the honey-hued light buzzing from the sconces above the bed. In that moment, I would have told her anything. I started with the Roxy watch, how I had copied everything Ivy did as a kid, how we became friends, our fights, our late nights sneaking out, kissing Jesse, how the cheerleaders hated me and the collages I'd made of her for the ice-cream shop, and finally how I'd followed her to New York. Hailey drank it up.

'Were you in love with her?'

'No – I guess, I was more fixated with her – we were best friends.'

'You get *fixated*, don't you?' Hailey paused, licking her purple teeth, 'You're fixated on me now, aren't you?'

'What?' I asked, a lump of shame forming in my chest.

'I know you wore my clothes to that party in Prenzlauer Berg.'

I scoffed, unsure of how to answer.

'You told Devin Kenter your name was Hailey. He friended me on Facebook, then messaged, confused – and then I saw a photo from the party of you in my clothes.'

I sat, drunkenly scratching for words; her name had just slipped from my lips in that instant, I hadn't imagined the drugged-out Marxist would remember what I said, let alone look me up.

'It's OK, I like that you're obsessive – so am I,' she said, turning to me, kissing me on the cheek before she swung out of bed. I couldn't sleep. I lay next to her, trying to be still, as heat radiated from her body.

The next morning was New Year's Eve, we swam and napped poolside. Hailey had requested a late check-out so we didn't have to be downstairs until 3 p.m. We discussed our options for the evening. Constance had told us about a studio party in Kreuzberg hosted by the DJs from the *Star Wars* bar. And Jens had invited us to a party at friends of his, Manuel and Bärbel, who lived at Alexanderplatz in one of the tall buildings that had a view of the large square.

'So I did some research on Manuel and Bärbel – apparently Bärbel's brother runs a project space in Mitte and I think there might be some *interesting* people there.' She paused to sip from her water bottle. 'Bärbel summers in Capri.'

'How did you—'

'Light googling and cross-referencing their friends list.'

'I think the studio party could be fun,' I added.

Hailey scoffed.

We walked to the sauna for one last sweat. I lay on the top bench still in my swimsuit. Hailey was buck naked adding water to the rocks with an oversized wooden spoon, mid pour she turned to me, 'I've been thinking about it since everything you told me last night.'

I opened my eyes.

'Did you kill her? Ivy. To get with Jesse?'

I took an angry hot breath, 'No, I fucking didn't. They were long broken up by—that's insane, Hailey.'

'I'm sorry. I know. I'm in *Law & Order* mode.'

'Well, don't,' I snapped, wrapping my towel around my chest.

'I said I was sorry,' she called as I left.

I jumped into the pool and swam to the other side, when I came up for air she was standing on the tiled edge, still naked. She cannonballed in. I dipped under, sucking a mouthful of chlorinated water, then spat it in her face when she surfaced. She took it, her punishment, then softly said, 'Let's go.'

When we emerged from the subway, an old man shot a firework at us from a second-floor apartment, he whooped when he saw me buck like a horse and drop my duffle on the sidewalk. It was a booming battle ground. I couldn't understand how a city that had been bombed to smithereens would enjoy producing such a violent New Year's symphony.

I grabbed the mail and filtered through bills we'd have to forward to Janet, several innocuous white envelopes, and opened one addressed to us.

Girls, a friendly reminder.

The boiler is not meant to be left on for long periods of time. One should simply turn it 'on' before a planned bath, and then 'off' directly after taking said bath. Thank you for your understanding.

Warmly, Janet.

'How do you think Janet knows we've been leaving it on?' I asked.

'*Warmly*,' Hailey laughed, then shrugged, handing the letter back to me.

I went to the bathroom, the fuzzy red light of the boiler was off. I looked around uneasily. 'Didn't we leave it on when we left?'

'Honestly, I don't remember, sometimes I turn it off,' Hailey called back.

She rarely did. I became frantic. The tremor of Beatrice being in the apartment returning. 'Beatrice or Janet must have been here while we were out.' Hailey was already engrossed in a gossip website. 'There's no other explanation, right?' I pressed again.

'Oh chill. I think I turned it off.'

'But how did she know we were leaving it on?'

'The bill from last month was probably higher. I'm sure Janet has nothing better to do than analyse our electricity usage on the lonely island of Sylt.'

109

I walked through the apartment looking for more evidence of entry but everything seemed in place. I sighed, then opened my laptop and found a series of progressively more agitated emails from Jesse. I'd forgotten to tell him I was going to the hotel and would miss our Skype date. At first he was just sending pictures, but the last few were angry.

Why aren't you responding to me?? What the fuck? Are you with someone? Please come back. Buttercup?
I need you.

My mom had sent photos of her firespike plant blooming on the patio. And I had an email from Ana Noble, Ivy's mom. I knew what it was and didn't want to open it – an invitation to a remembrance ceremony in their backyard on the fourth of January, Ivy's birthday.

My computer was a wormhole back to America, I closed it hastily and tried to relax into the empty evening. Even with the windows closed the sulphur from the fireworks crept in. Pulling my duvet tight, I moved to the window, staring out at the street while digging my thumbnail into the waxy skin of a Navel orange. I inhaled deeply. The smell of Florida, another wormhole, I was transported far from the Day-Glo bodies of the prostitutes strolling Bülowstrasse. I could see the sun-baked parking lots of my home state, the baroque mangrove marshes, bleached docks and the sandstone shopping mall with its skunked fountain glittering with oxidised pennies.

Imagining the hot wet landscape made me feel fresh with guilt, no distance would change the fact that I had pressed that bracelet for Grandma Jane into Ivy's hand, telling her to go back to Sebastian for the weekend.

I dug my thumb in so deep the orange bled. I inhaled again. There had been no news about Ivy's murder. Nothing from the cops. Nothing in the newspapers. Before his emails had turned resentful, Jesse had sent a photo of her grave. He had bought a bouquet of tulips, they wouldn't last five minutes under the harsh afternoon sun. He should have bought a vase. He also sent pictures of his family dog. The 7/11 near his house. A T-shirt he'd found at a thrift shop. His new uniform for work at the marina: khaki shorts and a blue Hawaiian button-up. I didn't know what to say to any of it.

Hailey had torn up the apartment looking for her diary but still couldn't find it. Among the debris was one of Zander's packages, in the shape of a cat, lying on its side, unopened in the hallway. Hailey saw me kick it gently, pushing it towards her open door.

'I got it from the Zollamt before I left. Honestly I can't even keep up.'

'Can I open it?' I asked.

She was spoiled by mail, she'd thrown a fit two weeks before when a package from her mother arrived and she'd forgotten to include Hailey's La Mer foundation, which apparently cost over a hundred dollars an ounce. Hailey had begrudgingly bought a jar of Maybelline Dream Matte Mousse, which she called *peasant primer*, slathering it on with a look of defeated disgust.

'Be my guest,' she said curtly.

It was much heavier than expected and built with intricate cardboard scaffolding and superglue. I went to the kitchen to find the one good knife, dutifully serrated, and returned to open the flap on the left leg. After a minute of serious sawing, the leg tore, and spurted green Jolly Ranchers. 'Ohhh Zander you shouldn't have,' I cooed. I began working on the other leg, a hail of pink Starbursts fell to the floor. I could imagine Zander, *The Genius,* at the Kmart on Astor Place, buying a discount Halloween bag and faithfully separating each colour at his desk before filling the cardboard chambers. Jesse probably couldn't even manage mailing a letter.

'Throw me a green one.'

The time between the rolling firework booms was getting shorter. We began to prepare for battle, holding shimmering shirts up like armour.

I was inspecting my yellow top we'd tried to dye black that was now swamp green.

'The dye didn't hold because it's cheap material,' Hailey said, winding past me to get to the mirror, a tepid insult. I pulled a sweater over my head, trying to get out of her way as she began ripping red hairs from her brow.

'And that studio party in Kreuzberg is probably going to suck.'

'Why?' I asked.

'I looked up the artists who work there, they've never done any real shows.'

Hailey shot an eye at me, struggling with a nearly invisible hair, 'But don't worry about Devin, I told him he was confused, that he must have been too fucked-up. And that your name was Zoe.' I smiled, relieved that she had smoothed out the situation with the Marxist. I busied myself with applying plum-coloured lipstick.

The train was psychotic, packed with people drunk out of their minds firing bottle-rockets off in the train car. We pressed our heads against the glass, trying to avoid the path of the speeding sparks. It seemed no one would survive the night.

We were four stops away when Hailey turned her head to me, 'Do you ever think about – never mind.'

'What?'

'Ivy's last moments?'

I watched a teenager with a sparkler run off the train.

Hailey continued, 'I mean, her body was found in a sand dune next to a highway, do you think she knew – *this is it* – these are my final moments, this is my resting spot.'

'I hope she could feel how many people loved her,' I said

softly, then stopped myself. I didn't want to think about it. I hadn't read the interviews with the retired accountant who had found her, I wanted to keep Ivy on the sand dune like every other collapsed body on *Law & Order*, fake, so that Ivy, the actress, could just get up after the cameras had stopped rolling and wash the cornsyrup blood off. Before Hailey could ask anything else, the doors to the subway whirred open, and we were expelled into the madness of the night.

Manuel and Bärbel's apartment was full when we arrived, the square windows of their concrete-slab *plattenbau* already frosted with cheerful condensation. I left Hailey and searched for drinks, winding my way through the tasteful silver garlands that dipped from the ceilings. When I returned with two flutes, Hailey was already deep in conversation with a bearded guy, touching her collarbone and laughing. She hardly acknowledged me as I pressed the glass into her hand. I stood awkwardly at her side, withstanding several drumbeats of jealousy. Finally giving up, I found Jens on the balcony resting against the sliding glass door. I joined him, and he awkwardly tried to tell me something but the fireworks were so loud I couldn't hear a word. I retreated.

Viola was pouring champagne near the sink.

'Where is Constance?' I asked, holding my glass out for a refill.

'She's with some Belgian guy, he got a hotel room for them at the Park Inn.' She pointed across the square where the glass skyscraper was barely visible through the fog and explosions. I shrugged.

Viola was staring at Hailey on the other side of the room. 'You know that guy with the beard is a von Habsburg?'

'What?'

'Otto von Habsburg. Like the last Austrian ruler – he's a direct descendant,' Viola said, jealousy flaring.

It all made sense. Of course Hailey was after the Austrian

113

prince, she must have recognised him from trolling Bärbel's contacts.

I almost called Jesse at midnight but it was his 6 p.m., he would be at the marina, mooring a pontoon in his blue Hawaiian shirt. Our phone conversation earlier had been short and terse. I didn't want to hear about his afternoon crying at Ivy's grave and I could tell he was annoyed at my improved mood from the hotel stay with Hailey, he preferred me depressed.

I scanned the room, everyone was in their early twenties and mostly dressed in black with a few stray sequins. They all seemed to have gotten tattoos from the same shaky-handed friend: dodecahedrons, golden ratios and crooked arrows running up forearms. Viola was now trying to edge into conversation with the von Habsburg, her hands moving like an airplane controller as she talked. Hailey wasn't having it, slowly turning her shoulders, shifting Viola out. A familiar feeling washed over me, which I recognised from countless high-school parties when Ivy would disappear into the mesh of cheerleaders; *there was nothing for me here*. I slid in behind a clump of girls in silky outfits with matching red lipstick to get within earshot of Hailey. She tossed me a frustrated look for interrupting then shook her head, she was staying. I trudged out.

I had always been annoyed at the pressure of New Year's Eve but the battle-ready rollicking of the city made me feel up to the challenge. A new year. A new war. I was thankful I'd worn my knee-high Wyoming riding boots as I waded through cartridges and broken bottles. The party was in an old 19th-century horse stable that had been converted into studios. It cost ten euros to get in. The techno was thudding and crashing, it sounded like being in a submarine during a storm. The Croatian dancer from the *Star Wars* bar was selling shots with two big duct-taped X's over her tits. We hugged.

She gave me tequila in a plastic cup and I found a corner to stash my coat. Above the DJ booth an image of a snake eating its own tail was drawn out in plastic tube lighting. Devin, the Marxist, greeted me with a monster's grin and placed a pill of ecstasy into my palm with his wet fingers. He winked, too high to talk. I thanked him and he lumbered off, his eyebrows fused to his scalp in a look of surprise. I felt the shape of the oval, wondering briefly if it was a sleeping pill, then swept it down with a spike of tequila.

Twenty minutes later the light in the space started to feel thick and watery, my jaw began careening back and forth. Every sweaty body was a tropical island, everyone existing in their own libertarian state of bliss. I felt truly happy, my brain riding the cresting waves of serotonin. I let myself go and closed my eyes.

A girl with a shaved head bumped into me, she seemed to be on the same stuff. We grinned at each other. This was our island. She slid her hands down my butt while we danced, I ran my hands through her fuzz, it was the nicest thing I had ever touched. She kissed me. Her tongue was warm and wet and her mouth felt as though I were hopping into a perfect bath. Every inch of my body felt good. The shaved head kept disappearing into the crowd, then returning to make out. It felt like Christmas morning every time she reappeared.

When my feet became heavy I searched for the shaved head, she was nowhere. The duct-tape X's had long removed themselves from the Croatian girl's tits and she was throwing bottles against the back wall screaming as each glass orb burst. She didn't hear me say goodbye.

Sifting through the tired morning light, the city seemed exhausted, everyone on the streets still drunk, tinsel spilling from trash cans like the evening's charred intestines. I was tingling. My skeleton felt like it was still on the dance floor, still grinding. Hailey wasn't home yet. I had a pang of resentment that she was still out, still going. I made my fire, then went into her room to check on hers. I sat on her bed. I noticed for the first time that the moulding was made of little rosebuds connecting and reconnecting infinitely, same as the snake eating itself at the party. I was still high. Hailey's fire was out, I went looking for the *New York Times* to burn.

Resting on the corner of the table, casually left askew, was Hailey's diary. Its soft orange cover a hot burning button. I knew I couldn't touch it. Something was wrong. My brain was fizzing, trying to trace the timeline – we had cleared the table after dinner then gotten ready together. I'd reapplied the plum lipstick sitting right there before leaving. The diary had not been there. I sat down and stared at the disturbing object as if it would eventually explain itself, knowing full well if Hailey had found it, she would have told me. Maybe I was just high. I should call Hailey. I went to look for my phone. It wasn't in my coat, I realised I must have left it at the party where I'd stashed my stuff.

The apartment was off, suffocating. I found my Advil bottle, which was running low, and took two, then laced my boots and went outside for a walk. It was cold and grey, I wished I could lie down in grass or sit in the sun, winter felt endless. Going back to the party felt too far so I went to the abandoned train yard just down the block and perched on a fallen lamp post above the harsh white snow. My brain glazed over, a doughnut. Who was that girl I'd made out with? She was British, she'd screamed her name over the music but I hadn't caught it. Holly or Helen or Hazel.

Something shifted inside of me when I thought of her, I had never danced with a girl like that. I'd certainly never kissed a girl like that, baptism by spit. I traced my lips with my finger, they felt the same but I knew they weren't. I wished I'd brought her home, then I wouldn't have noticed the diary. Then I'd be warm.

I had no idea how long I'd been on the lamp post but when I finally pushed open the door I was freezing and Hailey was in bed listening to R. Kelly.

'Did you see your diary?' I asked.

'Yeah. Where'd you find it?'

'When I came home an hour ago it was sitting on the table. I didn't touch it . . .'

She shifted her chin to the side, as if to ask *really?*

'Unless you and the von Habsburg came back here and did a late-night reading.'

'We went to his place,' she had a hint of pride in her voice, which I hated her for.

'I don't want to be the psych patient, but it had to have been Beatrice. Who else would have put it there?'

Hailey looked at me like I was insane.

'Your pupils are huge. Are you on something?'

'Beside the point,' I said as straightly as I could. Hailey *mmmhmmm*'d me.

'So you really don't think it's Beatrice? I mean – I think she's watching us, it would make sense that—'

'No. You're high, go to bed.'

'Fine – how was the prince?'

'His apartment was heated,' she said, then pulled the duvet over her face.

Lying in bed staring at my own ceiling, I noticed where the moulding intersected at the corners was messed up, as if a little deer had tramped through the perfectly pruned hedges. Would I ever fall asleep? My room was bright. I tied a pair of leggings that smelled of old cigarettes from the jazz cafe over my eyes and tried to recount every conversation I'd had in the new year. I woke up around 4 p.m. feeling as if all the liquid had been drained from my body. Remembering I had to go to work, I forced myself out of bed, the apartment was freezing, my fire was out. I gulped water from a tea-stained mug, then wandered into the bathroom to fill the tub.

While I was waiting for the steaming bath I opened my computer. I had an email from Jesse. I forgot that I'd never called. He was furious. He spelled it out: if I couldn't at the very least manage a conversation with him on New Year's, we shouldn't be together. I tried to remember the Jesse who sang on the road trip. I tried to remember the Jesse who cried for Ivy. I was fragile from the drug. All I could think about was the girl with a shaved head, her tongue outlining my teeth. I closed my computer and decided I would deal with Jesse when I got back from work. Get it together, then deal.

The gentle rocking of the train vibrated through my body, a cosy echo, as I walked to the Breitbachs' house. It was my third time there, and Beata, the housekeeper, still greeted me like the Unabomber. The girls were fully charged, somehow I wrangled them into the toy room and we played *The Mountain*, where I lay down, my cheek pressed against the grey carpet, while they trotted plastic horses over my unresponsive body and then would eventually roll over screaming, 'Earthquake!' It was the lowest-energy game I could come up with and they seemed entertained. Dinner was yuca fingers and tamales, Claire hated the food in Berlin and insisted the girls eat Cuban at least once a week. I *oohed* and *aahed*, my mouth full, as the girls described the vacuum-sealed plastic bags that arrived weekly from Claire's favourite Miami restaurants.

Filling the clawfoot tub, I began to tell them the *Monster Story*, which I had made up on the first night, promising if they went to sleep and were good little monsters I would tell them the next chapter when I came back. I named all the characters in the story after my actual friends, and their corresponding monsters after their favourite alcoholic beverage, so I wouldn't forget them because the girls remembered every single detail and would berate me when things didn't line up.

'What happened to Jesse and his monster Jameson?' Laurel asked, dumping a silver goblet of water over her head.

At the mention of Jesse my face pinched up as if preparing for a massive cry. The two older ones, now wrapped in towels, stared confused. The youngest on the verge of joining my tears. I tried to remind myself my serotonin levels were at zero from the previous evening's drugs. I felt out of breath as it hit me – I didn't need Jesse in my story any more. Ever since opening up to Hailey about Ivy, Jesse had become unnecessary and I no longer required him as my instrument of mourning. 'It's actually a very sad story, that's why I look so sad. Should I tell you what happened to Jesse? Are you strong enough to know?'

'Yes. Yes. Yes,' they squealed.

'OK, so put your pyjamas on, and I'll tell you what happened to Jesse.'

Before bringing the older girls to their bedroom, I vengefully killed Jesse off in a vat of lemonade where he drowned trying to save a baby monster. This seemed a bit too depressing for them to handle and trying to abate any anxiety that would deter sleep, I added, 'But, maybe Jesse escaped to the kingdom of Lemondria, which is filled with lemon-headed peacocks and buck-tooth princesses with long spaghetti hair.' That seemed to work. The girls drifted off and I climbed down to the sunken basement to watch SportsCenter on their international cable. Basketball made me feel closer to my dad. I had never met him but *liking basketball* was one of the stray facts my mom had let slip. During the commercials I inspected the framed photos of the Breitbachs. Vacations to Bali. Hiking the Great Wall. Snorkelling in crystal-clear blue water, matching swimsuits, little hands holding up bright dying starfish. They seemed too perfect.

Tobias and Claire returned. I updated Claire on the state of the girls while she peeled off her Louboutins and poured herself a glass of wine, 'Well, good. I hope they got the next installment of the Monster Story, they won't stop talking about it.'

I nodded and she went upstairs to check on her brood. I headed for the door. I could sense Tobias's potato shape lumbering after me. He had a tendency to lurk in the shadows of the house, only appearing when Claire was out of sight, emerging from one of his offices, replete with bear rugs and framed records, droning minimal techno. He often cornered me to ramble about his many *interesting* investments, including a food-delivery service still in beta, which I admitted was a good idea for Berlin. Locked in this process, I once asked if he collected art, to which he responded, 'I collect experiences and hand-blown glass, but my dad bought Richter early.'

Tobias was indeed behind me. One hand rubbed at his moustache, while the other was shoved deep in his signature red cashmere hoodie, 'Do you gamble?'

I had no idea how to answer the question. I missed a beat. 'Simple question Ms Zoe. Do you gamble?'

I supposed you don't end up a millionaire without a little risk, so I said, 'Yes.'

'Great, I'm cleaning out a room on the second floor, there's a roulette table, maybe you want it?'

'Yeah . . .'

'Claire, I'm showing her the table,' Tobias called over his shoulder, too softly for her to hear.

He piloted me through a series of large, nearly empty rooms on the second floor decorated with bent steel and leather furniture, glass tables hidden under plastic drop cloths, and a few stray abstract paintings, no Richters. At the end of a hall lay a dark wooden door, upholstered with velvet and an Art Deco door handle. He turned the knob, holding it open, a glass chandelier shrieked on. The room was a disjointed movie set covered in dust; deep green velvet couches, crystal ashtrays glistening on a wooden bar surrounded by sturdy leather stools that looked like spiders.

'It's a bit ridiculous I know, I moved all this stuff in here from my dad's old office in the West. The casino thing was in fashion, I guess. I'm ready to let it go now, turn it into my mixing studio.' A mahogany roulette table sat under a low-slung copper lamp in the corner of the room. 'There she is,' Tobias pointed towards the table. 'If you're into it, I could have it sent tomorrow.' I walked over, it looked as if it had been pulled up from the sunken depths of the *Titanic* with red inlays and jewel-toned lettering, I spun it, a hummingbird's whirr filled the air. 'Yeah, I mean it's beautiful, are you sure you don't want to sell it or just . . .?'

'I don't need the money, and most of the other stuff is getting repurposed for the remodel. You will be doing me a service.' I nodded dumbly. Tobias slipped behind the bar, 'It's still stocked, you want a drink?' he asked, inspecting the row of bottles. I agreed with a twitchy smile but was suddenly struck with the strangeness of the situation, the remnants of the ecstasy still circulating my brain like loose electricity. He poured something brown into two small glasses with long flowery stems, babbling about the *pioneer life* in Mitte, Love Parade, and a DJ I'd never heard of named Westbam. When he dipped his head to inspect the pour, I could tell his remaining patch of hair had been recently dyed. The smell of breath-mints wafted as he slid the shot towards me. I lifted myself on to one of the stools and he leaned over to clink my glass. After a few seconds of holding my gaze, he moved around the bar and slid his puffy wrist over my waist. I froze. Of course, this is what he had expected in exchange for the strange and extravagant gift. Why the fuck was I sitting here?

'You know you are beautiful, don't you?' He adjusted his hand down my thigh. I sat numb, staring at a marble lamp.

My mind felt cast in resin, fossilised for all eternity. His pudgy lips blew a small burst of air into my ear to get my attention. I shuddered, coming back to life. The whole situation seemed so archetypal. The babysitter straddling a leather stool in this ancient man cave. I released a short laugh then caught myself. I wondered how many servers, secretaries and nannies before me had been in this exact position.

'That is very kind of you. But I have to say, your wife is more my type.'

'Oh?' His voice reverberated somewhere between intrigue and disappointment that I had brought her up.

'Yes, I'm gay,' I said, straightening myself. I was surprised at the taste of the words on my tongue. Metallic and certain. As if they were owning up to an ore buried deep inside of me, that I hadn't been able to extract till now.

'Why didn't you say so?' He laughed, relaxing into a gooey slump. 'Do you want another shot?' he offered, abstracting his disappointment with hospitality. I shook my head and spun off my stool and headed for the door.

'I'll see you next week.'

I dashed through the empty rooms, flying down the stairs. The cold air outside slapped me. I ran to the train not wanting to feel my own thoughts. Not wanting to feel the edges of my hangover meeting the fresh liquor in my veins. Finally in the safe yellow light of the subway I played through what had just happened. Tobias had acted predictably. I should have known, I should have never gone to the second floor. I wondered if Claire knew he was like this. But I had told him I was gay. I felt as if something inside of me had been re-set. Plugged in for the first time, fully volted. I laughed out loud in the train car, startling an old lady death-clutching a KaDeWe shopping bag – the insect with tits, the good lord's cheerleader, Chelsea Benedict, had been right about me after all.

By the time I'd made it back to Bülowstrasse my fire was out. I balled up a *New York Times*, watching a photograph of the chemical-green outfield of Yankee Stadium disappear into flames, then fell asleep. When the electrocution buzzer rang at 9 a.m. I tried to ignore it. Hailey opened the door then yelled to me, a gust of Siberian air blew in from the hallway.

'Zoe? What the fuck is this thing?' I rolled over, groggy, the hangover's claws still deep. I pushed my face into the warm pillow trying to ignore her.

'Zoe, what the fuck is this giant thing? They say it's for you.' I bolted up. The roulette table.

'Uh, just bring it in here,' I called, pulling up my sweatpants as four men moved the table into my room. Hailey quickly closed the front door behind them, trapping our precious warmth. The men asked me something in German, I stared blankly back. Hailey stood, her duvet wrapped around her chest like a strapless ball gown, 'Zoe, they are asking you if they should set it up.'

'*Ja, bitte,*' I said with a foreigner's lunatic smile. They began to pull tools out: screwdrivers, a tiny hammer. I went into the kitchen to explain.

'The guy I work for. He asked if I wanted it. I said, *yes*. And then he tried to hit on me.'

'Really?' A bitchy tinge of disbelief and jealousy fused in her voice.

'He's gross, a techy-butterball. He was getting rid of a bunch of stuff, I guess.'

Hailey's jaw fell slightly open as it was flipped over, revealing the wheel.

After the movers installed the table and left we both sat on my bed staring at the magnificent object. It was so deeply masculine and sad, like a mid-gallop buffalo petrified in amber. Hailey decided it would be a great centrepiece for a dinner. 'It can be *Casino Royale* themed,' she said, flicking her hands into the air imitating a flamenco dancer. 'Does it have chips and the little ball thing?' I shrugged, eyeing a little leather case by the door. Hailey lunged at it, undoing the buckles and revealing stacks of blood-red, white, and green chips all with MDB embossed in silver.

'Why are rich people so into their initials?'

'Oligarchical branding. He's Swiss, right? I bet he made his money off the Holocaust, they all did,' Hailey said while digging through the leather case. She removed a bag of white balls, and then a note. Giggling, she opened the envelope, reading with Shakespearean pentameter.

Dear Zoe. My sincerest apologies.
Let's please keep our conversation between the two
of us. I'm afraid I'd had a bit too much to drink.

'Fucking creep. You could totally blackmail him with this letter.'

I snatched it from her, examining the heavy rectangle. She was right, the letter was more incriminating than his fumbling attempt at hitting on me.

'He's like really rich? Right? Like Viola rich?'

'I don't want to blackmail him. I just don't want to lose my job.'

'He should at least buy your art.'

'He only collects experiences, and hand-blown glass.'

'*Experiences*. He's definitely talking about hookers,' Hailey said, she then turned towards the roulette table that stood before us. 'Let's try it.'

'OK, ten on red six,' I curtseyed with my sweatpants, taking ten blue MDB chips from the case. 'And ten on black eighteen.' Hailey pulled red chips from the case then dropped the ball, it landed on black twenty-six.

'Constance said she worked at a casino, right? She should come over and teach us.'

'I think there is literally nothing to teach.'

We sat around dropping balls and picking numbers till Hailey finally got an eight on red.

'Finally, I win,' Hailey said, zipping up her jacket. 'I'm going to Peres Projects.'

'I have to go back to sleep.'

'Wasn't an invitation.'

I looked at her. She made a head-tilty smirk, she was joking or maybe not. I was too tired to decode.

Thchüss.

8

Jesse and I were two bloody open wounds, bordering on turning a violent green, neither of us able to heal as long as we had each other. Since his email on New Year's introducing the notion of breaking up he had stopped writing me back, wouldn't answer my Skype calls – and as with all open wounds the risk of infection increased with each day. We'd succumbed to the inevitable. He finally wrote me: *just read my texts. i said everything i needed to say.*

I had to find my phone. It was a long shot, but I prayed it was still at the studio from the New Year's party. I traced my route back in the wet snow. The city was so grey it seemed flat, a depthless world. I couldn't stop thinking about the shaved-headed girl. Jesse probably would have found us making out hot, I knew he enjoyed lesbian porn with slutty school teachers and co-eds in pigtails. But Jesse already felt like the past. A footnote to a diseased time. When I finally found the low brick stable I banged on the green studio door. A guy in a Nike windbreaker answered, he was holding a Japanese sculpting-knife in one hand and a joint in the other. The studio was littered with bits of blue foam, which had been carved into an oblong column in the middle of the room. He introduced himself slowly as 'Ben from Denver'. I asked about my phone and he disappeared into a back room.

'It keeps beeping,' he said, handing it over, miraculously still charged.

He motioned to the sputtering snow outside and offered

me some of his joint, 'You can dry off for a second if you want.'

I sat on a raspberry exercise ball and took two deep hits. My lungs erupted in flames. I coughed, and he went back to hacking the block of foam. I had twenty-two angry messages from Jesse. *Bullshit girlfriend. Fuck You. I hope you burn in hell.* I guess my horror was plastered on my face because Ben asked, 'What's up?'

I was suddenly very stoned, I told him I had been dumped on New Year's.

He laughed, 'Long distance never works.' Taking a deep inhale he added, 'I was dating a girl back in Boulder for a while. Now I'm seeing this French girl – she's a painter.' He exhaled, passing the joint back to me. I nodded, not sure what to do with this information. Silence fell, I thanked him and walked back towards home, stoned, single and relieved.

Freezing, I jammed my hands in my pocket and discovered the Polaroid of Hailey playing piano at the hotel. I stopped on the sidewalk and stared at it, there was something about her body cast in emulsion that made you want more. She wasn't a supermodel swimming in the infinity pool of capitalism – that quicksilver that made purchases seem inevitable and easy. No, she inhabited a stranger space – she had the smile of the debutante in dirty pictures, a Midwestern mall model, an actress whose lines were written on her hands. She was *just* barely out of reach and that made her even more desirable. I turned into the Spätkauf near our apartment, and laid the Polaroid on the glass bed of the ancient black-and-white machine. I blew Hailey up and shrank her down, making copies of copies. Disintegrating her smile.

When I got home Hailey was gone. I closed my door, and laid out the black-and-white versions of her on the floor and took out my scissors. Maybe it was the weed, the trance came easy. I cut her thighs into round shapes. Her arched feet into spiked triangles. Her gold bikini into glitzed diamonds. I filled in the green space of the collage with the silvery planes of Hailey's skin. The Dada groceries now barely visible, their bright colours peeking out in splinters, like lost punchlines. It felt good. When I was done, I rolled up the collage and stuck it behind my bed. I didn't want Hailey to know.

School was back in session, meaning I had my one class for the month. Group critiques are already a strange ritual, but my German was so scant everything floated into abstraction. I wondered how an alien would interpret the situation; sixteen people standing around an overturned trash can filled with silver spray-painted popcorn. Would the alien assume the group could talk about any earthly object with this amount of focus? I nervously pinned up four photographs of the collages I'd made for Ivy and burned, as well as the one I'd just finished of Hailey.

I didn't know what to say about the prints to the class. I didn't know how to describe my practice of burning the collages. I didn't want to talk about how I thought of them as offerings for Ivy. I didn't believe in an afterlife, I wasn't even really spiritual. These collages were airplane trails – white smudgy lines between myself and a bigger world, water and sky, living and dead. I was half hoping the fifteen people would have recognised my need for an intervention. I was a bulimic alcoholic – or maybe those things cancel each other out, I still wasn't sure. I let the democratic group of fifteen deliberate over the details of my prints. The quality of paper, the shapes the flesh were cut into. A pink-faced boy in a fleece brought up a series of collages that dealt with the Vietnam war but couldn't remember the artist's name. I assumed Martha Rosler, but he insisted not. Everyone agreed they liked the one of Hailey the most. I understood. There was a violence to her image, her body begged to be looked at – to be reproduced. Obliterated into a million pieces. Klaus, the democratic dictator, cut in to end the discussion; he thought they could be bigger.

Our group of sixteen moved to a sculpture of a painted chair with seven plaster eggs resting in sanded-out indentations. I understood nothing. They were arguing in German. I went to the bathroom and exhaled, looking at myself in the mirror. I didn't want to go back. I was floundering and had nothing to add. The group of fifteen was better off without me. I walked to the train station.

Since New Year's, Hailey had twice stayed until the bitter end of gallery openings, hoping to score an invite to the afterparty. Both nights she'd been left on the sidewalk as the crowd filtered into taxis, whisked off to a destination printed on small pieces of paper that she had never been handed. Adding insult to injury, the von Habsburg, who hadn't been replying to her texts since they fucked, ignored her as he'd breezed into one of the waiting cars. She was livid, and in a rage, decided she needed a new strategy – and began scouring the internet for internships and jobs in art-adjacent fields.

'I mean Constance got one internship and she met like – everyone,' Hailey had moaned, slouched over her computer. In the end the only place that wrote her back was advertised on Craigslist as a '*Bohemian Artist Bar in Neukölln*'.

Stefan, a middle-aged sculptor, and the owner of Der Wald, had been deeply relieved when the efficient and punctual Hailey sat down for her interview in a black turtleneck. And after only one weekend of barely competent work he'd trusted her to run the place on her own.

'Amanda Knox also worked at a bar in Perugia,' Hailey had said, trying to repackage her disappointment after her first night. 'And I stupidly told my dad about the job and now I can't quit – at least for a few weeks. I don't know why he thinks I *need* to work. I mean, we *have* money.'

The train burrowed into Neukölln and I eventually emerged on a dark cobblestone street strewn with sun-bleached desktop computers, graffitied mattresses and music playing from apartments above, reminding me of Brooklyn. I hoped it would be a slow night. There was something deeply bleak about Der Wald. The ancient wooden bones of the *Kneipe* with its stocky carved tables and nicotine-hued ceiling obstructed any attempts at updating. And despite Stefan's efforts, decorating with Duchampy bike-tyre lamps and Kunsthalle posters, the lonely candles sputtering in golden holders still felt more depressed-Rembrandt than hipster-chic. As soon as she saw me open the door Hailey began pouring a lethargic beer, the bar was empty except for an old man slumped at a stool snoring. I pointed to the drooping shape that was rhythmically releasing phlegmy bursts of 'huggghrrr eeee uggghhherrrr'. She shrugged, 'He's harmless.'

'How was school?'

I scoffed, 'Shitty.'

Hailey laughed but her face was tight and twitchy, she burst out, 'I have been thinking you might be right about Beatrice.'

'What?' I sat up.

'You know how I'm obsessed with everything she writes. And I just googled her this afternoon, and I found a new interview, where she's asked about her next book, and get this.' Hailey balled her hand up then pushed her fingers out into a little explosion as if she were about to blow my mind. 'She said she's interested in "the complexities of a contemporary twenty-something female friendship", and that she's doing research, AND it's supposed to be set in Berlin.'

'Show me.'

She pulled out a folded sheet of paper. I mumbled while reading. She nodded along, her arms tightly folded. 'Two twenty-somethings in Berlin . . . roommates . . . artists . . .

'See. It has to be about us. And when I came home the

other day, the apartment smelled of flowers, just like the night we came to meet her. She *had* been inside. I know it.'

Hailey sensed my excitement and continued, 'I'll be honest, I thought you were making up the whole *Beatrice stopping by* thing to cover for the fact that you stole my diary.'

'What?' I flushed red. 'Why would I—'

'It all seemed a little convenient, especially with the diary reappearing when you knew I wouldn't be home. Sorry, I don't know, you can be—'

My jaw clenched.

'I thought you took it, and read it, OK? It's why I've been annoyed with you. But it doesn't matter now, if you swear you found it where you found it – I believe you.'

'I swear.'

'OK, then. I know for a fact the diary wasn't on the table when we left on New Year's Eve because we took that stupid picture with my Photo Booth. Remember: *the last photo of 2008*? Hailey made air quotes around '2008' as if it were a million years ago. She pulled over the bar's PC, which was plugged into the sound-system gently pumping No Doubt. There we were on her Facebook page. Hailey was making a pouty face with her eyes closed, I was kicking my leg out of the frame, my lips covered in that sticky plum colour, we had our coats on and she was clutching the bottle of Rotkäppchen we'd brought to the party. The table in the background was empty.

'See, it wasn't just because I was high.'

'You were very high.'

We both stared at the photo. The last picture of Amanda Knox's roommate Meredith Kercher drifted into my mind. Hailey had shown it to me weeks ago – it was taken on Halloween 2007, the day before her death. Meredith looks drunk and is dressed in a cheap vampire costume, smiling next to someone wearing a plastic scream mask. It's an incredibly doomed image. Our 'last photo of 2008' had the same improbable unfortunateness with our over-painted lips and trashy poses, destined for some disaster.

'So if you believe me now, then answer me this: why wouldn't she add the diary to one of our piles of shit? Make it look like you just misplaced it? Why leave it out on the table?'

Hailey was twisting a chunk of hair, 'She wants *me* to be suspicious, possibly, driving a wedge between us.'

I thought about this. 'What's in your diary?'

'Everything. I write every day. Ever since I was a kid and heard that Lewis and Clark brought the same amount of parchment as ammo on their journey West, I started to take it really seriously.'

'How old were you when you heard that incredibly colonial piece of American lore?'

'Twelve.'

I was staring into the white beer froth, mutating microbes under a lens, I was the skeptical one now. 'You really think this is about us?' I motioned back to the interview.

'You said you thought she was *watching us*.'

I should have mentioned Beatrice knowing about my email to Molly Webster. I should have just told her about the drafts folder, but I was embarrassed – the pit of bullet-holed bulimics flashing.

'Yeah,' I mumbled. The fridge gurgled. Hailey pulled out two shot glasses and poured thick frozen vodka from an icy bottle.

'Maybe we'll be famous,' she said, eyes glittering.

'This doesn't freak you out?'

The sleeping guy let out a giant snort and we both jumped. I shifted my back towards him as he returned to his phlegmy tempo. Leaning her weight onto the counter Hailey held her glass up, 'It doesn't freak me out, because we recognised it was happening, and I don't know,' she became serious, 'after all my reading, I think I sort of understand Beatrice. We can take control of our own narrative.'

My fingers were pressed into the curved base of the shot glass. 'How?'

'She has no idea we are aware of her watching us. Her books are trashy and seductive and dangerous, and I *want* one to be about us.' She mopped the sweat from the glass off the bar, 'But it can't be about our depressing nacho life and Skyping with our boyfriends.'

I gave her a look.

'Sorry, RIP Jesse. But you know what I mean – our existence here is mortifying.' She dropped her head, nearly whispering, 'We've never been invited to an afterparty, we have like – no friends. This can't be it.'

It was true, our lives were a montage of monotony punctuated by the shallow thrill of grocery theft. But I also wasn't sure exactly what type of character I wanted to be, or if I even wanted a novel written about me.

Hailey could see my hesitance. 'Come on. What else are you doing?' She flicked a straw in my direction.

I shrugged, but knew she wasn't wrong.

'If Beatrice writes *this* book,' she pointed at herself then me, and back to herself, 'we are immortalised as losers, we *have* to become spectacular.'

'How?'

'It will be a performance. Like Studio 54 or Warhol's Factory or – Max's Kansas City.'

'What does Studio 54 have to do with Beatrice's book?'

'Come on,' she continued. 'We live in a ballroom, we have no neighbours. We could throw epic parties. We could have a novel written about us like Gatsby. Otto could play the piano. We have that roulette table . . . we could build a real spectacle,' she paused, 'a society of the spectacle.'

133

'So you want to open a club? Or you just want to be Patti Smith at Max's Kansas City?'

'I want to be Max. I want to be Warhol – fuck all those other clubs here, they're all annoying.'

I was genuinely surprised.

'You want to open a club in our house? In Beatrice's house?'

She looked at me with her puritanical determination. 'Yes. I spent all yesterday thinking this through.'

An image of blood dripping from Hailey's nose at the Berghain door popped into my head. This had to do with rejection. If we were running the party we could never be shut out. I lifted my eyes up at the ceiling, 'What about her stuff? The red couch . . . all the nice—'

She cut me off, 'We cover it with sheets or move it to the basement.'

'And you do know Gatsby doesn't end well.'

'I know. But this will.'

'Who would we even invite?' I asked, chewing on the straw Hailey had flicked.

'Constance, she knows everyone and word will spread.'

I leaned back, knowing she already had an answer, but asked anyway, 'So, what do we call it?'

'*Beatrice*,' Hailey said, hands planted firmly on her hips. The righteous pilgrim.

I smiled as a current pulsed between us.

'You said it yourself, you've met all these people but don't know how to make anything stick, we just float in and out of things. We would control the scene. Be *it girls*. We can even make some money.'

'How?' I asked, cringing at the term *it girls*. Hailey's aspirational-new-student-in-school side was showing. Sometimes I tried to picture how she had done it – moved around with her parents to all those states as they expanded Biggles. I imagined she'd set up her locker the same in each place, with ripped-out pictures of Josh Hartnett, Bath & Body Works hand lotion and colour-coordinated schedules.

'We charge cover at the door. Duh.'

I was thinking it over, 'So it's like,' I made bunny-ear air quotes above my head, 'reality TV? And we are the main characters, acting out our fantasy versions of ourselves?'

'Yes, we control the narrative, so Beatrice writes our version.' Hailey hopped onto the bar, pulling her knees to her chin, 'I am so excited. And anyway what's the worst that can happen, we have a really amazing winter and then we go back to school in New York.'

'And you think it will work?' I asked.

'*Art is what you can get away with.*'

I looked at her blankly.

'Warhol.'

I stayed while she closed up. On our way out we helped the sleeping man to a bench, leaving him with a Berliner Pilsner for the road. We had hatched a plan. Hailey would write in her diary and I would take pictures and leave them on my laptop for Beatrice to find.

'And we can't tell anyone, it has to seem natural,' Hailey said with finality as we were swallowed into the stairwell of the train station. I nodded.

Under the guise of trying to fulfil our New Year's resolution of *wanting to be more social and make money*, we filled Constance in on our plan for opening a club in the apartment. She was excited. She offered to run the roulette table and steal the contact list from the gallery where she interned. We discussed how to structure the party, settling on a ten-euro entrance, which would include a stack of three €1 chips and champagne. 'Roulette is all about the house making money. It's the dumbest game. But it's fun to watch, and half the people won't use the chips so you just keep the money.'

Hailey made a bulk order through Der Wald, fifty bottles of the second-cheapest prosecco to be delivered next week.

'So it's not really champagne?' I asked, trying to get the wording right for the email.

'No, but it looks good in a glass and tastes fine.'

'How do you say black tie in German?'

'*Schwarze Krawatte.*'

9

If we were going to build a new frame for our narrative we thought we should also work on our own performances. Hailey had naturally done improv workshops in high school.

'The first rule of improv is never say *no* to another actor. Instead you say, *Yes, and* . . . It allows for the scene to never get shut down.'

We'd just finished a gruesome *Law & Order* so my mind was in the gutter. 'What if someone in improv says, "I want to rape you?"'

She didn't miss a beat. 'You could say, "Yes and . . . now I'm going to get in my time machine and kill you before you rape me."'

I stared at her. 'Wow.'

The theatricality of our new lives was rapidly building. The Russian girl in Klaus's class had mentioned there was a costume sale at the Deutsche Oper and she'd warned us to go early because it got crowded. Hailey and I found a long and quiet queue already wrapped around the brick building an hour before the doors opened at 10 a.m. 'This must be it,' I muttered. Hailey held our place in line while I traipsed off into the statuesque slice of Charlottenburg to find caffeine. When I returned Hailey filled me in on the history lesson the tall woman in front of us had given her.

'Apparently the opera does this every year, and things range from five euros to four hundred. There are pieces from historical operas as well as more contemporary, she suggested we make a pile which we trade off protecting. She said it can get a bit *nasty*.'

As soon as the doors opened, we knew our budget of €100 was too small. Mustard-coloured fat suits hung next to brocade ball gowns and ancient-cupcake tutus. The bundled forms that had been patiently lined up had now aggressively thrown down their jackets to stake small plots of wall space. 'This feels like *Supermarket Sweep*,' Hailey said, pausing to relish the intensity of the room. 'My aunt was on the show, she said all the food was fake and gross, it's shot in a warehouse and they re-use the food for every episode.'

I had never watched it, but I recognised the pro-sumer athleticism in the crowd around us; a mixture of renaissance festival girls lacing each other up in corsets, serious seamstresses inspecting zippers, club kids looking for gear, those only interested in resale value, and us.

We began fondling lace fabrics and gargantuan feathered sleeves, trying to ascertain what or who it was we wanted to be in our hypothetical novel. I was magnetically pulled towards a slippery golden dress that burst into sequined flames, replete with a shawl of woven gold laurel. I slipped the dress under my jacket in the corner, our pile commenced. Hailey tried on an emerald-green dress with a hoop skirt. I found a rack of chainmail, selecting a long-sleeved silver sheath. Hailey pulled two matching David Bowie-esque turquoise suits.

Competing against one of the more diligent seamstresses I had narrowly gotten my hands on a light-pink suit with a stiff cream Elizabethan collar and matching flamingo-feathered shoes. The last costume Hailey picked was a black bustled dress that made her the lead contender for the madam of the sleaziest brothel in the Old West.

'This is it,' she squealed.

We added up all our precious items together totalling €380. Hailey had the idea to peel the tags off the more expensive pieces and take our chances with whatever prices the old ladies at the register would make up. When they rang us in at €160, Hailey shot me a look of deserved pride.

On the train, with our garments packed tightly into white garbage bags, we sat like two proud chickens protecting their eggs. At home we laid each costume out on the floor and then began an elaborate fashion show. After the Polaroid collage I knew I wanted to use Hailey's image again, but this time I'd get her consent. I nervously asked her to pose. She agreed, babbling about her teenage model years, lying back on the lip couch, her freckled legs climbing arrogantly out of the black bustled dress. She was a natural.

When Hailey went to the bathroom I looked through the images, zooming into the display at her contorting body, wondering what shapes I wanted to cut from her.

'Hard to pee in a hoop skirt,' Hailey called, the door to the bathroom open.

I put my camera down. Still dressed in chainmail, I added another brick to my fire. Watching the wedge of marshmallowy kerosine burst into an apocalyptic blaze, I sensed our literary transformations had truly begun. I reluctantly wiggled back into my jeans for work, leaving Hailey re-reading one of Beatrice's novels, the red couch barely visible under her elephantine dress.

As the golden door in Mitte swung open, the youngest – by two minutes – Leia charged at me with a pink plastic wand. I jumped out of the way, but was quickly ambushed by three more girls all with the energy of having just chugged a case of Red Bull. Serena trailed them with a unicorn head attached to a stick, cackling at the top of her lungs. Claire was picking out a purse for the evening from the drawer in the hallway, when she held up a yellow clutch made of buttery soft leather, I nodded approvingly. 'All the moms wear black here. It's very *Addams Family*. I would have never believed you ten years ago if you told me I could be edgy by wearing turquoise.' I laughed, happy to know Berlin's dress code of all-black-everything extended to the upper echelons. Claire turned and her fragrance descended on me as if by crop-duster. Unmistakably Chloé Eau de Parfum. It was a perfume I had sold to young beach wives who preferred their tanned skin to smell chemically clean as if they had no genitals. I usually disliked the women who bought it, but it seemed fitting on Claire and softened her steely aura. I suddenly thought about Tobias. I wondered if I should tell Claire about his indiscriminate hand on my thigh, or if she already knew.

'Well, I'm sorry to report the girls had a carnival at school today and by the looks of them they were doing rails of sugar off their PSPs.' I laughed an unexpected jerky laugh. Claire asked what I had been up to, and I blurted something about the costume sale. She looked up from unwrapping an AstroTurf-green ostrich bag. 'Why are you buying costumes?'

I didn't have an answer so I made something up, 'We are doing a film shoot with a Monte Carlo theme. We're using the roulette table as a set piece.'

'Wait, that's amazing. That's totally so cool, Tobi is going to love that. Tobi? Tobi?' she called, my body seized as she clacked into the kitchen. He wasn't there. I sighed with relief and Claire proceeded to show me what the girls would have for dinner.

'You know, I have a ton of old Monte Carlo-esque clothes, really more Baden-Baden, from Tobi's mother, would you want them? They just sit in boxes in storage. I don't wear other people's clothes, *vintage*.'

She said *vintage* as if it were an STD, then touched her ear signalling Bluetooth, her clicking heels fading into the hallway.

I served the girls cut-up bratwursts, which they inhaled in mere minutes in hopes of having more TV time. After a few episodes of a sparkly-super-hero show, I chased them into the bathtub where I regaled them with the next chapter of the Monster Story.

'So is Jesse in the golden castle in Lemondria? Did he survive?' the girls asked in squawking harmony. How they remembered the nuances of each world I would never understand. I was feeling bad about the real-live-human Jesse. So I told them, 'He was in Lemondria and he was recovering from his near-death experience, training, getting his strength back at the house of a very nice old Kung-Fu master.' Savannah and Serena did Karate chops and squealed with pleasure. 'But tonight we will talk about the Creepy Owl. The Creepy Owl is watching over Hailey and she doesn't know it yet. But there are clues . . .'

'What clues?' Leia asked, submerging a Barbie in the tub, its crimped hair forming an algae blob at the surface.

'Simple things, a door open that she had left closed, or a glass sitting in the drying rack that she knows she never used, or one day she comes home and her diary is in a different place.'

'So the Creepy Owl is just watching her and Zinfandel?' Serena was getting suspicious, maybe edging towards bored.

'Yes, don't you know how much you can learn from watching? You can discover strengths and weaknesses. You can discover their Achilles heel.'

'WHAT is an Ack–KILLEYS heel?' Laurel screamed with disgust.

What was I doing? These poor girls. I explained the Greek myth of Achilles in as boring a manner as possible. Trying to maintain the slow trot towards sleep, I segued into a detailed description of the dense and populated forests of Lemondria. When they lifted off to their own dreams I waded downstairs to the TV room.

Hours later, Claire and Tobias came tumbling in. They were tipsy from a charity dinner and arguing about whether or not they should go to Zurich the following weekend. My whole body recoiled at the sight of Tobias in his wrinkled tux, a wine stain creeping out from under his suit jacket. He gave me a nod as he slipped past me at the sink, his whale belly casting a shadow on the floor. I focused intently on washing a plate smeared with ketchup. Claire went tottering up the stairs to check on the kids. Dreading being alone with Tobias, I put the last dish down and tried to escape to the pantry but he threw a loafered foot in my path, stopping me at the edge of the counter.

'Who's your favourite artist?'

I shrugged.

He took his Hermès scarf out of his pocket and dramatically wiped the table down before sitting at one of the oak chairs. 'Who is it?'

'Right now, Hannah Höch, I guess. She made collages also.'

'She's German. I know who she is,' he paused, 'also a dyke.'

He released a chuckle as if to say *only joking*. He was testing me. I returned to the dish, picking at a crusted French fry. Silently Claire padded in the room holding her heels, Tobias jerked up when he saw her in the door frame.

'Stop with the dishes. Join us for a last splash?'

Tobias looked nervous, he hadn't anticipated her return. He quickly mixed three gin and tonics in etched crystal glasses while Claire grilled me about the *film project*. I filled her in on some loose ideas as best I could, eyeing her to see if she noticed my discomfort, but she seemed distracted, her nails clicking on the bevelled edges of her phone. I was relieved her perfume had worn off.

Tobias had shifted into an overly-cordial voice that seemed reserved for school teachers, tutors and fellow parents, 'Well, I'm delighted Claire will be passing along the clothes from my mother. She literally went to Monte Carlo all the time in the '80s. It's so fantastic that that roulette table gets another

142

life, this is exactly what I had in mind.' He walked towards the fridge, 'I've got your address on file.' He winked at me, and my stomach dropped.

Claire was staring at her phone oblivious. I felt trapped. 'I'll have my guys bring the clothes in the next few days.'

I thanked them and headed out.

When I got home Hailey was standing in the doorway with her arms folded. 'Sit down.'

'Why?' I asked, following her into her room.

Hailey made her serious face, a divot appearing between her eyebrows. I leafed through our last interactions. I couldn't think of anything that would warrant the divot. I became anxious. Hailey went into the kitchen, leaving me to tear at my cuticles. A train rushed by, the room shifting in light. She returned with two full glasses of wine, I relaxed.

'Spit it out,' I begged.

'OK, so I was bored after you left and decided to call the Austrian Federal Chancellery Writers' Schloss. I spoke with Annika Wetzler, who organises the residency programme – and she informed me that Beatrice Becks is not there for this session.'

Hailey held her eyes on mine, wide and bright, as she broke into a smile. I felt a cold flush, goose bumps travelling down my neck and back.

'So this is real.'

'It's real. She's not there. She's watching us.'

I sat up in my chair, 'OK but like – do you think there are cameras? I mean, seriously.'

'There could be,' Hailey said quietly.

We spent the remainder of the evening silently inspecting the apartment, checking the shelves and pushing around the furniture, but all we could find was an extension cable leading to nowhere in the kitchen.

10

Since New Year's, every shaved head I spotted was Helen or Holly or Hannah from the studio party. Usually it was just a teenage boy confused by my desperate stare, but on Wednesday, inspecting hairdryers in the Karstadt appliance section, I looked up and did a double take – there was a shaved head bobbing in the electronic toothbrush aisle. The real one. Even more beautiful than my drug-soaked brain had remembered. I couldn't find my voice so I waved.

'Hi,' she said. She was so casual, so cool, I became instantly self-conscious.

'I'm not sure which one to get,' I said, motioning stupidly to the display of gun-shaped devices in front of me, which wasn't true – I'd get the cheapest.

'Just shave your head.'

'Good idea.' She was escaping again, heading towards the kitchen appliances. I called after her, 'We're opening a club on Friday at our place, you should come. It's called *Beatrice*.'

I still felt weird saying it – *Beatrice*.

'OK. Put me on your list.'

Her phone rang. I was worried I would lose her without telling her where it was and I couldn't add her to any list without her name. I followed her, pretending to read the back of a sleek Philips Turbo Haartrockner box as she confirmed what appeared to be dinner plans. When she finally hung up I called after her, 'Give me your phone number and I'll text you the address.' It was a ruse for her name. I handed her my Nokia and she punched in: *Holiday Roberson*. Was her name actually Holiday? No wonder I couldn't remember it. She twisted a lock of my hair around her thin finger, smiled, and strutted off.

I was left in the aisle, ecstatic. I walked through the remainder of the store imagining the pillow cases and china sets Holiday and I would pick out for our future apartment, wondering what type of lighting fixtures she preferred, probably nothing overhead. My retail fantasy dulled when the woman manning the register refused my payment for the hairdryer because the signature I'd made on the receipt didn't match my Florida State ID from when I was sixteen and looped the Z. I tried to calmly explain my signature changed yearly, I was an artist, but she huffed and called her manager, who agreed to accept my payment only after inspecting my Gold's Gym membership, New York Public Library and a Kim's Video card, each with a wildly different signature.

'You have to decide who you are,' the manager chided, shaking his head, as he retreated to the stationery aisle.

At home I told Hailey about Holiday Roberson. 'She's cute and British with a shaved head.'

'Hot,' she said dismissively. 'Holiday sounds like a fake name.'

'She's really cool—' I was a schoolgirl gazing out the window, wondering how I should interpret Holiday's flippancy.

'So you're gay?' Hailey clucked, moving a stack of Beatrice's books she'd just added to her spreadsheet.

'I was high.' I flinched, not ready to tell Hailey what I'd told Tobias Breitbach. I still wanted to keep the words for myself.

'Well, good you're over Jesse.'

'Yeah—'

'What would Ivy think?' She had the clinical tempo of a doctor inquiring about side-effects, she hadn't asked about

Ivy in a while. And I hadn't been thinking about her as much either. I felt bad. As if she could sense my lack of mourning.

'She'd probably just want to know all the details and then start planning our wedding . . . rainbow cake . . . matching dresses . . .'

Hailey cut me off, no longer interested. 'Have you decided what you are going to wear on Friday? I think we need to make sure to mix time periods. And, whatever we do, we should both be wearing an element of Beatrice's. I was thinking we could cut the cuffs from the Oxfords in the closet and wear them as bracelets – symbolically it feels important.'

The idea of slashing the few pieces of clothes Beatrice had left in the apartment seemed excessive, but maybe that was the point. There was no going back.

'OK – and I was thinking chainmail.'

She shook her head and slid into her bossy voice, 'Wear the gold dress. Chainmail will make it seem like a Halloween party.'

I rolled my eyes while walking to my room to throw a few lumps of coal on the fire.

The electrocution buzzer jolted us both out of bed, a man in paint-covered overalls delivered three boxes with my name written in clean black marker.

'Dear Lord,' Hailey belted, tearing open the biggest box before the door shut, pulling out a wad of brightly patterned scarves with the fervour of a magician on a cruise line.

'The perks of this man's creepiness are spectacular. Why would Claire be OK with you getting all this stuff?'

'She said she didn't wear other people's clothes – *vintage*.'

Hailey nodded, 'You know Britney Spears wears a new pair of underwear every day.' She was already trying on coral-pink pants with fringe at the bottom. I joined her in the mirror, inspecting a shimmery hazel dress; I'd popped a blood vessel

146

in my eye throwing up the previous evening's baked ziti, but I felt, new – somehow even more beautiful.

'Very few people actually know us here, we could just start wearing this stuff every day,' I said, slipping a cranberry bolero over my shoulders. 'This, this could be me.' The colour exaggerated my haemorrhaged eye, I took it off.

'That is you,' Hailey said confidently, edging me out to check herself in a canary-yellow turban.

In the mirror I admired Hailey's long fingers as she repositioned the head-piece, her nails were tipped in white polish, classic French. I appreciated the girlish seriousness of her manicures. I'd spent the previous evening focused on them while snipping her limbs from the dozens of photocopies I'd made from our photo shoot. Patiently freeing each digit with an X-Acto blade, collaging her hands like trees at the bottom of the page and then gluing seven circular cut-outs of her chest in a lunar arc.

'What we need now is more chairs and champagne flutes,' Hailey said, settling behind her computer, still wearing the turban, her reading glasses reflecting the chunky font of eBay. We only had three wine glasses left in the apartment. I'd broken yet another, calling out the customary, 'BEATRICE IS GOING TO KILL US,' much to the delight of Hailey who loved the maintenance of our inside jokes. Hailey tracked down a restaurant that was going out of business and arranged to buy twenty black chairs, eight bistro tables, and twelve boxes of champagne flutes all for under four hundred euros.

On Thursday, Hailey and I met at Der Wald to discuss further preparations for Friday. Even though we hadn't found any cameras, it still felt better to plan our 'narrative' outside of the apartment. Everything was in motion. We would use Der Wald's tax ID, Hailey having successfully convinced the suppliers to deliver straight to our apartment where we'd pay in cash, certain that Stefan wouldn't notice the tax discrepancy until we were long gone. Hailey pulled out the red diary I'd gotten her for Christmas and I swelled with satisfaction knowing that I had selected the vessel for our story. She cracked the spine, smoothing down the first page as we prepared our opening lines.

We have decided to open a private club. We are inviting the most interesting people we have met thus far in Berlin; artists, writers, musicians, DJs, thinkers; and allowing each one of them to bring one guest. Otto will play piano. Constance will run the roulette table. And Zoe and I will alternate working the door and hosting. We are pulling from the salons of Paris, the cabarets of Berlin, the poetry clubs of the East Village.

I tossed back the last of my beer, making my final edits, 'I hate the term *thinkers*, why is *thinkers* a separate category, is an artist not a *thinker*? It seems corny.' Hailey was annoyed I was questioning her.

'I know what she appreciates, I've read all of her books, this is the type of scenic description she would totally love.' Hailey was already pouring me another frothing beer, her hair pulled back in a brightly patterned Emilio Pucci scarf – she had the look of a movie star or crazy person, maybe both.

By Friday we were buzzing. Jens had come over to help. We moved extraneous things from the apartment into the basement: plastic tubs full of Beatrice's more unattractive periodicals, wicker baskets, an oversized watering can, a collection of small brass statues, anything that seemed too pedestrian or could get easily stolen. Our own valuables – passports, laptops and nicer toiletries – were moved into the pantry, which boasted a brand-new combination lock. We rolled the piano to the centre of my room and finally, barely managing, lifted the heavy roulette table into the niche of the bay window.

I was cleaning the last remaining things from my room, when Hailey came in, noticing the pile of collages I'd pulled out on my bed.

'That's my chest, isn't it?' she said with vain glee, pointing to the arc of her collarbones. 'And those are my hands, aren't they? Creepy.'

'Sorry—' I mumbled, trying to move the stack.

She grabbed the paper, 'No, creepy in a good way – but I like the other one.'

'Which?' I asked.

'The big one you made, that you keep hidden under your bed.'

'How did you—?' I asked, embarrassed.

'No secrets in this house,' she laughed, then extracted the tube from my hidden tangle of art supplies and unrolled it – we both stared at the black-and-white collage.

'It's amazing. Can I have it?' Hailey asked. I nodded, singed with pride.

'Oh and do you have any more tampons?'

I pointed to my backpack. We were vibrating on a new level. Even our periods were synced.

The buzzer rang. Constance stood in the hall, her brows raised as I opened the door.

'Did you guys start a metal band or something?' She tossed her coat on my bed. 'Your eyeliner is a bit – thick.'

Constance pushed past us into Hailey's room, her gaze falling on the roulette table. She lit up, clicking her tongue against the roof of her mouth, then confidently dragging her index finger down the length of the edge before beginning an investigative series of drops and spins.

'Do you have a level?' she finally asked. I dug one out of the closet in the hallway, Constance placed it on the green felt and made a dissatisfied frown. 'It will do for tonight, but in the future everything should be precise.'

'And how many chips do we have? We need to make sure people can't fake them.' I handed her the leather bag that held the engraved stacks of MDB chips, adding, 'I don't think we have to worry about anyone faking chips.'

'You never know.'

Hailey shot me a smirk, Constance's professionalism was a new look.

'God, but what if no one comes,' I moaned.

'Babe, people will show. It's new and something to do, everyone is sick of always going to that same bar in Prenzlauer Berg,' Constance replied confidently.

Hailey dragged an armful of clothing options for Constance to the couch. She was already wearing a belted Nirvana shirt and seemed offended by Hailey's insistence she change, but her mood shifted when she inspected the pile. Constance held up a strapless cream dress biting her lip, then throwing it down with the apathy of a used tissue. She poked at the Elizabethan collar and checked the tension on a pair of moss-green tights, then held up Tobias's mother's red pantsuit.

'Claire, the woman who gave me the clothes, said her mother-in-law *snogged* Mick Jagger in that pantsuit.'

Constance laughed at the term *snog*. 'I don't think my ass will fit,' she said, lifting her shirt. She stepped in. It fit perfectly. Despite regularly photographing herself nude for her artwork, Constance was careful to keep her looks iced, hidden under fashionably oversized T-shirts and baggy jeans – but she was a Bunsen burner, a controlled flame, turned on.

Hailey returned to the room with a bottle of prosecco. Popping the cork, she filled four glasses and handed them out. Constance clinked her flute with a metal tube of mascara, signalling a speech, 'To Beatrice.'

'Every night you miss in Berlin is a night you miss in

Berlin,' I added. Hailey dropped her chin in salute, 'To Beatrice.'

I took a picture for Facebook, frozen smiles with glasses extended. Otto arrived. He chatted with Jens in German while warming up on the piano, testing the weight of the keys, moving his left hand over his right working his way up.

Sucking in, I zipped up my gold dress, then switched my lipstick to a nearly black red and put on a pair of oversized hoop earrings I'd bought on St Marks in New York. Hailey was melodically practising her Western accent, belting, 'Haaaallllllo, Haeeeeeaaallllllo, Heaaaallllllo,' as she strutted about the apartment in platform heels and a rhinestone choker. I was concerned her look was too theatrical, but she seemed at ease in the tight corset, there was even an impossible naturalism to her hairsprayed curls, which hung heavy as genetically modified roses. She came over and helped fasten the final touch to my look: two of Beatrice's white cuffs.

'The stricter we are, the more people will talk,' Hailey said, in prep for the door. 'The most important thing about tonight is to be controlling.'

I had the initial shift, it would be the slowest. Everyone is late in Berlin.

Travis, a Canadian musician who we'd met through Jens, was the first to arrive with his plus one, a German sound designer named Steel, who seemed bored in a leather trench coat and fishnets. They each paid with crumpled bills. I handed them their chips and Hailey turned on her lunatic hostessing charm, clearly nervous they had arrived to an empty party. But all awkwardness dissolved when Travis caught sight of Constance on top of the roulette table – he strode over and introduced himself, she hopped down and dramatically spun the wheel. On cue, Otto began playing 'Umbrella', and Steel slapped a prosecco glass into Travis's gawking hands. The next to arrive were Bärbel and Manuel, they looked ready for a funeral or political fundraiser, Manuel in a dark-blue button-up and a thin tie and Bärbel a demure turtleneck dress. They were clearly uneasy when they saw Hailey in her mountainous hoop skirt throttling towards them. It hit me how over the top it all was. There was something demonic in Hailey, I flushed with embarrassment, which I escaped by downing another drink. Soon there was a steady stream of people willing to press ten euros into my hand at the door.

I hated the idea of rejecting people, but eventually a drunk guy in a neon polar fleece showed up. His hair was shaggy and his teeth deeply wine stained, he wanted to get in for free, he was leering.

'Come-on-iths – iths a house party,' he motioned behind me. 'You're being an asshole.' This could have been Hailey or me on any other night after too many bottles of gluhwein. I channelled the beefy-necked bouncer from Berghain, delivering a firm *No*, then quickly looked down at my clipboard as if there was an urgent message that needed attention. He left. Others sifted in, a blonde with the soft features of a toddler explained he was the director of a gallery in Charlottenburg, and wasn't on the list but 'was willing to over-pay.' I told him he would have to wait until someone came without a plus one. He looked at me with private-school disbelief but agreed to smoke a cigarette and come back and check. Sure enough Viola's cousin Colin had showed up alone, and I allowed the gallerist in.

Most people in Berlin don't actually get dressed up, they simply have a plastic or leather version of the black outfits they wear all week. Devin, the Marxist, showed up in a pair of latex sweatpants and a mesh T-shirt. The Croatian dancer trailed him in a leather minidress and giant hoodie covered in studs and clothes pins, which she tied around her waist like a wrestling belt. My hour at the door was up. Hailey and I switched.

Relieved to be back inside the apartment, I observed the

group gathered around the roulette table where Constance was holding court. She'd flash a tough smile, fishing bets from those gathered round, then spin the wheel, the room erupting in loud cheering no matter where it landed. Otto was rattling away at the piano, some beer-hall song I didn't know, while a Swiss painter with a voice like a canyon bellowed, barely able to keep up with Otto's flying fingers. *Well, show me the way to the next whisky bar.* I watched as a joint made its way clockwise around a circle of art-bros, each recipient ashing nonchalantly on the floor.

Looking around the crowded rooms, I realised the spectre of Liza Minnelli's bowler hat loomed closer than I had anticipated – the apartment's lights were hazy with smoke, and the Weimar-1920s-cheesiness clung to the ornate moulding of the rooms, but the party didn't seem to be taking itself seriously. It still had a stink, a house-party grunge that made it seem young. Wading through the charged bodies I thought about Ivy, she would have loved this, she was a perfect character for this narrative. They were similar in some ways, Ivy and Hailey, both prisms, able to refract everything into more colourful and big shapes.

I was loading glasses when a graceful hand extended towards me, 'Hi, are you Zoe?'

I nodded.

'Hi, I'm Sam Cassady.'

The name set off a car crash in my brain. Who was it? I knew it was wrapped up in something awful. It hit me. Sam Cassady was the girl who had been fucking, or at the very least texting, Nate – *Leather pants and white button-up.*

'Hi,' I said, gathering my balance and what was left of my composure.

'Constance invited me, she said this was your place and I wanted to thank you. I just got to town – so it's really nice to be here.'

I laughed a weird nervous laugh that didn't sound like my own. She was hot in an airbrushed way with glossed cheeks, perfect posture, peppermint teeth, her black hair sculpted into an intricate braid running down her back. What did I want to say to this person? Nate felt like a character from another universe, but I still boiled with something. Not hatred. But frustration. She recognised my discomfort, and nodded towards the tray in my hand, 'Hey, you look busy. Nice to meet you, and thanks again for having the party.'

'Oh, yeah sure.' I handed her a flute and quickly spun away to do a round of the room.

A Dutch artist I'd met at the *Star Wars* bar screamed into my ear, 'YOU'RE OUT OF TOILET PAPER.' I grabbed a twenty from Hailey at the door and ran outside in the freezing darkness. On my way down the street I paused and looked up at the apartment, which hovered like its own bright star. I wondered if Beatrice was also out here, watching from the safety of the thick shrubs, violently scribbling notes. It was bizarre to imagine all of this was for her.

After I delivered twelve rolls to the bathroom line, I went to Constance, who was collecting chips at the roulette table.

'You know that girl Sam Cassady?' I whispered into her ear.

Constance lit up, 'Yeah, I thought you guys would love her. I met her at a dinner party the other night.'

I pulled my head back, so I could gauge her reaction, 'You know she used to fuck my ex-boyfriend?'

'What? No. I had no idea. Talk to her about it – she's cool – I swear,' Constance said, turning back to the wheel.

Hailey was standing at the door, arms crossed, 'People want to drink something other than prosecco,' she said, matter-of-factly.

'Should we get something at the Spätkauf?'

'The guy who runs that gallery just went to buy a bunch

of vodka. He keeps talking about how he was roommates with Mary-Kate in college.'

'The girl who was sleeping with Nate right before we broke up is here,' I lobbed,

Hailey made bug eyes, 'You should beat the shit out of her.'

'Right?' I said, grateful for her reliable malice.

I took over at the door, by midnight the apartment was crammed and it seemed as though the train tracks outside had been installed for the sole purpose of bringing people to the party. A girl in a shiny faux-fur coat started shouting when I told her we were at capacity. The door was cracked, and Sam, who had been standing in the hall, slipped out and coolly talked her down. The faux-fur coat apologised and squeaked off.

'Whoa. You're good at that.'

Sam snorted, laughing, 'It's sort of my speciality. Sociology major with a minor in psych.'

Noticing her glass was empty, I poured half my vodka into hers. I stared at Sam and tried to imagine why she would ever fuck debate-champ-dork Nate. She was clearly far outside of his league, or maybe she too was into conspiracy theories . . . *Leather pants and white button-up.* The vodka had lubricated my mouth. 'I'm sorry to do this. Were you sleeping with Nate Kai last spring in New York?' I paused, there was no turning back, 'I was his girlfriend then.'

She sucked air into her mouth with a dismissive click, 'Oh, god, no. Is that what he said?'

I was shaky, 'Uh, well he didn't actually tell me anything. I found some texts, and then, yeah, he essentially admitted to it.'

She took a deep breath, then touched my arm, holding eye contact, 'I'm sorry. I was a verbal dominatrix last semester. And he was a client. I have no idea why he would say we were dating. Text messaging was a part of his package.'

'Oh.' I was floored. I took a few seconds, remembering his mind games. 'Leather pants and white button-up.' It just plopped out, a fish, that she was now holding with a strange smirk. Sam laughed and took a sip of vodka, 'Yeah – I had to tell him what to wear. If we are being frank I did you a favour, he was a bit of a—' she looked up at the ceiling, searching for words, 'privileged bitch.'

She wasn't wrong. It was Friday and Nate was probably slurping lobster bisque on the Upper East Side. His eccentric aunt owned a brownstone across from the Met, and one of his favourite after-school weekend moves was inviting select guests for *lunch tours* of her Picabia collection. I exhaled quickly, then began nodding along, pretending to be cool. 'Are you still . . . a . . . domina—' I could barely say the words.

'No, I wrote a paper on power dynamics, race and the art world, and I was done. Everything is about sex, except sex.'

This was not how I imagined this going. 'Yeah – I would love to read that paper,' I added, trying to seem casual, as if I, too, had a thick thesis tucked away ready to validate my horrible relationship to Nate.

She cracked a sideways smile, 'The paper won't grab you any clarity on your shitty ex-boyfriend, but I'll send—'

Before she could finish, a tall guy in a navy parka came running up the stairs screaming belligerently. I recognised him, one of the guys I'd rejected earlier, and now he was roaring at me in German, finishing his tirade with perfect English saying: 'You dumb American bitches are why Berlin is dead.'

Sam straightened her already ramrod spine and addressed him in his native tongue, the navy parka's hands went from clenched to relaxed, he muttered something in my direction that appeared to be an apology before turning away.

'And you speak German?'

'Army brat. I lived on the Rammstein Air Base for two years in middle school.'

I stared blankly.

'It's near Heidelberg.'

'Wow.'

'Yeah. It's weird to be back in Germany,' she said, looking over her shoulder back into the party. 'We should get a drink soon when you're not working.'

It didn't feel like work, but I was tinged with self-importance at her saying it, then, swiftly, a kick in the bladder. I hadn't peed all night.

'Hey, would you mind watching the door quick, while I go to the bathroom?'

'Not at all.'

I hugged her, charged with new-weird-friend energy.

The Dutch girl, who had screamed about the toilet paper, was at the front of the line. I asked if I could pee in the bathtub while she used the toilet. She shouted, 'YES.' I held my gold dress up and squatted. She offered me a line of coke, making the constant near shriek of her voice make more sense. I obliged.

'FUN PARTY,' she said, checking her nostril in the mirror.

I found Hailey in the kitchen and pulled her head towards me. I told her about Sam and Nate, the dominatrix thing and her perfect German.

'Oh my god. We need her.' She paused, ingesting my coked-up eyes, 'You OK though?'

'Yeah, I'm into her – which I can't believe, she seems smart. She's working the door, while I pee.'

I fished my candy-apple-red Nikon Coolpix out of the pantry to prepare my photographic breadcrumbs for Beatrice. The first image, Hailey insisted, should be of her. I agreed. She paced the room looking for the right backdrop, then moved a clump of guys from the roulette table, taking her position reclined against its edge. She pulled up her skirt, revealing the crook of her leg. Looking through the viewfinder, it reminded me of the old-timey photo studio that Molly Webster had dragged me to in Kissimmee, Florida, where high-school seniors posed in Velcro-backed period costumes with prop guns and ceramic mugs of moonshine painted with *XXX's*. The sepia-toned images had always struck me as strange, an unsettling formulation of nostalgia and narcissism. *What had Molly wanted from a picture of herself dressed as a saloon whore? Who was it for?* The same questions were posed by the crook of Hailey's knee.

In my room Otto had just begun playing a German song, and was ramming the notes with such violence that a champagne flute teetered off the top and burst into hundreds of pieces on the keys. In tandem, a tall British girl with greasy hair was screaming out the lyrics while extending her hands towards the ceiling, half sexy, half menacing. Otto kept playing despite the bits of glass that were now tearing at his fingers. Sensing the demonic shift, the British girl jumped on a neighbouring bistro table and began striking poses while the song rang from her huge open mouth.

I took a picture. *Bella, bella, bella Marie, bleib' mir treu.* Blood was spurting from the pads of Otto's fingers. The greasy-haired girl continued contorting. When Otto lifted his hands from the piano, the keys were covered in blood. The room erupted in a thunder-drunk applause followed by demands for an encore. With a T-shirt I quickly wiped up as much as I could. And like a dog swimming in a stream, Otto began to bang his bloody paws on the piano, starting the song over again, and the girl returned to her perverted gestures and cawing.

The few Germans I knew in the room seemed uncomfortable.

'It's sort of a Nazi-era song,' Jens said, reluctantly bobbing his head.

'Yeah, I had no idea Otto was such a performer. He's still bleeding.'

Jens grimaced, but still looked oddly proud. I took another picture then went into the kitchen to stash my camera. Hailey swung in the room, her Western voice see-sawing, informing me that she'd officially hired Sam. 'I adooore her. She's brillieeeant. If it's OK with you, she said she'd love to work the door for the rest of the night.'

I was relieved.

Two hours later and the party slowed. Steel tugged Travis's arm and dragged him away, Hailey cashed out chips for those who remembered. 'Y'all come back now,' she cackled down the hollow staircase. When everyone had gone, Constance, Jens, Sam and myself gathered around Otto, who was now fully bandaged. Hailey was counting the mound of money on the top of the piano, looking satisfied.

'I think it was a great success,' Jens said with comical certainty.

'Well, next time you need a full bar with bartender. People shouldn't be able to walk in with their own booze,' Sam said smartly.

Hailey nodded.

'Are you doing this every Friday?'

'Yes,' Hailey said to Sam, without looking at me.

It hit me I hadn't really thought about *next time*. I glanced around my trashed bedroom, paper towels and spilled drinks. I wasn't completely sure I wanted to do it again. I didn't enjoy hosting and hated the door. I was happiest handing flutes of champagne to alcoholic smiles, hiding behind a liquid.

Hailey slipped her hand around Sam, they were laughing about something. I became annoyed at Hailey for liking her so much. 'I guess I'll bartend,' I said.

Hailey seemed pleased, 'Perfect, I can teach you,' she turned to Sam, 'and would you work the door again?'

'Easy, yes.'

'I want to run the table again,' Constance said.

'Duh—' Hailey said, beginning the process of undoing her corset. Joining her, I peeled off my gold dress, letting out a gulp of relief. The electrocution doorbell rang, I jumped, spilling tequila down my leg. The Dutch girl blasted into the room, a jackrabbit with huge expectant drug eyes. 'I LOST MY PURSE.'

'Is it blue?'

'IT IS!'

'It's in the kitchen.'

'THANK GOD. I LOVE YOU. COME TO BERGHAIN WITH ME. I'M ON THE LIST SO WE CAN JUST WALK IN AND I HAVE A TAXI OUTSIDE!'

Jens and Otto already had their coats on. 'Too tired,' they chimed in haggard unison. Sam, Constance, Hailey and I exchanged looks.

'We need to change,' Hailey said. We were only in our black tights and bras, and the thought of picking out an outfit seemed daunting after our previous rejection at the club's door. The Dutch girl ran into the kitchen to get her purse. 'YOU LOOK PERFECT, IT'S BERGHAIN. JUST PUT ON YOUR COATS. I'M LEAVING, THE TAXI IS WAITING.'

Hailey shrugged, then nudged me, saying the improv line, *Yes and . . .*'

I put on my jacket and slipped out into the dark hallway. Constance and Sam followed, Hailey grabbed two fifties from the shoe-box in the pantry, releasing a cackle as she locked the door.

The sky had already split into its deep morning-glory blue. The taxi ride was a giggling blur until we saw the line outside the sprawling ex-power plant, three hundred people stood, placid as cattle, their breath white and round like hovering speech bubbles in the frigid air. After slamming the cab door shut, the Dutch girl flicked back her auburn hair and marched past every tourist, technohead and party-kid to the door, the four of us sheepishly trailing. After minor intimidation by the hulking bouncer, he thumbed through the guest list until he found Milla Haas. The Dutch girl now had a name. And just as she'd said, we walked right in.

Once in the concrete entrance hall I handed my parka over to a severe pixie-brunette in exchange for a plastic number on a leather string that I slipped over my neck, the smell of weed and sweat washed over me. In stockings and a bra, I was still wearing more than most people. We twisted upstairs to the main dance floor where the techno was crashing. Sam and Hailey began jumping up and down, Constance sped off to buy a round of beers. Hailey looked at me with a triumphant smile. The music was so loud, it felt as if the air itself was being thrown around the room, on the dance floor leather daddies lorded over us on cement slabs like prized cars at an auto show. After an hour or so of shuttling my neck back and forth over my careening limbs I broke from our euphoric female formation and began to explore.

A metal stairwell led up to a smaller dance floor where the shutters on the windows thumped in time with the music, releasing the glare of the morning in rhythmic waves. I walked past a stream of niches, replete with pleather benches holding bodies moving in slow tangled units. Winding my way up and around through an unmarked doorway, I accidentally found myself in one of the dark rooms. I thought I could see a man bent over with a fist up his ass, but wasn't sure, the shape was moving, groaning, I turned to leave. I put my hand on a wall, unsure of the depth of the space, and touched something wet. It could have been beer, it could've been spit, but it was probably cum. I made a mental note in my mother's voice to *not touch my face*. When I finally found a soap dispenser, it was broken, and I pawed out the blue liquid, a cartoon bear in honey. The bathroom was clearly the highway of the club, bodies whizzed by smoking, snorting, laughing, coughing, and at the end of it all there was man on his knees by the big stainless-steel urinal waiting to drink the piss of whoever was willing.

With my newly clean hands I worked my way through an amoeba of bodies, up another metal staircase and into a bar with a glassed-in ice-cream freezer. An impossible oasis. With only one way to test this mirage, I ordered one scoop of pistachio. It was real, and it was Friday – I felt a wave of chaotic grief – I was continuing the tradition. Grandma Jane would approve, maybe not of the context, but of the cone. I sat on a stool slurping while swimming in music, a choir of electric eels. She was here. I could feel her wrapped around me. Ivy always came to me on dance floors, I think it's because that's where she was happiest – surrounded by others in motion. I closed my eyes and I could see the coiled strength that lived in her limbs, her arms floating, legs extended, back arched; a spinning chandelier of blonde hair suspended over the sweaty heads of the club.

I sensed someone was looming, when I opened my eyes Holiday was standing in front of me with a big goofy smile, I jerked back in surprise. She was wearing a black halter top and tight black shorts that cut up into her crotch in a V shape.

'Are you really that fucked-up?' she asked.

'The real question is – is this ice cream that good?'

She poked my side, seemingly amused with my dumb response, 'And, is it?'

'Absolutely,' I said, offering her some. She took a lick.

'You didn't come to our party,' I said, an eight-year-old at Baskin-Robbins.

'People are talking about it.'

I sat up with pride, 'So why didn't you?'

She was winding her way between my legs, her face was only a few inches from me, 'Art people scare me, I prefer music people.'

'Why do art people scare you?'

'Because they're all so caught up about how everything looks they can't have fun.'

I shrugged her off, but knew I understood. All our time in the mirror perfecting our looks flooded back. The endless discussing of the positioning of the objects in the apartment.

'So show me,' I said, wiping ice cream on my stockings and offering my hands, a sacrifice to be dragged to the dance floor.

When she was in sight Holiday kept her hands on me. Slinking them down my stockings, winding her thin arm around my sides. She was exquisite, spitting on the floor before kissing. Confusing, fast bursts of spitting, kissing, then disappearing.

I wanted to reach inside of her and learn everything. I wanted to consume her. To cut her into pieces and eat her. To become her and be owned by her. As we danced I worried she could hear my thoughts. She moved her hands down my back, pulling me close, our chests pressed against each other. I tried to memorise everything I could about her face in the strobing daylight. Her crooked nose. Her dilated brown pupils. Her pierced ears, the right, higher than the left. We grinded on each other. I was wet. After a few hours or maybe minutes, she evaporated. I could feel her buzzed hair on my fingertips but she was smoke. I texted. U STILL HERE? No response. I stalked the club looking for her, then began the walk to the train in the afternoon's putrid glow, everything ringing with disappointment that she was, again, not with me.

11

The hangover lasted the full weekend. My slippers made thwapping noises through sticky patches on the parquet. Hailey had counted the money three times while sitting cross-legged in bed, we'd made enough for rent and then some. Only on Monday afternoon did we feel strong enough to start cleaning. I scrubbed the cigarettes petrified in prosecco on the floor with steel wool while Hailey mopped. Our Nokia bricks had been bleeting and buzzing on and off, and we'd gotten at least two dozen Facebook messages.

'When is the next Beatrice party?'

'Why wasn't I invited?'

'Have u found a black swtr?'

We responded to nothing. Hailey said building suspense was important. I scrambled to my phone, every time hoping it was Holiday, a fact that Hailey somehow knew.

'So I googled your bald girlfriend,' Hailey said later that evening, while sautéing mushrooms.

I coughed, 'How did you—?'

'You told me her last name, *Roberson*.'

'Either she's a serial killer or a complete loser, she doesn't even have a Facebook page. And you said she's a music person? Doubt it. The only thing I could dig up were sound-mixing credits on an *extremely* indie film.'

'Hailey, that doesn't matter.'

'It should,' she called as I left the kitchen, irked.

We weren't sure what Beatrice had seen or how closely she

was surveilling us. Hailey had bought a pair of binoculars at a second-hand shop and took to watching our street while eating cereal from the box, spotting several blow jobs in cars, but no Beatrice. Hailey had written a thorough diary entry, but we hadn't left the apartment for longer than a grocery run, so there was no way for Beatrice to inspect any of it. But we assumed she must be watching us on Facebook, and discussed the need to watermark our images so everything was traceable. We settled on a Helvetica *B,* in the right-hand corner of each image.

I had shot twenty or so that felt worthy of the *B.* Our criteria were that they needed to capture the aura of the party, and also have *punctum.* We'd both been forced to read Roland Barthes freshman year and we sat together under the duvet in full photo 101 re-enactment, arguing over *the accident that pricked* – the point in an image that draws you in. With the photo of Celia on the table, arms stretched out – we both agreed, the *punctum* was the T-shirt, wet with Otto's blood, that lay at her feet. With the photo of Sam standing at the door, the line a shadowed mass behind her – Hailey argued the *punctum* was the way the flash reflected off her glass, I argued it was the way her head was cocked as if she was still keeping watch over the line even while posing. And with the photo of Hailey leaning against the roulette table – Hailey insisted the *punctum* was the way her leg pointed towards the body of a girl in the foreground, creating a triangle between the two. But I knew it was the obvious hunger to be photographed that seeped from her eyes.

I woke on Tuesday with a headache, Hailey was out so I rummaged through her toiletries for Advil. I assumed she was off trying to ingratiate herself to the red-roped world of the Charlottenburg galleries – checking to see if any of the gallerinas knew about our party. She was determined to be remembered. Always asking questions to the bored girls at their laptops because she knew it wasn't enough to just float through the exhibitions nodding at the frames.

Anyone could do that. So she would request the text, reading up on the *juxtaposition*, *tension* and *material fluidity* of the displayed artist. Our bathroom was littered in folded-up A4's with gallery names printed at the top. I was fairly certain Hailey read the press releases while she shat, which made me hesitant to handle them. Visual toilet paper, *material fluidity*.

I was staring at my computer when the buzzer rang. Hailey regularly forgot her keys, so I absentmindedly opened the door, heading back to my bed without even waiting for her to appear. 'Hallo?' a male voice called over the *bop bop bopping* of Joni Mitchell.

I jumped up, letting out a small scream.

In the doorway a wild-haired man in a little brown vest began speaking in a thunderstorm of German. I shook my head to slow the gush of sound. 'English?' I finally pleaded.

He registered my lack of registering, holding his hand up as if trying to stop a car, then bent over, pulled a plastic tube on a leather strap from his back. He spun open the tube's cap, and retrieved a roll of papers – architectural plans. He began pointing to a blurry photocopy of a hand-drawn, cursive-adorned document. The plans looked vaguely like our building.

He pointed again to the paper. More German. I shook my head. He looked exasperated. 'I coming. I, Fritz Weigel. Must – look.'

That was all the English he could muster.

Varoom, I knew meant, *Why?*

I asked. He seemed extremely pleased by my attempt at his mother tongue. He responded in another deluge of long unknowable words. Where was Hailey when I needed her? He made an opening and closing motion with his forearm. Fritz Weigel looked too buff to be an architect. He made another forearm gesture, affirming that fact. I had no idea what he wanted.

I knew too well that this sort of charade only came to an end when someone caved. I would either slam the door, or he would soon be in my apartment. There was no in-between. He proffered a laminated card with his face on it next to the words *Baugruppe Schöneberg*. I sighed, caving.

Frazzle-haired Fritz entered without pausing. I followed as he turned towards the back of the apartment and into the kitchen. As a precaution, when he wasn't looking, I slipped the knife from the dish rack into the pocket of my hoodie. I could go *Kill Bill* if I needed to. Fritz took in the surroundings. It was still a mess. Remnants of the party still clung to the table, a pile of dishes in the circular sink, and the washing machine's mouth stood open, barfing a twist of soured fabric.

Fritz, unfazed, seemed grateful to be able to perform his mystery of a task and was cheerfully studying the walls. The wallpaper of dippy daisies and bowed willows was mostly obscured behind the rows of books and boxes that I knew from our digging to be full of edited manuscripts. I appreciated the chaos of the room, it felt cosy. He pointed to the table. I understood, and we began decluttering, first moving a collection of beer bottles to the floor, the tea pot and Hailey's scraps of toast to the sink. When we were finished and I'd dry wiped, he unrolled his architectural plans, standing with authority, staring at the ancient document, muttering more foreign words.

Fritz then promptly turned and began knocking on the half-wall next to the window. The wall was patterned in the same yellowed '70s paper, and home to a series of twelve cheap-looking L brackets, packed with more books, mostly classical romances including *The Emerald Peacock* and *Gone with the Wind*. Dust fluttered like dandruff from the edges of the wall. Fritz then knowingly pushed at the right side, and it popped open, romance novels swinging in tow – a perfect hinged rectangle. Without looking back, Fritz removed a flashlight from his pocket and ducked his head into this dark new world.

It hit me. A week or so prior, Jens, who had just moved apartments, explained that these types of buildings, which had survived Allied bombs, all used to be much bigger. Often the whole floor would have been connected in one sprawling compound. The owners living in the front, and their servants in the back. The *Berliner Zimmer*, as it was warmly referred to by real-estate websites, was the highway-like room connecting the servants to their employers, usually with a singular window that looked into the *Hinterhof* with its trash cans and rusting bikes. Our *Berliner Zimmer* had been cut in half to create the kitchen and bathroom, with the coveted trash window in the kitchen. But apparently we still had a door leading to the apartment in the back.

I was now alone in the kitchen. The air rushed in from the new door, stony and cold. Would Beatrice be in there? My stomach flipped. Had she been there this whole time? Is that how she'd known I was vomiting? Was there a peep hole? I pressed on the flat blade of the kitchen knife through the hoodie's pocket, trying to muster courage. I had to go in. Sacrificing my wool socks to whatever lay beyond, I stepped through the door. All I could make out was Fritz, on his knees, the flashlight in his mouth – inspecting a fuse box with wires poking out. He removed a small camera and took several pictures. From the camera's repeated flash I could tell it was a one-room apartment, much rougher than ours, with crude slabs for floorboards and no decorative moulding.

Fritz saw me in the doorway, motioned around the room, and called, 'Sur-prise!'

I grimaced at the English word, which was terrifying in this new context. Fritz saw my fear and laughed a hearty, *hurr-hurr-hurr.* I choked on a wave of dust, and he motioned for me to follow. '*Komm, komm . . .*' he said. Was this our punishment for the party? Would chortling Fritz lock me in here forever? I was too curious not to follow. I pattered behind him on the straw-like floor runner, following his tight circular flashlight down a windowless hall that led to a tiny room with a toilet in it – one would have to cower to piss, knees to chin. Spiders visible at the edge of the light ring shifted towards the walls. Fritz made a universal sound of disgust, 'Eeeuuuugrhh.' He then spun his light to the right, revealing a doorway to a graveyard of a kitchen with an oxblood floor pockmarked with grease from long-gone appliances. In the kitchen stood a less dignified version of our front door, presumably opening to the back stairwell. I frowned, knowing perfectly well who had the key. Fritz took a photo of the door, and removed a measuring tape. He wrote down a few quick numbers, then turned to leave, signalling for me to lead the way.

Once back in the safe glow of our kitchen, Fritz swung the hidden door shut and slipped his papers into the rubberised tube. I had ten thousand questions to ask and no way to do it. There was no mime skilled enough for the task. I stood frozen and wide-eyed, staring at what I had once thought was merely a bookshelf. Fritz continued his work, spouting words while measuring the width of the kitchen doorway, noting it on a graph-paper notepad. In the hallway he jovially knocked on the wall to my bedroom with his fist. Maybe that was also a trap door. Maybe Beatrice was curled inside. German Narnia. Anything seemed possible with Fritz. He stuck out his hand as if to give me a balloon animal. I stared at his rough palm, cocking my head to the right, unsure of what he wanted. He laughed, then jerked his hand up and down, gesturing shaking. I smiled, feeling like an absolute moron, and shook it. He left *hurr-hurring* down the stairs.

In New York I'd had a perennially sawdust-encrusted sculpture professor, who told my class, 'You'll know you're a New Yorker when you have a dream where you discover another room in your apartment, through a closet, or behind a chest of drawers – if your subconscious is carving out legroom, you're one of us.' Berlin had an excess of space. Maybe it's actually what people feared here – that you'd pop open the attic and discover an extra twenty square metres – because it would inevitably come with a skeleton. I couldn't stand to go back into the new room alone, but couldn't stand to sit in the apartment either. I called Hailey.

Throwing on my jacket, I waited in the bakery down the street chewing a croissant until I could see a smear of red hair booming down the train steps. She waved, and I joined her. Breathlessly describing Fritz and *the room* as we mounted the apartment stairs.

'You really brought the knife with you?'

'I did.'

Hailey's and my matching and otherwise technologically minimal phones had LED flashlights nestled into their tips – Hailey sat in the kitchen flicking hers on and off as I popped the door, just as Fritz had an hour earlier.

'Holy – fucking – shit.' Her words fell like dumb-bells.

In our pathetic phone lights, the apartment was barely visible, but it didn't matter.

'Isn't it insane?' I asked, feeling privileged to be the tour giver. 'And there is a disgusting toilet in a cupboard in the back.'

Hailey *mmmhmmm*'d while examining the edges of the room.

She bent down to flip the switch on an extension cord. Two work lights, caged in wire, roared on. The walls were turmeric yellow, an old shelf and a pile of lace curtains lay heaped towards the left side of the room next to a rusted pail of orange coal dust. In the corner, beneath a window so grimy it was opaque, sat a neat desk and a Danish-modern wooden chair. I walked over and examined it – the surface of the desk was littered with stacks of index cards, no dust.

'Beatrice,' Hailey whispered, 'that's the extension cord we saw leading to nowhere in the kitchen.'

We both took a moment, letting the snaking cord and its current sink in. 'What do the cards say?' Hailey asked.

I inspected the stack. They were indecipherable, covered in scratchy shapes – orbs and x's. 'It's not – legible, maybe this is German shorthand or something?'

Hailey walked over, took a stack and shuffled through, shaking her head. 'Weird, like really – weird.'

'I mean they must be notes, right? Like about us—' We looked at each other.

'That's a Montblanc pen,' Hailey said, reaching for the sleek object on the desk, removing its cap, and inspecting the tip. 'You don't just forget a Montblanc pen.'

I shrugged, I didn't know what that was.

'They cost, like four hundred dollars, my dad carries his around in a case. It means she'll be back.'

Hailey placed the pen how she'd found it, taking care to angle it just right. I split into a hacking cough from all the dust and ran to get water from our kitchen, ducking through the small door. I drank straight from the arched tap, which felt dramatic and matched the moment. Hailey followed me, and closed *the door*, which became unrecognisable once sealed. She let out a fast exhale, then bee-lined it for the fridge in our uneasy kitchen, pouring two large portions of Korn vodka into water glasses. It was still daytime, and we were out of ice, but neither of us cared. We sipped cautiously, settling into the transformed space, now sensitive to every creak in the building, every car door slammed on the street. We drank a quarter of the bottle down.

'So, what do we do?' I asked from the deep end of our pooled silence.

'We have to pretend like we never saw it. I keep writing in the diary, and you keep taking photos at the parties. She obviously can't see shit from back there. It's just how she comes in to go through our stuff, and maybe where she works.'

I let Hailey's words and another pull of vodka soak in. A few seconds later, I bolted upright – 'It's why she wasn't wearing a coat the day I saw her here.'

'What?'

'When I came home and found Beatrice on the couch, she hadn't been wearing a coat, she must have left it *in there*.'

Hailey nodded.

We'd barely left the apartment since the party. But Beatrice would have a prime opportunity to enter that evening, as we were headed to the Volksbühne theatre to see *Berlin, Alexanderplatz*.

With my limited knowledge of spy movies, I carefully laid a small white thread ripped from my duvet over the edge of my laptop so there would be no way to raise the screen without disturbing the string. We turned off all the lights, something we rarely did, signalling our exit to the street.

We had selected our outfits with dramatic consideration and were wobbly from the vodka and unexpected expansion of the apartment. Everything felt heightened. Hailey did a ridiculous faux strip-dance on the train, her right foot tucked under the yellow metal pole, back arched. A man clapped. An older woman in a potato-shaped coat yelled at us.

At Rosa-Luxemburg-Platz the theatre loomed before us, as if each stone had solemnly given its life to the building. On the stairs we split a pretzel with spiky granules of salt, trying to soak up the booze. Entering the theatre's doors was like slipping into a glowing lantern, an ancient threshold of magic preserved just for us. We checked our coats, revealing our costumes; I was in a halter-top one-piece covered in tiny fake black pearls and Hailey was in a shimmery short blue dress with black tights and a New York Yankees baseball cap. We took our time finding our seats, ogling the glass chandelier that stared down at us like a twisted love child of a firework and a palm tree.

The curtain rose and I squeezed Hailey's hand, buildings spun on the monstrous stage as if it were an entire movie collapsing before our eyes. All of the American theatre I'd seen had the dull lustre of NEA austerity; shoestring budgets worn as clunky jewellery by underpaid actors. This was different. The actors screamed in a psychotic chorus of German while they climbed a mountain of gold coins as tall as a house, simultaneously sucking down hundreds of cigarettes, then disappearing only to reappear in a fast rotation of gaudy costumes. We sat in rapture. Hailey kept leaning over to whisper translations. But I'd looked up the premise on Wikipedia before leaving. I knew we were in for several hours of 1920s Berlin, following a man's release from prison, after serving four years for murdering his girlfriend with an eggbeater – yet another night's entertainment played out on the female form.

The actors were filled with rabid energy and it was impossible not to fall into cycles of disgust and love with each of them. Franz is the bumbling anti-hero floating through Berlin, an ex-con trying to find his way. Can one ever return to society after killing someone? Rolling in the waves of indecipherable German, I thought about Ivy's murderer. Whoever they were, they had never been asked to leave. They were out buying milk. Or getting gas. Breathing air. Maybe the only return for a murderer is through extravagant theatre same as this, a fire baptism into reality. For Amanda Knox it had been the contemporary-media-gore-circus-twenty-four-seven-camera-hell. As the play floated deeper into abstraction I filled in the blanks, imagining Amanda playing Franz, screaming in German running around the stage throwing coins with her big watery eyes. 'Welcome back!' We would scream and clap as she bowed, a fresh civilian born again from the flames.

My attention ebbed and flowed over the four-hour play. I'd never sat for anything that long and kept needing to readjust myself because the fake pearls were digging into my ass. Even if it had been in English it would have felt psychotropic. When it ended the actors ran off, and then on to bow for a thunderous applause, then off again, a second bow, a third. Hailey nudged me and told me, 'Germans love applause,' she looked down at her own moving hands, 'to the point where it hurts.' The curtains opened and closed several more times, a fourth bow. More bowing. More clapping. My hands still tingled when we were spit back out on the steps of the theatre. We wanted more.

'I read on a blog that you can go to the Kantine for after drinks,' Hailey said, looking at the cold street.

'Where—?' The building looked dead. But it seemed obvious that all the energy from the stage must have gone somewhere. 'The back of the building?'

We walked around the dark side streets of the theatre where a small door opened, casting a yellow rectangle of phosphorescence onto the pavement, and five drab pea-coats moved towards it. We ran to catch up.

'Kantine,' they said to the doorman. We nodded along, trying to fit in with our adopted group. I discharged a sigh when we were through the door, relieved to be returned to the precarious world of magic.

The wood-panelled Kantine filled up. When the last empty chairs left were at our table, two guys sauntered over wearing little black tool belts and clutching Berliner Pilsners, eyeing us kindly. '*Hallo. Ist hier noch frei?*' the older one with grey hair asked.

'*Ja,*' Hailey responded with zest. The guys sat down and chatted among themselves. Hailey leaned in, giving them her signature – *fuck me* – look, then asked for a cigarette, flipping her red hair back. They nodded. We were integrated.

'*Hast du das Stück gesehen?*' the older one asked.

'*Ja, es war so schön!*' Hailey said, her hand slapping the table, imitating one of the gestures from the drunks in the play. I sat there quietly, trying to build a response in German, then gave up.

'Sorry my German sucks. Yeah, it was amazing. Did you see it?' I asked, even though it was obvious he was an employee.

'Well, yes and no – I work here,' he said, puffing out like a bird.

'Oh. What do you do?'

'Prop master.'

'What does that entail?'

'Well, I have to know exactly where every object an actor uses is on stage, all the cigarettes that get smoked, the glasses, coins and all the fog machines . . .'

'That beer must taste good after all that,' I was beginning to flirt. He was hot in a dorky-bad-boy way, with long black hair, thick stubble, mud-brown eyes and a constantly lit cigarette. I imagined he probably had a tattoo of a wolf or a hawk somewhere on his body. Being prop master seemed like a less egotistical form of being a sculpture-bro – at least in the theatre everything had a function and served a greater story. The Slayer T-shirt started talking proudly about the history of the Volksbühne, which was built by workers for workers in 1913: *The People's Theatre*. Hailey wasn't listening, she had slid into conversation with one of the actors sitting at the adjacent table. The actor who had played Reinhold poured her a shot, their German grew riotous – at one point Hailey stood on her chair and belted the opening lines of 'Seasons of Love', *Five hundred twenty-five thousand six hundred minutes*. The table burst into laughter. It was unclear if the laughter was *with* her or *at* her – either way, she took a proud bow.

Being in the Kantine felt like passive time-travelling; tubing down some underground prehistoric Berlin river. Hailey and I kept shooting each other full-moon eyes. It matched our energy, our new theatrical identities. I exchanged numbers with the Slayer T-shirt and excused myself. After the buttery-yellow light of the Kantine, the bathroom's sharp neon and white tile felt futuristic.

While I peed I stared at the prop guy's name spelled out in the Nokia's Pac-Man-ish font: *Mathias*.

We stumbled back into this century well past two in the morning. The night bus felt like a campus party bus. Everyone was drunk and young, squawking in different languages as we drove down to Schöneberg. We reeked of cigarettes and were babbling with excitement until we got to our front door. The chemical lily smell was razor sharp. We exchanged looks, cautiously slipping in the key.

The thread was no longer on my computer. 'Hailey,' I screamed, 'she was here!'

'Shhhhh—' Hailey hissed.

I filled with panic.

Hailey walked towards me, whispering, 'My diary has been moved, it's barely noticeable but I know it's not in the same place.'

There was a part of me that had assumed we were just being crazy. That there could have been ways to rationalise it all, but not now. I sobered up. How would she react to the diary entry and photos? The outrageous party. All of those people in her apartment. She could kick us out, or worse. Only then did it hit me, how vulnerable we were, playing this game.

'She's clearly taken the bait. This is – amazing – amazing.'

My stomach tightened, 'Why are you whispering? Is she still in there? What do we do? God, she's probably just pissed we threw a party in her house.' I was spiralling. 'We should check if she's in the back room, right? Or maybe she added cameras.' I began running around the apartment looking for more signs of entry.

Hailey charged at me and grabbed my wrist, her voice barely audible, 'We already checked. We know she's just sneaking in. We have to keep going. We have to build an *amazing* arc and we'll get our novel. She can't know that we know about the back apartment, you are never to mention it again. Promise me.'

Hailey wouldn't let go of my wrist till I promised. So I did.

Madness lingered in her eyes as she went to the bathroom and began violently brushing her teeth, spitting a red crescent of toothpaste into the sink. I went into my room and shut the door, I tried to think about what sort of arc could possibly make sense. Maybe it could be like *Berlin Alexanderplatz* and we could twist our hysteria into our own secret language that would be impossible to comb out, let Beatrice try. I burned my theatre ticket for Ivy in the coal fire. Crouching, I watched the smoke bend up into the back of the oven, sending what I imagined was an interesting package of German theatre to the afterlife.

At the Breitbachs' golden apartment door, Beata gave me her usual grimace, which I had grown to enjoy. I slid my coat onto a hanger and was nearly knocked over by Savannah, brandishing a sword-like unicorn on a stick, 'I need to know what happens next in the Monster Story. What happened to Hailey? Is she still in the Cotton Ball Monster Universe? I don't understand why no one can speak in that universe. And what about the Creepy Owl watching Hailey and Zinfandel. Is he good or bad? I bet bad.' All four of the girls shared their mother's intensity. And despite their insistence on dressing as powder-puffed princesses, there was a fierceness, a no-bullshit attitude, which was nearly untameable in arguments about homework, TV privileges and narrative constructs.

'All will be revealed, but first we all have to make sure homework is done.'

I checked the backpacks, then opened the fridge looking for whatever dinner was instructed. Claire and Tobias had a German cook, who came every other week to fill their freezer with glass containers neatly labelled: 'Maultaschen, pan fry for 10 minutes.' Idiot proof. I wondered how it would be to have grown up like this. Everything prepared. The girls would inevitably turn into power-suited femmes fatales, real-estate titans, lawyers, maybe diplomats with medicated trophy husbands and pre-planned vacations with dozens of Rimowa suitcases in tow. They would never steal cheese. They would sleep comfortably forever on Tempur-Pedic mattresses with well-moisturised skin. I almost felt sorry for them.

After dinner I chased the girls into the mausoleum of a bathroom, giving them each a vitamin gummy and taking one for myself. In the medicine cabinet I pocketed a handful of imported extra-strength Tylenol for my headaches, which were nearing constant, I assumed a symptom of all my drinking and barfing. Once the youngest girls were tucked in bed, the older two curled on the child-sized floral sofa, and we got right down to the Monster Story.

'Well, this is the thing. Hailey thinks the Creepy Owl is watching her. And Hailey becomes very suspicious. She notices things – a missing book or weird smell – and she thinks that Creepy Owl must have just been there.'

'So is the Creepy Owl evil?'

'She isn't sure.'

'Does she set traps?'

'She does.'

'What does the Creepy Owl even want?'

'No one knows yet. But she has a secret room . . .'

The girls eventually fell asleep, I lead Serena to her bed and tucked her in. She grabbed my arm, muttering in thick baby sleep, 'I hope Hailey isn't crazy.'

I was startled. 'Me too,' I whispered.

I took a bag of dried pineapple from the pantry and wandered down to the TV room for my ritual of SportsCenter. When the alarm system hiccuped I knew Tobias and Claire were home. I sat up, straightening the wool blanket at the foot of the couch. They idled in the entrance, their voices ricocheting, clearly fighting. It was a good ten minutes before her ticking stilettos became audible, his heavy dress-shoe clunks about thirty seconds behind. Tobias nodded towards me with the grunt of an ill-tempered hippopotamus before waddling down the hall. Claire went straight to the fridge and pulled out a tall bottle of wine.

'Do you want a glass?'

She seemed desperate. I nodded, she filled two stemmed orbs big as my head, letting out a sigh. 'Sorry, I'm tired. Actually – I'm fine. Tobias is just – in a mood. He can be a fucking dick,' she said, motioning towards the hall where he'd retreated.

'I – know—' The words fell out with too much meaning.

Claire stopped in her tracks, then released a sad laugh, 'What did he do?'

'Nothing.'

'Tell me,' she said, now severe.

'Really it was nothing.'

'I'm not stupid, Zoe. Do you think I'm stupid?'

'No.'

'So tell me the truth.'

'He – sort of, came on to me in the old-timey bar-room my third night here.' I could see her silvery eyes glassing over, near tears.

'He does that,' she caught herself, smoothing a crease in her dress.

'He put his hand on my thigh, that was it.'

She released another sigh and looked out, staring at the shadows of trees below, ebbing mercilessly under the street light. 'That's good,' she paused, 'I mean, if that's all he did. And let me promise you – I will make sure nothing else happens.'

'But you're OK?' I whispered.

'There is a man inside of him that I truly love who is my intellectual equal. But ever since he sold his shares he just wastes his time on expensive hobbies – and girls. It's like being married to a nineteen-year-old.' Her voice became mechanical as if she'd rehearsed the speech in the mirror, 'Look, I'm not interested in monogamy. You have to understand. I fully grasp the complexities of carnal greed, I was a very high-powered lawyer, that's how I met Tobias – divorce court. I advised. We have rules. I also have my fun, but I don't like it when it's close to home and I am truly sorry you had to deal with that. I thank you for being so forthcoming.'

'I told him I was gay,' I blurted.

'Are you?' Her tears were settling back into their window-less vault.

'Maybe – he was the first person I'd ever told.'

'That is sort of humorous – not that you are, just that you would come out to him.' She paused and I could feel something shift between us, we were treading new territory, the velvet edges of friendship appearing.

'Well, tell me about your life, it'd be nice to hear about someone else for a change.' Claire presided over the silence between us with expectance.

After a few sips of wine it all just sort of fell out. I told her about Jesse. About how Ivy was murdered. How my school in Berlin was basically non-existent. About Holiday. She

180

refilled my glass as I explained that the woman we were renting our apartment from was coming over while we were out. Sitting in Claire's stone tower in Mitte, I felt far from my reality of the city, it seemed OK to confess all this.

'But – you really think this Beatrice woman comes in and reads your roommate's diary and checks your emails?'

'Yes. I do. We found an apartment in the back, it's connected – through a second door.'

'That's unsettling and certainly illegal. You should gather evidence.'

I nodded. We'd drunk the whole bottle and she went to the stainless-steel fridge to retrieve another, swaying as she walked, 'You know. I was a good lawyer. Actually, no – I was the best.'

'Why don't you do it here?' I asked.

'I can – I passed the equivalent of the Bar here, but—' She waved her arm around the room as if the gleaming kitchen would finish her sentence, then she added, 'Fucking Tobias wanted me to focus on the kids while he worked, and now look at him, bleep blooping on the computer. If he shows up to one of your parties, 'cause he will, you have to reject him. Promise me.'

I swore I would. Halfway through another glass I remembered that I needed to catch the train.

Viola was back from her *research trip* to Barcelona, and we were all meeting at Der Wald to catch up. I hugged Claire goodbye.

It was Hailey's last night working at the bar. Now that we had the *Beatrice* parties she felt Der Wald had 'served its purpose'. When I walked in Hailey looked bored, asking only the bare minimum to Viola while still performing her forced bartender-sociality.

'So how was it?'

'D-a-z-z-l-i-n-g.' Long pause.

'And what did you do?'

'I collected samples from the city.'

When Viola said this it usually meant taking photographs on her expensive Hasselblad camera. She pulled out her new iPhone and began showing pictures. Gaudi architecture. Churches jutting into an ultra-marine sky. Little copper plates loaded with greasy food.

'The tapas was so good.'

'Didn't Gaudi get hit by a car when he stepped into the street to look at his own building?' I asked.

Viola ignored me, 'Oh, here, see, paella.'

'I want an iPhone,' Hailey said, her voice leadened.

Constance breezed through the door, headphones still in, loudly repeating German phrases – '*Wollen Sie mit mir kommen? Können Sie mit mir kommen?*'

'Are you practising pick-up lines?' Hailey yelled, visibly relieved to no longer have to continue her questions for Viola. She poured Constance a red wine.

'Yes. Pick-up lines are the foundation of *The Michel Thomas Method*. And I dumped Lucas so it's urgent.'

'I've been thinking that we should rent a fog machine for the next party,' Hailey said, switching gears.

'Maybe that's a bit extreme,' Constance laughed. 'I don't think so—'

Viola opened her mouth, then paused, spinning her wine glass between her thumb and forefinger, then asked, 'Aren't you worried Beatrice is going to find out?'

'Honestly, I think she would be happy for us,' Hailey said with a smirk.

'I mean, *happy* might be a bit of an overstatement – but you do have to be some brand of freak to be an adult and own a lip-shaped couch,' Constance said, winding her headphones around her wrist. 'Oh by the way, I stole some books from Beatrice's, I'll get them back to you when I'm done.'

'You better,' Haily clucked. 'What did you take?'

'Euripides, *Medea*, and some weird '80s thriller I can't remember.'

On the walk home from the bar Hailey was recounting all the ways in which life had been better while Viola had been gone.

'Like. Don't show me a photograph of *paella*.'

I took a pause from applying chapstick, 'You do know, we don't have to be friends with anyone we don't want to.'

Hailey snorted, 'We're all victims of circumstance here, Zoe.'

We had forty-two RSVP's in fifteen minutes for the next party. I'd spent most of the week practising bartending with Hailey, resulting in a near-perpetual state of drunkenness or hangover.

We found Jaques, our wine supplier, through Adnan, the guy Constance was renting her place from – an aging punk covered in tattoos, who specialised in good-tasting but cheap German wines and enjoyed waxing about his club days running the sound board at SO36. After lugging the dolly loaded with our first delivery up our stairs, he asked if he could come by the party with a friend – we said, *yes*.

'Is it weird to sell a glass of wine to the guy who sold you the bottle?' Hailey asked after we heard his truck tear down the street. I shrugged, and popped a Tylenol.

She was inspecting the labels with the precision of a pharmacist, then looked up, 'You do understand that we need to create conflict.' She still felt we needed to settle on an arc for our characters for Beatrice's novel, I thought there was enough narrative in throwing parties. 'We're just trying to build a better frame, no? And now we have the frame,' I motioned around the room.

She snorted dismissively, 'We need conflict, we need something to really pop.'

Done washing glasses, I wiped my hands on the rag at my

hip and turned to her, 'I was thinking if we need to add something – maybe we could start hosting performances, or readings, create some sort of focus for the party? I met this Croatian dancer . . .'

She looked repulsed, 'No. We need a literary-worthy conflict, we need a love triangle or murder or incest.'

'Gross.'

She sighed, 'I mean we *could* do an Amanda Knox crime-scene-themed night. Everyone would have to play their part, there is lots to choose from, dramaturgically speaking. Caution tape as streamers, we could dump fake blood all over the floors.'

I turned away, digging at my cuticles.

'Foxy Knoxy is probably the only other exchange student who will be as famous as us,' Hailey called after me, 'once Beatrice writes her book.'

Friday arrived. We built a make-shift bar with a wooden door and two sawhorses we'd found in the basement. And after much debate, we decided on wearing the matching baby-blue David Bowie suits. I'd unearthed the wigs I'd stolen from the costume sale in the bottom of one of my tote bags: a short black bob similar to Beatrice's hair and a long wavy red one, almost identical to Hailey's. I put on the red wig, pinning it down, mimicking Hailey's messy bun. We could have been sisters.

Sam showed up next. Digging through the boxes of clothes from Tobias's mother, she settled on the black halter top covered in fake pearls, the one I'd worn to the Volksbühne. It looked better on her, which I quietly resented her for. Sam was already the smart Spice Girl, it seemed excessive that she should also be the hot Spice Girl. Who was Sexy Spice? *Ginger.* That would have to be Hailey. Viola was Posh, obviously. Was there even a smart Spice Girl? I was probably Sporty or Baby – the lessers. The nothings.

The electrocution buzzer rang and a minute later, Constance entered lugging an Ikea bag with a house plant whose glossy leaves framed her face. 'You look hot,' she said to Sam, out of breath. Pointing to Hailey and me in our matching outfits, Constance added, 'but you two, you're like those Diane Arbus twins – that wig is creepy.'

Sam laughed, 'What's with the plant?'

'I picked it up from Craigslist. I didn't have time to bring it home. Also I got you guys something.'

Constance set the plant down and pulled out a soccer-sized disco ball from the blue bag, 'It's left over from an installation at the gallery.'

We giddily installed the shimmering orb over the piano.

With my MacBook propped on the vanity, open to a photo of Bowie, we tried to match his bright turquoise eyeshadow and flamingo-pink lips. Meanwhile, a pimply teenager in a T-shirt emblazoned with *Ice Man* wandered in with three Styrofoam boxes the exact same shade of blue as our suits. We paid him, and then took photos straddling the coolers for Facebook. Otto arrived next. I made him a neon-orange spritz. He quietly thanked me before turning towards the piano. The party took off at 11 p.m. Bartending was the perfect dress of shadows, retreated but still in demand. I was surprised at how subservient I was, when anyone ordered a drink I responded with – *of course*.

Mary-Kate's alleged roommate, the blonde over-grown-toddler gallerist, who had bought the ten bottles of vodka at the last party, came up to the bar with two well-coiffed men in heavily starched shirts. Apparently they were his bosses, also very gay. They ordered three vodka sodas with extra slices of lemon. The bosses were excited, moving around the room like sharks. 'We have all of her books in our summer house in Provence,' the short brunette cooed, his skin stretched thinly over his expensive-looking face. Slipping on a pair of gold glasses, he began surveying the titles on the wall, 'Aren't you nervous someone is going to steal something?'

I made a pensive grimace, 'You are the only ones I'm worried about.'

They laughed and began doing figure eights in chatty high voices, 'Beatrice really is the perfect blend of trash and class, we are obsessed with *On Blue Peak*.' I nodded, as if I, too, had read it and adored it.

A girl in a sheer mesh bomber jacket began performing an ass-drop dance on the couch, each plummet pulling the covering further down, revealing the crooked upturned smile. I ran over to fix it and her eyes caught mine, wide as saucers, greasy with drugs, affirming my suspicions about the guy she'd come in with wearing a cheetah-print backpack. When Hailey shot by I tried to ask her who he was. She shook me off, busy sorting the change, but when she came over to exchange a handful of bills I had my opening.

'Hey, is the guy with the ugly backpack *selling*?' I pointed to the guy who was now busy telling a story to a wax-tweaked moustache.

'Oh! That's Mel, he's on exchange too – from Providence.'

'Is Mel selling drugs?'

'Just ecstasy. I heard he's a Kennedy.'

'Why would a Kennedy be selling ecstasy?'

Hailey shrugged, 'I am going to write a character profile on him for my diary. I think it's good to have drug dealers. It seems *noir*,' she waved a wad of fives at me then flitted off. Ecstasy explained the crowd's energy, everyone looked suspended in jello, dumbly shaking about and touching each other.

A guy in a yellow cardigan wandered up to the bar, standing behind two lanky brunettes. He began looking around the room, stretching out his lower lip and nodding as if he had just been shown a fancy hotel suite and wanted to wordlessly

186

say – *not bad*. He ordered a Moscow Mule, and while I scooped ice he made jokes about *Berlin, the last stop off the L train*. I ignored him, not looking up until he raised his voice in rehearsed humility, explaining he was writing a profile on the city for the *New York Times*. I gave a polite smile. He promptly began asking questions about Berlin as if she were a young woman who'd grown tits over the summer and didn't realise she was hot yet.

'Why are all the young artists so into her?'

'What do you think she is going to become?'

'Is she really as fun as everyone says she is?'

'What happens in ten years, when she grows up?'

I remembered back to my drawing professor in New York saying, 'The problem with the art world was not the artists but those around them. We are the sheep, you see. And the gallerists and the critics, they shear us down and then spin all this yarn about our existences, and then what are we left with? Nothing but a bad haircut.'

I told the yellow cardigan to talk to Hailey. He nodded and sauntered off, sipping his drink while continuing to make his – *not bad* – face around the room.

The party hit capacity at around two in the morning. The beer was no longer cold and what was left of the ice was a watery minestrone, meanwhile Sam was holding off about twenty people at the door. The piano in my room mixed with the techno crackling the computer speakers by the bar. Hailey briefly took over so I could use the bathroom. Walking through the clumped bodies felt like canoeing through a loud jungle full of bull frogs, crickets, and sloppy parrots.

Constance, still running a steady game at the roulette table, added a peculiar glamour, channelling the psycho-chicness of Sharon Stone in *Casino* with her hair in an oversized looping ponytail. Travis the Canadian was fixed at the corner, this time without Steel.

Viola was next in line for the bathroom, I went in with her, fully prepared to wait, rather then defile the tub. I checked my lipstick in the mirror, then glanced over at Viola and burst out laughing, her pale white ass was hovering more than a foot above the toilet seat, knees bent, ankles pigeon-toed holding up her black pants.

'Viola – you can sit down on the seat, it's still my house.'

'I never sit on toilet seats, not even in my own house,' she said, ceremoniously wiping herself. I made a point of plopping down on the seat while she washed her hands.

Viola began applying mascara in the mirror, her mouth puckered in a taut circle. 'Is Hailey a star-fucker?' she asked as she finished, capping the black wand.

'What?' I asked, stunned, Viola never swore.

'I mean like, first the von Habsburg and now she's obsessed with Mel, who by the way isn't a Kennedy. I know she's your roommate but—' She pulled a safety pin from her purse, holding the point up to her eye, separating each lash, 'Why are you even throwing these parties? Don't you want to be an artist?' Her lashes now looked like plucked spider legs, she shifted one eye to meet mine in the mirror, 'I mean – don't you want to take yourself seriously?'

'Hailey's not a star-fucker and the parties are – art.'

Viola smiled, then pressed her purse closed, 'No, they aren't.'

She left me in the bathroom, I looked in the mirror and smiled. She was just jealous. I felt a pang of gratefulness towards Hailey, for the parties and our friendship, this big world we'd built together. Fuck Viola.

When I finally returned to the bar I spotted Mathias from the Volksbühne prop department, I'd almost forgotten inviting him. He was wearing a Nordic-looking metal T-shirt from a band I didn't know, and his long black hair was pulled back in a ponytail. He lit a cigarette as I walked over.

'Hi, Mathias.'

'Oh,' he paused, 'wow, hi – the wig. I thought you were – Hailey.' He cracked a smile, he was nervous.

'I didn't think you would come,' I said, unexpectedly flustered.

'Well, I was very curious.'

Mathias looked dorky next to the fashion types and grungy art people, which helped me relax. I made him a Club-Mate vodka. He slowly edged in, eventually leaning against the wall behind the bar. We talked about the theatre, I told him I thought the Kantine was a time machine. He made a joke about that being a very American thing to say. We both awkwardly laughed. He launched into talking about his parents' house in Mecklenburg.

'Everything happens in Mecklenburg fifty years later, so if you're ever in the mood for some rural time travel, it's really the place to go.'

I did the rough calculation, 'So it's like 1958 in Mecklenburg.'

He looked at his watch, 'Haven't even built the Berlin Wall yet.'

I laughed shakily. Hailey had spotted us and swayed over. She looked Mathias up and down, 'I see you're prepared.' She pointed to the pocket knife he was wearing on his belt, the same one from the night we'd met him.

'Ah, yes, I am a Boy Scoot.'

'Yes. The mighty Boy *Scoots*.' Hailey was being snarky, but I reasoned that maybe she was allowed to tease his English because she actually spoke German.

Hailey and Mathias began a round of gun-fire German, I couldn't follow. I had been taking online 'classes', which mostly consisted of a bright-green worm that poked its head out of an apple and delivered quizzes, but thus far the worm had focused only on the transactional, and Hailey didn't seem to be buying a loaf of bread from Mathias. After some back and forth it appeared Hailey had given him a challenge, which he accepted. Walking over to the one 'real' oak cabinet, he swung the glass door open and dropped to his knees. Pulling out a pair of dainty tweezers, he began working on the locked drawer. Nothing happened. He got up, turned around, and walked towards me at the bar, our eyes locked. He ran his fingers through my red wig, tugging out two hairpins. Watching the action, Hailey's eyes lit up like street lights. I flushed red. He set back to work on the lock and someone began playing Michael Jackson's 'Thriller' on the speakers. Forty-five seconds later the drawer popped open.

Hailey clapped and Mathias made a proud bow. She walked over to inspect. Resting in the drawer was a stack of papers, she lifted them and began leafing through. With everyone high on ecstasy the drink sales were sparse, so I took the moment to slip out and peer over her shoulder. Some sort of legal documents. And receipt of payment for two hundred and fifty-thousand dollars to a *Betsy Conely* in North Carolina.

'BUM BUM,' Hailey squealed.

I was hit with a cinderblock of foreboding. 'Put it back,' I pleaded.

'No – let's keep it.'

'Hailey please, just put it back,' I hacked, terrified that we had crossed this line in front of a room filled with people. Hailey gave in and asked Mathias to lock it, then turned away as if she had never really cared. We both returned to our posts.

At around 4 a.m. there was a mass exodus to a club. Coats, bags and gloves were finding their owners. A girl in a vinyl hoodie explained it was a *literal underground club*, as in the club was in a basement. Constance had already abandoned her house plant, leaving in a cloud of toxic-plastic perfume to meet up with an artist who made digital scans of Greek sculptures. I was in the kitchen with Hailey and Sam, they wanted to go, and were reapplying lipstick with art-school conviction.

'Also Hailey, you were right – fuck Viola.'

'What happened?'

I recapped our conversation from the bathroom.

'We need revenge. Let's take her off the guest list next week.'

I agreed, then performatively yawned and told them that I would close up. They raised their eyebrows and looked at each other with their over-painted smirks, fully aware that Mathias was quietly playing snake on his phone in the other room.

'Bye—' they clucked, bouncing down the stairwell. When the door finally shut behind them, I turned to Mathias, who'd begun pouring the ends of the remaining liquor bottles into a glass, topping it off with his half-drunk Club-Mate.

He presented the concoction to me, 'It's – what do you call it? – Long Island ice tea.'

I took one sip and spit it back out. I tried to set the drink down, but dropped it, the contents inking out on the floor. I would clean it later. As we tumbled to my bed he began sneezing in tiny volcanic eruptions. I laughed and he defensively explained that he sneezed when he was 'horny'. Loosening the buttons on my blue pants, he jammed his hand down pressing wildly as if still playing snake. Maybe if I was drunker it would have felt better. I missed Jesse. I wanted Holiday.

The only time the apartment felt warm was after parties. I hadn't lain in bed with my skin visible since moving in, the grey light refracted through remnants of sweat and breath on the windows made my legs look alien. The train rumbled by, turning my thighs yellow. I looked over, I had been right. Mathias, whose long black hair was now untied, had a tattoo, a fist-sized spider straddling his shoulder. He woke up and we rolled around, he was strong, he pinned me down.

Having someone else in the apartment helped ease the pressure of *the door*, which was poised similar to my headaches, always ready to fracture any thought. Ever since Fritz banged it open, being truly alone was impossible. Beatrice always hovered. And maybe she was there, hunched behind the romance novels at her Danish-modern desk, listening to Mathias and me moan. It reminded me of the performance piece by Vito Acconci we'd seen in art history class, where he'd built up a ramp that extended the gallery floor, just high enough so he could lie beneath it and jerk off while narrating the movements of the viewers above him via loud speaker.

Mathias was telling me about his metal band DEATH LORD. He had my laptop balanced on his bare chest playing a music video when the electrocution buzzer rang. The ice cold of the hallway poured in around me as a short DHL delivery man handed over a cardboard object in the shape of a manatee, or maybe a deformed whale.

Mathias tugged the blanket back over me, taking the package from my hand, 'This is incredible, it's a *Seekuh*.'

I repeated, 'Zeeee-kuh. Sea cow?'

He ran his index finger down the seamed cardboard, 'It is very well made.'

'It is . . .'

I looked at my phone, the glow of our morning faded. Maybe it was the hangover, maybe it was him, but the dog-whistle of nausea hissed – I wanted to throw up – and I needed him out. I told him I had school.

'On a Saturday?' he said, surprised, hunting for his shirt in the bed.

'Yes,' I lied.

He offered to sneak me into a play at the theatre next week.

I said I'd check my school schedule, which I could tell he knew for sure was a lie. He kissed me goodbye.

After he left, the stench of the apartment hardened, cigarettes and foul booze. I went back to bed and closed my eyes. A few minutes later, I heard a thud in Hailey's room, but I knew she was still out partying. My throat tensed. Was Beatrice there? It dawned on me that it might be relieving to catch her, I could put the kettle on, and we could sit for a moment — talk through the book, brainstorm together. I heard another thump and snapped with fear. I gathered my courage and crept towards Hailey's room.

'Beatrice?' I asked softly as I opened the door, the sound of my own voice terrifying me. But the room was empty, just the mess of the previous evening. I plugged my laptop in, turning Lil Wayne up, drowning the sounds of the house. In the bathroom I wiped down the bathtub with a dish towel, turned on the water, then made a two-fingered salute towards *the door* before gagging myself, releasing a triumphant slosh of yellow bile.

While I was soaking, Holiday finally texted me back.

Want to get a drink next week?

12

The next morning I woke up to a nasty string of comments under several Facebook photos of me from the last party. *Btch used me like a napkin, hope you fcking nvr leave Berlin. Hapyp to see you're soo fuckng happy.* I asked Hailey if I should delete them, they were all from Jesse who had clearly been drunk, or stoned. It wasn't hard to imagine him ripping from his gravity bong in his dad's garage, sluggish yet enraged, he couldn't even spell *bitch*. The comments had sparked traffic, and the thread, below an image of me and Sam in the bathroom mirror, was now twenty-two comments long, with a litany of responses riffing on Jesse's dilapidated spelling. 'You absolutely can-not delete. It's gold. They invigorate the images, and if you remove them – then he knows you care. If you leave them, he's immortalised in his impotence.'

I had foolishly assumed there were no hard feelings between us. He had dumped *me*.

Later that morning, while I was debating the eventual regurgitation of a bran muffin, Hailey squealed from behind her computer, 'OH MY GOD *PURPLE MAGAZINE* WANTS TO DO A SHOOT AT OUR NEXT PARTY – *THIS* FRIDAY.'

Even I knew *Purple*, a downtown staple. The French art-culture-fashion magazine always featured either a near-nude gamine or well-clothed male movie star on its cover, with Chloë Sevigny in heavy rotation. Hailey turned up the music and began dancing with both middle fingers extended. I had never seen her so happy.

'Bitch, we're almost there,' she kissed my cheek and ran to the kitchen to make coffee. I tried to imagine what that meant. We're almost there. I assumed she was referring to our narrative. Was this the cresting apex? Or maybe once we'd been photographed like wisps of vain smoke, we'd be fully realized — finally there.

It had to be our best party yet. We ordered real wine glasses and a proper spotlight to point at the disco ball. I insisted we buy another fridge for under the bar. Hailey found one on eBay. We picked it up from an ancient lady whose apartment stank of rotting apples. Before letting us leave she made us promise we would wait two full days to turn it back on after moving it, we promised with no intention of doing so, then ferried the small fridge out the door.

'So, are you in love with Mathias?' Hailey asked while we hauled the fridge up our staircase. I stopped, trying to catch my breath, 'I don't think so. I mean I like him – he's fine. But I'm into Holiday, she's just hard to read – she disappears.'

'Well, when it rains it whores.'

'Anything from the von Habsburg?' I asked, as we picked the fridge back up.

Hailey grunted, 'Once he sees me in *Purple* I'll probably have the privilege of ignoring his texts. Is Holiday coming to the party?'

'She doesn't like art people.'

Hailey dropped her lower lip in thought, 'Fuck her. Music people are snobs. It's like Otto, he thinks he's so interesting and altruistic because he studies a useless medium.'

'*Art* isn't really hyper-functional either.'

'Bad art isn't.'

'I'm getting a drink with her Sunday . . .'

'Oh—' Her voice had stiffened, her eyes no longer willing to meet mine. For whatever reason, over the course of several similar conversations, it had become clear that Hailey did not

195

like Holiday. Maybe she was jealous. We had one more flight to go.

Later that night, cutting photos out of the newspaper for a collage, I could see the pink screen of Perez Hilton reflected in Hailey's reading glasses. She turned the computer towards me, 'Look at Britney—'

A video played of a pants-less Britney Spears shopping at an empty store in LA in what appeared to be the middle of the night – her black aviators reflecting the paparazzi's strobes, her overly tanned legs squeezed into ripped fishnets and her panties smeared in something.

'Is that period blood?'

'Maybe it's barbecue sauce,' Hailey released a seal laugh. 'You know she shaved her head on my birthday last year?'

'I didn't.'

'It was a cosmic sign.'

'For what?'

'That we are aligned. What most people don't get is that she is brilliant. She has no manager, no agent, no publicist and clearly no stylist. This is all one hundred per cent her.'

I nodded, half listening, watching Britney inspecting a white sneaker while paparazzi yelled questions. Hailey continued, 'She deserves more credit for this. She's just out there living her fiction.'

We spent Thursday setting up the apartment and Friday we planned our outfits with the fervour of the Bennet sisters preparing for the Netherfield Ball in *Pride and Prejudice*. Only after the apartment was littered in fabric lumps did I finally settle on chainmail paired with a lacy black bra and tights. Hailey slinked herself into the green Victorian dress that made her eyes pop like two tiny Jupiters shooting out of her sockets, topped off by a crystal choker and fake eyelashes. She was stalking around the apartment in commander mode, barely even saying hello to Sam when she arrived.

'Zoe, clean up the bathroom,' Hailey bellowed, motioning to the vanity strewn with make-up. I exhaled, silently telling myself *namaste*.

Constance came over and slid into her red suit, 'Can we get this dry-cleaned?'

'That's expensive,' Hailey clipped.

Constance pinched Hailey's ass, 'Cost of doing business, Madam.'

'Zoe, make me a Club-Mate vodka – and pre-cut more oranges, we ran out last time,' Hailey barked. There it was, my unflinching, *of course*. I plucked four cubes from the fresh bag of ice and tilted the bottle of Absolut, watching the liquid round the edges. Sam eyed Hailey until she disappeared into the other room.

'You let her dominate,' she paused to tug at her stockings, 'but you know that.'

'I have a tendency to say *of course* when I make people drinks,' I said defensively.

'That's economic subservience. That's normal—' She pointed to Hailey who was strutting around the other room, 'What you guys have is different, it's not my business – but it seems like some sort of *transitional dependence*. You should deal before you snap.'

I knew I had been rudderless since Ivy died. I'd let Jesse drag me to Wyoming, and now I was serving cocktails dressed in costume in Berlin. Sam wasn't wrong, but I was having fun. And I needed Hailey. I reminded myself that Sam was dosing me with her psych 101 and it required a margarita rim of salt. I wanted to change the subject.

'What was Nate's fetish?' I asked, surprising myself.

She narrowed her silver-lined eyes, assessing if I could handle whatever she was going to say. 'The usual Oedipal complex.'

I nodded, making a *not surprised* face.

197

'All rich boys have mommy shit, well, really it's nanny trauma. I only did verbal work, so it was just a lot of your typical school-boy humiliation, *where's your homework bla bla.*'

'I let him fuck me with a zucchini because he wanted me to have a fetish – and wouldn't tell me his unless I had one, so I made up *vegetables*. Then he still wouldn't tell me.'

Sam let a little dribble of her drink return to her glass before she let out a snort of laughter, I felt my face turn scarlet.

'I know, it's insanely embarrassing.'

She caught herself, 'You were trying to participate in something you thought was important to him which he was not strong nor intelligent enough to communicate with you.' Her clinical certitude reassured me. 'Anyway – forget what I said about you and Hailey. What you guys are doing here is great.' She squeezed my shoulder and left for the door.

People began to filter in, discarding their coats and adopting ice-filled glasses. Otto was playing a song I couldn't place that made everything feel as if it were moving in fast forward, voices and piano galloping together full trot. Mel *the Kennedy* ordered a whiskey soda, then settled in the corner guarding his cheetah-print backpack. A handful of guys I recognised from the *Star Wars* bar had plugged in their iPod, Soulja Boy crackled and they began dancing in a tight circle, arms bobbing up and down with pre-teen vigour. *Now watch me yuuuuuuu.*

And then as if a skip in a record, four large policemen were at the door. A hush rippled through the party. The Soulja Boys hastily ripped the jack out. Mel scooted his backpack under my bed, I hid the menus and the cash box, repeating the lines Hailey had made me memorise: *Das ist nur eine private Party* – or was it – *Dies ist nur eine privat Party?* Hailey had been patient with me, her pretty mouth pushing out the foreign sounds: *It's just a private party.* I spiralled into inky doom. Maybe we would get kicked out the apartment. Maybe we would get kicked out of the country.

Hailey marched over, the bustle of her Victorian dress swishing confidently behind her. She greeted the officers with a tight nod and professional smile, accompanying them as they toured the apartment. I stood off to the side of the bar, keeping my foot on the hidden cash box. My phone bleated, a text from Sam: *They got two calls?? sound complaint + illegal club* :(

I later learned Hailey addressed the men in their bullet-proof vests, saying something along the lines of: *We are students from the Berlin art school and we are producing a film. Tonight we are shooting a scene at a party. As you can see, we are doing a rehearsal, we will be filming later this evening. Is there a problem?* The cops looked confused, but our period-specific costuming supported her claim, and after a few minutes of back and forth they tentatively accepted the situation, insinuating that they would stop by again to follow up.

Hailey closed the door, her composure melting away, 'Fuck – the photographer isn't here, right?' I shook my head.

'Is Jens?' she asked, careening off like a race car driver through the thicket of bodies, Constance pointed to Jens, who was sitting on the ledge of the bay window staring at his phone.

'Jens! We need to go to school, we need to check out lighting and camera equipment.' Jens looked perplexed.

'I'll explain in the cab.'

The party carried on with the electric current of illicit activity. Constance motioned towards me from the roulette table, she wanted a drink. I added her usual liquids: vodka, soda, lime. There was a lull so I walked it over.

'*Danke*, pick a number,' she smiled, motioning towards the table. 'Red, six.'

She spun the wheel, it landed on red twelve. 'Close.'

'There is no such thing as close.'

I rolled my eyes. 'You say that one a lot?'

'All the time,' she laughed.

Before turning back to the bar I glanced out the bay window, and was struck with a bolt of white heat. It was her. On the train platform. There was no question. That Uma Thurman helmet of hair and red lips. It was Beatrice in a sleek brown floor-length jacket. I stood petrified, unsure of how to respond. Her eyes were fixed, a beam of focus on the window of the next room. I wondered if I should hide, duck below the ledge or she would surely see me. A second later, something cracked across her alabaster face, she looked strange, suddenly older – she cocked her head and stepped backwards, absorbed into the darkness of the station's stairwell. I stood, waiting for her to return, terrified she might appear in the street and head for the door.

'Zoe, they're going to start making their own drinks if you don't—' Constance snapped her finger in front of my face, breaking my stare. I nodded, taking one last moment to scan the empty street. She was watching us. *She must have called the cops.*

About fifty drinks-served later, Hailey and Jens returned with nine hard-plastic suitcases from the video department. Jens began stretching out metal tripods, Hailey popped reflective umbrellas, screwing on light fixtures, her knuckles white, wrist spasming as she tightened bolts. 'Hailey, I saw Beatrice. She was out there – looking in,' I said, pointing to the platform.

The piano lurched into a torrid version of Guns N' Roses, 'November Rain', and the Swiss painter with the canyon voice was leading a rough choir. Hailey nodded, 'Of course she was. She probably called the cops to create narrative tension. I knew something like this would eventually happen. She wants to see how we react.'

'But doesn't that mean she's mad? Shouldn't we stop—'

One by one the white-hot studio lights flashed on, and the crowd morphed into sexed-up moths revelling in their final flaps before incineration. I tried to reiterate my concerns, but Hailey shook me off, 'It's good, it's what we want—' Her dress thwapped as she turned, ceasing any further conversation of Beatrice.

The photographer, with slicked-back hair and big beady eyes, entered just as Jens was adjusting the last metallic parasol. I offered him a drink, he declined. Draped in black fabric and silver jewellery he had the look of a gothic squirrel, he turned his unpleasant smile on the overlit room, and asked, 'Dolls, did you do this all for me?'

Hailey flashed a coy but unhinged smirk, and in one seamless gesture, The Squirrel whipped the camera that hung from his neck to his right eye and began clicking. The Swiss artist hung from the door frame. Sam posed arms on hips. Three girls, understanding it was a photo shoot for *Purple*, had drawn a bath, their nipples peeking out from the sudsy water, still wearing their black stockings and making duck faces for the camera.

When the cops returned, the party fell silent. Jens hopped on a chair in front of the video camera and began pretending to direct while holding his hands up like Nixon exiting an airplane. 'Now, Zoe, I need you to speak loudly here,' Jens called. 'When I say action you yell towards Constance. Do you remember your lines?' I nodded, but of course had no idea. 'Action.'

'Red, six,' I called to Constance.

Taking the cue, Constance spun the wheel. 'Black twenty-two.'

'Close,' I yelled back.

'There is no such thing as close,' Constance smirked.

Jens began moving his hands, 'Cut – everyone else, please

just carry on, don't forget – you're at a party, act like it. And action.'

The cops stood silently as the fake film shoot unfolded. In between cuts they politely asked Hailey to *keep it down*, to which she curtseyed. The Squirrel even persuaded the four uniformed officers to pose for him, Hailey proudly nestling herself in-between their stiff vests, her lips pushed out in two satisfied sausages. When the door finally banged behind the officers, the party erupted in applause and Jens took a deep bow from his director's perch. The remainder of the night screamed by. The extra fridge kept the beer cold, we didn't run out of ice, and the room was so bright no one felt morning creep on.

My bed was wet with beer so I threw a towel down. We slept without cleaning, waiting until the following evening to begin the rancid affair. I was amazed that people were willing to ash in anything even vaguely concave – a bottle cap, a spoon, a banana peel, each object transformed into an ashen bomb waiting to explode when swept up. Hailey found a vial of what appeared to be coke wedged behind the couch. I dotted some on my thumb, testing the bitter chemical. 'Yup.' We cut lines on the cover of one of Beatrice's novels and cleaned the apartment like robots.

The next morning our *Purple Diary* post was up:

BONFIRE OF THE VANITIES: It's an extremely exclusive party and you're terrified: Were you even invited? Who'll be there? What will you wear? What is this place? Is it a house or a club? All you know is that you'll do anything to get in. EasyJet tickets litter the floor, the bathroom line is longer than Berghain and it's lit up like a detergent commercial. Time to strike a pose and grab a drink. You won't regret it.

The text had the sophistication of a 6th-grade birthday party invitation but, thankfully, The Squirrel made everyone look like the type of people who belonged in the pages of a fashion magazine.

'In the future we have to control the language. This is beyond lame,' Hailey whined.

'He must have done something to my cheekbones,' I said, pressing my face to my laptop. Hailey's glasses were reflecting the manic speed she was cycling through, as she started mumbling, 'This – is – us. This – is – us.'

I pointed to my screen, frozen, 'Hailey.'

'What?' she asked, breaking her chant. 'That's her.'

'Who?'

I dropped my voice, 'Beatrice.'

I turned my laptop to Hailey wordlessly. In the background of one of the photos, in the corner of Hailey's room, was a mushroom of jet-black hair, her back angled towards the camera, face hidden behind the shoulder of a tall guy in a green sweater. It was the exact same floor-length brown jacket I had seen Beatrice wearing on the train platform.

'Are you sure?'

'Yes.'

We looked though all the other photos, the brown jacket never reappeared. 'She was here.'

I got up from my computer.

'She definitely called the police to create narrative tension,' Hailey shouted after me, ecstatic. I walked to the position in the corner of Hailey's room where Beatrice had been standing, and tried to imagine it. What had she been thinking? Watching all of these people in her bedroom. Was she worried we would see her? Or was that why she was here?

Hailey followed me.

'What are you doing?'

'I'm thinking about her – here.'

I felt another kick of uneasiness. The fact that Beatrice was willing to come to the party meant something had shifted. I became jumpy. The back of a chair, a pile of clothes in the corner of the room all morphed into Beatrice — her shadow now everywhere.

'It feels wrong,' I said.

'Honestly, I enjoy the feeling of being watched,' Hailey laughed as she strode to the bathroom, turning the tub's tap, stripping naked and not bothering to close the door. Performing for me now too.

The next night I went out with Holiday. She wanted to meet at a gay bar at Kottbusser Tor. I got there early because I was nervous and assumed that, as usual, I would get lost. I found the bar at the mouth of an enormous yellow and white housing complex. I peered in the corner window, I couldn't see Holiday, and didn't want to be caught waiting outside. There were two doors – I pulled the left one but it was locked. The bartender pointed to the other door, I flushed red. Taking a deep breath, I pulled the handle, trying to seem confident. It was Sunday, early evening, and nearly empty except for a few strays quietly sipping drinks. The bar was lit by a line of spinach-hued bulbs fastened to satellite dishes, under which the wooden stools glowed like wayward jellyfish. I ordered a beer and sat down. A silver-haired man two stools down smiled. I reciprocated. We sat in silence. After what felt like an eternity, Holiday slid up to the stool next to me winding her arm around my shoulders. My heart began clobbering and I prayed my nerves weren't plastered on my face.

'I see you met Oscar,' she said, motioning to the silver-haired man. 'He's an excellent poet. Was he hitting on you?'

'Oh. No . . . he wasn't,' I stammered.

'I was joking,' she chuckled, ordering a beer by coolly sticking her index finger in the air.

'Do you like poetry?' Oscar asked.

'Yes – I do,' I replied.

Holiday shot me a devilish-yet-kind smile, the answer seemed to satisfy Oscar as he returned to his beer in feline silence.

'So your budget Moulin Rouge is going well,' Holiday snickered, and imitated one of the more ridiculous poses from the *Purple Magazine* shoot, her thin legs sticking wildly towards the satellites above us.

'Yeah, yeah, yeah.'

She kept posing, looking more and more like a young Madonna, I started laughing and felt something – *relief* – to be with someone who had no interest in art, or Beatrice, or the trajectory of our *narrative*.

'I want to hear your music.'

'No one gets to hear my music.'

'Oh,' I said, surprised, 'and why is that?'

'It's not ready,' she said with a dismissive flip of her hands before ordering two vodka shots.

When Holiday got up to go to the bathroom, I took a long look at her. She was wearing the same black halter top she'd worn to Berghain, with tight camouflage pants and plasticky red Doc Martens. Her silhouette made me feel fluttery. I missed her in the few minutes that she was gone. How was that possible? The bar was starting to fill up. When she finally returned to her stool she had a fresh pack of cigarettes. She knocked two out. I didn't smoke but accepted, she flicked a flame from a pale brown lighter, I inhaled and began coughing. Her face creased laughing. The door of the bar swung open and a tangle of British 'blokes' sauntered through, stinking of Ryanair-pre-planned-pub-crawling. The bartender stiffened. Holiday ducked her head closer to mine, explaining that ever since the *Lonely Planet* had christened it 'the best bar in Kreuzberg', the staff had adopted an aggressive attitude towards outsiders, especially straights. The group was preppy in a distinctly date rape-y way, with ugly colourful button-ups and popped collars. They ordered beers and settled in a corner where they began yelping at each other.

Holiday leered at them, 'These are the same illiterate apes that called me a faggot and beat the shit out of me in Brixton. They don't get to drink here.' I couldn't imagine anyone wanting to hurt Holiday, she was such an obvious gift to the world. She opened her mouth startlingly wide and pointed to one of her teeth, tapping it. It was brighter than the rest.

'They may as well be the same assholes that knocked it out.'

As if on cue, one of the guys began grinding his butt against the wall, pretending to be effeminate.

Holiday snapped, 'Nope. Not while I'm here.' She swung off her stool, a wrecking ball, gliding to their table, 'You do realise this is a gay bar.' Stunned, the table fell silent. Holiday seemed to triple in size, her words popping out of her mouth like slaps, 'And because it's a gay bar, you're making people uncomfortable.'

The least aggressive of the group began to whisper to the rest, he looked embarrassed, his cheeks pink and sweaty. They sucked down their pints and began putting on their jackets.

Holiday returned.

'It was 50/50 chance, either they yell back and we fight or they just leave. They weren't that drunk so—'

The poet Oscar leaned over, 'She does this every night.'

I was worried I wasn't gay enough and she'd kick me out.

'Thanks for nothing,' the tubbiest of the popped-collars bellowed as the door slapped behind them.

'Suck my cock,' Holiday called. Everyone in the bar laughed. I ordered another round, we got drunker and drunker, and eventually Holiday followed me into the bathroom and fucked me against the sticky semi-reflective wallpaper that hugged the stall. Without warning, I came – like a SWAT team bursting through a suburban door.

13

At first it had been mostly artists and students, which made sense, but now gallerists and curators were messaging, asking if they could have their afterparties at *Beatrice*. As the Fridays marched on, a steady stream of 'suits' poured in with coke-crusted nostrils and steak bouncing in their stomachs. It was all speeding up. I was constantly scanning the room but Beatrice never reappeared in the crowd — a near-blind gallerist broke his nose jumping from chair to table, a German artist set off a fire extinguisher in the hallway, and a painter from Boise 'ironically' drew a swastika in the bathroom, which took four layers of paint to cover up. And one Friday Tobias Breitbach showed up with a squad of dinner jackets and I was able to fulfil my promise to Claire, having Sam reject him at the door, despite his protests.

We celebrated Hailey's twenty-first birthday — I baked her a red-velvet cake — and she cried in the kitchen because she felt that Europeans, who'd been legally drinking from infancy, didn't grasp the full monumentality of a twenty-first birthday. And Hailey discovered *Deko Behrendt*, a one-stop shop for party decor, a few blocks south of our apartment that even rented props, including a giant burlesque martini-glass, which I insisted was too cheesy.

'Is she supposed to be the physical manifestation of a champagne bubble?' I asked, looking over Hailey's shoulder, indicating the woman on the website's advertisement doing the splits while inside the large plastic glass.

'What good is sitting alone in your room?' Hailey crooned.

'What?'

I stared at her blankly.

'It's from *Cabaret*.'

I rolled my eyes, no longer caring to mask my irritation at her over-the-top-ness.

'We wouldn't dance in it – we'd just fill it with fake blood or Campari or something.'

I shook my head.

Hailey had developed a child-like habit of decorating on Thursdays, a full day before the parties, tinsel curtains duct-taped above doors and cartoon hearts dangling in our bedrooms before Valentine's. Helium tanks and fog machines arriving in the afternoon's flurry, balloons gently bumping above our sleeping heads.

The weekdays between parties were a blur of nachos, planning drink orders, cleaning grime off flat surfaces and answering messages. We were in demand. And so was Berlin. You couldn't open an American newspaper or magazine without a yuppy-ready report from the nightlife capital of Europe. There was something in the water. Berlin had the post-Wall residue of the '90s with the hedonistic wells still running deep, but the hotels were plush and the taxi drivers spoke enough English. Hailey was perfectly poised for the moment, she loved PR and her flawless German made her seem *integrated*. Hailey had developed a mystic sensibility, an astrological sixth sense for saying the right thing. Always prepped with zingy one-liners, which she paired with photographs from our trove that perfectly illustrated the quixotic quest of the party-goer in well-balanced chaos. Mostly, she was just always willing – and the illegal party scene wasn't really an industry booming with rapid email responders. But she saw it as an appetiser. 'Any cretin can get press,' Hailey had said, looking up from painting her nails a burnt-crème-brûlée orange, 'we're going into the books.'

On Tuesday Hailey was particularly excited because *Interview*, the magazine Andy Warhol started in the late '60s, had just included us in their article – '10 New Best of Berlin Nightlife'.

'I don't understand why they aren't actually interviewing us,' she'd said while re-reading the magazine's email for the fifth time.

'It's a listicle,' I chided.

'Well, *Interview* is famous for its interviews. I want an interview.'

Hailey was never satisfied. The previous evening she had folded into possessive indignation when Sam let slip that the focus of her thesis was shifting to Berlin's ex-pat community, something about the 'performance of professionalism within the culture industry'. Later, Hailey yelled over my running bathwater that she felt Sam was using the parties to get access to 'the scene', something that was *ours not hers*.

Despite our new-found presence in the art world, I wasn't making much art. I wasn't even collaging any more. All I really did was photograph the parties. Berghain and most Berlin clubs had a no photo policy, but ours was different. Every night was an image – I loved the flash-drenched frames of people in line for the bathroom, Constance applying green lipstick, Hailey's crystal choker resplendent, Mel making a scrunched face from behind a glass – often, in the empty hours of the afternoon, I would scroll through the albums as if they were silent films, each night available for infinite replaying.

But no matter what I did – mindlessly touch up my blonde roots, sift through my receipts, scrape peanut butter on toast, scroll Facebook – I was waiting for Holiday to text me back. I felt dumb, an adolescent in braces again. I worried I wasn't cool enough for her. At the department store she'd told me to shave my head, hadn't she? I ran my hands through my hair, my skull was too lumpy. It had been almost five weeks since she'd fucked me in the bathroom of the bar. And three weeks since her last text. I sent another. What if next time I needed to reciprocate? I'd never fingered anyone but myself. I googled tutorials on 'how to go down on a girl'. *Go slow. Circular motions. Consistency. Teasing.* Another five days later and still no text back. I thought about just going to the gay bar. Would it be strange if I went alone? I couldn't bring Hailey, she would want to dress up and make a scene. After some white wine meditating, I decided to take it as what it was – Holiday didn't want to see me – I needed to move on. A few hours later Mathias wrote, asking if I wanted to sneak into a play, I decided why not. Fuck Holiday.

It was a cold black night and the Volksbühne theatre still burned like a lantern. The play was set in a hotel lobby and followed a volatile female night porter. Again the actresses screamed in a near constant wall of sound. I assumed they were talking about sex or maybe politics. I didn't understand much but I loved it, I felt transported to another, better, planet, where only extreme feelings were traded.

When it was over I was clumsy, as if returning to land after a year at sea. I found Mathias near the exit. He led me to the Kantine through the twisting channels of the theatre – an impossible maze of ladders, set pieces, crooked stairwells, costume racks and chunks of wood painted black. We drank golden beers at a corner table, and he complained about a 'lightning' technician who was always late. After I was good and drunk I asked him where the best place to fuck in the theatre was. He laughed. I told him I was serious. He erupted in a flutter of sneezes and then took my hand, leading me back down one of the crooked stairwells.

I felt cheap. On the way home, my eyes focused on the train seat upholstered in blue, black and red camo-print, I drunkenly swore I would never fuck out of spite again. Sex with men had always been a gear shift, a way to control direction. I felt childish, and with Holiday I had felt different, closer to myself. I didn't hide behind clothes or stories or false motivations, even if she wasn't texting back – there would be other Holidays.

When I opened the apartment door Hailey was crying. Big sloppy throbs. I assumed, as I always did since Ivy, that someone had died.

She slurped out her words, 'My parents just called,' another air sucking snot sob, 'Biggles is bankrupt – they're all closing – and they can't afford to keep me in school. They lost the house – and the cars – and—' she sloped her shoulders towards me, snot pooling in the depression under her nose, 'that's why my mom stopped sending LaMer.'

I hugged her, then quickly opened a bottle of wine. Her eyes were crazed as she watched me pour, I handed her the glass and she sipped it down silently.

I took the pause to calmly explain, 'There are scholarships. I'm on a scholarship. I know there are ways to figure it out with school.' I rested my hand on her knee. She shook me off, picking herself up from the couch, and began lunging, a caged tiger, her wine glass near spilling at each curve of the room.

'You don't understand,' she stopped and took a shrill breath, 'I came here to this fake school for a year and paid full tuition, it's theft. You know how much they charge students here in Berlin? €285 a semester.' She was seething. 'My parents paid what? They paid $42,000 dollars to a school in New York so I could come here for this bullshit year.' She pointed at me.

I sat frozen. Why was she angry at me? She walked to her door and slammed it shut, switching into a hissing whisper, 'It better be fucking worth it. This all has to be worth it,

Zoe.' She spat my name out. 'This is my piece. This book Beatrice is writing. It's based on MY diary. My story. You see that right? It's MY ART PIECE, and it's all I have now.'

Hailey was seething, her eyes dark, borderline homicidal. I leaned back in my chair, trying to glue it all together. I didn't really see *this* as art. The parties at this point were just something we were doing. I hadn't cared, or even inquired, what she was writing in her diary since the first entry we'd written together. She was the one who had pushed everything. For me, Beatrice's looming presence had become an excuse, an abstract and terrifying deity we nodded to on our path to reverie.

I tried to speak calmly like the hostage negotiators I'd seen in movies, 'Look, Hailey, this thing she is writing, is all yours. Whatever that means to you – it's yours.'

Relief settled across her face, I couldn't believe this is what she needed to hear, she sat down and poured herself more wine.

I was unable to sleep, my mind retracing the oil slicks of Hailey's meltdown. I opened my computer and watched an episode of *Gossip Girl* with headphones, the Upper East Side soap seemed tame compared to Hailey's implosion. I still couldn't sleep. Around 4am, I heard footsteps in the kitchen. Hailey rarely got up at night. I braced with fear then closed my eyes, too exhausted to inspect, unsure sure who I would be more afraid to find.

The photographer was supposed to show up at noon for *Interview* magazine, so I padded into the kitchen a little before eleven making sniffle sounds. Hailey was brewing coffee. 'Hey, I'm not feeling well. I think you should do this alone. I'll help you get the place up and ready, then I'll just lie down.' I was trying to softly hand her the spotlight. She glowered. It wasn't a lie, my face was gaunt with matching liver-coloured crescents under my eyes.

213

'What, do you not even care any more? You want to abandon me the second things get hard. We have the *Beatrice* image to uphold. The image is both of us.' I nodded and dug my tea box out of the cupboard, unable to reconcile her current words with her previous evening's insistence on solo ownership.

She continued, 'You should wear the Elizabethan costume.'

I shrugged, and walked into my room to get dressed. Whatever had been fun about doing this had entirely evaporated, I was trapped in the looping spider silk of Hailey and Beatrice.

The photographer, an hour late, was an elegant Italian man, who looked as if he'd just stepped off a yacht at Lake Como, reeking of a grapefruity-turpentine cologne.

'*Ciao, Belle.* You make my job so easy!'

He began setting up lights, his citrus skunk made me open a window. Hailey stalked over to him. 'Why doesn't the magazine want to interview us?'

'Baby, that is not my department. I'm just here to make sure you look stunning.'

'Can I speak with your editor?'

'Baby, it's really not my place.'

Hailey reluctantly accepted, and retreated to the mirror in the bathroom. When she returned she was wearing her crystal choker and the black-bob wig I'd stolen from the costume sale. She glared at me. I said nothing, she'd even drawn on a mole – Beatrice with a side of Liza.

The magazine wanted two photographs: one 'playful' at the roulette table and one 'serious' at the piano. Hailey was caked in her now usual foundation, which, in the light, seemed three shades too dark. She popped two Advil, then caught me staring and pointed to the piano. I took a breath, walking over, I looked absurd with my giant pink ruff – a bargain-basement Shakespeare, a collared dog.

The term *party* felt wrong. It started to feel like what it was: a rave in my bedroom that I had to clean up before I could go to sleep. I was still happy to bartend, and happy to see Constance at the table in her red suit, and with Sam working the front door I felt safe, but Hailey floated through the nights, a ghost refusing to work or do anything other than socialise with people she thought were important. When she did talk to me, Hailey babbled in snobbish tones about how Beatrice's novel would make her an 'art star'. She wanted to be as mainstream as possible – in-flight magazine features, Urban Outfitters tote bags, and Absolut Vodka sponsorships. She was always waxing about the divide between fake artists, real artists, and the worst breed: *middle-class artists*, whose work only mattered in the art world.

The end of Biggles had tripped something inside of Hailey. I assumed the volcano would cool with time, but her anger only seemed to build. And as her control evaporated, the PR work accelerated. She began sharing photographs from our parties on random Facebook pages, spamming blogs. Even, unprompted from the magazine, submitted an interview to accompany our photo shoot for *Interview*.

'They would be stupid not to use it. I took the questions that Glenn O'Brien asked Andy Warhol in their iconic interview and answered them myself. I put myself in Andy's shoes. What would he have done? He would have done a fucking interview. I recorded it, then transcribed it so it has their *off-the-cuff feel*. They'll run it,' her voice had an air of desperation that made me nervous.

I didn't know what I wanted from the *Beatrice* parties. I wondered if this made me a middle-class artist. Everyone seemed to know what they wanted. Sam's thesis research had escalated and she was now writing down nationalities and professions next to the guest list and googling them later.

It was early on in the evening and I had just finished installing our brand-new speakers with Jens. Hailey had only agreed to purchase the Easter Island goliaths after we'd gotten bad press in *Electronic Beats* online magazine, which under a photo of a packed dance floor posed the question: 'The parties are good, but how much fun can you really have dancing to desktop speakers?'

Sam was sitting on the couch, killing time before she headed to the door, while I sliced limes. 'It's funny how many Swiss people there are, right?' she said, without looking from her clip board.

'What's wrong with Zurich? Is it boring?' I asked.

Sam huffed, 'Berlin is just a good place for rich people to hide.'

'How?'

'No one is judged for not working, because no one really works here. You know – like if you move to New York and do nothing but snort ketamine and read Picasso coffee-table books you're an asshole. But here it's totally normal. There isn't much you can even spend your money on, there's only like one nice restaurant—'

I laughed. Sam checked her watch then sauntered off towards the door.

It was a fairly nondescript *Beatrice* night, until a smiley girl came to the bar to inform me that someone vomited into the bathtub. I looked around to try and find Hailey, this would fall under her jurisdiction, but she was – of course – conveniently tucked away and out of sight. I sparked with rage. Constance agreed to watch the bar and I headed to the bathroom. As I was lifting the vomit from tub to toilet with yellow gloves, the red-faced girl who has released the pineapple-chunk-slop apologised effusively. When I gave her an earnest *it's OK* nod as I truly had plenty of empathy for puking in that windowless bathroom, she weakly smiled and wiped her face. Attempting to make conversation, she asked what I did. I told her I was an artist, she asked what type of work

216

I made, I laughed and motioned towards the third handful of vomit I was transporting from tub to toilet, 'This is it, it's right here.'

Holiday finally texted. She said she'd had the flu and apologised that she hadn't written back. I didn't really believe her, or care about her excuse. I was desperate to get out of the apartment, away from Beatrice's shadow and Hailey's aspirational melancholy.

Holiday and I began seeing each other almost every night. We'd meet in dive bars and make out, sometimes sneaking off to the bathroom to fuck. She loved the jukebox at Rote Rose, where the heavy drunks drank all day and night with no interest in linear time. She'd put on Tracy Chapman's 'Fast Car' five times in a row and spin in a circle until she cried. She told me about her dad who had early-onset dementia and how her ex-girlfriend Irena, one of her original roommates, was finally moving back to Spain the following week. I told her about Ivy, how I'd pretty much stopped making art, and how the parties had taken over my life. I didn't want to tell her about Beatrice, I didn't want to betray Hailey, and at this point it all seemed impossible, even ridiculous. I imagined Holiday would have just laughed it off as some narcissistic fantasy. Maybe it was.

At home, Hailey's whole demeanour had shifted, not only was she indifferent to working or doing anything other than 'press', but when the parties were over and we'd finished cleaning she kept her door closed. She stopped leaving the apartment except to buy groceries and endless packs of gum. Her preferred Dentyne Ice was impossible to find so she switched to Airwaves, sharp and cough drop-ish. In the apartment I could always smell the edges of her minty cloud, a prickly green storm front that never blew in. She left a trail of chomped gum on everything. White sticky barnacles on plates, floating in the soap dish, pressed under the window ledges, thumbed into scraps of paper and spun around the ends of pencils. One night when cleaning up after dinner I broke yet another of Beatrice's octagonal wine glasses while trying to scrub a petrified wad off its base. I teetered into Hailey's room holding the stem like a lifeless rat, just as she had all those months ago, the old joke: 'BEATRICE IS GOING TO KILL US.' Hailey was hunched over her diary, she raised one eye to meet mine, then released a long sigh mixed with two singular 'Ha's. I closed the door.

Holiday took me to an LGBTQ solidarity march. She wore a bright-green wig with short choppy bangs. She looked like a lollipop. Walking arm in arm with her, with everyone there – the shimmering flags, plastic flowers and rainbows – I felt closer to myself. I was finally somewhere I wanted to be, with someone who I actually wanted to be with. The self-loathing finger-throat-fucking bulimic was a blurry stranger. I wished I could talk to Hailey, about Holiday, about everything, but I was afraid of her – afraid of her strange focus, whatever she was doing behind her closed door. And when I did say anything, tell her where I'd been, or what Holiday and I were up to, she'd roll her eyes. I stopped saying goodbye when I left, trying my best to hush the lock as it clacked shut.

The following Tuesday night I got home around 2 a.m., reeking of cigarettes after a few rounds of Polish beer at the gay bar. Once in bed I reached for my computer, cloudily remembering I'd told my mom I'd email. The screen took a second to load, then Ivy's Facebook page lit up. It felt like a slap. Ever since Beatrice had read my email to Molly Webster, I had been extremely careful in remembering what I was leaving on my desktop. The image staring back was from a homecoming photo album; me in a hideous lilac dress with spaghetti straps and Ivy in a denim halter dress, both of us with butterfly clips in our hair, and Jesse, Ivy's date, in the background smirking. I knew I hadn't left the tab open. I also knew Hailey hadn't left the apartment so there would have been no way for Beatrice to enter. It had to have been Hailey.

Unsure of how to confront Hailey about whatever she was doing on my computer, I ignored her, and she seemed perfectly happy to accept the silence. We set the next party up on autopilot, only exchanging words when absolutely necessary.

Constance could sense something was off, 'All good at chez-Beatrice? Hailey seems a bit ehhhh—' she cocked her head, making a sideways frown to the kitchen where Hailey was going over the guest list.

The catalyst for Hailey's new dour mood, I still assumed, was her parents' financial situation – which she had made me swear to keep secret, so I just huffed indifferently.

'Well, if you need to talk. You've got me,' she paused, looking earnest, 'you know that, right?' I was surprised. Surprised that things were bad enough to be outwardly apparent, and also, that she was friend enough to see it. I squeezed her hand.

Two people were celebrating birthdays that night, and by 11:30 there was already an obnoxious after-gallery-opening crowd. The apartment was packed. I was busy decanting bottles into flutes to the mostly shirtless crowd, everyone sweating like furnaces, nipples out, techno thudding from the loud new speakers. Mid pour I saw Mathias in the hallway. Sam knew I didn't want to see him, normally she would have texted for my approval.

He sauntered over to the bar. I gave him a cordial European kiss on the cheek. Hailey recognised Mathias from across the room and perked up. Running over, she made a big show of cinching her hands around his neck and collapsing into him. They looked like they were dating. She began speaking in German, they both laughed, he traced the outline of her collarbone with his index finger. It was borderline pornographic. The techno grew louder, as if someone were spanking a metal rod suspended in water, fleshy human cannonballs began throttling around the room in rhythm. I felt overwhelmed. I could barely hear the drunk Serbian girl order a gin and tonic right in front of me. I loaded cubes into her glass while trying to keep an eye on Hailey and Mathias. It appeared she wanted him to open the locked drawer again. He dug in her hair for a bobby pin, I turned hot with anger. Just as he had all those weeks ago, he swaggered over to the locked bookshelf to perform his trick, dropping to his knees. After a beat, Hailey's face radiated terror. The drawer was empty.

Across the chaos of the room Hailey looked me in the eyes, for the first time in days. Why was this so alarming to her? I didn't understand. We knew Beatrice was watching us. If I woke to find her looming over my bed I wouldn't have been surprised. Why did Hailey care about these papers going missing? Nothing was sacred. Hailey, ghost white, asked Mathias to lock it back up, then jammed her tongue down his open mouth. The Serbian girl tapped the bar with her wallet. I had forgotten to give her change. A fresh wave of rage crashed over me, what was she doing? Mathias moved into the other room. I lunged out from behind the bar and grabbed Hailey's wrist, pulling her towards the bathroom, screaming, 'ARE YOU FUCKING HIM? REALLY?'

I pushed a group of four waiting in line out of the way, and swung the door open. 'Hailey, are you fucking him?'

She ignored me, reapplying lipstick. I asked again. She continued smearing her satisfied pout with a salmony colour. I hated the way she looked at herself. It was the same way she checked her reflection in the window on the train, moving her chin down and pursing her lips out with a sex doll's dead stare.

'Who I'm fucking is the least of our issues. Beatrice—'

I cut her off, my blood swelling in my wrists, pumping with anger, 'I don't care any more about this game. I don't care about Beatrice – or what she is writing behind her little door. I care about you, and our friendship, and our actual lives. Are you sleeping with him? Is this why you've been so weird?' I pointed towards the party, to an out-of-sight Mathias.

She stared at me, closing her tube with a bitchy *snap*, 'Why do you care?' She made sarcastic bunny ears, 'You're gay.' She slammed the door.

Alone in the bathroom I texted Holiday. She was at Berghain. I stormed out, leaving the bar unguarded, knowing Hailey would be pissed and forced to work.

When I got to Berghain, the line was at least two hundred people deep. It would give me time to think. What was going on with Hailey? She was acting insane. If she was fucking Mathias it was annoying, but it didn't matter – it was everything else, the way she looked at me filled with resentment. Her creeping on my laptop. Her insistence on drama. What had happened to us? Surrounded by tourists and club kids all crowing and swaying, I felt sick. I always felt sick. I popped DayQuil, the last of my stash from America. I imagined the neon-orange pills exploding in my stomach, running through my veins, a super power. German over-the-counter drugs were a joke, all sage tablets and eucalyptus drops. I missed home. I got to the door and the pirate bouncer with face tattoos nodded me in. A rush of vindication. I thought about the Australians at the hostel, and getting rejected with Christopher from Connecticut – and the propulsion of water that still felt like it was pushing me over a cliff – *Every night you miss in Berlin is a night you miss in Berlin*.

Topless was the theme of the evening. I found Holiday on the strobing dance floor with her perfect tiny tits out. She jumped up when she saw me. After dancing for a few hours Holiday took me to her house. Irena, the ex-girlfriend, had been replaced by a musician from Thailand, so I could now enter without fear of flying objects. Holiday called their place a 'WG', which meant shared apartment, and explained that all the roommates self-identified as queer. They lived in one of the tall buildings right near Kottbusser Tor, or as Holiday said, 'Kotti'. It felt like entering a church, everything full of gravity – the stacks of dishes meaningful, the mess of books in the kitchen sacred.

We brought a bottle of schnapps into her little room, barely bigger than her mattress, filled with dead flowers. It was heaven. We fucked blissfully, her thin neck dipping down below my *cunt*. I loved the way she said *cunt*, as if it were both a place and an action. A private island and an assault rifle clipping the sky. In the morning we ate cantaloupe with globs of yogurt and listened to one of her roommates talk about how his new bisexual boyfriend was in the process of trying to impregnate his ex-girlfriend who wanted kids – and he couldn't understand why they had to actually sleep together, why they weren't just turkey basting. Holiday thought it was hilarious. We went back to bed.

I walked home in the early-evening fog, replaying the previous hours, coasting on happiness that Holiday had finally let me in. Once I opened the front door I heard a crash, then an exasperated wail – Hailey was crying. I assumed more drama at Biggles. From the stench of rotting beer and cigarettes I could tell she hadn't even cracked a window since the party. I took my coat off, preparing myself for whatever miserable tale she would spin, then gently knocked on her door frame. Hailey looked up, ghoulish and disoriented, surrounded by the shattered remains of champagne flutes and sodden confetti.

'Look!' she said breathlessly, thrusting a tortured piece of printer paper at me. I grabbed it, flattening it on my thigh. It took a second for my eyes to focus – it was another interview with Beatrice from some blog, her bitter stare mutilated from the page's creases. I scanned the page.

> BB: *I mean the next book, at its core is about narcissism and desperation. The two main characters are impossible to love because of their sheer obsessive desire to be loved.*

> QL: *So who are they?*

> BB: *Two young girls who get wrapped up in partying in a desperate bid for recognition. The book follows their thought process . . . how they unravel, dissolve into themselves . . . they see themselves as celebrities . . . but of course, they are not.*

> QL: *So is it more of a psychological drama?*

> BB: *It is principally a psychological drama — isn't it always with roommates? But there is sex, it is quite a juicy love triangle. But I think it's important to recognise that the sort of behaviour the Facebook generation is built on is a doctrine of performing for one another, and see it for the darkness that drives it. It's a cautionary tale about who NOT to be, what NOT to do! [laughter]*

> QL: *So it's a bit of a modern tragedy? And where did you draw your inspiration for this book?*

> BB: *I'm a lint roller for this sort of drama, but I think this behaviour, and more importantly these sort of young women, are everywhere. All you have to do is open your eyes. I am shining a light on the underbelly of banality. [laughter]*

> QL: *But is it completely finished? The big question, I know.*

BB: I'm still working on the ending, I can't resist a juicy ending. You'll have to pick up the book to find out . . .

QL: Last question. What's the title?

BB: Great question, The Dull and Dead. *Of course it's a play on the classic* The Beautiful and Damned.

QL: Fantastic. We will look for The Dull and Dead *on the shelves next fall.*

'She thinks we're idiots. *The Dull and Dead* – she doesn't realise – I know all about her—'

My hangover was setting in, I was having trouble following what she was even saying.

'I'm not stupid and I know what she did with her other book,' Hailey was speaking at a violent pace, 'she thinks she's so smart – and can get away with it. Stealing – stories and twisting – them into – this – into—'

Whatever seams had been loosely holding Hailey together had torn. She walked into the kitchen and ripped open *the door*, romance novels toppling onto the linoleum. I followed her into the back apartment where she turned on the caged work lights. The room initially appeared untouched, Hailey bolted towards the desk. Then I saw, there was nothing. No notes cards, no Montblanc pen. She took a heated breath, then used both of her hands to flip the wooden desk, which thudded uneventfully into the centre of the room.

'I want her to know we know,' she said, motioning towards the belly-up table. 'I'm going to beat her at her own fucking game.'

Hailey stormed back into our apartment. I followed. In the light I re-read the article, trying to make sense of it, and flashed with hatred for the entire situation. It could have been about any two girls in Berlin. Everyone partied. Everyone posted pictures to Facebook. I took a deep inhale to steady myself, the stenched air made me nauseous. I went to open a window, Hailey followed, slamming it shut, nearly catching my fingers in the frame.

'She can't take my story and turn it against me. I am not *dull*. I'm a fucking genius.' Her angry freckled face was operatically stretched. She had turned a corner that I didn't know existed, she was living in a world I no longer understood, imagined or otherwise. And I no longer cared.

'Hailey, I'm not following you, this is, whatever. Let Beatrice do whatever. You're taking this way too far.' I was shaking my head, while ripping at my cuticles with my index finger.

She glared at me, 'Oh, Zoe – what did they call you? Dumpster? You think you're so cool – and sure, you can abandon me and our story, and start sleeping with *Holiday* – we all know you're just trying to be more interesting.' A look of disgust ran across her face. 'The only interesting thing about you is that you fucked your dead best friend's boyfriend the night of her funeral – honestly, you're lucky Ivy died so you even have a story.'

I wanted to smash her jaw with my laptop and shove the Beatrice interview down her throat. I wanted to kick her teeth in on the edge of the piano bench and ladle her brains out with the wooden spoon. I wanted to suffocate her with Saran wrap and inflict ten thousand episodes of crime-show violence on her taut flesh. Instead, I took another deep breath, and turned to walk out the door, throwing my gnarled cuticles in the air.

'You're a crazy bitch, Hailey,' my voice echoed over the stairs, still littered with empties and cigarette butts.

The air outside was relieving. Bülowstrasse had turned green black. The street lights danced a wild can-can as I weaved my way back to Holiday's. Her roommate Laith answered the door in a Ren & Stimpy T-shirt with a groggy

'Oy'. I crawled into bed with Holiday feeling safe. I told her about Hailey. About how I wanted to kill her for what she'd said and how I was never going back. Holiday purred, half asleep, 'Straight people are mental.'

Sunday morning Holiday cooked butternut squash risotto and we lay in bed alternating between making out and looking through books about the occult. Eventually, she slipped two fingers inside of me, we tried to be quiet because her room-mates were home. But Holiday was never quiet. When it got dark we went to the gay bar, where Oscar did a reading. He stood on top of the concrete bar with one hand outstretched from a metal pole while holding a thin grey book, gently swaying, pausing between beats from his heavy baritone to make a sphinx smile at the audience below. I missed twenty-three calls from Hailey and I didn't care. I wanted to live inside of his poems, inside of that bar, inside of my beer glass.

Holiday and I spent the week in bed. My whole body relaxed. No headaches. No paranoia. On Friday I didn't show up for the *Beatrice* party, instead I popped the battery out my phone and watched Wong Kar-wai movies. Holiday's Israeli roommate Yael helped me dye my hair a toxic shade of blue. I wanted to be new. To shed that dry ravaged skin I had shared with Hailey. I went to the bathroom while Holiday made popcorn, everything in their yellow-tiled room was covered in grime, the mirror glazed in bumpy toothpaste. I stared at myself. My uncombed hair, the freshly minted blue-Medusa. I loved being framed in their filth. Whatever I had with Hailey was over, this was me.

The next morning over puffed quinoa cereal, Yael, who was short and muscly from countless hours of warrior pose, informed me she was going to a meditation retreat for two weeks, and offered me her room. I looked at Holiday who had clearly already discussed this with her, she smiled expectantly.

'Come on, if you're going to be here every day you should at least have some space – Hol's room is what we call the *Besenkammer*.'

'What's that?' I asked Yael.

'Means broom closet.'

It was blissful. I emailed Constance and Sam, telling them I was on vacation. It was almost true. I told Claire I needed to focus on school and wouldn't be able to babysit. Holiday and I watched movies, ate food, fucked, and smoked cigarettes. The days were getting longer. Spring croaking – shoots of green peeking from the hard black earth, birds warbling. I was happy.

But after two weeks, I couldn't help myself. I didn't want to talk to Hailey but I needed to know how they were doing without me. I checked what was posted from the last *Beatrice* party. There was nothing. Not even a page. At first I thought maybe Hailey had rage-deleted it. Holiday explained that if someone or something disappears, it usually means you've been blocked. She had plenty of experience with Irena the ex, who had a convenient way of vanishing and reappearing on mood. I went to Hailey's page, nothing. As if she never existed. I had been shut out from *Beatrice*, and from Hailey. I should have known to expect one of her slow-motion slaps.

On Thursday, a techno label Holiday loved had organised a party at KitKatClub, and she was bouncy. She'd bought us both tickets and matching beers to drink while we waited in line. 'Sex clubs always have the best parties,' she'd said, popping my beer open with a lighter, the pilsner foaming over onto my boots. We sipped and observed the line behind us, leather straps snaked out from under coats, platform heels, fishnet and smears of bright body glitter. When we finally got in, we took off most of our clothes, checking them into a clear plastic bag. My Gap thong had a hole in the crotch but no one seemed to notice my pubic-curl escaping in the cavernous space. The club stretched out for a full city block. We wound our way deeper through a series of small grottos and bars that were hidden in corridors underneath the main dance floor, eventually finding ourselves at the foot of a turquoise swimming pool where slug bodies oozed around the edge.

'Don't swim in there,' Holiday said with a smirk that sounded more like a dare, 'but it would look good with your new hair.' I promised her a body of water in a sex club was not where I wanted to find myself, ever. Jens had told me about a meningitis outbreak there a year ago, which made me shudder.

KitKat was an impossible place to be with Holiday, who was startlingly fast and loved jumping from room to room. In a black-lit alcove she found her favourite ketamine dealer Donnie, who looked like drugs in shag carpet pants and an electric-pink fishnet tank top. We bought a small bag. 'Just enough to dance,' she said, offering it to me from the little indentation at the end of the silver Venus symbol she wore around her neck. When she snorted it, she took off. Tinker Bell on jet-fuel. I scrambled after her shaved head, always just bouncing out of sight.

Soon the floors began to curve and the walls felt soft as a body. I lost Holiday. After wandering around for a while, I sat down, resting my head against a metal guard rail. Time was slippery. I felt sick, the drug had loosened my insides. Clutching my stomach, I got up and pushed my way through the main floors where hundreds of people were dancing to splintering techno, then dragged myself through a bar in the basement. No Holiday. I ducked under two spurting fog machines surrounded by fat bears bumping into each other, their hairy bellies catching my shoulders, still no Holiday. I had to sit, I lowered myself down on a stone staircase. I was going to pass out or shit myself. After a few minutes I got up, and swivelled through a room with loud group sex on hospital stretchers, and finally the lethargic drug pool, where a girl was dipping her foot, watching the indigo ripples. Then on a red pleather bench in the corner, I saw the back of a shaved head – blurry and moving. Her legs were wrapped around another girl, they were making out. Holiday paused, then turned her head in my direction but didn't see me. My stomach cinched.

Should I confront her? Should I just walk over? I felt my asshole dilate. I wanted to die. I could barely wait in line at coat check. I knew I had no choice, I would go to Bülow-strasse. Even in my hollow state it stung to go back – but it was better than collapsing on the street or going to Holiday's. I walked to the train.

From the sidewalk, I could see the apartment was dark, I was too fucked up to hesitate. When I finally pulled myself up the last set of stairs, I quietly slipped my key in and went straight to the bathroom. The cold ceramic rim of the toilet under my thighs was the last thing I remember before everything went black.

I came to stuck inside of a washing machine – everything spinning, sweating, my face pressed against the bathmat. I lifted myself up, the walls still seemed curved and my hands were sticky. My eyes could barely adjust to the bathroom lights, I bent over and splashed water on my face. Feeling a little better I walked out, then caught myself on the door frame of Hailey's room, wetness soaking into my socks. I looked down, red liquid splotched the floor. The drug pool from earlier surfaced in my mind, I must be hallucinating. I flipped the hallway lamp on. I could see that *the door* to the back apartment was open, caution tape was draped like streamers and red balloons bobbed throughout the apartment. What was going on?

Then I saw the giant martini glass in the middle of Hailey's room – and on her bed, under the duvet, one leg dramatically sticking out. Her freckles, her beaded anklet. I knew what she was doing – *the crime-scene-themed night*. That psycho bitch, she must have been decorating for days. I walked through the puddles, pulling a chair to face Hailey's bed. It felt good to sit. The edges of the room were fluttering, as if they could fold in on me at any moment, the train went by sending a strobe of yellow light. Everything felt elastic, I sighed.

I'd been waiting for a chance to confront Hailey, to unpack our fight and the rot between us, but this was not how I had imagined it – then again, maybe it was perfect, her penchant for the theatrical – the stage set of the slain foreign exchange student, sure. I bent down to put my finger in a puddle of red, it was sweet, like the sugar that came in pink packets at diners.

'It's stage blood? Hailey this is so – weird.'

It felt good to finally be talking to her, 'I know we aren't good. And we both said things . . . I just don't really get how this is supposed to make me feel,' I said, looking around, books, papers, all of her clothes dumped out, her computer a smooth stone in a pool of red.

'Do you want an apology?' I paused for her to answer. Nothing. 'I mean. I'm sorry. If that's what you want. I am sorry—'

The room was spinning again, I was tired. Maybe I was already asleep. The train splashed by, the floor lit up again, it could have easily been a dream.

'How are we going to clean this up?' I needed her to answer. 'I know you hate Beatrice but this is a fucking mess.'

She hadn't moved, had she? I couldn't remember. I felt my brain returning, slowly booting up. I needed her to reply.

'Hailey. Come on, this is too much—'

I gave in. I dropped to my knees, releasing a splatter of sugary blood, and crawled to her bed half hoping to snuggle in, half wanting to smack a response out of her. I tore the duvet from her body, her face was white-blue, and there was a series of reddish-brown gashes on her chest. It was different, it smelled metallic, real. It snapped me, I grabbed her shoulders. She was limp, I dropped her back to the bed.

I didn't even know the number to call the police. I remembered the word *hilfe*, staggering out to the steps, I pressed the creaky sound from my mouth. Outside my *hilfe* found an old woman walking her dog, she dialled the police, her fingers shaky while her dachshund tongued the red splatter on my legs. When the street was finally swimming in blue lights, I closed my eyes.

14

The officers were antsy to begin, pacing just outside of the door while a tall, ungainly doctor briefed them on my condition in German. For one week I had been in and out of consciousness. For one week the story unfolded without me, snippets floating by as innocuous soap bubbles of information, while tubes and needles were inserted into my body. The only reason the two detectives were allowed to be present was because the hospital had buckled under the pressure of the police department and approved the visit.

The officers entered my little room, I smiled. Hailey would have loved the young one, he had a swath of thick hair and too many TV-white teeth. He looked at me kindly. I knew instantly he was the good cop, my Olivia Benson. I waited for the 'Dun Dun', signalling the beginning of the episode.

In soft British-style English, Olivia Benson offered me a glass of water in a paper cup. A stocky bald man sauntered behind him, he was the tough cop, my Ice-T, with his ill-fitting button-up and food-stained pants. Ice-T nodded towards me without pleasantry and held up a glossy rectangular photo. The long fluorescent tubes on the hospital ceiling reflected across the image, he adjusted it, Hailey's twisted torso in a valley of blood came into focus. I released an involuntary sputter of soft laughter, which Ice-T noted with the half-turn of his lip towards his partner. I hadn't meant to laugh but there was something so high fashion about Hailey's contorted skinny body in all that liquid crimson, like a Christmas spread in Italian *Vogue*. She would have loved the glamorous image.

'What's funny?'

'Sorry,' I said, snapping into the situation.

'Your friend is dead.'

I nodded solemnly and looked down at the photo again.

'We are trying to put together a timeline of what happened, there are some things that we need help understanding,' Olivia Benson said, moving cautiously to remove a pen, as if not to disturb a frightened animal.

'When did you get home last Thursday?'

'Around 4 a.m.—'

'Why did it take you till 5:15 to call the police?' Ice-T asked.

'Maybe,' I paused, 'I'm wrong? It's all a bit blurry. Maybe it was five.' The officers exchanged looks.

'When was the last time you saw Hailey?'

'A few weeks ago, at the house.'

'And?'

'She seemed fine,' I lied. The last words I'd said to Hailey came rushing back — *crazy bitch*.

'People say they saw you fighting at the last party you attended.' The sternness in his face made my feet go cold, panic creeping. I remembered back to the party, to grabbing her wrist and pulling her into the bathroom, screaming.

'We were just having a conversation.'

'About what?'

'A boy, it was stupid,' I said, trying to end the subject.

'What boy?'

'Mathias Fischer. He works at Volksbühne, in the prop department.'

Olivia Benson made a note.

'On Hailey's phone we found text messages she sent you, reaching back days. You never responded. She seemed upset.'

'I took the battery out of my phone – I told you, I hadn't

seen her for weeks.' The defensive twang in my voice surprised me.

'Did you know about the book?'

'What book?'

'The one she planned on releasing.'

I dug my index finger into my thumb, blood ringing the nail. 'I hadn't talked to her. I have no idea . . .' I trailed off, my mind whirring, 'I was with Holiday Roberson. Hailey had been acting I don't know, weird – I needed to get away from her. You can ask Holiday,' I said with a sour pang, thinking of her mouth locked on that other girl at the club.

'Oh, we did,' Ice-T said smugly. I hated imagining him near her. What had she said? Did she know where I was? Did she care? I assumed the cops must know about the ketamine. I wondered if I should tell them that I had blacked out, that my timeline was a nervous leaking river.

Ice-T motioned back to the photo of Hailey, 'The majority of that was stage blood. Do you have any idea why?'

I remembered the pink-sugar-packet taste. I closed my eyes. I told them about the crime-scene party and her obsession with Amanda Knox and Hailey's plan to fill the martini glass with blood.

'And when you got to the apartment. Were you looking for anything—?'

'What?'

'The apartment was,' he paused, searching for the English word, 'torn apart.'

'Beatrice Becks killed Hailey,' I said.

Ice-T looked at Olivia Benson. 'Can you explain why you think that?'

I patiently explained that Beatrice had been sneaking into the house when we weren't home, using the back apartment to spy on us. That she had been reading Hailey's diary, and Hailey had effectively been writing directly to her. And

Beatrice's next book about us. Olivia Benson and Ice-T exchanged glances, the curl of Ice-T's lip rose again, this time a cresting shark fin. It hit me slowly, as if my reflection was finally coming into focus in a foggy bathroom mirror – I sounded completely crazy.

Ice-T said something in German. Olivia Benson's phone rang, he answered gruffly and walked into the hallway. Ice-T seized the moment, he turned his inflamed face towards me, nearly spitting, 'Hailey thought you were planning to murder her.' He let it sink in, then added, 'Her words, not mine,' throwing a stapled booklet in my direction.

Ice-T motioned to the pages on my lap, 'It's all there.'

He looked out the window, 'And one more thing, the stab pattern on Hailey – is nearly identical to your friend Ivy Noble.'

I felt sick. Was this a joke? I didn't even know Ivy's stab pattern.

I looked down at the pages on my lap, the cover was a scaled-down photocopy of my collage – the one I'd given Hailey, made from the Polaroid shot at the hotel. In large German Gothic font, the title had been written at the top: *HOSTEL STAR by Hailey Mader.*

A beige machine started beeping.

After passing out in the street I had been taken to the hospital and my unconscious body wheeled to a hyperbaric oxygen chamber where I lay on a stretcher receiving pressurised 100% oxygen in rounds of three hours. When I finally came to, I had watched with a helmet of confusion as the nurses and doctors moved like unaware sea creatures through the small circular windows – octopuses and busy squid with clipboards. When I was moved to my hospital room, I was told I was lucky. Lucky that I'd spent time in the past weeks outside of the house avoiding the worst of the effects. Lucky that I'd left the apartment to dial the ambulance. Lucky to have been locked in that hyperbaric submarine.

My blood had tested positive for ketamine, trace amounts of cocaine that I didn't remember doing, and carbon monoxide poisoning. Paranoia is a side-effect of CO poisoning, as are many other forms of mental deterioration, which was all calmly explained to me by a short doctor with a big sunburnt nose three days after arriving at the hospital.

'You see, the pipes and chimney system from your apartment hadn't been cleaned in years and the two of you were living with low-level leakage.'

Everything went silent. I closed my eyes and thought about all the glowing winter fires that had been eroding the fragile passages of our brains. The twists of *New York Times* bursting orange. The mountain of greasy coal in the basement. Our life had been condensed into those black bars, one after the other, the measurement of our friendship. One ton.

'Did you feel strange in the house at any point?' the sunburnt nose asked. Everything had felt strange in the house. I nodded.

'Headaches? Weakness?'

I nodded.

'Hallucinations? Voices? Unusual sounds?' I remembered back to the rumblings, the strange cries, what we had chalked up to the cold creakings of an old building. 'Nausea or vomiting?'

The tempting white toilet bowl at Beatrice's flashed into my eyes. The hours I'd spent facedown, coaxing my pharynx into relief.

The doctor was blabbering, I half listened, 'Hundreds of people die every year from this sort of thing – last winter we had a dinner party of sixteen – the host tried to brew coffee on a coal stove. Two died, and the others were extremely sick.'

I nodded, trying to imagine the dinner party. Had they been like us? In costumes? Posing for cameras? Playing some hideous game? Who was the first person to feel sick? Mrs Peacock in the dining room?

'Proper ventilation is critical,' the doctor was still talking.

All those cold hangovers in that poisoned jewel box, of course we never felt good. Of course we flew through the plastic bottles of pain relievers, temporarily slowing the swell of our choked brains.

I had tried to quiz myself. Who was the president? What year was it? What were the opening lines of *Pride and Prejudice*? I had most of it. But some things had just disappeared. I couldn't remember the address of our apartment, or where I went to school in New York. And names, which I had never been good at, seemed like balloons without strings, just out of grasp. But I knew Hailey had been stabbed fourteen times, just like Ivy. I tried to keep the number out of my thoughts. No matter what I did, it kept popping up, ramming its pointy head against my skull. I inhaled – oxygen – I felt like I would never get enough, then turned towards the packet of pages in my lap.

HOSTEL STAR
The window is pitted with drops. From what Zoe can remember, it's been an endless string of these sort of nights since leaving her small backwater town in Florida. Zoe contemplates herself in the reflection of the darkened window, she is beautiful but no Helen of Troy – she'd be lucky to launch a singular kayak. It's a fact she has known since she was young. She has brown hair, fair skin, and the temperament of a maid; always one to fall into the shadows of a boisterous room. Zoe inhales, turning back to her messy dorm-room desk, and strums out a sad chord. This is not the life she wanted, not at all, but she isn't lost, she just simply wants someone else's.

*She has tried, truly. She watched all the episodes of Sex
and the City, swaying into the downtown bars and ordering
a cosmopolitan, wondering if that's all it would take to
make the confetti of young adulthood start falling. Zoe
often reminded herself that art school is a good place for
the disturbed, and she is, in some ways, feeling more at
home than ever. Yet there is a dark shadow dancing in the
corner of her eye – her best friend.*

*Ivy and Zoe had grown up together, competitive and
fused. The two girls spent their youth walking arm in arm
through the palm trees and perfectly planted tropical
flowers of Sebastian. But Zoe had always been the beta,
eclipsed by the shadow of her blue-ribbon best friend, Ivy.
The prima ballerina who spun her way to first place on
the state stage at age 12, then captured the coveted early
acceptance to the best dance college in the nation at 16.
She was the girl everyone wanted to be. Strong, funny,
beautiful. Couldn't Zoe have just been fine being her best
friend, her closest confidante? Couldn't she have been
happy picking out clothes with her at the mall? Riding
shotgun? Laughing at her jokes? She always had been –
until Jesse.*

It went on and on. My blood boiling, then cooling. It was
brilliant to a point. Hailey had begun by reading all of
Beatrice's twisted books and when there was nothing left,
she'd catalogued the library, so the next step was to write
one. Why not? A perfect little conceptual loop between the
two of them, in which Hailey stretched our lives into faintly
recognisable pulp-trash alongside painfully detailed accounts
of the parties we threw – all with me as the bright sparkling
villain. I sat back in the hospital bed, as every secret I had
whispered to Hailey clanged, an angry bell on the page.

At the funeral Zoe does her best to seem sad, but she knows the truth and she wonders if the others can see it reflected in her pupils. It had only been nine days since she'd ripped her uncle's hunting knife through Ivy's pearly skin, and she has no remorse.

Zoe politely refused to eulogise her best friend, citing shyness, but she knows her guilt would simply be obvious. At the first words of the sermon she tried to cry but it was no use so she settled on a grimace. Inside she is buzzing. She slips from the pew to check her make-up in the bathroom. She knows she is nearing the fateful moment when Jesse will finally look at her – not through her, nor beyond her, but at her. She pats her mousy-brown hair down, practises her sad, dutiful frown and returns to the service, which she finds excruciatingly dull, asking herself: why does everyone always love a dead girl?

Big breaths. Zoe calms herself, she has it all planned out. Now she just has to be patient. Soon enough she'll dye her hair blonde, start wearing Ivy's clothes – and be with Jesse.

Hailey had chopped it all into bizarre pieces, a meta-soup. Mathias, who had meant so little to me, had been cast as my great love. Holiday, who Hailey had no interest in, was absent. I was deranged, and naturally obsessive. The story hinged on our love triangle – Mathias, me and her. What did Hailey want? Drama. That's what she'd told me over and over. I hadn't listened or hadn't cared. But Hailey didn't stop at just describing our contemporary life in Berlin, she had rendered my past in scalding detail farmed from Facebook photos – down to the purple orchid corsages and the thunderstorm that forced our homecoming photos to be taken in Ivy's garage.

Mathias is in love with me, and I with him. I am terrified, as I have the sinking feeling that if I do not act I must come to expect the same end as Ivy. I try to shake the feeling. I go for a run, I fix a salad, I pour myself a glass of dry white wine. I'm usually too anxious to even eat the salad. Mathias comes to me at night, he throws rocks at the window, I quietly open the shutters hoping not to wake Zoe. He stands below beckoning for me to come down for a romp in the snow, I sink down the stairs thinking to myself – she is going to kill me. My roommate is going to kill me just like she killed her best friend Ivy.

The book culminates in a final party at *Beatrice*, in which Hailey performs a reading perched in the giant blood-filled martini glass, red balloons clinging 'suspensefully' to the ceiling and caution tape blowing in the 'uneasy' wind. She had it all planned. And in the big reveal, she informs the crowd that I killed Ivy – and tells the harrowing story of how she averted her own death, by outwitting me. And of course it ended with me locked in prison.

A nurse with frizzy hair, who looked like *Cathy* from the eponymous comic strip, whispered in and took Hailey's book from my hands.

'That is enough.'

I didn't protest. It was.

'If you are feeling strong I will take you to the phone,' the nurse croaked.

I tried moving my legs, then nodded. My muscles still felt weak but I was desperate. My Nokia brick had been confiscated by the police, and I needed to talk to my mom. The nurse helped to heave me into a grey wheelchair and pushed me down the hall to the phone booth.

'Mommy.'

'Sweetheart, I'm so sorry.'

We both sat silently on the line, comforted by each other's breathing. 'How are you feeling?'

'I'm OK—' I lied.

I wanted her to talk about the flowers in her backyard, and know if she'd been to the beach and if the weather was nice and if she'd been to the burger place she liked with the curly fries. I wanted to entirely ignore my reality.

'I'm so – sorry about Hailey. I can't imagine what her parents are going through.' She paused, 'But what she wrote in that book about you is horrific.'

'How do you know what's in her book?' I asked, shocked.

'Honey—' she said too kindly, clearly nervous, 'she mailed them out to newspapers in weird animal-shaped boxes. It's all over the news.'

I let my head fall against the glass of the booth.

'Sweetheart, just take care of yourself, OK? Drink fluids. I'm trying to find a lawyer, but it's very confusing – I'll be there as soon as I can.'

Maybe if I had been left alone to dwell on her betrayal, or even on her death, I could have found forgiveness. I could have at least mourned. I knew Amanda Knox had her prison diaries leaked but at least it had been her voice, her own sad poetry in her own bubbly American handwriting, at least she got to write: MY PRISON DIARY *IL MIO DIARO DEL PRIGIONE*. I wouldn't even know how to say *prison diary* in German. It hadn't taken long for the magazines and newspapers to groggily realise the photocopied books lodged inside the cardboard Noguchi sculptures and surreal animal-shaped boxes were a posthumous gift from the dead girl they'd all been reporting on. I couldn't sleep. How could I shut my brain down? Hailey had framed me.

My mother trying to find a lawyer scared me. Was she just googling *lawyer Germany*? Would they speak English? Could she afford it? Were there public defenders? Did they have the death penalty? I was spiralling. I needed to be proactive. I tried to play through the events. I knew Hailey would have done anything for her *narrative* but I also knew she hadn't meant to end up dead.

I waited till after dinner and lifted myself from the bed, padded down the empty hallway and sank into the glassed-in booth. I began thumbing through the yellow tissue-paper pages of the phone book. The Breitbachs were listed. She was the only one, she had been drunk, but I had told her about Beatrice.

'Hi . . . Claire, it's me, Zoe.'

'Oh my god. Are you OK? Where are you?'

'I'm in the hospital.'

'I can't believe all of this,' she said as if her eyes were glued to a TV and my life was being spliced and montaged as we spoke. 'You're everywhere. It's – bizarre – Hailey – your roommate—'

I wondered if she'd read the book, but didn't want to ask.

'Claire, you're the only person who I told about Beatrice.'

She paused. I could hear her thinking. The girls began shouting in the background, I continued, 'I know Beatrice did this—'

'We can win this,' she cut me off, 'I'm so excited,' her voice exuberant, like a volleyball coach.

Claire showed up two hours later in an electric-orange power suit, holding an iridescent silver briefcase, her hair swept back into a semi-serious half-ponytail so stylish I wondered if she'd stopped at the salon before coming. My own defence Barbie. Her eyes focused on me, 'Sorry it took so long, Savannah and Serena hid my car keys and I ended up in the world's slowest taxi. You have to tell me everything,' she said, leaning in to give me a hug. She was drenched in Chloé Eau de Parfum, which felt somehow comforting, a reminder of female vanity, an idiotic world to which I hoped to return.

I stammered out a *thankyou*.

'Zoe, your hair,' she said, obviously disappointed with my blue dye-job. I had almost forgotten.

'So I've read some excerpts from the book Hailey wrote. I've followed most of the press; what's on TV, and in the newspapers. It's a very flammable situation, legally speaking. I'm glad you called, you need proper representation. Hailey's diary paints a very damning picture.' Claire began clicking around the room, she was jittery, flipping her ponytail, listing off the articles she'd read, her opinions on the journalists, *rotten like everywhere*, the police department, *lazy and under-staffed*, the justice system, *broken and slow*, and all the possible outcomes. 'I'll take you on as my client. Pro bono is illegal here – hilarious, right? We can settle for something very low, but you have to do exactly what I say, OK?'

I nodded, but her buoyancy made me nervous. 'Beatrice did it,' I blurted.

Claire paused, her eyes plunging into my own, searching for something. 'Remember when you told me about this – I told you to gather evidence that she was entering, tell me you listened.'

I shook my head, embarrassed.

She pulled her phone from her opalescent bag, set it to record, then slid her chair in front of the door. 'OK – we let the police find Beatrice. What we need to do is build a defence. You should know German law is different from American. There are no juries, which in your case is good. And there are no plea bargains, and it all moves, well – glacially. This could take years. Jail time is comparably mild, murder will only run you five to fifteen years but – we won't worry about that.'

I sucked in a blip of air.

'Firstly where were you the night of the *incident*, and were there witnesses?'

'I was at KitKat with Holiday—'

Claire raised her right eyebrow, she knew the club. 'Holiday is a person?'

'She's the girl I was – seeing.'

'Not an ideal location but good there were plenty of witnesses.' She looked up from digging through her bag, 'What was your last interaction with Hailey?'

I told her about the fight, about Hailey and Mathias. About missing all her calls. My voice cracking with her last words to me – *you're lucky Ivy died so you even have a story.*

'That bitch, and leading up to that?' she asked, coaxing me like a girlfriend about to order another round of tequila on ladies' night. I tried to think about the other words Hailey had screamed but they were hollow, empty shells.

'And what about Beatrice – were there tangible signs she was entering?'

'There was a stack of papers in a drawer. We popped the lock in February and they were there, and a few weeks ago when we opened it – they were all gone. And her note cards in the back apartment, also disappeared.'

'OK—' Claire pursed her lips.

'And she came to one of the parties, we only found out because she was in a photo – you can't see her face, but it's her. It's on *Purple Magazine*'s website.'

'OK – and when you found Hailey's body, what happened? Take me through it step by step.'

I told her about Holiday. About KitKat. About the train ride home. And then I stopped. I didn't tell her that there was a chunk of time missing. I didn't want to give her, or anyone, a window of doubt. I remembered the curved walls, balancing on the ledge of the tub, sitting on the chair in the puddles of red. But I couldn't remember the actions that linked them together. This was normal, the nurses said. This is the reality of my condition. Disturbances in attention, mood shifts, weakness, inability to retrieve memories.

'CO poisoning is not a concrete science,' a maroon-haired nurse had said as she checked my chart. 'There is still a lot we do not understand. Brain damage can permanently impair your ability to work, your relationships – everything,' she looked up from reading, registering my horror, 'or unlikely, you get better.' I longed for American bullshitting, for the glass half full.

Claire nodded for me to keep going.

'I came home a few weeks after moving in and Beatrice was sitting on the couch. I think she was reading Hailey's diary.' I paused, 'And she was reading emails.'

'How do you know.'

'It's dumb.'

'Tell me.'

'She said something to me, that *an eating disorder was a serious thing.*' Claire frowned.

'I was throwing up. I wrote my friend about it. She had to have read the email. It's the only way she would have known.'

'It's going to be hard to prove that – but bulimia could help bolster a drug-induced-psychosis plea – although that's getting ahead of ourselves. For now, let's get back to the timeline.'

I zoned out while staring at the bright jade beads that clung to her neck on a twist of thick silver. They looked expensive. Probably a gift after one of Tobias's infidelities. I wanted *that* timeline: tennis bracelet for the bartender at King Size, a Mercedes-Benz S-Class for the stripper in Basel, an Oscar de la Renta gown after the stewardess over the Atlantic – or more likely Claire had a contract drawn up demanding a cheque be deposited in her personal bank account for each indiscretion. Claire cleared her throat to get me to return to her questions. I tried to focus but everything seemed wavy.

'When I last saw her, she said she wanted to catch Beatrice.'

'Doing what? What was her and Hailey's relationship? Were they corresponding regularly?'

'Yeah, Hailey did all the emailing about house stuff, but with Janet, Beatrice's mom.'

'We are going to need copies of all the emails that you were included in. What could she have *caught* Beatrice doing?'

'Spying on us?'

Claire began pacing, her white pumps making sucking noises on the hospital floor.

'Zoe, why the theatrics? The fake blood? The Amanda Knox stuff? Sending the diary to all those magazines?'

'Everything Hailey did was a performance for Beatrice. The parties were just a way to make us better characters for the novel.'

'What novel?'

'The one Beatrice was writing about us. We read her interviews and it was obvious it was about us – the book followed two American art students in Berlin. And then in the latest interview, she said the book was going to be called *The Dull and the Dead*, and would make us look – like idiots. Hailey was pissed.'

'Then why would Hailey frame you for her own murder in the diary?'

I blew a jet of air, 'She wanted a better arc – she was just inflating things.' Claire frowned.

'And Beatrice killed Hailey, why?'

'Because she was releasing her book first?' I responded shakily.

'Why? Isn't all press good press?'

I shrugged, 'She did it.'

'And so – then we assume Beatrice used the same stab pattern as Ivy to throw suspicion on to you, Jesus.' Claire's tone shifted volleyball-coach chipper again, 'Well, we will try to keep this from even going to trial. It's a real PR disaster—' She looked down at her phone, 'In my mind, it's very unethical of these news outlets to release it pre-trial. We are going to

246

have to go through it page by page and discuss what is true and what is fiction and set the record straight.' She shut her briefcase and stretched her arms to the ceiling while taking an exaggerated exhale, 'God, it feels good to be back.'

The general consensus in the press was that I had left the sex club – the words sex club were hissed by the reporters like a snake striking, *sssssssex ccclub* – gone to our apartment in a ketamine-induced rage, found Hailey preparing for her book-release party, and stabbed her. It didn't help that everyone had seen us fight weeks earlier, me dragging her by the wrist to the bathroom screaming about Mathias at the party. But it felt good to try to remember that argument, Hailey's insistence on ignoring me while she looked in the mirror. Imagining that moment made me feel like we could still make up. If I could go back and watch her twist open the tube of salmon lipstick and glide it across her stiff frown what would I say to her? I had no idea. I would tell her to open the window.

Hostel Star had its genius. It was a series of tabloid-gumdrop half-truths dipped in cyanide: had I dated my best friend's ex-boyfriend after she died? Yes. Was it wrong of me to sleep with Jesse the night of Ivy's funeral? The world seemed to think so. *Perez Hilton* seemed to think so. Did I dye my hair to look like Ivy? I mean, I did. And mere months later did I wear Hailey's clothes to a party and introduce myself as her? There were Facebook pictures to prove it. Were Hailey and I sleeping with the same man? Apparently. Did Hailey and I have a publicly fraught relationship? Sure. Was I obsessed with her? Did I make collages with photos of Hailey? Yes. Amanda Knox looked like a lightweight.

At Claire's insistence I deleted my Facebook, trying to slow the race to corroborate Hailey's tales with photographic proof, but if I was tagged in an image anyone could still find it. I thought back to the slideshow at Ivy's funeral of all her proudest moments, this was the opposite: me in a bikini smoking a cigarette and giving the middle finger, me dressed as a zebra on Halloween holding a paper-mâché zombie over my head, me with smudged eyeliner drinking from a bottle of vodka. And meanwhile Chelsea Benedict, the cheerleader, whose once-boyfriend, Brock, I'd conveniently also fucked, had finally found her outlet and was busy giving interviews and posting her recipes of equal parts salvation and *I told you so.*

John 3:20
   For everyone who does evil hates the Light, and does not come to the Light for fear that his deeds will be exposed.
   ****Just a morning reminder that all truth comes to light – sometimes we grow up with the dark ones, but we are united against evil, and it's our job as a united community to punish those who work for the devil. We demand justice for ***Ivy
   **** Stay Classy Sebastian and listen to my interview, where I share my thoughts on Zoe Beech and the recent murder of her roommate in Germany: Airing on Wild95.5 this afternoon at 3pm!

It had always been easy enough to prove I had no role in Ivy's death, but still the intense media speculation had warranted the involvement of the Sebastian Police Department, who had sent over an official form for my statement. I was thankful to see the plain English and ugly decorated shield *TO PROTECT AND SERVE* of my birth city on an 8.5 x 11 piece of American paper. My statement of alibi for Ivy Noble: *I was in New York City. I was seen that night at Erica Oh's for the birthday of Jessica Easter.* I had never liked Erica Oh or Jessica Easter, but in that moment, I missed them both deeply. I copied each of the witnesses' names I could remember, in loopy font as if inviting them to my own birthday. The fact that Ivy had been wrapped into this nightmare made me feel like I had radioactive bugs living under my skin. Ivy did not belong in Berlin, in Europe, on newspaper covers or foreign lips.

I tried to hold the real Ivy in my mind, whole and human. She was not the cheerleader in the obituary – pixelated in black and white. She was a world of motion. Sweaty and muscular. An athlete with bandaged feet. A friend who always texted back. A girl with erratic music taste, who'd burned Modest Mouse's 'Float On' twenty-three times to a single CD. I tried to remember our last afternoon sitting together at the froyo place at Union Square – she'd ordered a twist of cake-batter flavour and I'd made fun of her. I was a classicist and ordered plain.

What would have happened if I had never given her that bracelet for Grandma Jane, or encouraged her to go back? What if she'd never slipped the little gold nameplate on her wrist? Never admired it in the window? What if I had told her to focus on finals. I could have saved her.

My release from the hospital was imminent, but I would still be returning for bi-weekly appointments to track my progress. I was suffering from memory loss, and had slowed motor skills from the CO poisoning. I could get better. I could get worse. The fork travelling to my mouth might take less focus in a week, maybe more. My mother arrived, finally. She looked small and lost in the hospital's taupe hallway but I was hit with a thunder-bolt of relief. Moms fix things. I wondered if we could just escape. Take a taxi to the airport and never mention Berlin again. I collapsed into her arms. While embracing she held a clump of my blue hair up and frowned. I told her I was sorry. For everything.

Instead of the airport, we packed into a taxi and drove to the Park Inn, the same hotel where Constance spent New

Year's. From my mom's room on the thirty-second floor the whole city looked fake. Fake tiny people with fake shopping bags, even the pillows seemed fake, too thin and too wide. Once my mom unpacked, she sat down on the bed and I rolled into a ball, my head resting on her lap.

'What happened?' she asked through tears, stroking my forehead.

I had no answer.

'Zo—?' she pleaded.

'I don't know – I don't,' I whispered.

'It's OK—' she said gently, but we both knew that wasn't really true.

I was exhausted and so was she. She slept. I couldn't, I just stared at the ceiling listening to her wet breath rising and falling, I was grateful for my mother, grateful for her seashell-embroidered suitcase and pelican necklace laid out on the bed-side table.

Three days later Olivia Benson and Ice-T came to visit me at the Park Inn. The small room filled up with their foreign man smells: woody aftershave, currywurst, cigarettes, sweat. I was terrified, unsure if they were there to chain me up or let me go home. Claire was late.

'I'm Officer Müller,' Olivia Benson said, extending a courteous hand to my mother.

'And this is Officer Graf,' he said, pointing to Ice-T who was busy on his phone. I hated that they were real now, this was no longer just an episode. They had names.

Graf still wouldn't look up from his phone.

'How are you feeling?' Müller asked kindly.

'She's not answering questions until her lawyer arrives,' my mom said tightly. She was nervously moving back and forth in the swivel chair by the window in a hibiscus-print tunic. Neither she nor the tunic was built for this sort of stress. We sat in silence. The rumblings of an airplane mixed with the gentle squeaking of the chair until Claire flew through the door looking like an NFL commentator in a Mountain Dew-hued pencil skirt and jacket.

'So – we – begin,' Müller said gently. 'We have a few questions but first—' he let the room get quiet before dropping the bomb, 'Hailey's official death has been ruled as carbon monoxide poisoning.'

I looked at Claire and flared with hope. Maybe the stab wounds had been silicone gashes applied with stage glue and Hailey had simply floated off in an accidental toxic cloud – a tragic misunderstanding. Not another Ivy.

'So murder is off?'

Graf snorted, 'She was still stabbed post mortem.'

'Post mortem?' I asked.

Claire shot a silencing look.

'Yes. *Someone* stabbed her dead body fourteen times,' Officer Graf added.

'So murder is off the table?' Claire asked again harder.

'Why would someone—' I muttered.

'This doesn't make sense,' my mom whispered, grabbing my hand.

Müller regained the floor, 'As you well know, the whole house had a problem with the build-up of soot. But the blockage itself in Hailey's coal oven is still *suspect* – tampering is a possibility. Which brings us to our first question, we need to know if she was having any trouble with her furnace. Did she say anything to you?'

'Are you insinuating Zoe had something do with the blockage?' Claire asked.

'Nothing is *off the table*,' Graf said, spitting Claire's words back at her.

'Were you having issues?' Müller asked again. Claire grimaced, then motioned for me to answer.

'The furnaces were annoying but we thought we had the hang of it. So *no*, she didn't say anything to me out of the ordinary.' The reality is she hadn't said much of anything to me over her last weeks. 'Did you find Beatrice?' I asked.

Graf let out a huff, 'Beatrice was seen every morning for the past five months at the Cafe Mozart in Vienna. She has multiple witnesses corroborating her whereabouts for the entire duration of her stay. Beatrice is not a suspect.'

I felt like I'd been hit by a truck.

'But she lied – she said she was at a residency.'

'She *was* in Vienna,' Graf shot.

'What about the apartment in the back?' I asked angrily. The apartment alone seemed like enough to put her away.

'The back apartment was freshly cleaned. We assume by Hailey, as we found it decorated with streamers and balloons.'

Müller jumped in, 'And, Beatrice says she was not aware of the back apartment, or the entrance between the two.'

'That's impossible,' Claire snapped.

'She had to have known—' my mother huffed.

'Beatrice let herself into the apartment on several occasions without permission from Hailey or Zoe,' Claire said, looking to me to speak.

'I came home, around Christmas, and she was on the couch. She took Hailey's diary, she wasn't in Vienna.' I was stuttering. 'Also we found something – there was a stack of papers – we popped the lock on her drawer, it was there, and we checked again and it was gone. She took it. She had to have been in the house.'

'What sort of papers?' Müller looked slightly intrigued.

I was still drawing a big wide blank about what had been folded inside. 'I don't remember.'

The officers exchanged looks. A silence fell, then Graf cleared his throat, 'And, we need to inform you that your prints were the only others found, beside that of the victim, on the knife used to stab Hailey.'

Claire's eyebrows raised, 'Of course they were. Zoe, how many knives were in the apartment?'

'One—' I responded.

'Exactly. You'll have to do better than this.'

Graf scoffed, 'Did you read Hailey's book?'

I nodded and looked to Claire.

'It's a fictional diary written by a mentally unstable young woman suffering from the long-term effects of carbon monoxide poisoning,' she said, moving her hand to my shoulder.

'It's also evidence,' Graf added. 'There were two hundred copies, which are missing, along with the original.'

'So?' Claire asked.

'I'm saying we have a receipt from Trigger Copy Shop, for printing two hundred and fifty copies of her diary. Fifty have been accounted for as having been received by various press agencies. The two hundred we assume, based on her posts, were intended for distributing at her release party on Friday – they are missing. And so is the actual diary. Zoe, do you know where they could be?'

'I have no idea,' I said bitterly. Imagining Hailey hauling two hundred copies of that psychotic book up the apartment stairs to hand out to our friends made me violent. How was it supposed to have played out in her ideal world? Was she expecting a slow clap while she twisted around in a cartoon martini glass reading aloud? What did she think I would do when I found out? Silently take it? Go in a rage? Laugh at her artwork-cum-Becks-book like a big fat joke. 'Beatrice must have dumped the two hundred books, not realising Hailey had already sent out the others. And she probably tore the apartment apart looking for the original,' I said aggressively. It all seemed so obvious to me.

Claire squeezed my shoulder to shut me up.

Graf asked to use the hotel room's tiny glassed-in toilet, we all sat there listening to him piss in loud dribbles. He didn't flush or wash his hands. After he re-emerged Müller informed us they would follow up if they had any more questions. They thanked us and left. My mother disappeared behind the opaque glass and flushed the toilet, then hung her head releasing a silent exhale, her hair seemed to have suddenly turned grey.

Claire took a breath, 'OK – there is a lot to process. This is good. Really. There is no fucking way they will be able to prove foul play with the coal-heater, that's clear. I'll be surprised if this makes it to court as murder. This is worth celebrating.' She paused, 'They will go for corpse mutilation.'

'What?' my mom choked, startling both Claire and me.

Corpse mutilation, the words felt cast in bronze.

'Well, Zoe's prints *are* on the knife.' She took a breath, 'Essentially this is good news.'

'Someone still stabbed that poor girl,' my mom added.

I wanted to correct her. Hailey was not a *poor girl* – she was a monster who had built her stage, nail by nail – but I stayed quiet.

'And Beatrice with a solid alibi, that's complicated,' Claire looked at me, searching for something.

'She did it. Beatrice—' Claire checked her phone. 'You believe me, right?'

'Zoe – my job is to simply create enough doubt.'

My mother threw nervous eyes in my direction, 'But she can't be a *corpse mutilator*, there has to be some way to prove that.'

'The judge, Viktor Hofmann, who has been assigned, he's going to be assessing if this case, and more importantly the evidence, is even worthy of trial – but I know Viktor. Berlin is a small town, judicially speaking, and he was close with

Tobi's father. They knew each other from their Cold War days,' Claire said.

My mother looked anxious for her to get to the point.

'I mean – it's a bit of a Hail Mary but I know Viktor watches Greta Meyer's show religiously. If we are going to shift dialogue, we do it there. *Hail Meyer*,' Claire said. Her phone rang, a mechanical burst of beeps. She silenced it.

'Usually I would stay away from the press at all costs, but this is about proving your sanity and giving our side of the story. Also we need to shake Beatrice out of whatever tree she's hiding in.'

'Corpse mutilation,' I repeated, in shock.

Claire nodded as if she'd just confirmed the time.

'And we need to dye your hair brown, natural, trustworthy, normal – I'll book you an appointment with Udo, the girls love him – he's in the West.' She paused, adding the note to her phone. 'Is what Hailey wrote true? Did you really dye it blonde to look like Ivy?'

I nodded, it wasn't worth rationalising all the versions of myself.

No one wanted to risk getting photographed, so we ordered room service. Lunch arrived. My mother, animated, pulled out place mats and began decanting sandwiches and greasy chips onto paper napkins. As she busied herself, Claire explained that under German law, she, as my attorney, had access to the files of the prosecution, including the witness testimonies. Pulling a slippery piece of paper from her bag, she informed me – after a dramatic pause – that Holiday could not confirm my alibi at the *ssssex club*. Claire took a bite before explaining that Holiday could corroborate my entering the club at 23:45, but insisted she could not remember the time frame of when exactly she had seen me, or when I had left.

I stared out the window at the foggy city. She was out there.

Ordering a falafel. Watching a movie in bed. Did she even care? I had desperately searched only to find her sucking some other girl's face. I knew it was a sex club. I wasn't an idiot, I shouldn't have been shocked. It had been my decision to leave – if I'd just been happy to find her locked in pleasure, maybe even joined in, then I wouldn't be here. We could have all gone home together. The threesome-that-wasn't played out in my mind. Cunts on cunts. In her statement Holiday told the police: *we waited in line, we went in together, we did drugs, we saw each other on and off.* It sounded like a description of our actual relationship.

'Here's the worst part,' Claire said, bringing a napkin to her mouth.

'"Why did Zoe move in with you?" Holiday's response, "*Tension with her roommate, Hailey Mader.*" "Did it ever appear she wished her harm?" Holiday's response, "*Yes, she came home once and said she wanted to kill her.*"'

Claire looked up at me, 'Tell me this is not true.'

'It's a fucking turn of phrase – I was just angry over what Hailey had said. I didn't mean it.'

'It's bad.'

'I know.'

15

After the final autopsy, Hailey's body was sent back to the United States. Her parents couldn't decide where to bury her, so they'd settled on cremation, spreading her ashes in each of the states where she grew up; Rhode Island, Nebraska, Kentucky and Colorado, tiny specks of her being forever marking the trail of the collapsed Biggles empire. I didn't think that's what she would have wanted, but I was also tired of burning things. Tired of watching flames lick at collages, and bodies and bricks of coal. Her parents didn't want to meet me, or hear from me, a request that was relayed to Claire, which I was happy to respect.

It was hard for me to process Hailey. *I was heartbroken.* I had lines I said when I was asked. But the truth was I still sucked on a cherried cigarette of hatred. She had twisted my grief for Ivy, my love for Jesse, into something that was cruel and dark and all for her. It was impossible to unbraid the girl who had written those terrifying things in her diary from the girl who waved me down with a freckled arm at Hauptbahnhof. But Hailey felt like she was still with me, smirking at each little plot development as if every question from Officers Müller and Graf, from the doctors, from my mother, from Claire, were all part of her plan and soon enough she'd waltz out from behind the curtain at the Volksbühne and demand her applause – and we would give it to her like horses galloping over a tin bridge. It would be thunderous. She would take her bow, relishing the stinging fingertips celebrating the world's most important conceptual artist: *Hailey Mader*, who had faked her own death rigging the theatrics of contemporary-media-gore into a plot destined for the silver screen. All of her PR madness working just as planned – each strange wire live, rigging a delicate bomb with an explosive plot.

My mom, despite her constant complaints about money, was stress shopping. She'd discovered the German version of T.J. Maxx, and our small carpeted hotel room was quickly filling up with non-slip baking mats, chunky-knit bathrobes, polar fleece zip-ups, and ugly table cloths. I wasn't sure what future she was preparing for, mine or hers, or maybe she thought we would never leave the little room. We rarely did. We watched hours of daytime TV, sitting silently side by side. And over our meals, which we always ordered in, we talked. I laid it all out, bit by bit – from my first day arriving in Berlin to now, and she swore she believed me. She even wanted to see the photos of the parties and learn everyone's name. She thought *yes* Viola looked like a snob, Constance at the roulette table looked *fun*, and Hailey was clearly *insane* – but she couldn't wrap her mind around why Beatrice would murder her.

I had another check-up at the hospital. I was getting better. But my memory was still deemed *unstable*, and the doctor with the sunburnt nose was concerned for my 'psychological state'. He needed to give a report on my condition to the judge, and wanted to bring in a specialist. I had no choice.

I waited in a sage-coloured room covered in posters of aerial views of the Black Forest with my arms folded. As the minutes dragged on, I began picking at the white lacquer on the arm of the chair. I had never gone to therapy, I was nervous. I knew it was important to seem sane. What did sane people act like? I tried to remember back to BD Wong, who played the psychologist on *Law & Order*. He always knew if the criminals were nuts by asking about their parents. I wondered what I would say about my father – if I answered honestly, that he had another family three states over, and my mother had never let him know I existed – I would certainly seem like a psychopath. I would have to lie.

When the door opened I was hit with a rush of disappointment, Frau Klein was no BD Wong.

She didn't belong on TV. She was flat-faced with loose skin and baggy clothes. She looked at me only briefly before clearing her lungs, asking me how I was feeling. I nodded, saying I was *well*. She cut right to the point, asking me about my relationship with Hailey. I smiled calmly, sane people smiled, sane people had no reason to be nervous. I told her the basics, how Hailey had been my roommate – how I hadn't really known her before Berlin. Frau Klein nodded, scratching in a little notebook with a blue pen. I told her everything. How Beatrice watched us from the back apartment, how she communicated with us through interviews. How she'd read our emails. How it had all been a performance. Hailey's book an artwork. How the note cards with their strange language had disappeared, and the apartment would reek of her perfume. When I was done, I felt relieved, like I'd gone to confession or taken a big shit, she never even asked about my parents.

Back at the hotel Claire let me sift through the witness statements. I released a hiccup of surprise. Viola, before packing up her khakis and escaping Berlin, informed the police that *she* had in fact called *them* on our behalf months ago – the night of the *Purple Magazine* shoot. It had been her. Not Beatrice. I forgot Hailey had taken her off the list. Viola wrote a lengthy tirade on how if the police had simply shut down our parties as she'd demanded none of this would have happened. If only.

I had at least received a direct email from Sam, saying that she needed to keep her distance from 'the situation' as she had already sold her thesis to a publisher and didn't want to, 'emotionally or otherwise', contaminate her research. She hoped I understood her need to 'stay impartial and not take sides.' Her email made me tired with rage, as if the whole thing had been a science experiment and I was just an over-fed lab rodent that had simply taken a left turn in a maze that I couldn't see. Yet another story spun, and Sam had all the real dirt if you paired her time verbally dominating my ex-boyfriend Nate with her detailed notes from running the door at the parties.

I'd even told her about the zucchini.

One early evening, desperate for some air, I agreed to go to a wine bar with my mom. It was only two blocks away. We wore baseball hats and I kept my sunglasses on. None the less, we were unwittingly photographed through the window. The morning's headline read: KILLER ENJOYS VINO WITH MUMMY. Claire had left a blistering voicemail about *optics*, ending in a near scream asking us *how hard is it to just stay in your room?* I imagined Amanda sitting back in her Italian prison releasing a belch of relief – there was some other American girl even more evil than her with more salacious pictures, more incriminating quotes, and an even longer list of ex-lovers.

I was barely sleeping and my face was starting to look severely emaciated. Claire thought it was important to seem healthy, 'not goth', and insisted I wear make-up. I felt clownish. The next morning, over breakfast arranged by my mother on newly purchased floral plates, Claire explained that I wasn't 'naturally sympathetic', and that my mouth tended to fall into a thin frown when I focused, which made me seem 'untrustworthy'. We practised serious smiling. 'You need to seem like you're processing the pain, but not guilty. Sadness not shame,' Claire said, putting down her fork and heading

260

to my closet where she began selecting pieces of clothing she thought were acceptable.

'She seems like she's enjoying this,' my mother said after Claire had left the room.

'What do you mean?' I asked.

'I don't know, like she's happy this happened because it gives her – power.'

I scrunched my face, Claire was all we had.

'I mean she's never represented anyone in Germany, right? Does she know what she's doing? It feels like she's treating this like some sort of pageant.'

Unprepared to entertain another route forward, I slumped and turned up the TV.

At night I trolled the internet for news, surfing the slippery currents of our repurposed photos. One of the tabloid favourites was Hailey and me side by side in our David Bowie suits, my wig matching her lava hair, with captions about *obsession* and *hysteria*. We looked good. Young and glossy. My mom tried to keep me from reading press, but I saw online that *Interview* magazine ended up printing the full transcription of Hailey's unprompted interview. I snuck down to the Alexanderplatz train station and bought a copy and read it in the locked bathroom of the hotel.

GLENN O'BRIEN: What was your first work of art?

HAILEY MADER: My diary.

GO: How old were you?

HM: Twelve.

GO: Did you get good grades in art school?

HM: Yes. I was good at school. I'm good at whatever I decide to do.

GO: *What did you do for fun when you were a teenager?*

HM: *I made movies in my basement.*

GO: *Who was the first artist to influence you?*

HM: *Britney Spears.*

GO: *Do you think the art world is dead?*

HM: *Of course. It's a walking corpse. But walking corpses are more interesting than most people.*

GO: *Who do you think is the world's greatest living artist?*

HM: *Me.*

Curled on the tile I couldn't finish it. She had succeeded, she was an art star. It had cost her everything, but in that moment, my cheek pressed against the cold floor, I knew she would be happy. Happy to have exited this world in such a ferocious ball of fire.

Constance came to the hotel with a greasy plastic bag tucked under her arm, she had been steady. My only real friend. She had even told the police that Hailey had been *losing it*, showing signs of paranoia and hostility in the weeks before her death. She pulled out three cold falafels as my mom readied the napkins, plates and place mats, I sat back and waited for the room to fill with Constance's dumb dating-chatter and fried chickpeas. 'Sharon, here's yours, extra spicy.'

'Thanks, sweetheart.'

'So, Andrea, it sounds like a girl's name, I know. He's Italian, he's the best. Also apparently the worst. And I've been dating him for a few weeks. Well . . . not dating, sleeping with. Sharon, you're cool, I can say that, right?'

My mom nodded, deeply thankful for Andrea, for his girlish name, our current distraction.

'Well, Andrea, he's a writer.' This impresses my mom, she makes a face.

'He sends me books via courier. He's done this three times and it's quite romantic, and the books always have a little inscription.'

She pulls a poetry anthology from her tote bag, cracking it she reads aloud.

'*Dearest Constance, I think you will enjoy "The Lady of Shalott", there is something of you in her pearled crown, hope you are feeling better. Dinner soon xx Andrea.*'

She paused to take a sip of water then let out a dainty burp, 'And it should be known that Lady Shalott is really a depressing poem about a woman stuck in a tower, and he sent this after I was home sick for a week. Anyway, yesterday, he sent me this—'

She pulled out a brand-new copy of *Lolita* and I released a dark snicker, Constance shot me an – *I know right* – look, and handed the book to my mother, who paused to inspect the cover, which depicted a young salivating open mouth with a heart-shaped lollipop resting just inside. Constance read the inscription, '*Dearest Birgit! I was thinking of you while reading this, there is something of you in here. Dinner soon xx Andrea.*'

My mom clasped her hands over her mouth. We all laughed. 'So that's over.'

'Poor Birgit. Do you think she's twelve?'

Constance shrugged.

After Constance left, my mom fell asleep, and my brand-new Nokia buzzed on the table still greasy from lunch. A blinking unknown German number, I recognised his voice instantly. It was Mathias. He was nervous. He talked about the weather, *yes*, Berlin was warming up, *no*, I hadn't been to any of the lakes. He went on to describe how Officers Müller and Graf had questioned him for two hours. He admitted to stealing the jugs of theatre blood at Hailey's request from the state-funded Volksbühne theatre, and Officer Graf made a comment about how, 'It wasn't going to be taken lightly because it was the taxpayers' blood.' Mathias laughed. Then, in a more solemn tone – as if finally getting to the point – he reported that his semen was found in both of our beds, a fact that I had already been informed of by the police. There was a hint of pride in his voice as he explained the cops had given him my new number because he wanted to be *the one to let me know*. I almost laughed when I realised his phone call was a perverted apology. Didn't he know he'd merely been a chorus member in Hailey's lunatic version of *Cabaret*? Or did he think he'd had a leading role? I shuddered, imagining that horrid shade of CSI purple scanning over the intimate surfaces of the apartment illuminating his spunk. He ended the conversation with a joke about staying away from American girls in the future, sneezing. I hung up.

The Greta Meyer interview was the following morning and I knew everything hinged on it. I took a sleeping pill that I found in my mom's plastic make-up bag. It did nothing. Using an anonymous account, I spent the early hours clicking through Facebook photos from the parties. By sunrise my eyes were bloodshot.

As the clock flipped to 8 a.m. Claire came charging through the hotel door, followed by an assistant with a large purple birth mark below his eye. 'The taxi is here, let's go.'

My mom and I put on our coats.

The paparazzi had swarmed outside the hotel. A small army of men with lenses pointed towards the revolving doors greeted us with eerie cheer and an assault of questions, their clicks grammatic ammunition.

'How you feeling, Zoe?' Click-click. 'What really happened to Hailey?' Click-click. 'Zoe you look great, over here.' Click-

click. 'Have you talked to her family.' Click-click-click. 'Have you read her book?' Click-click.

My mother and I ducked our heads, keeping our eyes fixed to the ground. After we tumbled into the taxi, Claire walked up to the wall of flashes, tipping down her black Prada sunglasses, 'Please save your coverage for Greta Meyer later this evening, all your questions will be answered.' She held a tight smile until the van door slid shut.

When the photographers and their phallic instruments faded out of sight, Claire began her monologue. 'I meet with Viktor, the judge, in two days. What we want to do is shift the conversation. He will watch Greta's show tonight, it's very straightforward – you will tell your side of the story, providing a concrete version of events. We need to fight narrative with narrative. Nothing that sounds too paranoid. Simply that you were aware that Beatrice's next book was based on your lives, point to the suggesting evidence – of which there is plenty. And most importantly that Hailey's diary, *Hostel Star*, is a work of fiction and a pre-emptive strike against Beatrice's own. I've made you flash cards with potential answers and approved questions.'

I nodded, accepting the stack of cards.

Q: *How would you describe your relationship to Hailey?*

A: *Loving, friendly, supportive. She could be challenging, but in an exciting way. You never knew what was next . . .*

Q: *What drove Hailey to write her book implicating you in Ivy's death?*

A: *It was a conceptual art piece. Hailey was a gifted storyteller. I assume she was just having fun, creating a work of fiction with our lives, I don't think she imagined it would ever be taken so seriously.*

I rolled my eyes, sliding the stack into my pocket. Claire was convinced the press conference should take place somewhere with *stature*, and the taxi soon pulled up at the Ritz Carlton where she'd organised a suite. We walked towards the spotless glass doors, Claire took a deep inhale, visibly relieved to be breathing the Ritz's oxygen.

'The make-up artist will be here in twenty. So let's get upstairs and changed.'

The concierge ushered us into a carpeted elevator and we silently rose through the building until the doors opened on a gallery-white wall with seven abstract canvases framed by thick curtains and two leather-upholstered armchairs. I ran my fingers along the bronze sculpture that led into the sitting room.

'Don't touch that,' my mom softly snapped.

Everything in the room felt as if made by some other species with access to superior materials. The birthmarked assistant, once alone with me in the bedroom, introduced himself as, 'Josef, and I totally believe you.' He pulled jumbles of fabric from bulbous garment bags, which were tropical explosions, bright and colourful – just like Claire. I smiled at Josef's resounding belief but it did nothing to buoy my nerves.

'Oh fantastic. Zoe, I'd like to see you in that number,' Claire called, motioning towards a two-piece suit that looked as though it should come with matching butterfly wings.

'You don't think this is over the top—' I asked, nervously pinching the stiff sleeves. I had a flashback to prepping for the parties with Hailey, her bossy tone – *wear the gold dress.*

'We are trying to shift your public image. We have hundreds of goth-drugged-out Facebook photos to compete with.'

'It's pink . . .' I muttered, which seemed an obviously inappropriate colour. 'It's a loud nude.'

I grimaced and began to change. The pants fit, but the jacket was tight and itchy, covered in tiny feathers that danced about the structured shoulders. Claire was nodding approvingly when she put her hand on her ear to signal Bluetooth, I zoned out into the mirror trying to make my face look more sympathetic, I looked tired. I tried pushing my bottom lip out and dropping my chin, I shuddered, a not-quite-full-grown JonBenét Ramsey.

Kora the make-up artist arrived with a suitcase of slimy product and began to prod my face with a sponge.

'Are you sure this is a good idea?' my mom asked Claire, motioning to my pink outfit, but I knew she was also referring to whatever was about to happen next live on camera. 'Maybe she's not ready for this?'

Claire looked at me, 'Zoe, do you feel prepared?'

I shrugged towards my mom from underneath a powder brush, too exhausted to argue. I never understood the kids in college who could stay out all night and show up to class forming complete sentences. I needed sleep or my brain didn't function. I checked the clock, it was 8:45 a.m., and I couldn't remember the last hour of sleep I'd had in two days. 'Look, Sharon, I appreciate your concern but Greta is the German Diane Sawyer. She's a heavy hitter with a light touch and she's on our side – people need to see that Zoe is trustworthy. Not the monster Hailey made her out to be.'

My mom was about to say something but let it go and walked off.

The hotel room soon filled with white light from the TV crew, Claire was tweaking the angle of the sofa, my mother receded into a nook near a dragonfly Tiffany lamp.

'Sit there and we'll test the shadows. Remember to seem assertive but not aggressive, don't forget your chin,' Claire said, checking my image in the screen. I felt anything but assertive. I tried dipping my face. I was searching for a Mona

Lisa smile, wondering why all the great art history smiles connoted secrets, when Greta Meyer entered the room. All eyes snapped to her.

She looked like the human embodiment of education and enlightenment, a tiny towering Athena, I straightened my spine. She smiled.

'Hello, Zoe, I'm Greta.'

'Hi, Greta—' I responded, trying to seem more alert than I was.

Claire shot in, extending her hand, 'And I'm Claire Breitbach, her lawyer.'

Greta and Claire discussed the questions while I lay on the bed in the adjoining room, blearily flipping through flash cards above my head.

Q: If you could say anything now to Hailey what would it be?

A: I would tell her I loved her.

Eventually we took our seats in the living room, Greta sat on a tweed scalloped couch, me in a leather armchair. The lens tensed into my face, we began. She introduced me, I pushed my lips out, sympathetically nodding, chin down.

'The world has read *Hostel Star*, released posthumously, by Hailey Mader – your roommate,' she tossed a sympathetic nod in my direction, '– and friend.'

I nodded back. She continued, 'The story itself, is complex. Essentially rendering a disturbing portrait of your relationship, but it is clear Hailey took some liberties with your portrayal; for instance, it can easily be proven that you had nothing to do with the death of your close friend Ivy Noble, in Sebastian, Florida, in May of last year, which is of course what Hailey bases most of the book around.'

'Yes, I was in New York at the time of her murder – and I was devastated, I went back for the funeral.'

I could see Claire nodding along, I was doing well.

'But in her odd blending of fact and fiction, there are of course some truths. This is a bit uncomfortable, but you did begin dating Ivy's ex-boyfriend directly after the funeral.'

I gulped, 'Yes.'

'And you did seem to alter your image, to reflect that of Ivy's, which we know from many photos, such as this one, just as Hailey details in her diary.'

A photo of Jesse and myself perched on the hood of his car somewhere in Nebraska popped up on the playback screen to my right. Jesse smiling, running his hands though my blonde hair, the thumb of the gas station attendant who'd taken the picture clouding the top right corner.

'The story has captivated the globe – but it's also the photographs of the parties you threw here, in Berlin. The excess of the young foreigners, the drugs, the drinking—'

'Yes, well, we were throwing weekly events. It really wasn't *excessive*. It was in response to Beatrice Becks, whom we were renting our apartment from – she was watching us, and we wanted to perform, for her, as we understood her next book was about us—'

A photo of Beatrice's apartment swarmed with twenty-somethings snapped onto the playback screen just above the live feed of the camera pointed at me. I looked at the small, live version of myself in the 'loud nude' suit bobbing just below the photo. My face looked demented. Greta lobbed another question. I didn't hear it, I was lost in thought staring at my mouth. Panic crept across my face, she repeated herself.

'I think what we all want to know, is what drove Hailey to write this diary?'

I couldn't take my eyes off the playback screen, watching my mouth move, as if a hand had been inserted up my ass and I was now a puppet with no cognitive system of my own. I tried to explain, lips flapping. It seemed impossible.

'Beatrice was watching us, she was there – if you read an interview with her she mentions her next book was – uh—'

Was I talking in a Southern drawl? My mind began to run. An image of *Sesame Street* with adults hidden under tables and behind fake trees animating those bizarre soft creatures. Who was animating me? Greta asked next what happened the night I found Hailey. I tried to think back to Claire's flash cards – nothing. Was this an approved question? So many people had animated me. So many people's hands jammed up my own ass.

'What was your mental state.'

'How did it feel?'

Greta was like a can-opener, my puppet mind, full of fuzz, spilling out answers. But all I could think about was how Hailey had set this up – it was her hand in my mouth, her body concealed behind the couch. And now no one would fucking believe me. Why had she done this? I was just a character in her narrative, an obtuse felted version of myself with button eyes, forced to defend myself to everyone.

'Hailey got what she wanted,' I choked aggressively. The camera man panned back to me. As the shaft of the camera zoomed in I panicked, picking up my water glass and throwing it at the lens.

16

On camera, I had what was described as *a psychological break*. The judge, and the doctors, and Frau Klein, who already suspected I suffered from some sort of paranoid-narcissistic disorder, all decided it would be best to commit me to an institution while the trial dragged on.

'It could be years,' Claire had said heavily as she teetered down a jagged hallway in the brick courthouse. I nodded, having heard the jokes about German bureaucracy, imagining my paperwork floating from office to office like scum in dead water. Both Claire and I knew there wasn't much she could do for me after my having said, on live TV, that Hailey had *gotten what she wanted*. My mother, who couldn't afford to stay in the country indefinitely was, of course, devastated, she thought I should be returned home – but I assured her, being institutionalised in Germany was probably better, less cult-ish, less Christian than Florida. I told her it would be *just like a spa*. So that's what we called it.

Constance had been promoted from intern to paid assistant and spent the summer in Berlin working at the gallery. She'd kept busy with her *lovers* and photography and visiting The Spa, updating me on whatever the nurses and Frau Klein weren't willing to tell me. She was honest. She didn't treat me like I was psychotic, happily listening to my theories and sharing her own, but she had a return ticket to Montreal. I waited patiently in the common area, trying to ignore the moving shapes around me.

I normally avoided the shared spaces, preferring the comfort of my room or innocuous corners where it was easier to imagine I was somewhere else. Visitation days at The Spa were the worst, they crackled with outbursts. Most were parents and siblings who only saw what their child or sister no longer was – tears flowing before, during, and after visits, the nurses scurrying to bridle the chaos while the parents gawked.

Constance walked into the common room wearing her signature black sweater, her hair in a loose bun held up by a pencil, eraser pointing due north, carrying an armful of books, which she dropped on the plastic table in front of me. I recognised a few of the battered covers. Some, including *Medea,* had been nabbed from Beatrice's library. And several, I knew, would have inscriptions from Andrea the Italian ex-*lover.* I cracked *Sentimental Education,* and sure enough, in a self-conscious boy handwriting – *Dearest Constance, here is a little Flaubert to wet your palate. Shall we try Paris Bar later this week?*

We exchanged laughs.

'I have too much shit to bring with me, I hope you don't mind,' Constance said, re-stacking the books, adjusting herself in an armchair that was both the shape and colour of an overcooked carrot.

Most of the furniture in The Spa had the texture and hue of a boiled vegetable. One of the girls told me the whole place was like what Berlin looked like before the Wall came down.

'So, what sort of work are you making in the darkroom?' I asked, envious of Constance's impending return to Montreal, a life of two-for-one drinks and shopping for art supplies.

She looked at her chipped purple fingernails while she spoke, 'I've actually decided to switch majors.'

'Oh,' I said, surprised.

'I want to be a lawyer.'

'You don't want to be an artist any more?'

'I literally spent part of my summer boiling cough drops in the back of the gallery to make drugs for one of the artists, and after all this,' she waved around the room, 'I think I'm good . . .'

I laughed, then thought about it for a second. 'You will make an excellent lawyer.'

'Also, look at this,' Constance pulled a cracked BlackBerry from her quilted bag. 'It's Beatrice on a morning show. It's really weird. Do you think you can handle it?'

'Yes. Show it to me.'

I could feel my temperature rising, Beatrice had kept a low profile since Hailey's death, not taking interviews, not even releasing a statement. But on her last visit Constance had informed me that Beatrice's new book tour had been announced. Constance tilted her head towards mine, turning the volume down so as not to attract attention from the blue-smocked nurses guarding the exit.

Beatrice was sitting in a tall director-style chair on a news-room set, her black helmet hair shiny under the lights, lips blood red, her nose powdered to near absence and her ankles lightly crossed like the Queen of England. The anchor, a sturdy woman with a tight ponytail and a wide sympathetic face perfect for processing the pain of others, sat to her right.

'Welcome, Beatrice Becks.'

The audience clapped. Beatrice nodded, her well-powdered reserve melting away as soon as she opened her mouth, 'Thank you for having me here today, I'll make this brief – I would like to take this moment to announce that I will not be releasing my forthcoming book, out of respect for the Mader family.'

The ponytail frowned, 'Beatrice, that comes as a complete surprise.' She pulled a piece of paper from behind her chair and waved it at the camera, 'We received this press release from your publisher just this morning, saying quite the opposite.'

273

Beatrice looked off set, took a breath, then pursed her lips, 'I have decided, *today*, to permanently cease publication of anything related to the case of Zoe Beech and Hailey Mader.'

The anchor nodded with a look of astonishment, then tapped her finger on the desk as if speaking some off-camera language, a photo popped up of a white book cover adorned in arched neon-pink lettering, spelling out: *Blood-Sex-Death-Berlin*.

'So, you're telling us that *Blood-Sex-Death-Berlin* – the book that even just five minutes ago you were in the process of promoting – is no longer going to be released.'

Beatrice nodded, asserting herself. The ponytail turned her attention to the paper in front of her, 'Your publisher claims it's *the book of the century*, and we won't ever get to read it? *A tragic, and true tale, set in my own living room, my side of the infamous—*'

Beatrice cut her off, 'Like I said, I will not be releasing it out of respect for the Mader family.'

In an effort to save the interview, the ponytail shifted to a serious tone, 'OK then, let's talk about what brought you to that decision this morning, of all mornings? Have you spoken with the Mader family?'

'I've said everything I need to say.' Beatrice stood and removed her lapel mic then exited the frame. The anchor did her best to wrap up the segment before a cut to commercial.

Constance silenced and pocketed her phone. I sat up in my egg-yolk beanbag, 'Why?'

'Well, the weird thing is, the publisher issued a statement the next day saying that they *would* release it. She must be contractually obligated, but now it's delayed.'

'Why would she change her mind?'

Constance shrugged, 'Maybe she discovered a shred of decency?'

'Doubt it.'

We both sat in silence, 'I'm sorry to do this, but I have to go soon and I hate goodbyes.'

'Will you write me?' I asked, pathetically.

'Of course.'

We hugged. I sank back into the beanbag and watched as she walked down the hall, her black bun bobbing out of sight in the rectangular window of the security door. She was gone. In the vacancy of that moment, the volume turned up. This was no spa. I had been trying to normalise the sounds – the freak-outs, the twitchers and scratchers and yellers – but now they were all around me, a choir of the disturbed, my crescendo.

What was Beatrice doing? It was too late for decency. And why now, after murdering Hailey for the story? Beatrice was ruthless, she didn't care about the Mader family. It had to be a game. Maybe for more press. But why? In a dull rage I knocked over the stack of books Constance had left on the table. A nurse scolded me and I dropped to my knees to pick them up. I noticed an index card had fluttered from *Medea*, the same type that had been on the desk in the hidden apartment covered in strange symbols. I hungrily picked it up, desperate for an answer – but the card was blank, its thin turquoise lines pulsating like guitar strings waiting to be strummed.

I walked to Frau Klein's office for my therapy hour. What my rehabilitation at 'The Spa' was supposed to look like I wasn't sure. There appeared to be no real plan. Frau Klein told me over and over that I was there to *get better*. From what? Hailey was gone. Ivy was gone. I couldn't talk them back into being. The physical therapy and memory exercises I understood. I could do that. But sitting with Frau Klein in her oatmeal-coloured room with grey carpet and plants in bumfuck Brandenburg seemed grotesque. Whenever she became bored, or rather, tired of hearing my detailed explanations about how Beatrice had been spying on us, Frau Klein would lift her potato-sack frame and pick up a silver jug with a long spout and begin slowly watering the green stalks. Each plant felt selected for a specific pseudo-therapeutic reason, as if some garden guru told her the slick monstera plant in the corner had a calming effect on alcoholic depressives.

Frau Klein wanted to pick up where our last session had left off, and continue talking about my relationship with Hailey. I was having trouble focusing, the interview Constance had showed me looping behind my eyes.

'Zoe, are you listening?'

I nodded.

'We see this often in people who have not fully embraced their sexuality – there can be a type of,' she paused, her lips disappearing like Ms Potato Head mid-makeover, 'there can be a form of transference, within friendships of the secretly desired sex,' she exhaled, lips returning.

Frau Klein noted my eye roll in her notebook. She was wearing a burlap dress over a white turtleneck, I found her interest in my sex life predictable as she clearly had none of her own. My gayness – whatever that meant – had been publicly dissected as part of the hysteria around Hailey, but the reality was I had hardly even begun to understand it myself, and I was in no mood to unpack it with Frau Klein.

'Your relationship to Ivy, and to Hailey, from what you have told me – they both bear markings of obsessive and absorptive behaviours. Do you recognise that?'

I shrugged. I knew she wasn't completely wrong. I'd even moulded myself into a blue-haired nymph for Holiday, but there was no reason to add another transformation to Frau Klein's deck. She already thought I was loony enough to stab the corpse of my best friend fourteen times. Cuckoo enough to believe that Beatrice had been watching us, and far enough gone to complain about the smell of lilies – Beatrice's perfume – in the hallways of the The Spa, which triggered my now-regular panic attacks, confirming Frau Klein's belief that I should indeed be taking anti-psychotics. No matter what I said, Ms Klein thought I had stabbed Hailey's body out of repressed rage for Ivy's murder. *PTSD: rage within trauma*. She loved those words, cooing them like the bridge of a soft rock ballad.

I returned to my room irked and was greeted by the stack of books Constance had brought. Reading was the only activity I enjoyed, but it felt wrong to have something of Beatrice's in my room. I poked at *Medea* with my index finger and debated shredding it. *Beatrice*. What was she doing? If she wasn't releasing *Blood-Sex-Death-Berlin*? Was she no longer writing? I suddenly realised I'd missed a piece of the puzzle. I had never read anything written by Beatrice. Hailey had spent all those nights consumed on the smirking couch, the thriller-suspense-romances had been the bridge between the two of them. Two days later Frau Klein agreed, saying, 'the only way out is through,' nodding, that Beatrice's books could be part of a path to recovery, 'to transcend my' – and fuck her for this – 'swelling paranoia.' The reality was I had no interest in my recovery, I wanted to understand Beatrice's voice so I could understand what happened inside of Hailey's head. Frau Klein made the order.

A week later a box arrived, filled with the same bright spines that had lined the shelves of Beatrice's apartment, the strips of colour had only been abstractions to me, a backdrop to a horrible year. I took a moment to stare at the choppy rows of tangerine, red, baby blue, gum-ball pink, all set with the same embossed font. Impressed with the sheer volume of her writing, I pulled a strawberry spine out: *Roses for my Dead*. Why not? The story was set in California and each time the state name was printed I imagined Beatrice's mouthy pronunciations of *Calii-fourn-nia*, how it wrung with an elegance I had no taste for.

Roses for my Dead spun a gory and glittery portrait of

Lila DeFranc, a '70s movie star who murders critics who write negative reviews of her films. Lila is smart and cunning and eats lots of salad and drinks an inordinate amount of dry chardonnay, which made Hailey's own prose start to make more sense. Lila naturally seduces the detective on her case, eluding capture, but – in a dark turn – gives an insecure soliloquy to her own bathroom mirror and thus Lila DeFranc decides as her final act she must kill herself.

I pulled the next book out, titled *Breathing Bottles*. Set in the late '90s, on a vineyard in *Calii-fourn-nia*, the book follows a young vintner from an old wine-making family named Bryce who falls in love with Lander, the darling daughter of his rival vineyard. It was a fairly cheap rendition of *Romeo and Juliet* with a twist of a jealous ex-lover-cum-soil-scientist, ending with Lander and Bryce dead and both family vineyards barren. The books were like Girl Scout Cookies, calorically vacant but disturbingly addictive. I cracked the next spine: *Closed Blinds*.

I read six of Beatrice's books in under four days. Next up was *On Blue Peak*, the famous one. The first-person voice of Frannie the young girl from the Blue Ridge Mountains is so loud and sharp it felt like she was in the room with me. The story begins when Daniel Dupree, a rich young man from North Carolina, falls in love with Frannie Colins. Frannie is only seventeen, she hesitates, but they soon get married and decide to move to New York City. Frannie is a Southern belle, frank and good-humoured, who charms the frigid Northerners with her honey-syrup storytelling and ends up writing a column for a famous New York magazine. Half the book is her penning and editing essays for her column and the other half is her describing how she feels as if she is losing touch with her husband. Then one night Frannie comes home and finds her husband Daniel sleeping with his best friend Hank. Frannie, in a fit of rage, pulls a gun on Hank but her pistol misfires and she kills her husband. Frannie goes mad and is put in a sanitarium where she continues to write, filled with remorse and guilt, but also sharp witty love. I devoured the rest of her formulaic murder-romance stories and they were addictive and dumb – none of the characters had the cut or humanity of Frannie in *On Blue Peak*.

I wasn't in the mood for therapy, I was about to get my period and it was schnitzel night, which I hated, but mostly I was annoyed that Beatrice's books hadn't revealed any underground tunnel between her and Hailey. Frau Klein was disappointed the books hadn't given me a sense of *closure*.

'Were you able to see the books as fiction?'

I shrugged.

'I'm curious, because we've discussed this slippage before.'

There was no point with her, I leaned back on the couch and refused to answer any more questions.

I went to dinner feeling lost, the smell of grease was thick. I took my favoured place at the corner table nearest the bank of windows, which were always closed and provided no relief from the scent of hammered pork that would soon fuse to my scalp only to be removed with a scalding shower the following morning. The food was usually brown or beige with brown or beige sauce, but the evening's schnitzel stood out in a nicotine-hued umber with greenish gravy, I ate slowly.

I had made a conscious decision not to learn the name of any of the other women at The Spa, living instead in chosen isolation. However, there was a new girl, with wild bleach-blonde hair and pillowy lips, eating at the other end of the bank of windows. I'd seen her a few times as she shuffled around, shoulders slumped, gnocchi pout pushed out. She, like me, was quiet with no visible outbursts. I dubbed her Scarlett Johansson and pretended we were both starting our freshman year at Oxford, both new to a foreign country so we'd simply chosen not to speak to anyone – just trying to make the Dean's List and be home for Christmas ham.

After my silent dinner, back in bed, I stared at the ceiling trying to remember the moulding at Beatrice's house. I missed drinking. I missed talking with friends, the late nights, snorting things, fucking people. Then as if a slide in the darkened room of art history class, the bright-red image of Hailey's body in a room of fake blood flashed. I sat up, I needed a distraction. I rifled through my shelf, pulling out the thin paperback of *A Room of One's Own,* by Virginia Woolf. The book had arrived two weeks ago with some of my other school things that my mom had packed up in a desperate attempt to normalise my time.

The book's lemon-yellow sticker from The Strand glared back at me, a reminder of the doe-eyed art student whose biggest fear was being laughed at by a group of sculpture-dicks. I scanned the first page, unable to remember what class I had ordered it for, maybe the feminist seminar I'd dropped. I read the introduction, explaining the book was based on a lecture Woolf gave when asked to talk on the subject of women in fiction.

The title 'women and fiction' might mean, and you may have meant it to mean women and the fiction they write; or it might mean women and fiction that is written about them; or it might mean that somehow all three are inextricably mixed together . . .

I kept reading. Woolf was angry. Angry at being shut out of the great libraries, angry for the difficult centuries all her sisters had faced, unable to afford a moment of quiet to write, unable to feed upon the knowledge that was readily available for men and angry at the scholarly disdain for their voices when they did manage to use them. Woolf described Charlotte

Brontë's longing through Jane Eyre to experience the world beyond her roof, to the cities, and people and stories that lay just outside of reach of women of her period. How Jane Austen, relying on a rusty door hinge, hid her writing from whomever entered her parlour, allowing interruptions to punctuate her process. And how if Shakespeare had had a sister just as talented as he, should she attempt to follow her desire for theatre, she would have been kicked out of her home, raped by an actor, impregnated, and eventually, out of desperation, taken her own life.

> All I could do was offer to you an opinion on one minor point – a woman must have money and a room of her own if she is to write fiction; and that, as you will see, leaves the great problem of the true nature of woman and the true nature of fiction unsolved.

I put the book down. Unlike Brontë, I had gone abroad. I was the foreign-exchange student for whom every corner of the earth had been open and I still ended up here, gagged. And I may have experienced the world but the world had also experienced me, whatever had transpired in the past year and a half had been severely public – everyone had their version. I tried to imagine what Amanda Knox would have to do, what lengths it would take for her to reclaim her own story. How long would she have to wait till the dust had settled on the hundreds of bizarre versions for her to tell her own? Would anyone believe her? She was a better demon than saint, and so was I.

I took a deep breath, floating back into Woolf's anger, a jacuzzi of spite where I felt at home. I read on. A few minutes later I burst out laughing, realising that, in fact, I had the support of the German State. I had a room of my own and I didn't need to worry about cooking or cleaning or the rearing of squawking children. Not only was I free to write, I had been involuntarily bound to fiction through the bright kaleidoscope of insanity. Any words I wrote would be the dribble of a ravaged brain, clinically dismissed – so be it, that was my answer to the question of women and fiction. I slid from my bed and looked for a pen.

17

On Monday, the smell of lilies was so foul and so bright in the L-shaped hallway leading to the cafeteria, I snapped. The scent, which seemed to be radiating from the freshly cleaned floors, sped up my usual slideshow of Hailey and the year's horrors into a terrifying blur, I needed air. I ripped at the handle of the window nearest me, though I knew, even at the height of summer, they remained locked. The lily smell began itching at my lungs like loose fibreglass as my mind swam backwards. Hailey's eyes flashed across my own, images of Beatrice's apartment – the parties, Hailey in her pyjamas, Hailey on the smirking couch, hunched over her desk, surrounded by a puddles of blood. I needed it to stop. Desperate for oxygen, I picked up a baby-shit-brown plastic chair with metal legs, and began banging it against the window. Despite repeated blows, the glass remained un-bothered and I began shrieking. A fat nurse with neck acne lunged from the cafeteria, grabbing me by the shoulders, trying to drag me away. I punched her square in the beak, she fell, and I went back to banging the chair. It was logged as a suicide attempt. Frau Klein upped my anti-psychotics and I was locked in my room on *watch* for the remainder of the week, meals delivered, pens and other sharp objects removed.

Whatever lint-coloured pills I was now taking made me too loopy to write, and without a pen I couldn't do much anyway. I stared at the stack of pages on my desk. Over the last weeks I'd written two hundred and in the process things came back to me, pot-holes from the year smoothed – but I still didn't have an ending.

In my stoned haze I often envisioned what Klaus Simons' class of fifteen would say if they were circled around me in my miniature room, excavating the meaning in the positioning of objects: the haphazard stack of books and my messy hamper. The Russian girl would think it was sad. The swan would suggest I read Sylvia Plath's *The Bell Jar*. Someone would probably tell me I should keep going, and Klaus Simons would suggest everything could be bigger and this time I would agree.

I wasn't completely without company in my daydreams. Even on *watch* I still received mail. Most of it, I assumed due to the lack of English spoken in the mailroom, was handed over without censoring – marriage proposals from men, and a few women, letters from satanic groups and angry church-going Midwesterners. The nurses checked the packages for weapons and contraband, without care to what might be emotionally triggering, but I was generally grateful for the entertainment – even the postcard of the Statue of Liberty from Carol Gaynor, my guidance counsellor: *Hope you get well soon and enjoy Berlin!*

It was barely September, still the dog days of summer, so I knew someone had to be *enjoying Berlin*. There were lakes outside of the city, Mathias had talked about them. And before she'd left, one of Constance's *lovers* had driven her out to Liepnitzsee, only thirty minutes from The Spa. I could hardly imagine; people on rafts, floating around, blaring techno and doing drugs in the sun. To me, Berlin was supposed to be cold and grey, the partying hidden so deep underground it formed its own nebulous body. I wondered if Holiday was out there on a raft. She would probably refuse to wear a swimsuit and it pained me to imagine her gumdrop nipples burning just minutes away. I told myself it was fine, I had no interest in witnessing bare legs littering the sand, I wanted Berlin to stay frozen. Calcified in darkness. And luckily, even with the farmland churning green outside, the walls of The Spa seemed to absorb all colour, dampening whatever stray beams slithered in.

My door remained locked except when the nurses checked on me, roughly every three hours. Despite my chair-dance-routine with the window, due to my relative good behaviour, I was considered low risk. When I wasn't smashed out of my mind on anti-psychotics, I tried to style myself into what I felt were 'non-nuts' poses for these visits: propped in bed reading a book, studiously at my desk, doing yoga, but if I was narcotised – I did not give a fuck.

The following day, I was indeed blitzed. I tried to masturbate, not caring who saw. No matter how hard I rubbed my clit I never came, I wondered if Scarlett Johansson was also mastur-bating in her room. I blearily fantasised about fucking her in the cafeteria, pressing her pool-toy lips against the bank of windows, slamming my weight into hers until we broke the glass, escaping on a bed of clouds and cum – but I still couldn't.

Wednesday morning I was woken by a gentle knock on the door, I barely registered. My consciousness had been hiber-nating, a crippled crab on the bottom of my drug lake. I nodded blankly towards the nurse delivering breakfast, who smelled of talc and hairspray and handed me the morning's limp cheese sandwich. Before leaving she disappeared below her plastic-wheeled cart, returning with a beat-up cardboard package in the shape of a cat. I thanked her, and she wheeled off. I sat thunderstruck by the object in my lap.

The cat, surprisingly heavy, was a zombie piñata covered in customs stickers and choked in black and white *Zollamt* tape. My mother's address in Florida, where it clearly had never arrived, was legible in Hailey's handwriting – and according to the layered labels, the package had been returned to Beatrice's house where no one claimed it, then forwarded to *The Spa*. The nearly decapitated animal had been inspected by customs, then searched for contraband by the nurses – but there it was, in one piece, the same feline that had been stuffed with Jolly Ranchers and Starbursts. I took a deep reverent breath.

I placed the mass on the desk and sat on my bed. My head was pounding. I tried to fight the ethereal dumbness of the drugs, forcing myself to stay present, move slowly, to think of myself like Molly Webster the bulimic veterinarian with her painted fingernails and surgeon's patience. I began dissecting the beast. First removing several layers of tissue paper from the head that had already been opened and taped back on by customs. I moved forward with the assumption that everything I pulled from the cardboard body was important. A possible clue. Dozens of *New York Times* clippings from before Hailey had died were scrunched in balls. I carefully unfolded each. Obama. Bear Sterns Bailout. Suicide bomber at a Marriott Hotel in Islamabad. Large Hadron Collider. There was something heavy at the bottom, Hailey's leather diary fell out – my collage glued to the front.

I sat on my bed with the red object, it felt heavier than when I'd bought it at the flea market, maybe the added ink, or maybe the damage it had done. I took a breath then opened it, turning over the smooth pages, ridged with her handwriting, reading a few sentences, it appeared, page-for-page what had already been published – Hailey's demented version of our lives. I flipped to the back, there was a note scrawled on the inside paper of the cover and pasted across from it, rippled from glue, was *the last photo of 2008*. Our party-girl smiles wet with anticipation, arms wrapped around each other, legs forever kicked towards that brand new year. Underneath she'd scrawled, *The best thing about a picture is that it never changes, even when the people in it do.*

I sighed, another Warhol quote. My eyes ingested the photo – in that moment she had only been mine, before everything soured. I couldn't stand to see her, or us, happy. I hid the photo under the crescent of my sweaty palm and read the note.

Zoe,

I'm writing you at Trigger Copy, there's a bunch of hippies in front of me. It always takes forever here, and the hippies are all indecisive and bad with technology – so I'm left to wallow in patchouli. You're probably wondering why I'm writing. It's not that I'm apologising, I would never do that. It's because I'm bored (the hippies, the paper jams, the toner cartridges) and because, well – I know you won't believe this – but I love you.

The release party for Hostel Star is tonight, I wish it were at Barnes & Noble Union Square, but Beatrice's apartment will suffice. If only these hacky-sack-playing morons could hurry up with their anti-nuclear pamphlets. I'm printing two hundred copies of Hostel Star and planning on doing the whole Amanda Knox-cum-crime-scene party, decorating with fake blood, maybe a plastic turd in the toilet AND I'm renting the mammoth martini glass. Splash. I wish you were coming, but your absence, and insistence on dodging my calls – makes it pretty clear you won't. Anyway, I know after you've read the book – you probably hate me. You have to understand, we were supposed to write this together, become famous together, but you left. You disappeared when I needed you.

Is the book revenge? No. I wouldn't call it that. It's merely a rearrangement of the facts. Your facts, my facts. Collage really, you can appreciate that. You did most of these things, so did I – our lives were merely the stretcher bars for the canvas. And I was acting it all out for Beatrice, for each other. Planting the goalposts for the game. I never broke character, unlike you. I even fucked Mathias for no reason other than to cause drama, which, lol, it did. The moral of the story is exactly what I kept telling you: we needed a better arc! And Zoe, you must understand, what I wrote is not about Ivy-Ivy, it's about the condiment of Ivy – tragedy transformed her to public domain, mustard and mayonnaise, Britney and Lindsay, Amanda and Meredith.

I made us readable. I made us fantastic! And I had no choice – I had to finish my book before Beatrice released her version and I needed it to pop. I hope you can come to see it as funny as I do, relax Z – take a breath, enjoy our glory.

Anyway, I have been dying to tell you, that I've been doing some digging on Beatrice and that mysterious disappearing file folder we found in the one locked drawer. Apparently – god it's so juicy – I have goose bumps – this has happened before. On Blue Peak was based on a diary she pilfered while on vacation in the Blue Ridge Mountains. And she got busted! Settled with the rednecks out of court, all it took was a little calling around and bingo, I found one of the plaintiffs, drunk at home, who told me everything despite very obviously signing NDA's. Here's the kicker, the drunkard kept bringing up Janet. Blamed the whole thing on her, kept calling her a stealing devil-whore bitch. And if you think about it, it makes total sense, Beatrice couldn't write that many books a year — they were doing it all together.

So to kick off my taking control of the narrative, I invited Beatrice and Janet to the book release party tomorrow and signed the invite Lucille Conely, which

*is the real name of the girl whose diary she stole. I'm
going to bring her down – let the press junket begin, the
pot has officially been – stirred.*

*I'll be sending a copy to every magazine I can think
of and I'm repurposing all of Zander's freak animal
boxes, I think they will make a statement in the mailroom. Also, I'm using your collage for the cover, so I
thought it was only fair to send you the original – you
gave it to me, after all.*

*PS. I guess I'm sending this to your mom's, cause I
have no idea where you are.*

*Love and kisses, and never forget – every night you
miss in Berlin is a night you miss in Berlin*
    Hailey

A slow coldness traced up my spine, my hands began to
shake. Hailey had not only threatened to release her diary
as her own before Beatrice's version, but she'd threatened
On Blue Peak – the last shimmering piece of the puzzle, and
what surely pushed Beatrice over the edge. Even I had realised *On Blue Peak* had a cadence all its own. I tried to
imagine Hailey, the brooding Nancy Drew, calling around
trailer parks in the mountains of North Carolina putting
the pieces together.

I remembered back to finding the photograph of Janet and
five-year-old Beatrice by the pool, the crispness of their
matching shirts, the perfect bite of Beverly Hills sky, and the
cloud of unhappiness that hung around Janet. What had
happened? The teenage widow with a baby. I knew the
vacuum, I had grown up alone with my mom – I recognised
the sacrifice, the mirroring, and directness; my mother's long
hours of work were my long hours alone. I wondered whose
idea it had been? Writing the mystery novels. Was it Beatrice?
A desperate plan to float the family? Or was it Janet, trying

to make their lives mean something? The first book had come out in 1987 when Beatrice was only twenty, and the next three books had followed in fast succession.

I knew it was my turn to move slowly and figure it all out, unravel the chain of events, but I kept filtering back up the note in the diary to the part where Hailey told me she loved me. Remembering how badly I had wanted, or needed, her affection in the beginning. I studied the stupid way she flourished her cursive, the slant of the letters increasing the same way her voice escalated as she got excited. I missed being alone with her in the apartment. I missed the way she could shift a day in a single breathless sentence.

I was holding proof. Not just that Beatrice was watching us but what we had been doing was real. And proof was Hailey's obsession. All the photographs. All the press. Maybe that's what we all want, some body of evidence to keep us alive. There was Ivy's Facebook, a digital graveyard, where our asinine youth was embalmed. Ivy would never have a session of cyber sage-burning in her late twenties and delete the pink-cheeked photos from our first night drinking wine coolers. But the impulse to return would fade, fewer afternoons would end with a dip in the nostalgia pool, and just like that, Ivy would dissolve, bit by bit, as Grandma Jane stopped posting e-cards, and I forgot to write on her wall for her birthday. The digital candle would flicker.

Hailey had no interest in a candlelight vigil, she wanted a blazing trash fire. Hailey wanted to char continents. Clutching her diary, I knew despite everything, all the manipulation and set-up, I'd still torch anything for her. And just like that, it all came rushing back, my intense love for Hailey, the control she had over me. Of course she'd sent the diary and given me my way out.

I waited for my next check, time slow as molasses, then finally, the silver handle bent – it was the wide-hipped nurse, who always opened the door gently, then *mmmhmmm*'ed when she clocked I wasn't engaged in any act of self-harm. As the door skimmed open, in my most polite German, or what I thought was polite, I asked – *Kann ich bitte Frau Klein sehen?*

The nurse *mmmhmmm*'ed and disappeared to make a phone call outside my room. I was soon shuffled into Frau Klein's porridge-hued office, where she and all of her melodramatic plants sat in audience. I stood at the corner of her desk.

'What is it, Zoe?' Frau Klein asked, without looking up from her paperwork.

'I have Hailey's diary.'

Her right hand was busy filling out a form. Maybe she hadn't heard me?

'It's her diary. The missing diary.'

'And what makes you think that?' she asked, nonchalant.

I dropped the heavy book on her desk. She finally looked up and registered the object, her brow furrowed at the now infamous collage, its edges flaking delicately. She reached for it, 'And how did you get it?'

'Hailey sent it to me. It must have gotten lost, in a cat, I mean box, cat box – the same ones that Hailey's boyfriend used to send her. The boxes always had customs problems, and this one never arrived—'

Frau Klein was not listening. She was carefully leafing through the pages. I watched as she flipped to the end, eyeing *the last photo of 2008*, then scanned the note.

I could barely contain myself as she read, I burst out – 'It proves Beatrice and her mom, Janet, knew about the book release. And that Hailey also threatened *On Blue Peak*, so there's motive. And I know they checked Beatrice's alibi, but did they ever check Janet? She killed Hailey.'

The words *slam dunk* floated to mind, I could feel my

slippered feet weaving down a lacquered gym floor, floating, towards the orange rim, ball in hand. Frau Klein sat tight. *Processing*, as she would say, her lips fully disappeared in thought.

'I don't want to service any fantastical narratives, but this does qualify as a *development*. I'll forward it to the proper authorities.'

I was ushered out of her office by a new nurse, with a button nose, grey hair and a smattering of moles on her forehead. The Spa was buzzing, or at least I was. It was *Käse Spätzle* night, my favourite.

I was on my second plate of Spätzle when Scarlett Johansson sat down just one table away. Her eyes were weary, but her feral blonde hair was tied cutely in a half-topknot. She was working on folding something, origami, maybe a rabbit or a seal. In my chipper mood I tried to imagine we were at a German restaurant in Kreuzberg, two lesbians on a second date, both creatives, who'd both just happened to order the same dish. Maybe she would tell me about her fairtrade jewellery line, and I'd tell her about my new collages. We could be normal.

'What?' Scarlett Johansson asked softly.

I jerked back to my egg-doughed reality, I'd been staring.

'What – is – it?' she asked again, her English was nervous but kind.

I shook my head, and returned to forking. When I looked back up her eyes were still on me, she held her hand out as if to introduce herself. A stroke of fear sliced through me – I picked up my tray and walked to the other side of the room. I had the diary. I had Hailey. This wasn't Kreuzberg and I wasn't going to learn her name.

18

Three days later I was called to Frau Klein's office ready for my parade, she was seated behind her desk, wearing what looked like a 17th-century monk robe. I thought the outfit was a good sign, procession ready.

'So—?' I impatiently asked.

'Zoe, please sit. The police followed the leads from the diary. They questioned Janet and I thought it was best to speak to you about it in person as I don't want the detectives disturbing your development.'

I could feel the orchestra swell. Strings. Percussion. It was about to happen.

'The police spoke with both Beatrice and Janet about the new information. However, there is no question, Janet was in Sylt, she had breakfast with a friend the day Hailey died, and was seen later that evening on a walk by several neighbours. She was not in Berlin. The police are looking into the plagiarism accusations but there simply is no proving—'

'No, that's not possible. She must—'

'I suggest we talk about what a nice gesture it is, Hailey sending you the diary. I hope it can provide a sense of closure.'

'What?' I spat.

'I'm sorry.'

'Janet killed her. With Beatrice. They stole—'

Frau Klein cut me off, 'I think it's best if we move in a straightforward manner. We've talked in circles around this. You are stronger now and so we need to speak directly – you found her body, and you stabbed her. It's time you make peace with your actions.'

I had hated Frau Klein because she was boring, and wore frumpy smocks, but at times she had been patient and listened and a part of me trusted her. Now I knew she would never believe me, and maybe never had. I sat motionless for the remainder of our conversation, my chin pointed towards the ceiling, her questions gliding past like paper airplanes. I limped back to my room. I wanted Hailey, my redheaded Kool-Aid man, able to break through walls.

In the galactic vacancy of my little room, for the first time in my life, I considered suicide. How would I do it? Bed sheets on a door knob? Suffocation by trash bag? Then I could at least join Ivy and Hailey. I wondered if they were together, preparing for our slumber party in the sky, popcorn spinning in the microwave and a movie perched in the VCR. The next few days were a depressed smear, everything an embossed invitation for the end – the slippery tiles in the shower, each bite of asparagus, the top of the stairs. Begging for a slip, choke or tumble.

Winter returned in a sweep of dirty frost. The fade of the landscape relieved me. I watched as crows picked at the farm outside the window, taking comfort in the sun's earlier and earlier disappearance. And in those dull mornings, sometimes I would forget. I'd wake up and feel fine. The sheets were nice enough. It was warm, there was no coal oven to tend to. I was rested with my life ahead of me, then, like a cement mixer of sewage releasing its contents above my naked legs, I would remember what had happened – and I would try to hold my breath until I choked.

There was no news. The *On Blue Peak* accusations had turned up nothing. Janet and Beatrice had alibis. I was still the corpse stabber. In my little room with mouldy sink I came up with my own theories, unravelling the ball of string, playing cat's cradle. I felt certain they had wanted me dead – Beatrice and Janet had expected to find me in the apartment. And curled in bed I imagined the mother-daughter duo scaling The Spa with nylon harnesses and black rope. What would they do to me? Most nights I wanted them to get it over with.

Claire had stopped coming on the weekly *visitation days*, which was fine, it meant I could hibernate without having to face the banal chaos of the weeping parents and stressed-out siblings. A tornado of disappointments. Mothers begging daughters. Grandparents' mute, extolling hugs. Cookies thrown. Juice spat. I called my mom every so often, but I had nothing to say that didn't scare her. She didn't enjoy my theories. My paranoia. Jens had come once. I'd been switched to a new drug earlier that week, which made me too tired, or maybe too depressed to rouse, so I'd just slept on a beanbag while he watched. He'd patted my head when he left. The feeling of his hand on my scalp had re-animated something cellular within me, but by the time I'd looked up, wanting to reach out, he was already walking down the hallway. I felt abandoned. Hailey's plan of sending me the diary had failed. The whispers trailing me around The Spa had quieted. Even Beatrice's perfume ceased to haunt me. I wanted to leave me too, jump off the TV Tower, exiting kraut country with a splat.

By New Year's Eve, I was on a drug that had at least stabilised me, now too numb to be depressed. After dinner, I hazily wandered down to the common area for the first time during social hour. Taking a seat on the mustard couch, I joined the choir of strange angels. Bobbing my head as a brunette counted her fingers loudly, each number dropping with a guttural thud in the middle of the room while another girl opened and closed the atlas making a loud whooshing sound, all peppered by an older woman sighing in little heaves.

295

There were a few stray party hats, and a nurse came by with a plate of marshmallow cookies.

As the rush of community gave way to boredom, I lifted the blue atlas, which had been discarded as a musical instrument, onto my knees and flipped to the map of Germany. I put my finger on Berlin, trying to read the energy pulsating off the red dot. Could I feel it? Everything that city was capable of? Without thinking, I traced the route to Sylt. I held my finger on the six-inch strip of green, leading from the capital to the far northern tip of the country. Had she driven with the windows down? Listening to Bach? Copies of Hailey's book banging around in the trunk, blood still wet on her hands as she strummed the steering wheel? I closed my eyes, trying to remember Janet's face.

'Seven and a – half – hours, from Berlin,' Scarlett Johansson said, startling me, peering over my shoulder, a conical silver hat strapped to her head. She swung around to sit down on the couch next to me, 'My grandma lived near there.'

'Oh,' I said, uneasily.

She settled in and began folding something from a ripped-out magazine page. It felt good to have her body heat next to me. I nervously shifted my attention back to the atlas, the fluorescent lighting, which was always violently bright, suddenly felt cosy – the faded twinkle of the holidays took over.

'I'm Zoe,' I whispered.

'I'm Stefanie,' she said, handing me the oragami crane she'd just finished. I had broken my rule and learned a name, *Stefanie*. Those gnocchi lips and empty eyes now belonged to a three-dimensional being with feelings and thoughts. No longer my vector. We would exist together in this deafening world.

After some shuffling, the older sighing woman put on an episode of *The Nanny* in which an over-dubbed Fran Drescher discovers she's pregnant, *schwanger*. Three girls began arguing. Two nurses jumped immediately to break it up. I knew tension was bubbling, the following morning marked the biggest visitation day of the year, the New Year's Day brunch. The Spa would be open for family and friends, with tours of the premises and even a promise of live music. I was happy I had no one coming, I wanted to avoid the mess.

The nurse who smelled of talc squeaked by with the mail cart. The older sighing woman got a letter. Then the nurse dropped an envelope in my lap, without picking it up I noticed there was no return address. I tore it open and a card slipped to the floor. Bending down, I saw it was covered in the same strange language that had been on the index cards in the hidden room of Beatrice's apartment, a chicken-scratchy string of orbs and x's. A thunder-bolt shot through me. I picked up the card and flipped it over. On the back, in red, fully legible English, was what appeared to be a translation.

#671

Potential murder plot: pipe carbon monoxide through already suspect heating system via canister and tubing from adjoining apartment, above or below.

*canned CO is used in metal fabrication and bio-tech, relatively easy to get ahold of, realistic for most characters, good for an engineer or chemist etc . . .

I heard the full explosion of the orchestra, horns, wind, string. Everything blaring at once. I screamed and suddenly there were two nurses at my side. Hot air was blowing out of my mouth. I tried to calm down, to explain myself, pointing to the card. They wouldn't listen, I jumped up on the couch.

'This is Janet and Beatrice, this has to be . . .'

'This . . . I need to talk . . .'

More screaming.

'Please . . . I need . . .'

'Stop . . .'

I began kicking. The talc-smelling nurse grabbed my leg, and I swatted her away, demanding to speak with Frau Klein. The other nurse, young and nervous, called for backup. Not thirty seconds later, there she was – the fat one with neck acne, whose beak I'd punched. Still eager for revenge and entirely unfazed by my theatrics, she clamped her pudgy hand around my jaw, using her right elbow and knee to pin me down, and tipped a paper cup with a quarter inch of a yellow cummy liquid.

'Swall-ow,' she cooed.

I tried to press my lips shut, knowing if I drank whatever it was, I would sink into the dark lake. Just before I felt myself go, Stefanie walked past and gingerly removed the note card from my near limp hand. She winked, and I closed my eyes.

I inhaled, my nostrils burned from the smell of lilies, scalding, chemical and clean. My lashes batted off whatever crud they were sealed in, and the room came into focus. I turned my head and saw one of the nurses on her hands and knees, leafing through a book. Maybe she'd brought me breakfast.

The nurse turned the book upside down, fanning out the pages as if looking for a long-lost pressed flower. To my right on my desk lay a silver paper plate, loaded with chocolate-frosted cake.

I took a breath still groggy, then looked back, jolted – it wasn't a nurse. It was Beatrice in a red and white Christmas sweater, her black bob deflated and unbrushed. I closed my eyes. Willing a different phantom. I could hear her jiggle the door handle, it was locked. She released an angry sound, tried harder, then moved to my clothes hamper and started digging through the pile, checking the pockets of my pants.

I jumped up, legs wobbly, and ran for the door. I didn't

know when my last check had been but in three hours I would be dead. Hacked to bits. In three hours Beatrice could eat my body and shit out the evidence. I tore past her to the door and banged till my knuckles burned.

'Please, please, please . . .' I begged, mouth shouting at the metal slab, but I knew after my meltdown in the common room it was no use.

'I just need it back,' Beatrice said sternly.

I mustered the courage to look back, heart in throat. 'Just give it —'

'What?'

'The index card. It was a mistake,' she said, turning to pull the blanket off my bed, followed by my sweat-soaked sheets, then shoving her hand flat around the edge of the mattress, 'I can give you money.'

I kept myself pressed against the door, pulling on the handle – it had been Beatrice who'd sent the card and now wanted to take it back.

'I don't want money.'

'Everyone wants money,' she clipped. 'Where the fuck is it?'

'I gave it to the police,' I lied.

It took a few seconds for this to register in her eyes. I thought of all the shapes Stefanie could have folded the card into – a swan or tug boat or kangaroo, it didn't matter as long as she still had it. How had Beatrice even gotten in here? Then it hit me – the New Year's Day brunch, in the vortex of familial drama no one would notice her sneak off with her plate of cake.

Beatrice moved towards me uncertainly, I dipped around her, and climbed on top of the now bare mattress. There was no escaping whatever she was going to do. I cowered against the wall, scanning the room for something to defend myself with. Her red lips stretched into a flat line.

She stared at me – a silence bellied up in the room. I needed to buy time.

'Tell me about the beginning,' I said, surprising myself, it was what Frau Klein had repeated during my first weeks at The Spa. *The beginning*. As if anything could explain why she and I were locked in this room together on the first day of the new year.

Beatrice said nothing, she was now leaning against the door, looking away from me. I asked again, then changed tactics.

'Do you write them together? Or are you just the face?'

Beatrice snapped, 'How do you know——?'

I gulped.

'Hailey told me – in a letter.'

She turned pale at the mention of Hailey.

'Tell me about the beginning.'

'No.'

I strained my ears, listening for the rubber footsteps of the nurses outside. Nothing. I needed to keep her talking.

'You killed Hailey.'

She flared, 'No I didn't.'

'Then tell me.'

Beatrice rearranged herself, then released a rough angry laugh – 'Fine. At first she wrote them, yes, but she had trouble finding a publisher so she had the idea to make me be the face of her mystery series, she thought a twenty-year-old *wunderkind* might have better luck.'

Beatrice took a gulp of air, then looked full of rage at the thought.

'We were good, we did well – but she always just got carried away.'

'How?' I asked, startled at my ability to prod.

Beatrice looked through me, 'We looked alike, she had me young – and so she started——' She paused. 'She resented me, and she started going to book signings pretending to be me. It was before the internet, and before everything was everywhere. She would wear a wig like mine, black – I found out by accident because my agent thanked me for making it to a signing when I had the flu. And my mom said she'd stop – but I knew she sometimes still did it. *Beatrice Becks* was an avatar in a way, for both of us.'

'Who did I see in the apartment?' I asked.

'She was doing it again – in the wig.'

I nodded, 'I didn't see her face.'

'I'm sure,' Beatrice cleared her throat, her voice full of blame, getting taller as she spoke. 'You gave her that rejection letter from the Writers' Schloss. That's how she found out I was lying. I was with Michael my partner, I just needed to get away from her. I didn't want to write another one. I hadn't even read the drafts she'd sent me.'

I nodded, still channelling Frau Klein, trying to stretch our time.

'I'd been fighting the release of the book – but the publisher – that's why I mailed you the index card because I wanted it to be over. I was tired. And the police questioned her but then, nothing—'

Her breath became choppy at the reminder of the index card and the action she couldn't take back. She stood up. I felt like Scheherazade, if I could just keep the story going – whatever terrible thing she was planning to do to me would be delayed. Even if just for another minute. 'She killed Hailey?'

Beatrice paused, 'I knew she'd taken her diary but wasn't sure if she had – until I found the card.'

Her eyes grew dark as if just realising something, moving towards me, 'You're lying, aren't you? You couldn't have given it to the police—'

I pushed myself against the wall, bracing myself for whatever came next. Then the door swung open, the wide-hipped

301

nurse appeared and *mmmhmmm*'ed. Beatrice flashed with panic then took the cue, assuming the role of doting aunt, handing me the silver paper plate of cake and patting me on the head. She moved out of the room, hiding her face from the nurse, wishing her a *frohes neues Jahr* as she disappeared down the hall towards the cafeteria.

'Stop her,' I screamed. The wide-hipped nurse appeared momentarily confused, then hushed me and entered the room, *tsk*ing me for the mess while fixing my bedding.

'Please don't leave,' I begged the nurse. I didn't want to be alone. The nurse just smiled then closed the door, sealing me in the lily-scented cell.

After two days of no sleep I was released from *watch*. There she was, heading to her usual spot by the windows, the elastic waistband of her pants rolled so low you could see her hip bones, and a shimmer of pubic hair. I trotted calmly towards her, sitting down, trying not to draw any attention.

'Do you have the card?'

She gave me a shrug and then winked, 'What – card?'

'Stefanie.'

She smiled at the sound of her name, then pulled a folded white rabbit from the inside of her pants' elastic edge and slid it across the table.

19

Sitting in the parking lot of Panera Bread on the south side of Sebastian, I had to force myself to get up, to get out of the car, cross the black asphalt, stand in line and, finally, order an antibiotic-free chicken salad on ciabatta. I was trying to return to 'normal', but even the simplest tasks took a type of energy I no longer had access to. There was a snaking line of ten or so tanned, mostly elderly, people now behind me, none I knew personally – but a handful whispered and stared with pity, which I despised even more than the blind disgust that had followed me in Germany.

I'd moved to Claire's house for my final days in Berlin, staying in one of their guest rooms on the third floor. Tobi and the girls were in Zurich. I took several baths a day in the Breitbachs' generous tub, admiring my naked body. I'd forgotten how I looked, the shape of my thighs and breasts, I seemed older. My skin had changed. I hoisted myself onto the granite vanity and inspected my face, prodding at my cheeks – then pushing my lips the same way Hailey had whenever she'd caught her own reflection. I could see her inside of me now too.

In Claire's tower in Mitte I was padded from the reality of the streets below. I knew I was free to do whatever I wanted but I was hungover from the seclusion of The Spa. Still afraid of crowds of people and honking cars. I could have taken the train to Bülowstrasse, stood in the street and confronted that year but instead I curled up in the tub.

On my last night before my flight back I'd shuffled into the flower-flanked kitchen holding my laptop open, my skin still hot from a bath, and a towel wrapped around my head. I poured myself a glass of wine. I'd spent my day watching and re-watching a twelve-second video of Janet being escorted from police car to precinct. She was handcuffed and wearing a yellow cardigan, a faint smile tugging across her face. The attention finally on her.

'Another bath?' Claire asked, emerging from the glass elevator. I nodded and the towel wrapped around my head loosened.

Claire was fresh from the office where she'd been going over Beatrice's testimony. She dropped her leather attaché bag and went to the fridge, pulling out a bottle of Pellegrino, then settled in on one of the stools and let out a sigh.

'It's really quite unreal. The type of relationship Beatrice and her mom had. It made me really look into the mirror. Maybe I'm pushing the girls too hard?'

I shook my head, impressed at Claire's ability to make this about her. She poured herself a glass of water, lost in thought.

'How is it going with the case?' I asked, trying to reel her in.

'Oh, it's straightforward but also not. Beatrice says she only found out *On Blue Peak* was plagiarised when a lawsuit arrived four years ago – they paid over a million in multiple settlements. So she *clearly* knew her mother had a history of this sort of behaviour, but she insists that she didn't know she was watching you two.'

I gulped my wine and nodded for her to continue.

'Claims that only after Hailey's diary had been posthumously published did she compare it to what her mother had been working on – and that's when she realised it had happened again. She said it wasn't unusual for one of them to focus on one book, while the other worked on another. Swears she had no idea, but I'm not sure I believe her.'

I yawned.

'Is this too much?'

'No it's just the drugs – still in my system. Keep going.'

'Where was I? Oh get this, *apparently* when Beatrice was young, Janet would not only read her diary, but edit it, giving her suggestions on how to keep the reader interested, along with grammar and punctuation.'

I shivered at the thought of Janet hunched with red pen over Beatrice's fluffy adolescent diary. Claire went on explaining how Beatrice admitted that she knew her mother maintained several false Facebook accounts, amazed at the people's willingness to give up the raw material of their lives for free. Often posing as a journalist probing grieving families for details on tragedies, or inserting herself into the universes of the unsuspecting – the party photos Hailey and I had added to Facebook had only fuelled the fire.

'And Beatrice says she went on that talk show to try and stop the release of *Blood-Sex-Death-Berlin*, because "on camera" was the only place she controlled their narrative,' Claire said, twisting her wedding ring. I kept my eyes focused on the red sediment on the rim of my glass. Did I believe Beatrice was blameless? When she'd come to The Spa, I knew she'd debated hurting me. Cleaning up one last mess for her mother. She hadn't. But she'd obviously known Janet had floated off into darkness – I had watched it happen to Hailey, and I hadn't stopped it either. In a way I knew we were all guilty of wielding the avatar of Beatrice.

'Apparently Janet swore to Beatrice that she had nothing to do with Hailey's death, and Beatrice believed her because there had been carbon monoxide issues in the past. So Beatrice insists that, like most people, she thought you came home blacked-out on ketamine, found Hailey dead from carbon monoxide poisoning, read her book and stabbed her corpse in a rage – then dumped the original and copies, and called the police. Until she found the card—'

'Fuck her,' I muttered, hating hearing it all spelled out.

'Yes. Total criminal negligence. Well, I still can't get over the fact that Janet would dress up as Beatrice, so perverse,' she laughed mid thought, 'I mean, kids steal your youth – so I guess that's one way to take it back.'

'What was Janet's alibi?' I asked.

'She gave the cottage to her cleaner for the weekend, in exchange for her promising to make her nightly walk dressed in her jacket and hat, and wave to a few houses. The neighbors never saw her face — they had no idea it wasn't Janet.'

Janet putting a black wig on in the bathroom of Books-A-Million for a meet and greet was absurd but I could almost empathise. I had pinned Hailey's red hair to my own scalp. It seemed impossible that we had all found each other, Beatrice and her mother, me and Hailey. We were the carnival women who'd been sawed in half and never put back together, banished to the hall of mirrors. I had hated Beatrice but she had taken the leap, she had betrayed her mother who had betrayed Hailey who had betrayed me. It was all so tightly braided, the imitations and their makers.

In turning her mother in, Beatrice had successfully blocked *Blood-Sex-Death-Berlin* from coming out. While holding my head under the faucet in my last bath, I'd wondered what Hailey would have wanted. Maybe she'd have preferred the book sold at airports all over the world, even if it had painted us as attention-starved morons? But after replaying the video of Janet in cuffs for the hundredth time, I had my answer – it was the perfect end to the drama. *Dun Dun*.

The final part of Beatrice's testimony, and in exchange for immunity, she had helped the police translate the many boxes filled with index cards found in Sylt. Revealing thousands of plot ideas, twists, character origins, and potential murder scenarios – poisoned tuba tips, neurotoxic incense sticks and cell phone tasers – as well as notes on real murder investigations, including Ivy's, with a notation of the exact pattern of her fourteen stab wounds, and the type of blade required to make them.

Claire was clicking her rose-coloured nails against the Pellegrino bottle's green glass, 'Oh, and we learned that weird symbology she wrote in was something she developed with her husband when he was serving in Vietnam. Beatrice claims her mother continued using it because she was terrified of someone stealing her ideas – ironic eh?'

I nodded. I had drained my glass and was walking to the fridge, realising I still had one last question, 'Did Janet dump all that fake blood?'

Claire nodded, 'She wanted to — *make a scene.*'

In the weeks after my return to Florida my mom's hair had returned to its bright espresso brown, she was tan, gardening, singing while she salted boiling pasta water and having friends – who knowingly put their hands on my shoulder – over for dinner. It hadn't dawned on me that she had been in hiding after returning from Berlin, ruled unfit by association, too ashamed to answer the phone or do showings of homes. A few weeks in, she made conch fritters, my favourite, we ate on the patio and when she leaned back in her chair she turned to me and said, 'I just never thought we'd get this. I thought it was all over, our life. And now we get to start again – maybe it will even be better.'

I had excused myself under the pretence of getting something from the kitchen, cooling myself in the yellow light of the fridge, unsure of what starting again would even mean.

My mom wasn't alone in her transformation – Claire's neon wardrobe had parlayed perfectly to the speedy news segments summarising the pulp case, she had emerged as the real winged creature, the one who had believed me all along, harnessing her fame into a new law practice. She had even sent me a selfie, taken in front of a pair of glass doors overlooking Ku'damm, cheekily etched with *Breitbach and Daughters*. She'd left Tobias. He couldn't handle her success, couldn't handle the power-suits return to work.

On one of my first days back, I'd gone to the mall, the same one where I'd worked, with its rank fountains and blistering AC. I wanted to wear something new and blank. I was drawn into Express by the electronic music zig-zagging over the speakers, and picked out a pair of black shorts and two unremarkable tank tops. The material was synthetic and clingy, which is exactly how I felt. After paying, I changed in the food court's bathroom and left my old clothes in the stall, then wandered to the perfume counter, recognising the listless daydreaming in the scrawny girl whose forearms were pressed into the underlit glass.

'Would you like to try Guerlain Cruel Gardenia?' she chirped, righting herself, bottle in hand. I shook my head, and asked for a sample of Chanel Mademoiselle.

Unlike Claire or my mom, I wasn't metamorphosing into a better, more vibrant version of myself. I could still feel the hole. The one where Ivy had lived and Hailey had followed. I sprayed myself with the tiny pastel tube of Chanel, letting Hailey's scent take over, relieved I could visit her whenever I needed to.

Constance and I kept in touch with late-night phone calls, she had a whole new life at the University of Ottawa studying poli-sci, prepping for law school – endless reading, and naturally, several boyfriends. And I had a new therapist, Dr Phillips, who wore sleeveless polo shirts to show off her muscular tennis arms and let me call her Angela. I didn't balk when she asked questions. I put in the work. And she was helping me deal with my feelings of guilt – for telling Ivy to come home, for dating Jesse, for not stopping Hailey spiral.

'How are you, Zoe?' Angela asked over the faint buzz of the lawnmower outside.

'Good,' I said, then fell quiet.

Jesse had texted me the night before and I wanted to tell her, but I knew she'd remind me to focus on myself. *Trauma recovery takes time*, she liked to say, *it's not all bubble baths and long walks*. Angela insisted I hadn't been insane for my attraction to Jesse, that I had merely been looking for a method of coping with *grief*. I never felt comfortable with grief. Grief had been the foreign substance slipped into my drink when I wasn't looking. Grief had made me dizzy. Grief had held my black dress up over my shoulders while I got fucked on the floor.

'What is it?' she asked.

'Jesse texted, he asked me to meet with him – I guess he joined some new-wave church and he's supposed to *make amends* to those he's harmed.'

'Do you think he harmed you?' Angela asked.

I looked at the ceiling, 'I mean – our break-up was messy.'

'Well, who does this meeting benefit?'

'Him,' I said with the certainty I knew she wanted to hear.

'Exactly, you don't owe him.'

I nodded, she went on to talk about the importance of cultivating new friendships and keeping them in check, re-iterating that my only responsibility was taking care of myself.

But I couldn't help it, I was curious. I texted him in the parking lot. Jesse suggested Captain Hiram's, he'd drive. At home I showered, then dug through the medicine cabinet, pulling out the electric-green aloe bottle and a tube of cucumber-melon lotion. I was red from the sun. I still felt like I needed to look good for Jesse, or maybe I wanted Ivy to look good for him, I did my eye make-up like her, heavy on the mascara, blue eyeliner.

The horn blared and I grabbed my purse. Jesse swung open the door from the inside and I stepped in. The smell of cedar and suntan lotion brought back the road trip, my chariot of sadness, all those pimpled chicken carcasses littering the highway and the endless guitar riffs. He lifted off his baseball cap and leaned in to hug me.

'Hey buttercup,' he whispered just before breaking into tears, assuming our old position; me uneasily cradling him in my lap. I froze, looking out the window at the neighbours' dead lawn, what was I doing?

Once in the restaurant we were handed two gigantic laminated menus, I ordered crab legs, and Jesse got a burger with extra fries. He pressed on the bridge of his nose while leaning back on his side of the booth, 'So how've you been since Berlin?'

I released a horse blow, lips fluttering, 'Great.'

He imitated my sound, 'Glad to hear it.'

'Is it new?' I asked, pointing to a stick-and-poke BMX bike on his arm.

'Nah, I always had it,' he laughed, throwing me a sideways look.

I fiddled with my fork. He filled in the silence, telling a story about a super-rich guy who'd gotten so drunk he'd forgot which marina he parked his boat in – freaked out and bought a new one in an attempt to hide his mistake from his wife, the boat's namesake. Madeline found out when they showed up to their slip finding the original *Madeline*. I could barely listen. In the greenish glow of the restaurant I could see him clearly. The smoke from Ivy had settled and I realised I had no idea who he was. We'd only found each other by reaching for something, or really someone, else. And it wasn't just the tattoo I didn't remember. It was the way he slouched, and the frown his lips fell into, his anxious energy and the way he incessantly flapped a sugar packet on the side of the table. Had I lived with this person? Had I loved this person?

'You OK?'

I nodded, unfolding my napkin in my lap.

I wondered if the same thing was happening for him. If he was looking at me, only now grasping that all those wild flowers he had picked had been for Ivy and that I was merely a stranger – a one-time nurse to his sadness.

Dinner began to stretch. He talked about deep-sea fishing. He was planning to start a charter at the inlet, taking tourists out to catch snook, red fish and the occasional cobia. I nodded along. He told me about a buddy who might lend him a boat. I wondered what would happen if I told him I was gay, or if I described the dark rooms at Berghain or the self-identified queers at Holiday's apartment. I knew it wasn't worth my time to describe the parts of myself that I had found and lost. He'd found God, and I didn't want to hear about that either. We paid, and walked to the parking lot. He'd never mentioned the *amends* and I didn't care. Maybe this was enough.

In the car, he dug out the *Californication* CD by the Red Hot Chili Peppers.

'Oh, no never again,' I pleaded.

'See, it really transports you. Just wait.'

He turned up the volume. The bass plunged, he began singing along. I gave in and joined.

Jesse stopped at the gas station for cigarettes, I waited in the car. It was Friday night and there was a line of Powerball ticket hopefuls and six-pack stragglers. I fidgeted with my seat belt, then checked myself in the overhead mirror. I looked wrong in Ivy's eyeliner, I didn't want to perform her any more, not for him. I popped the glove compartment, grabbing a Burger King napkin, wetting it with spit. Just as I was about to close the hinged door I caught the glint of a thin gold chain wedged in the far back. I yanked it, pulling out a bracelet holding an italic cursive nameplate – *Jane.*

Acknowledgements

Firstly I have to thank Max Pitegoff, whom without everything would be blank. I would also like to thank my mother, brilliant writer, Debra Frasier, who never balked at having to go to Staples to print the latest version. Likewise I thank Alex Scrimgeour, my editor-dramaturge and dear friend.

I thank those who read early – Patrick Armstrong, Fredrika Brillembourg, Caroline Busta, Skye Chamberlain, Peter Currie, Kim Everett, Georgia Gray, Natascha Goldenberg, Karl Holmqvist, Rebecca Hornbuckle, Clemens Jahn, Alexa Karolinski, Michael Ladner, Pablo Larios, Lily McMenamy, Theresa Patzschke, Ella Plevin, Billy Rennekamp, Starship Magazine, Emily Segal, Tobias Spichtig, Margy Stein and Everett Williams. And Tina Liebscher for explaining the German legal system.

I thank my agent Eleanor Birne and all of the PEW Literary team, along with Francine Toon at Sceptre, who truly understood the story and its time. As well, I thank my editrix, Lee Boudreaux at Doubleday, and her scalpel of a mechanical pencil.

And a deep thank you to the girls who made me, Claire Anderson, Madeline Brown, Jeffrey Easter, Erica Schaidler, Sam Sencer-Mura, and Lucy Voller.

I'd like to thank my full-of-plot-ideas, wonderful father, James Henkel – and my family in all it's forms – Jerry Stein and The Post, Beachcomber Lane, Isabella Bortolozzi, Joe Kay, the Summer Cousins, 12D, The Cooper Union, The

Librarians of Villa Rossi, John Snyder, JoAnn Verburg & Jim Moore, David Goldes & Sheryl Mousley, the Hornbuckles & Kramecks, Klara Lidén, Karen and the Roth boys, Peter & Eli Pitegoff & Ann Casady, and meine Liebe Stefanie Sprinz. Lastly I thank Mia Goyette, we never missed a night.